The Prince of Cleveland

DAVID W. STEPHENS

iUniverse, Inc.
New York   Bloomington

The Prince of Cleveland

Copyright © 2008 by David W. Stephens

All rights reserved. No part of this book may be used or reproduced by any means, graphic, electronic, or mechanical, including photocopying, recording, taping or by any information storage retrieval system without the written permission of the publisher except in the case of brief quotations embodied in critical articles and reviews.

This is a work of fiction. All of the characters, names, incidents, organizations, and dialogue in this novel are either the products of the author's imagination or are used fictitiously.

iUniverse books may be ordered through booksellers or by contacting:

iUniverse
1663 Liberty Drive
Bloomington, IN 47403
www.iuniverse.com
1-800-Authors (1-800-288-4677)

Because of the dynamic nature of the Internet, any Web addresses or links contained in this book may have changed since publication and may no longer be valid. The views expressed in this work are solely those of the author and do not necessarily reflect the views of the publisher, and the publisher hereby disclaims any responsibility for them.

ISBN: 978-0-595-52773-1 (pbk)
ISBN: 978-0-595-51754-1 (cloth)
ISBN: 978-0-595-62826-1 (ebk)

Printed in the United States of America

I dedicate this book to my dear wife, Iva, whose endless love and support have been deeply appreciated.

Dear Rick,

Thanks for visiting

Good Luck

Dave

Acknowledgments

To Donna Kominko, for her much-appreciated advice for the book as it grew, and for her generous support and endless supply of hot coffee.

To Timothy and Linda Tuthill, for their unwavering support, encouragement, and valued opinions.

To John Ackerman, for his many hours of computer expertise.

To William Greanleaf, whose valued guidance finally squared me away.

To Martha Jane Stephens (my dear mother), whose love, support, and encouragement helped me along the seemingly endless journey.

And last but not least to the many wonderful readers who took a chance on *The Prince of Cleveland*.

Prologue

Tom regained consciousness after taking two beatings. Alone and awake, his thoughts bounced in his head. He did not think he could survive another beating. He had not figured his lottery winnings could get him kidnapped, but it had, and he was helpless. He heard footsteps; someone entered the cold room. "Who's there?" His voice was muffled as he spoke through a hood.

"Thomas, you're awake."
"Who's there?"
"My name is Krueger. Lukas Krueger."
"Krueger, what do you want?"
"My men told you what I want."
"Thirty million? You must be out of your mind."
"On the contrary, my mind is lucid and clear and the thirty million American dollars is my price."
"Or what? You'll kill me!"
"Perhaps I'll start with one of your family members."
"Leave my family out of this, Krueger!"
"I can't. I've already kidnapped them."
Tom screamed, "Let my family go!"
"That'll cost you. Thirty million American dollars is my going price," chuckled Lukas Krueger.

Chapter One

Two Years Earlier, Autumn 2007

Yesterday Thomas Murphy couldn't buy bad luck, and now, today, still wearing his best cheap suit, he owns the city. But he did not figure his lottery winnings would get his family kidnapped by a psychotic killer.

But now, just standing to the right of the stage, he felt nervous and yet excited, scared and yet brave, all at the same time. He had never been on television before, and now he felt self-conscious, sticking out on the sidelines as if he were a sore thumb. Thomas was literally beaming. He stood next to his wife, Beth, in front of several large television cameras, where he anxiously held an oversized lottery check written for one hundred million dollars.

Thomas watched and listened while the master of ceremonies talked to the audience, just minutes before he and Beth were to go on. "Don't be nervous, folks," said the director. "Just relax and try to enjoy yourselves."

"Somebody pinch me," uttered Thomas. "I still can't believe we've won." His face was flushed red.

"You have won, Tom," reassured the director as he stepped up next to the camera and whispered, "Get ready. You're on in three, two, one, go!"

"Ladies and gentlemen, tonight we have the winners of last night's huge Mega Millions drawing. This is Tom and Beth Murphy, who are tonight taking home one hundred million dollars," said the master of ceremonies as the small studio audience clapped. The master of ceremonies had Thomas raise the impressive oversized lottery check so the camera could get a good view.

"How does it feel to be rich?" asked the master of ceremonies as he rudely pushed his microphone into Tom's face; he did not mind being the center of attention on such a celebratory occasion.

"It feels great," Tom joyfully replied.

"Are you going to work tomorrow?"

"Heck no! They can keep my coffee mug."

"What will you do with your fortune?"

"That is going to be a big surprise."

"A surprise?" repeated the master of ceremonies.

"I'm gonna surprise everyone," declared Thomas.

"We will all look forward to your big surprise, won't we, folks?" the master of ceremonies asked the audience. There was an uproar of applause.

Thomas was thrilled at the overwhelming response. "Audience, would you like us to bring up Tom's three kids?" asked the master of ceremonies, and again the audience applauded wildly.

Thomas handed the big check to Beth, then he ran down offstage to where his three children were sitting, and he gathered them up. Thomas and his children all returned to the stage where Beth was waiting. Once the five of them were on stage with the master of ceremonies, Thomas took back the long and awkward pretend lottery check from his lovely wife. Next, the three children hugged Thomas and Beth; as the show was ending, the entire Murphy family jumped up and down in celebration.

* * *

After they left the television station, Thomas took the family back to their small bungalow in Cleveland. Thomas drove, while Beth and the children all sang, "Happy days are here again." He drove home in the family's worn-out twelve-year-old Chevy. Beth jubilantly asked, "How much, Tom? How much money is it?"

"Fifty-eight million after taxes, honey," he replied, celebrating by doing backflips in his mind.

"What will we do with all that money?" asked Tommy, the oldest son, who sat in the backseat next to his younger sister, Jenny, and younger brother, Danny.

"Tommy, what we'll do with the money is spend it."

"Are we millionaires, Dad?" asked Tommy.

"We're all rich, kids!" shouted Tom. "We are surely millionaires."

"Tom, no more bill collectors," said Beth.

"No more selling life insurance," said Tom.

"No more scrimping to get by," said Beth.

"No more bosses," said Tom.

"Our kids can all go to college!" said Beth.

"We'll replace this old Chevy, honey," said Tom.

"Can we get a bigger house, Tom?" she asked hopefully.

"Honey, I'll build you a huge house in Bainbridge."

He pulled into the driveway and shut off the Chevy, but postignition rattle forced him to restart the old car and shut it off again. They sat there jubilantly thinking of all the wonderful possibilities that their future held, and she asked, "What do we do first?"

He smiled and said, "Let's go in and order a pizza!"

Tom helped his wife and kids get out of the old car. He walked them up the steps of their small home; as he opened the front door, the screen fell off of its rusty, worn-out hinges. "Don't worry about the screen," he said with a laugh as he caught and casually tossed it out onto the lawn. "Don't worry about the screen," he repeated. "We're gonna build a great big new home."

Once in the house, Tom asked, "What kind of pizza?"

In unison they shouted, "Pizza with the works!"

Tom called and ordered three pizzas with the works.

While they waited for the pizza delivery, Tom asked, "What does everyone want with our millions of dollars?"

Beth said, "I want a huge new home."

Tommy said, "I want a bright-red sports car."

Jenny said, "I want a state-of-the-art computer."

Danny said, "I want a colorful pinto pony."

Finally, Tom said, "I want to start a cool business."

While they all discussed their hopes and dreams, time passed; before they knew it the pizzas were all delivered along with three large bottles of ginger ale.

While they enjoyed the pizzas and ginger ale, Beth described the many details of the home she wanted built.

"Baby, we're rich!" shouted Tom. "You can have as many rooms in your new home as you wish." He knew he could finally afford to give his wife and his children anything they wanted, and knowing that gave him a great sense of accomplishment. "And you kids can have anything you want. Each one of you is going to the best college you can get yourselves accepted into," promised Tom.

Danny wiped the tomato sauce from his mouth with the back of his sleeve and asked, "Dad, what kind of business?"

"Yeah, Tom?" asked Beth, "what kind of business?"

Tom smiled sheepishly and said, "I have this slamming cool idea for a business."

"What kind of business?" asked Jenny.

"I wanna take some of the lottery money and hire an army of men to clean up the city of Cleveland," explained Tom as he anxiously waited for his family's reaction to his idea.

"Dad, that's a cool idea!" said Tommy.

"Yeah, that's cool, Dad!" shouted Danny.

"Is that the surprise you mentioned at the studio?" Beth asked with a sense of excitement.

"Yes," answered Tom.

"Can we help?" asked Tommy.

"Sure! The whole family can help," said Tom.

"Tom, I'll help you," promised Beth. She watched as he ran his fingers through his wavy copper-red hair, standing five feet ten inches tall and weighing a fit and firm one hundred fifty pounds, with a ruddy Irish complexion that was peppered with freckles. His cleft chin reminded Beth of a young Kirk Douglas.

"I really want to do this," he responded.

"Then let's do it," said Beth.

"Honey, I've got lots of good ideas," said Tom.

Jenny said, "Tell us about those ideas, Dad."

Tom sat on their worn-out, overstuffed wingback chair and said, "Just cuz folks from out of town think Cleveland is the poorest city in the country, doesn't mean Cleveland cannot be the cleanest city in the country."

"You tell it like it is, Dad," shouted Tommy.

"I'm gonna call my company, 'Just Clean It Up.'"

"Just Clean It Up," Beth repeated.

"Do you like the name?" asked Tom.

"Yes! I love the name," she replied.

"Yeah!" the children yelled in unison.

Tom's family celebrated as if he had discovered the cure for urban blight. And in Tom's mind he kind of thought he had the cure with the power of both his new company and his fifty-eight million dollars.

"Kids! Let's make a toast to your Dad's success," Beth said as she raised her glass of cold, bubbly, ginger ale. "Here's to Tom's success!" The entire family raised their glasses and drank to his success.

Tommy high-fived his father as they both jumped up and slapped hands together. Next, Danny high-fived his father. Jenny hugged him, and so did Beth. Tom knew that with his family's approval he could not fail. Tom and his family partied till midnight, then he carried Danny to his bed, tucked him in, and said a little prayer for his son's overnight safety.

When Tom entered their small bedroom, he found Beth in her nightgown waiting for him. She had a chilled bottle of champagne uncorked and waiting. "Come on in here, my millionaire boy toy," she cooed.

"Why, my dear lady," whispered Tom, "what do you have in mind?" He slowly climbed onto their bed next to her.

"Passion!" her voice vibrated sensuously.

"I don't know if I can afford you," whispered Tom.

"You've got fifty-eight million reasons why you can afford me, sweetie," she softly laughed.

"How about a dollar a kiss for the rest of your life?"

"Let me start collecting them," she said as she leaned close to Tom and kissed him passionately. As they separated, she said, "Would you like some champagne?"

He grinned, nodded, and took a glass after she poured it for him; then she poured a glass for herself. "A toast to our love," said Tom as he and Beth both tilted their glasses and took a small sip of the bubbly champagne.

She giggled, cooed, then whispered, "The bubbles tickle my nose!" She pulled the long-stemmed glass from her face, grabbed her pug nose and rubbed it.

"The bubbles tickle my nose too," whispered Tom as he also rubbed his nose. He again leaned over and kissed Beth tenderly. He wrapped his arms around her, pulled her down backwards onto the bed and continued to kiss her. "I love you, Mrs. Millionaire," he whispered.

"And I love you, Mr. Millionaire," she whispered back.

They both giggled, sat back up, and finished their glasses of champagne. He looked at her, saw her smile, and saw a gleam in her deep blue eyes. "Take off your clothes," she said gingerly as she scooted back up the bed until her back was up against the bed's headboard. "Hurry up, you Irish stud," she said as she laughed naughtily.

Once he was naked, he jumped onto the bed, and for the next hour they intimately celebrated their great fortune. By 2:00 AM they fell asleep after lovemaking.

By 3:00 AM, Tom was dreaming. The bedroom windows were heavily draped to create a total darkness. Tom was deep in his dream pattern. His dream mind drifted. He heard a raspy voice murmuring repeatedly,

"For you, we are coming."

"For you, we are coming."

"For you, we are coming."

"For you, we are coming."

"For you, we are coming."

Tom woke, and, in a clear whisper, he repeated, "For you, we are coming. For you, we are coming." What did it mean? he wondered. He sat rubbing his face with his hands, looked over at Beth, and wondered why he had had such a dream. Was this dream a premonition?

Chapter Two

Two Years Later, Autumn 2009

Monday, Day One

It was a Monday morning in 2009 and Tom and his bodyguard were jogging along Cleveland's Lake Erie. They came around the Cleveland Browns Stadium, then headed east toward the Rock-n-Roll Hall of Fame Museum. It was a sunny autumn morning. Both men approached the visitor benches outside the front doors of the museum. Sweat trickled down the men's faces as they sat down on a bench. "Let's take a break," urged Tom as he panted.

"Yeah. We could use a break," agreed Thornton Williams, Tom's broad shouldered, thirty-two-year-old, black bodyguard, who stood six feet four inches tall, and weighed a firm and strong two hundred twenty pounds. Thornton was a classically handsome dark black man, who kept his head and face clean shaven. He had a wide chest, deep dark-brown eyes, and a resounding baritone voice.

Tom sat on the bench while Thornton ran in place, headed for somewhere imaginary.

Tom watched as a group of tourists ambled out of the Rock-n-Roll Hall of Fame Museum and headed straight toward him and Thornton. Tom looked up, waved at them and said, "Good morning, folks."

"Good morning," they replied in unison.

"Dad, that guy is Mr. Murphy," whispered a boy in the group to his father.

"Are you sure?" asked the boy's father, who stepped up closer to Tom and asked, "Sir, are you Mr. Murphy? Thomas Murphy?"

"Yes, I am," replied Tom as he stood up and gladly shook the man's hand.

The boy's father looked at the group and said, "Folks, this here gentleman is the Prince of Cleveland."

"Wow! We've heard so much about you, Mr. Murphy. It is great to meet you," said the boy's mother. "Can you please sign my autograph book?"

"Sure, I'd love to sign your book," said Tom. "Where are you folks from?" He took the autograph book and signed his name; Thomas Murphy, the Prince of Cleveland.

"We're from Cincinnati," said the father. "We came up to see the Rock Hall, but we never thought we'd meet you, Mr. Murphy. We've heard all about you from all the way downstate."

"It is nice to be recognized," said Tom with a grin. "You folks relax and just call me Tom."

"Maybe after you finish with Cleveland, then you can come down and clean up Cincinnati," shouted one of the other tourists.

"You've done a great job," said the father. "This here city is real clean. You've done a great job."

"Thanks. I've had a lot of help along the way," said Tom. "You folks enjoy your visit here."

"Can we get our picture taken with you, Tom? Can your friend hold the camera?" asked the boy's mother as she held her camera, hoping to get a picture with the Prince of Cleveland.

"Folks, this is my pal. His name is Thornton," Tom explained. "Come on Thor. Help us out with the camera." Tom took the camera from the boy's mother then handed it to Thornton. Then Tom posed with the group from Cincinnati. Thornton took the picture, then Tom shouted, "Thor, take a second picture for good luck for these nice folks."

Tom touched an older woman who was using a walker, and he asked, "Ma'am, are you the boy's grandmother?"

"Why, yes, I am," she replied quietly.

Tom leaned over and gently took her hand and shook it and said, "It's nice to meet you."

"Jim, who is this man?" she asked her son curiously.

"Momma, this is Tom, the man who won the lottery and spent the money cleaning up the city of Cleveland," said the boy's father.

"You a janitor?" shouted the old woman as she leaned closer to hear.

Tom smiled and replied, "I'm something like that, ma'am."

The boy's father thanked Tom and wished him good luck.

After the photos, all the tourists shook Tom's hand, then Tom and Thornton restarted their jog up toward the eastern end of the North Coast Harbor. After they got away from the group of tourists, Tom looked at Thornton and said, "Those were nice folks."

"You enjoy being recognized, don't you?"

"Sure, why not?" Tom picked up his pace and said, "Sure. Those were good people."

Tom watched as Thornton picked up his pace to keep up.

"Boss, you're the most popular guy on the north coast," said Thornton as they both laughed and continued their jog. Up ahead was Tom's Cadillac Escalade with his driver, Bill, waiting for them.

Once Tom reached the vehicle, he tapped on the driver's window, startling Bill. "Wake up, Bill," shouted Tom as he jiggled the car door handle.

*　　　*　　　*

At the same time that Tom and Thornton were enjoying their jog around the harbor, they were being watched. A car was parked at the far eastern edge of the North Coast Harbor parking lot. The driver, Lukas Krueger, was watching Thomas while Lukas's partner, the lovely Dagmar, was snapping telescopic pictures with her high-performance camera. Lukas sat behind the wheel while he patiently listened to the sounds of the camera clicking off shots of Thomas Murphy. "Are you getting good shots?" asked Lukas as he anxiously tapped his fingers on the steering wheel.

"The bodyguard is huge," observed Dagmar as she smoothly clicked off several more shots after many hours of surveillance work.

"How many more pictures today?" asked Lukas as he impatiently exhaled blue cigarette smoke into the confinement of his black panel van. He wondered how skilled the black bodyguard would be.

"The bodyguard has gotta be at least six feet six," speculated Dagmar as she set her camera onto the floor of the van and lit herself a cigarette.

"I don't care how huge he is, I'm going to enjoy eliminating him," said Lukas, as he threw his cigarette butt out the van window.

"Don't litter," she said teasingly.

"Shut up," snarled Lukas as he ran his fingers affectionately through her pixy blonde hair. "Those are enough pictures for today."

Lukas was in love with Dagmar, and when he looked at her he saw she stood a taunt, muscular, five feet four inches and weighed one hundred twenty pounds soaking wet. She looked like a wavy blonde female Peter Pan with pixy hair, prominent cheekbones, a pug nose, a china-white complexion and dark emerald-green eyes. She displayed no scars, but she wore a small, red, rose tattoo on the upper part of her plump left breast.

"They are finished anyway," said Dagmar. "They are getting into his big, black car."

Lukas looked over at Dagmar and said, "Phase one is over. We are done with the surveillance of Thomas Murphy."

"Good. We have been following him for three months," said Dagmar, as she inhaled on her cigarette. "He is boring to watch."

"We are finished studying Thomas's habits. I feel that I know him," said Lukas. "Now on to phase two, the haunting, where I get to crawl under his skin and make him itch feverishly. I will plant tortured images of his dear family in his mind's eye." Lukas wondered how long would it take to break Thomas Murphy's spirit.

"Lukas, they're driving away," said Dagmar.

"Let them go. We'll return to the farmhouse." He started the van's engine, drove out of the parking lot and then drove to the freeway heading east back toward the Lake County farmhouse, which served as Lukas's central command center for the upcoming kidnappings.

"How are the teams getting to the farmhouse?" Dagmar asked as she swept her fingers through her short hair.

"Both teams are flying in today," said Lukas, "and they are taking airport limousines to the Willoughby Travelodge. We will all meet up this afternoon at the farmhouse." Lukas's thoughts were not on the meeting but on the haunting and the actual kidnappings. He looked over at Dagmar as he drove, and he said, "Thomas will be so scared after I haunt him that he will be eager to give us the money."

"I know you will scare him," said Dagmar confidently.

"The only question left is whether I will let him live," said Lukas; he stood five feet ten inches and weighed a tight one hundred fifty pounds. After years of facial alterations, to avoid the authorities, his face now looked tight, shiny, and inflexible like a face lift gone terribly wrong. After years of fighting, Lukas's surgically repaired perfect nose stood out as the hallmark of his face. Facial ticks caused his whiskey-brown eyes to blink sporadically and his mouth to jerk like a fish on a line. Lukas wore a tightly trimmed, thin-lined cheek beard with prominent chin whiskers and a cleanly shaven upper lip. He wore no imperfections.

As Lukas drove east on the expressway, Dagmar slept. His mind should have been focused on the kidnapping of Thomas Murphy, but instead his mind was idly wandering about his retirement plans. He knew his roots were in Austria, where he had been born, and he knew his base of operations was in greater Europe. America was foreign soil and a dangerous place to be, with

Interpol and the FBI constantly on his tail. He knew he was classified as an international super criminal who specialized in kidnap for ransom. He knew his targets were the American ultrarich. Thomas Murphy would be Lukas Krueger's sixth kidnapping in the last twelve years. His first five kidnappings were in New York, Miami, Los Angeles, Chicago, and then again in New York. He had been successful in all five scores, which accumulated him one hundred million dollars in his private Swiss bank account. Now, he knew he needed one last gig to fulfill a longtime dream of retiring to the Caribbean with his longtime lover, the lovely and seductive Dagmar. But he knew as he drove, he had never been in Cleveland; unlike the other cities, Cleveland he knew nothing about. But Thomas Murphy's high publicity lured Lukas into the unknown city. He wondered if Cleveland was unlucky,

* * *

It was noon, and, after a morning full of paperwork, Tom wanted to break for lunch. The weather remained nice, and Tom wanted to enjoy as much of the good weather as possible before the long, cold, northern Ohio winter made its appearance. Tom sat at his desk, where he had spent the last two hours working on paperwork, which was basically answering thank you letters from appreciative homeowners who had had their property cleaned up for free and were now writing Tom to say thank you. Tom usually had help with those letters, but that morning his secretary was off till after lunch. Tom dedicatedly answered each and every letter he received. He looked up at Thornton, who was sitting in the corner of Tom's large, cozy office, and he said, "Thor, let's go to Public Square for lunch today. We can get Polish Boys from one of the street vendors. What do you say?"

"Tom, I like that idea."

Tom had been trying to get out in the fresh air as much as possible, and he knew that Thornton also appreciated the fresh air. They had had their early-morning jog, which they both enjoyed. As Tom got up from his desk he looked at Thornton and asked, "Do you think we'll need our jackets?"

"Let's carry them just in case," suggested Thornton.

Just as Tom was getting up from his desk, his phone rang. He looked over at Thornton and said, "Thor, hold on!" Tom sat back down and picked up the phone. "Just Clean It Up. This is Tom Murphy. How may I assist you?"

"Is this Thomas Murphy, the owner?"

"Yes! Who's calling?"

"Thomas Murphy. For you, we are coming."

"Would you repeat that?" asked Tom as the phrase jogged his memory and sounded like a familiar quote.

"For you, we are coming."

"Who is this?" asked Tom, raising his voice just as he remembered the premonition dream he had had the night of the lottery show and the family celebration. "Who is this?" he repeated just as the telephone was hung up.

"Is something wrong?" asked Thornton protectively.

"No! No! It must have been a wrong number," replied Tom, who wanted to disguise the seriousness of the call from his bodyguard and to give him a moment to think about the threatening call and caller. He sat momentarily holding the telephone receiver before he returned it to its cradle. He needed a second to realize the phrase from the dream was the exact phrase the caller used. How could that be, he wondered?

"Are you sure everything is okay?"

"Yeah. Let's go," said Tom as he placed the receiver back onto its cradle and jumped up from his seat and proceeded to join Thornton on their way out of the office.

Tom and Thornton left the office and walked over to the company garage, where Tom's driver, Bill, was waiting in Tom's shiny, black Escalade. "Hey, Bill," shouted Tom as he approached his vehicle. "Let's head for Public Square. We're going to get some Polish Boys, and I'm treating."

"Great," said Bill as he held the back door open for Tom. "You've a good day to be out in the fresh air," said Bill as he started the Cadillac and proceeded to drive out of the garage.

"We have to take advantage of the good weather while it lasts, before the snow comes in off that lake," said Tom as he watched Bill pull out onto the street. Tom left his laptop alone; instead, he was thinking about the threatening telephone call he had just received. What did the call mean, and who had made the call? he wondered.

Before long they were at Public Square, and Bill was trying to find a parking spot. "There's a spot," shouted Tom as he leaned forward and pointed to Bill's right, where they saw the empty parking space. Tom leaned back and waited for Bill to park the SUV. Once out of the vehicle, Tom led them toward the Terminal Tower and the vendor with the food cart and the colorful umbrella. "Hey, Tony," shouted Tom once he recognized the food vendor. "We want three Polish Boys with lots of sauerkraut on top of them," said Tom as the three men reached the busy noontime vendor.

"Mr. Murphy, you done good cleaning up the city," said Tony, the food vendor, as he prepared the sandwiches for the three men.

"Thanks, Tony," said Tom with a broad smile. "We've had a lot of fun cleaning up the city. We've gotta get the city ready cuz the Browns are going to make the playoffs again this season. Right, Tony?" asked Tom as he pointed toward the stadium.

"That's right, Mr. Murphy," said Tony as he handed each man his Polish Boy. "You's want drinks?"

"Sure," replied Tom. "Three Pepsis."

Tom took the three drinks and handed them out. "Thanks, Tony. See you later." Tom led Thornton and Bill over to a bench, where they sat down and enjoyed their noon meal. Tom sat eating while watching all the pedestrians as they walked past him and his two friends. "Lots of folks out today," observed Tom.

"Good day for it," replied Thornton.

"It is a good day to be a freedom-loving American," Tom said with a big grin on his freckled Irish face.

Thornton looked at Tom, then Bill, then back at Tom, and he said, "It is also a good day to be a wealthy freedom-loving American." Tom laughed, as did his two friends.

Toward the end of the lunch break, Tom's smile suddenly faded into a frown. "Thornton, I'd like to speak to you on a serious note."

"Here?" asked Thornton. "Now?"

"Yeah." Tom stood up, walked over to a litter can, and tossed the last half of his Polish Boy into the can.

"Okay, Tom. What is on your mind?"

"Thornton, for the last month or so I've had the feeling that I'm being watched," stated Tom as he took a long drink of his Pepsi.

"Why haven't you said something sooner?"

"I thought it was my imagination," confessed Tom as he paced back and forth in front of his two employees.

"Have you seen anyone?" asked Thornton as he tossed his sandwich wrapper into the litter can.

"I thought I had a couple of times," said Tom, "but …"

"But what?" asked Thornton as he reached up and placed his hand on Tom's shoulder encouragingly.

"I can't put my finger on it," said Tom.

"Tom, hunches usually turn out to be real."

"What can we do?" asked Tom.

"Security professionals, like myself, hire shadows to check and see if someone is watching their clients," Thornton explained as he took a long swig of his Pepsi.

"Do you know of a shadow we could hire?" asked Tom.

"Yes. I'm close friends with one of the best security shadows available in this country. His name is Joe Brown, and he is based in Washington, D.C.," said Thornton.

"Can you contact him and see if he is available?"

"Yes. I'll call him once we get back to your office."

"Then let's wrap it up," said Tom, "and let's get back." Tom helped Bill wrap up his lunch, then the three of them walked across Public Square and back to where they had parked the Cadillac. On the drive back to Tom's company facility, he wondered how he could have dreamed a phrase which someone would later use during a telephone conversation. And he wondered who could have called and threatened him. He thought the phrase was unique. As they rode, he wondered if he should tell Thornton about the call. After all, Thornton was his bodyguard, and he was in charge of all of Tom's security. He decided, after they got back to the office, he would discuss the threatening phone call with Thornton.

* * *

Bill drove them back to Just Clean It Up, and Tom got busy dictating letters to Katelyn, his personal secretary, who had been off that morning but had returned to work the rest of the day. She was a tall woman with china-white skin and long, shoulder length, brown hair. Her eyes were light blue, and she seldom wore makeup. Tom sat behind his large glass top desk, while Katelyn sat ready next to the desk with her steno pad.

Tom kept reaching into his in-basket and retrieving incoming mail. Most were thank you notes, Tom thought. "Hold on, Katelyn," Tom instructed. "Thor, have you been able to contact your shadow friend?" Tom looked across the room to where Thornton was sitting.

Tom watched as Thornton looked up from what he was doing, and he responded, "Tom, I left a brief message and asked him to return my call. We may not hear from him until this evening."

"That's good, Thor," replied Tom just as the telephone on his desk rang. He had not yet spoken to Thornton about the earlier call, and now his phone was ringing again. He hesitated to pick it up. Would this be another threat? he wondered. He took a deep breath, then he picked it up and listened. For a second he was breathless. He listened then let out his breath. The call was from the company mailroom. Relieved, moments later he hung up, looked at Katelyn and said, "Katelyn, that was from the mailroom. Apparently, someone has sent me a large vase of flowers. Would you mind going down there and bring the flowers to me?" He was relieved it was not another threatening call.

"I'd love to fetch the flowers for you, Tom." He watched as she set her pad and pen down, then she walked out of the office.

"You've got an admirer, Tom," teased Thornton.

Tom looked over at Thornton and said, "The flowers are probably from my wife." While Tom waited for Katelyn to return, he quickly called home to talk with Beth, but all he got was a continuous ringing. "She must be out," he said.

"She is probably out spending your money," grinned Thornton. Tom saw Thornton put his hand over his mouth as if he had misspoken.

Tom pointed at Thornton's covered mouth and laughed. "She'd have to get started early to break my bank."

After a few minutes, Tom looked up from the letter he was reading, and he saw Katelyn returning with a cart with what looked like a huge vase full of flowers. Tom could not tell what kind of flowers they were because the entire vase was covered with a thin, green tissue paper.

"Katelyn, unwrap the flowers," said Tom as he watched her unwrap the bundle of flowers. As she was unwrapping the tissue paper she screamed. As soon as Tom saw the flowers, he jumped to his feet and shouted, "Thor, all these roses are dead!"

He saw Thornton jump up, rush over, and shout, "Wait! Let me check those first for a bomb!"

Tom motioned and shouted, "Step back, Katelyn!"

Tom and Katelyn stepped away while Thornton carefully pulled apart the many dead roses. Tom watched as Thornton carefully checked for a bomb inside the flowers. After several minutes Thornton shouted, "Damn, there is a dead red robin in the middle of these flowers." Tom watched as Thornton pulled apart the flowers, revealing the dead robin. "Its neck has been broken," said Thornton as he examined the bird. "This took some sick bastard quite a bit of time to think up and put together," said Thornton.

As Tom watched, he noticed a card and shouted, "Thor, there is a card next to your right hand!" He waited as Thornton plucked the card from the middle of the bunch of dead flowers.

He listened as Thornton read the card. "It says 'For you, we are coming!'" Tom grimaced as he listened. He looked at Thornton, who repeated, "For you, we are coming! Now that sounds like a threat." Thornton held the card. "Sure enough! It sounds very much like a threat to me," uttered Thornton as he handed the card to Tom.

Tom looked at the card, turned it over, and looked at the blank backside. "Maybe I am being watched."

"If you think you're being watched, and you get a bunch of dead flowers, a dead bird, and a threatening card, then I think there is a true security problem," said Thornton. "We may need more than a shadow to handle this developing problem. I'd better call Lockhart Security, the company you hired me from."

"Wait, Thor. I haven't been totally honest," said Tom. "There is more than just the feeling of being watched." He ran his hands with frustration through his long, wavy, red hair as he sat back down at his desk.

"What else, Tom?" asked Thornton as he pulled up a chair and sat down in front of Tom's desk. "Start at the beginning and don't leave anything out!" Tom could tell by Thornton's tone of voice he was serious and genuinely concerned. Tom seldom kept things from Thornton.

"If I start at the beginning, you'll think I'm crazy," Tom said with a sense of embarrassment.

"Try me, Tom!"

"It goes back two years."

"Yeah. And ... ?"

"It was the night of the lottery presentation." Tom stopped short of telling the story. He felt embarrassed.

"Uh huh, go on, Tom," urged Thornton.

"After the family celebrated at our home, well, we all went to bed, and I had a dream, which I didn't, at the time, understand."

"Yeah. What kind of dream?"

"It was a premonition."

"What was the premonition?"

"It was a phrase. It was repeated over and over. Maybe half a dozen times," said Tom with a sense of relief.

"What was the phrase?"

Tom hesitated, then shouted, "For you, we are coming."

"Tom, that's what is on this card with the flowers," uttered Thornton, who then silently stared at his boss.

"It was a very scary dream that made a strong impression and stayed with me." Tom wondered if Thornton believed him. He wondered if he thought he was crazy.

"And you haven't heard the phrase since the flowers showed up this afternoon?" questioned Thornton.

"That isn't true," Tom blurted.

"When else have you heard the phrase?" asked Thornton with surprise and concern.

"Today. Before lunch," said Tom incredulously. "The wrong number I answered just before we walked out. It was a man's raspy voice that asked for me. He repeated the phrase twice before he hung up on me," explained Tom with a sense of great relief.

"This is bad, Tom," said his bodyguard, "real bad." They looked at each other pensively. "Let's construct a timeline of events. First, there was the dream two years ago, then before lunch today you got a threatening phone call, and then after lunch today you received the dead roses. All three events had the phrase 'For you, we are coming' attached to them," explained Thornton as he rubbed his shaved head anxiously.

"Thornton, you've got the events correct," said Tom. He looked over at Katelyn, who had started to quietly sob. He rushed over to her, placed his arms around her and said, "Katelyn, don't cry! It's most likely some joker who is trying to scare us. I know it's upsetting. Why don't you take the rest of the day off?"

"Thomas, someone wants to hurt you," said Katelyn, who was loyal to her boss as well as concerned for his safety.

"Tom, she is correct," urged Thornton. "Someone wants to hurt you and has gone to a lot of work to tell you."

Tom walked back to where the dead flowers were setting. He carefully lifted the dead robin out of the flowers, and he set it on the flat surface of his glass-top desk. "Thornton, take some pictures of the flowers, the bird, and the written card," said Tom, knowing Thornton could take pictures using the photo feature of his cell phone. "Save the pictures. We may need them later."

"Okay, boss," said Thornton as he pulled his cell phone out of his pants pocket and proceeded to use the photo feature of the phone. Tom watched as Thornton took separate pictures of the dead flowers and the dead bird and then an additional picture of the threatening card.

Tom had Katelyn sitting on his couch while she composed herself. He walked over to the couch and sat down next to her and said, "Listen Katelyn, I get practical jokers sending me crazy stuff all the time. It's nothing to be upset over."

"I don't want anyone hurting you," she said sincerely.

"I really appreciate your loyalty, Katelyn, but no one is going to hurt me," said Tom. "Why, I've got big, old Thornton to protect me!" He looked over at his bodyguard's shiny, shaved, black head, and he wondered if he would put his life on the line for him. "Katelyn, I'll keep you on the clock. Why don't you spend the rest of the day walking in the park? The good weather won't last much longer."

"Are you sure you won't need me?" she asked as she sniffled and wiped the tears from her eyes.

"No. You go along," he replied. "We'll catch up on these letters tomorrow. Okay?"

"Okay." She smiled, reached over, and hugged him. She stood up and walked to the door. "Thanks, Tom!" He watched her leave.

He looked over just as Thornton was finishing taking the photos of the flowers, bird, and card. "Would you go down to the mailroom and see if anyone remembers who brought the flowers?" He watched as Thornton put his cell phone back into his pants pocket.

"Sure, Tom," replied Thornton, "that's a good idea."

Once Tom had Thornton go to the mailroom, he sat on his couch and wondered who sent the vase of flowers. Who would want to hurt him? he wondered. He walked over to his desk, and he started counting the number of dead roses. After several minutes, he confirmed there were twenty-four dead roses. Exactly two dozen. Next, he picked up the dead robin, and he carefully examined it. After a moment, he set the bird back down next to the large vase of flowers. Finally, he picked up the card. He reread it and wondered who had gone to such trouble.

As he sat waiting for his bodyguard to return, he thought back to the terrible dream he had the night the family celebrated the lottery winnings. There must be a connection between the prophetic dream and the arrival of today's flowers, he thought. Was someone coming after him and his family? he further wondered.

This line of thinking made him uncomfortable, and so he began to reflect back onto the time prior to Thornton's arrival. He thought back to a time when he had no bodyguard and the afternoon when he and his family were at a charity event. Tom and Beth had donated a sizable sum of money that afternoon. It was an outdoor event, a picnic type of thing. Tom and his wife were sitting at a picnic table, drinking lemonade, and watching the crowd walk throughout the picnic grounds. Tom's three children were in a tent watching clowns perform.

It was a warm summer afternoon, and Tom thought it was odd when he saw an elderly man standing at a distance, wearing a woolen poncho that looked terribly warm. Tom was about to mention the man to his wife, but he stopped when the man slowly started walking toward him. Tom looked down at his lemonade, then he casually looked at the man, who was coming closer. Tom watched as the man smoothly swung open his poncho and pulled out a sawed-off shotgun. The man aimed the gun straight at Tom, who jumped up and flung himself away from the picnic table, causing the poncho man to swing his aim more toward Tom's new position, further away from Beth. The first pattern of buckshot hit the ground between the picnic table and Tom, who by then was lying several feet away from the picnic table. Tom jumped to his feet just as the poncho man pulled out the spent round and quickly replaced it with a new shotgun shell full of fresh buckshot. Beth screamed as Tom scrambled toward the gunman, who was instantly ready to shoot again.

A good Samaritan stood behind the gunman. Tom saw him as he rushed the gunman and forced the shotgun to point down, with the explosive pattern of buckshot spraying downward near the gunman's feet. By that moment, Tom had reached the front of the gunman and struck him violently in the face. The gunman dropped his shotgun onto the ground, just as he fell back into the arms of the good Samaritan, who grabbed him and held on tightly.

A park ranger saw what had happened and had arrived just in time to arrest the poncho gunman, the man who had just tried to assassinate Tom Murphy.

Immediately after that episode in the park, Tom started interviewing for a bodyguard from a security company called Lockhart Security. After two mornings of interviewing potential bodyguards, Tom had the next candidate enter the interviewing room. Tom stood up, reached out to shake hands, and said, "I'm Tom Murphy."

"I'm Thornton Williams," said the tall, broad, black bodyguard as they shook hands. Tom was impressed. He saw that Thornton stood a tall six feet four inches and weighed a firm, strong two hundred and twenty pounds. His head was clean shaven, and he wore no beard, mustache, or sideburns on his exceptionally dark, brown, and small-featured face. When Thornton spoke, you heard a fine baritone voice. He was broad shouldered and had a wide, strong chest. He wore no scars, tattoos, or imperfections.

Tom remembered that after talking to Thornton for fifteen minutes, he was certain he had his perfect bodyguard. Tom looked no further.

After Tom's short reflection, he lay down on his long couch and within a few minutes he was sound asleep. The arrival of the flowers had upset him. They had created tension in his body, and his afternoon nap was not only relaxing, but also recuperative. He slept for nearly half an hour, then Thornton returned from the mailroom.

Tom awoke feeling a hand on his shoulder and the sound of Thornton's voice. "Okay, I'm awake. I'm awake," Tom uttered as he sat forward and looked at Thornton, who was standing over him. "What did you find, Thor?" asked Tom as he started to rise from the long couch.

"The mail clerk told me he remembered the man who dropped off the vase as a white man with a trimmed beard and a clean-shaven upper lip, who drove a black, paneled van without markings," said Thornton as he backed away from Tom and the couch.

"Was there any paperwork, something he had to sign for?" asked Tom as he walked back to his desk.

"No. I asked the clerk, but he said the man was in and out in a flash," explained Thornton, who walked over and sat down in a chair in front of Tom's desk.

"I guess there was no license plate number."

"No. There was nothing like that," replied Thornton.

"What do you think we should do with this vase full of dead flowers, the dead bird, and the threatening card?" Tom asked as he glanced at the vase.

"Tom, I've got pictures of all three items in my cell phone, so why don't I just take all of it and give it to a janitor to dispose of," suggested Thornton as he stood up from the chair and waited for Tom to agree with him.

"That sounds good," said Tom, "but don't lose the pictures because if this thing gets worse we may need them." Tom watched as Thornton lifted the dead bird and placed it and the card inside the vase. Then he watched as Thornton wheeled the whole cart out of the office and down the hall. It still seemed scary that someone was sending him such things. He wondered why. Then he thought about his wife and he wondered what he would tell her, if anything. He had a marriage based on truth, and he knew he would not lie to her, but he was not sure if he would tell. If he did tell her about the delivery, then she would be scared and worried. But would that be a lie by omission? He was getting a headache thinking about all of these things, and so he got up from his desk. He walked back over to the couch and lay back down. He told himself he would only rest until Thornton returned, but he fell back asleep. He did not hear Thornton when he returned.

At four thirty, Tom woke when finally Thornton shook his shoulder. "What time is it?" shouted Tom, who just realized he had been sleeping the balance of the afternoon.

"It's four thirty, Tom," said Thornton. "You were resting so well that I was afraid to wake you."

"Hell. We gotta get out of here," said Tom as he rose from the couch. He quickly walked to his desk and dialed Wanda in the phone branch to check on incoming calls. Once he was assured there were no important calls, he said, "Let's get out of here, Thor."

* * *

It was two o'clock, and it was a cool November afternoon on the north coast, but Lukas Krueger paid little attention to the weather. He had more important issues at hand. He and his assistant, Dagmar Stent, were introducing the team members for the kidnapping of Thomas Murphy by Team One and then the kidnapping of his wife, Beth, and their three children by Team Two.

Lukas had all the team members arrive from the airport by airport limousines directly to their assigned rooms at the Willoughby Travelodge. Lukas had arranged that when each team member arrived, they would find an informational package on their bed pillow. Once they read their package, they were directed to attend a 2:00 PM meeting at the rendezvous location, which was Lukas Krueger's Lake County farmhouse.

Dagmar was the closest person that Lukas would allow near him. The second person was Otto, who Lukas trusted with his life. The three of them had successfully pulled off all of Lukas's prior kidnappings. Lukas gave the lead position of Team Two to Otto.

By two thirty, Lukas sat behind a desk, drinking black coffee and looking over the two teams of professionals he had handpicked from all across Europe. They were professionals as well as cutthroats, thought Krueger. "Let's start folks. My name is Lukas Krueger, and this is my assistant, Miss Dagmar Stent." He looked over the men. "As you may have heard, I run a tight ship. Do as I tell you and we'll get along fine. For those who know me, thank you for coming. For those who are new to my project, I also thank you for coming. You each have had an informational package delivered to you. I hope you have read it and gotten to know the players in this project. Our target is Thomas Murphy. He is worth somewhere around fifty-eight million dollars and our goal is to relinquish approximately thirty million from him. This project should be easy and lucrative for every one of us. I operate on a four-phase approach. Phase one is surveillance, which has already been accomplished. Phase two is what Dagmar and I call the haunting, which is almost completed. It is where we get under the target's skin and make him want to give us his money. Phase three is the kidnapping, and phase four is the collection. All of you will be involved in phases three and four."

"Phase five should be celebrating," interrupted Alex.

"Very funny," said Lukas. "Do not interrupt me, Alex."

"Sorry, King Krueger," said Alex, laughing.

"I am not a king," snarled Lukas sternly.

"Sorry, Lukas," said Alex sheepishly.

"Memorize your packages and be prepared to execute phases three and four," explained Lukas. "Team One will kidnap Thomas and Team Two, led by Otto, will kidnap the wife and three children. Tom will be taken to the abandoned house on Franklin then released. We kidnap him for psychological effect. The real kidnapping will be the family, who will be first taken to the foreclosure in the Ohio City area, then moved ultimately to this location, our farmhouse."

Alex raised his hand and asked, "Have you finished phase two, and how soon will the kidnappings occur?"

"Phase two continues as Thomas remains free, and if you'd read your package you would know that your team kidnaps the family first on Wednesday morning," said Lukas, his patience toward Alex running thin.

Alex was cocky as he smiled and said, "Guess I ain't read enough yet. Maybe you could give us an extra day to prepare?"

Lukas slammed his clipboard down on top of the desk, stomped out from behind the desk and shouted, "I was told you were a professional!" Everyone in the room took a deep breath and looked expectantly at Alex.

Alex again smiled, leaned back his chair, and said, "I could kill you in a heartbeat, Mr. Krueger!"

Lukas showed no emotion as he drew his weapon, aimed pointblank and shot Alex between his eyes. Alex fell backwards onto the living room floor, then Lukas calmly said, "Otto, take out this trash!"

Otto, the leader of Team Two, motioned to two other members of his team to help remove Alex's corpse. They quietly but quickly picked up the body and carried it out of the living room.

Lukas calmly walked back behind the makeshift desk and continued his presentation. "Has anyone not completed their informational package?" asked Lukas calmly. No one indicated otherwise, and so he assumed everyone was prepared to carry out Wednesday morning's abductions. "Let me clarify. Team One will attack Murphy's black Cadillac Escalade at exactly three blocks from his business. We will kill both the bodyguard and the driver. We will not harm Murphy. All his injuries will be in a controlled atmosphere while we restrain him. Team Two will abduct the Murphy family. We will not hurt the Murphy wife or the children. Do I make myself clear? Initially, the Murphy family will be kept at the foreclosure in Ohio City then moved here later."

Lukas stopped and finished drinking his hot coffee, and then he said, "Most of you know me. You know I am a fair man. We have worked together before. So we can get along well, but as you may see, as we age, we tolerate less bullshit. Alex was bullshit. Don't make the same mistake."

He picked up his clipboard and asked, "Are there any questions?" He waited; when no one asked anything, he said, "See all of you in the morning."

Lukas collected his loose papers, clipboard, and empty coffee mug. He motioned toward Dagmar, and she rushed to go with him. No one spoke to Lukas or Dagmar as they worked their way out of the farmhouse and went to his black van. He pulled out and drove directly back to their room at the Travelodge.

He noticed, as they walked along the steps to their motel room, that the evening sky was full of bright stars. Once they reached their motel room, he unlocked the door and held the door open for her to enter. He closed the door and walked over to the big king-size bed. He looked at her with an unknown anger. "Lukas, do you want to order our dinner?" asked Dagmar as she slipped off her bright red leather bolero jacket.

"Not yet," he barked. "Go clean up!"

He watched her walk over to her overnight bag and slip a red satin negligee out of the bag. As she walked toward the bathroom, she seductively slipped off her blouse and let it fall onto the carpeted floor. While she prepared for her shower, she purposely left the door ajar so that Lukas could hear her singing to the pulsating shower water.

While he waited for her, he removed his suit jacket, shirt, and tie, then finally he removed his shiny black leather wingtipped shoes. Next, he pulled back the bedspread and fluffed the pillows with anticipation.

When she entered the bedroom she whispered, "Would you like dinner, darling?"

"Yes!" he roared as he stepped toward her. As they stood by the bed he slapped the side of her face, knocking her back onto the pillows of the bed.

"Don't hurt me!" she screamed as he jumped on top of her. He ripped the top of her red satin gown, then he buried his trimmed-bearded face in her long fleshy neck. Again, she flirtatiously screamed, "Don't hurt me."

Next, he jumped up, and with his two strong hands he grabbed her by her throat and began to choke her. As her head bounced up and down on the pillows and her eyes rolled back in their sockets, she screamed, "I love you, Lukas." They were both sexually aroused as they played the choking game.

* * *

By 5:00 PM, Tom called it a day. He and Thornton headed back to the parking garage where Bill was waiting for them. "Bill, it's time to call it a day," shouted Tom as he and his bodyguard entered the parking garage and approached Tom's black Cadillac Escalade. Tom saw Bill lazily sitting on the front fender waiting for them. "Let's head for home, Bill," repeated Tom as he watched his driver slowly slide off the front fender, then run to open the back door.

Once everyone was belted into the SUV, Bill headed for Tom's home. Tom watched as Bill smoothly pulled out of the employee parking lot, then Tom leaned forward between the two front seats and said, "Thor, I'm worried about the threats, and I know I'm being watched."

"Are you sure you haven't seen anyone?" Thornton asked again as he looked toward Tom in the backseat.

"No. Like I said earlier, my feeling of being watched is just a gut feeling, but the dream, the threatening call, and the flowers are all real," said Tom from the backseat.

"My experience tells me that your gut feeling about being watched is usually based in reality," said Thornton as he looked toward the backseat.

"Well it's just my feelings," said Tom. He leaned back into his seat, but he continued listening to Thornton.

"Tom, I'll talk to Joe Brown, but like I said before, we may need more help than Joe Brown. In the morning, I'll call Lockhart Security. Okay?" asked Thornton.

"Yes, Thor, but also call Joe Brown tonight."

"Sure. If we use him, it'll probably take him a couple of days to get here, but I'll call him again," said Thornton as he sat back in his seat and looked forward through the windshield.

Tom leaned forward and vigorously patted Thornton on the shoulder and thanked him. The remainder of the ride home was quiet. Thornton used his cell phone to again call Joe Brown, but all he got was another leave-a-message recording, which he'd left before.

Tom sat back and started inputting information into his shiny laptop computer, which he always carried inside the Escalade. Despite the rush-hour traffic, Bill still arrived at Tom's home by five forty-five. When Bill pulled into the driveway Tom said, "My wife has made a honey-baked ham. Can you two join us for dinner?"

Bill looked back and said, "Boss, I'd love to, but I've got a hot date tonight. Can I take a rain check?"

"Sure, Bill. How about you, Thor?" asked Tom. "Can you stay for dinner?"

Tom saw Thornton's big grin as he replied, "I'd love to stay. Thanks, Tom. Maybe I can reach Joe Brown from your home." While Thornton was responding, Bill got out of the Escalade and ran around to the back of the vehicle. He then opened the back door so Tom could climb out.

"Sounds great, Thor," said Tom eagerly as Bill helped him climb out of the back of the beautifully detailed black Escalade.

Tom and Thornton stood outside the SUV. "Bill, we'll see you in the morning. Have a good time tonight," said Tom as he and Thornton walked away from the vehicle. Tom waved at Bill as he climbed back in behind the wheel. Then they both watched as Bill pulled out of the drive and

proceeded to drive away. "Does honey-baked ham sound good, my friend?" asked Tom as they walked toward the house.

"Sure thing, Tom," said Thornton as Tom walked him up the front steps and into Tom's starter home, where he had decided to stay while his ranch-style home was being built in Bainbridge, Ohio.

"Pretty soon my family will be living in my newly constructed ranch home," said Tom as he and Thornton walked up to the front of the small house.

"Tom, how soon will your new home be ready to move into?" asked Thornton as they walked up the front steps of Tom's starter home.

"The contractor predicts one month," said Tom, "but you know there are always unforeseen obstacles." Tom opened the front door and shouted, "Beth, I'm home!" Beth came running from the kitchen. She hugged Tom. "Are the kids home? Thor is staying for dinner."

"Good. The more the merrier," said Beth as she released her husband. "Tom, you got some strange mail."

"What's strange about it, Beth?" asked Tom as he walked into the living room, tossed his suit jacket on the back of a chair and looked for the mail. Tom's eyes scanned the room but did not see the mail.

Beth was mischievously holding the mail behind her back. She smiled and said, "A big brown envelope came for you with the word 'private' scribbled on both sides. It was written with bright red crayons." She laughed as she pulled the envelope from behind her back, surprising him as he saw the large eight-by-eleven-inch brown envelope she had been hiding.

"That looks strange," said Tom as he took it from Beth. He turned it over several times, then he said, "It's addressed to The Prince of Cleveland, with our home address written in bright red crayon."

"I didn't open it because it had 'private' scribbled several times on both sides," said Beth, sincerely.

Tom smiled at her and said, "You did good to wait."

"Yes. Wait!" shouted Thornton, "Let me see it." He took the envelope from Tom. "It doesn't look safe." Tom watched as Thornton carefully examined the front and back of the large, brown envelope. Tom noticed it was taped shut, and he watched as Thornton used his pocket knife to carefully cut open the strangely marked envelope.

Tommy entered the living room and whispered, "Maybe it's a bomb!" The boy had seen the envelope earlier that afternoon when it was delivered.

"Shush, Tommy," his mother scolded.

Thornton stopped cutting, looked up, and said, "I initially thought it may be a bomb, but I don't feel any wires." He kept feeling the edges of the taped envelope.

"Thor, shouldn't you take that outside to open?" Tom asked as he thought about the safety of his family.

"No! It's already open," declared Thornton as Tom watched him gently pull out the paper that was inside the strange envelope.

"Holy crap!" uttered Tom as he gazed over Thornton's shoulder at the horrid faces that were scribbled on the paper. "It looks evil." The entire picture was done with crayons. It had ugly pictures. "What does it say at the bottom, Thor?" asked Tom with concern.

"It's scribbled, but I can make it out. It appears to say, 'for you, we are coming!'" said Thornton as he held the drawing close to his face. "Doesn't that sound familiar, Tom?" asked Thornton as he held the drawing.

Tom looked sternly at the picture and said, "That's certainly the same threat!"

"For you, we are coming," Thornton repeated the threat for Tom's sake.

Tom took the drawing from Thornton and laid it flat on the coffee table. He sat down on the sofa and briefly studied the many grotesque figures and frightening faces. "This drawing took someone quite a long time to compose," said Tom as he studied the drawing from different angles. Tom looked up from the drawing and realized he had forgotten that Beth was still standing there, and suddenly her arms were crossed over her chest angrily. Tom rose from the sofa, and he looked her in the eye and said, "Beth?"

"For you, we are coming," repeated Beth, "that is the same phrase you had in your dream the night we celebrated your lottery winnings two years ago." She stood staring him eye to eye.

"Beth, you remember that dream?" asked Tom, surprised.

"Yes, Tom. I pay attention to everything that affects us," replied Beth.

"Thor, I'm impressed that she remembered the dream from two years ago," said Tom, trying to change the subject.

"Thomas, don't try to avoid the subject," snapped Beth, who wanted to talk about the drawing. "Why did you dream the phrase, then why did someone use the same phrase on an evil drawing two years later?" He knew she would grab onto this like a terrier playing tug of war with a pull toy.

"I don't know why some freak sent us this evil drawing," said Tom defensively.

"Tom, this freak, who sent this drawing knows where we live because he has our house address, which, I repeat, means he knows where we live!" she said, pointing out the seriousness of the situation. He could immediately see that she was scared, and he knew she was correct to be scared. He tried to comfort her by placing his arms around her, but she pulled away and said, "Tom, for the safety of the kids and me, you've got to take this freak's threat seriously. Don't just blow it off!"

"Beth, you're right," Tom agreed, "and Thor is bringing in extra security people first thing in the morning."

"You've already talked about bringing in more security! How could you two have already discussed more security when you have just discovered the drawing?" she asked scornfully.

"We want to do what is best," stammered Tom, trying to avoid telling his wife about the threatening phone call and the dead flowers.

"What else is there, Tom?" she asked flatly.

Tom glanced at Thornton, hoping he would not mention the phone call and the flowers. "We think someone is following me," he said, dodging the real subject altogether. He did not want to scare her anymore than she already was.

"What're you going to do about it?" she demanded.

"Like I just said, Thor is bringing in an additional security expert tomorrow," said Tom as he finally hugged his scared wife.

"Tom, is there anything else you're not telling me about?" she wanted to know as she pushed him away, suspecting there was more to know.

Tom looked at Thornton, who said, "Tom, You might as well tell her everything. She needs to know."

"Okay ... Okay ... Before lunch today I received a threatening phone call. The caller said, 'For you, we are coming!' And then, after lunch, I received a vase of dead roses with a card which read, 'For you, we are coming!'" confessed Tom as he stood facing Beth and Thornton.

"Phone calls and dead roses?"

"Yeah. They had the same threat."

She started to cry. She was overwhelmed, and Tom embraced her gently. While they hugged, Thornton said, "I can take this drawing to the Case Western Reserve University tomorrow and have a friend of mine analyze it. My friend is a psychologist; he specializes in abnormal behavior."

"See, Beth, Thor can get it analyzed," said Tom as he released his hold on Beth, but he still held her hands in a gesture of reassurance.

"What is analyzing the drawing going to tell us?" she asked as Tom watched her gaze shift from him to Thornton.

"To analyze it will tell us what type of abnormal behavioral character we are dealing with," said Thornton.

Beth let go of Tom's hands, backed away, and said, "I'd feel safer if we were in the security of our new ranch home. Here I feel vulnerable and exposed." Beth started to cry as she left the living room and returned to the kitchen, where she continued preparing the family dinner meal.

Tom watched her stomp out of the room, then he said, "She's real scared." Tom started pacing nervously.

"She should be scared. This guy knows where you folks live," said Thornton. "He's got your home address."

"Yeah. You're right. He knew where to send the drawing," said Tom as he paced faster. After a few minutes, Beth returned. Tom looked at her as she handed him and Thornton each a cold beer. "Thanks, honey. How soon till dinner?"

"Five minutes," she replied. He watched her angrily stomp out of the living room and back into the kitchen. He knew she was scared, and so was he.

"Thor, try your friend again," urged Tom as he took a long, slow drink of his much-appreciated beer. He watched as Thornton pushed redial and waited for the call to go through.

After two minutes Thornton hung up the telephone and said, "Joe keeps strange hours because of the business. He'll check his messages in a little while, and then he'll buzz us." He finally took a drink of his beer.

"Do you think he'll be free to come help us?" asked Tom as he took another long swig of his cold beer.

"It all depends on what he is working on," replied Thornton. "If he can get away, then he'll come. We are good buddies."

"Thor, do you think I'm not taking this seriously enough?" he asked as he paced anxiously.

"Tom, I know this is a lot for you to absorb, but if I were you I'd move my family immediately," said Thornton. "Now we've got the flowers and the hideous drawing and the repetitive threats. I am truly concerned, Tom." Tom looked at Thornton and was a little surprise at his bluntness.

"Do you really think it is that serious?"

"Yes, Tom, I do think it is that serious!"

Tom rubbed his chin nervously while he contemplated the situation. After a moment's thought he looked directly at Thornton and said, "My family will be out shopping all day tomorrow, and then they'll be with us tomorrow night while we're at the City Club." He was talking out loud as he explained things to his bodyguard. "How about after the presentation at the City Club we move the family to a hotel?"

"Why wait?"

"Well, I think we're good for tonight, and we're all gonna be real busy all day tomorrow," explained Tom as he finished his beer.

"I see your point. Do you want me to stay overnight for added protection?" asked Thornton. Tom saw the concerned look on his bodyguard's face.

"No! I'll need you all day tomorrow, probably till after midnight, so you'll need your sleep tonight," explained Tom, who was avoiding moving his family that night.

A few minutes later Beth called everyone to the dinner table, and they had a enjoyable meal. The central topic of conversation revolved around the construction of the new ranch home in expensive Bainbridge, which had the entire family excited. Toward the end of the meal Tom said, "I've got good news. You kids have not been to the construction site for over a month and during that time a full-service barn with stalls and a corral have been built. You kids are each getting your own horse. I have hired a stable master to care for the horses and to teach each of you how to ride. The stable master's name is Gabby Hayworth. He has been around horses all his life. Hayworth is seventy years old, so take it easy on him." Tom watched as the three children erupted into cheers.

"Can we name our own horse?" asked Danny.

"Can we pick out our own horse?" asked Jenny.

"I want a black stallion," said Tommy.

"Tom, I think they are excited," said Beth.

"Yes to each of you," replied Tom as he looked at Beth and threw her an imaginary kiss. "Danny, what are you going to name you horse?" Tom took his napkin off his lap, wiped his face, and then placed it on the table indicating he was finished with his dinner.

"Dad, how about calling my horse Joy Boy?" said Danny.

"Danny, Joy Boy sounds great."

"Better hope you don't get a filly," said Tommy.

"What is a filly?" asked Danny.

"A filly is a girl horse," explained Tom.

"Dad, I don't want a girl horse," objected Danny.

"Okay, we'll get you a boy horse, Danny," said Tom as he got up from the dinner table. "Thor, let's talk in the living room. You kids help your mom with the dishes then get on to your homework."

After the dinner meal, Beth returned to the kitchen. The three children were hidden away doing their homework, while Tom and Thornton headed for the living room to discuss matters of security. The feeling of being watched, the creepy flowers with the dead robin, the creepy drawing, along with the phone threat, all concerned Tom. He wanted security and safety for his family.

By the end of dinner the sun had set; the house had a chill upon it, and so Tom started to prepare a small fire in the living room fireplace. Thornton stood while Tom made the fire. Tom placed the small pieces of kindling into the fireplace, then he crinkled some newspaper and placed it under the small wood, and struck a match, waiting for the paper to light. After the fire started, Tom walked over to the sofa and sat down next to Thornton, who was already sitting in the overstuffed chair next to the sofa. Tom did not speak at first. He was not sure what to say to his friend and bodyguard. He was thinking about being watched and how Thor's friend, Joe Brown, could help with that problem. But he thought the flowers and the drawing, along with the threats, were probably enough to move his family.

"Tom, what are you thinking?"

"I'm thinking your friend may help us, but now with these threats I believe we have a more serious problem. What do you think?"

"You know how I feel. Things have escalated."

"Yes! And I've decided I want a bodyguard planted on each member of my family. I'm taking these threats very seriously, Thor." Tom stood up and walked over to the fireplace to stoke the fire. "You can go ahead and have Joe Brown come help us, but I want you to get more bodies to help us," stressed Tom.

"Tonight, Tom?"

"No! Tomorrow morning we've got to go to my new home construction site. After that, when we get back to the facility, then you can make some calls and start to set up some arrangements," explained Tom as he returned to his seat on the sofa. "If these threats increase, then I might be forced to bring in the police."

"I agree. Whoever is threatening you knows where you live because he had your address to send the drawing to," said Thornton, who truly comprehended the seriousness of the situation.

Tom looked up, and he saw Beth had brought the two men a pot of coffee and two big coffee mugs. "Here! I thought you two might want some hearty coffee," said Beth as she set down her serving tray on the coffee table.

"Thanks, Beth," they both said in unison.

Tom stood up and kissed his wife, who then smiled and took the coffee pot and poured into both mugs. Then she asked, "Thor, black with one sugar?" Thornton nodded affirmatively, and she added the sugar and handed him his coffee. Tom took his with cream and one sugar. After they each had their coffees, Tom said, "Beth, I want to go over tomorrow's agenda. Tuesday is going to be busy. The first thing we've got to do is meet with the contractor at the construction site of the new home. After that, when we return to our facility, Thor can make arrangements for more security. At noon, I'm being interviewed by the newspaper people, and then that evening we have to be at the City Club for my award as Man of the Year. Beth, after that, we are gonna move the family. You all will be away from the house most of tomorrow during the day shopping, and so you all will be safe."

"When did you make this decision?" she asked hotly.

"Just before dinner."

"Where are we going?"

"I'll pick a safe and comfortable hotel, Beth."

"I'll help," added Thornton.

"Tomorrow, Thor is going to call Lockhart Security and get a bodyguard for each member of the family," said Tom as he sipped his hot coffee.

"Damn, Tom, this is serious," she shouted as she stepped up to him and gently pounded on his chest, making her point to him. "We gotta get out of here!"

"Calm down. We know it's serious. We'll be safe for tonight, and tomorrow we'll all be away from the house," explained Tom. "And tomorrow night after the City Club, Thor and I will move the family to a nice, comfortable hotel. Okay, Beth?"

"We gotta take the dog with us," she said, conceding.

"Of course! We couldn't leave Duke behind," confirmed Tom as he held her hands up against his chest reassuringly.

"The kids would hate us if we left the dog," she said as she slowly started to cry. Tom held her close to comfort her. "I know, honey!" he soothed her.

Tom looked at Thornton, who whispered, "My friend at the university who specializes in behavioral abnormalities will find the drawing fascinating."

"Show him the pictures in your cell phone of the dead flowers and the dead robin," said Tom as he held his wife close and comforted her. "You can fit that in while I'm being interviewed by the newspaper people."

"Oh, yeah, the pictures," uttered Thornton, "I almost forgot about the pictures in the cell phone."

"Will he freak?" asked Tom jokingly as he tried to ease the tension, more for himself than for Thornton.

"He'll probable freak, but he'll be able to interpret what we are dealing with," said Thornton as he then took a sip of his hot coffee.

"It would be good to know what we're dealing with," agreed Tom seriously. Tom and Thornton continued to discuss the situation while Beth pulled away from Tom and rushed out of the living room and into the kitchen.

By 8:00 PM Thornton was ready to go home. Tom gave him the drawing and the envelope, and he walked him to the door. Tom stood at the front door watching Thornton as he climbed into his car and drove off.

Next, Tom checked on his wife, who was helping Danny with his geography, and then he returned to his living room and the cozy, warm fire that was crackling in the fireplace. Somehow he knew he was being watched. He could sense it. And now that someone had delivered dead flowers and a freaky drawing along with written threats, he just knew they were all related by a common theme; For you, we are coming!

Tom decided to place a call to Mike Max, his business manager and overall supervisor of Tom's entire staff, to bring him up to date on the threats. "Mike? Yeah, Tom here."

"Yeah, what's up, Tom?"

"Mike, I've gotten a couple of threats today, and I feel I need to tell you about them," said Tom, who then went on to tell his business manager about the security problems that were developing.

After they talked, Tom felt reassured that Mike Max was aware of the situation, and he was feeling safer knowing someone who he regarded as a strong individual was in the loop.

* * *

By nine thirty, Thornton was just settling into his apartment, where he had a rustic, brown, leather couch and two identical overstuffed chairs with matching ottomans. The walls were all painted a cocoa brown color with black lamps. Just as he sat down on his overstuffed leather chair, his cell phone started playing "The Star-Spangled Banner." He quickly answered the cell phone, and he was happy to hear Joe Brown's husky voice. "How the hell are you, old buddy?"

"I'm good, Joe. You sound fit as a fiddle."

"Thornton, my health is good, my girl is good, and my business is good. What more could I ask for?" replied Joe.

"It's great to hear your voice," said Thornton with a chuckle.

"In your message you said you had a problem. What is it? Is someone taking pictures of your boss?"

"Joe, we think someone's watching him. Today he received a threatening phone call, two dozen dead red roses along with a red robin whose neck had been snapped, along with a card that said, 'For you, we are coming!' Then when we returned to his home tonight, he had a drawing delivered with evil faces scribbled all over the page. The drawing had the same quote. 'For you, we are coming!' These threats are unnerving him and his wife."

"What does the drawing look like?"

"It's a complex drawing of grotesque figures and hideous faces drawn with crayon and at the bottom it spells 'For you, we are coming!'"

"Thor, that doesn't sound good. I'm fortunately between jobs so I'm free, but I have a commitment which will keep me here for three or maybe four more days, then I can come to Cleveland to help you," explained Joe as he spoke into the phone. "But it sounds as if you need more than my help. From the description of those threats and the drawing, it sounds as if you have a psychopath on your hands."

"Joe, tomorrow I am going to take the drawing to the university to a professor who specializes in behavioral abnormalities. I'm going to get his interpretation of the flowers, drawing, and the threats, and see what he thinks," explained Thornton.

"Thornton, I'd be anxious to hear about his interpretation," said Joe Brown.

"I'll fill you in when you get here," said Thornton.

"That sounds great," said Joe Brown, "and in the meantime keep your client and yourself safe."

"Call me the night before you fly in, and I'll pick you up at the airport," said Thornton.

"Sounds great. Good buddy, I gotta go. My girlfriend just walked in," said Joe. "I will call you soon. Bye."

After Thornton finished with his call, he dialed Tom's house, and he got the answering machine. "Tom, I just talked with Joe Brown. He'll be here in three or four days. He is anxious to meet you. He is the best, Tom. Talk to you in the morning," Thornton left the message and hung up, then walked to the kitchen and retrieved a whistling teapot. Next, he poured himself a cup of green tea and went upstairs to bed for the night.

*   *   *

By ten, after Tom had gotten Thornton's message about Joe Brown's availability, he sat on their bed waiting for Beth to join him. Beth was in the bathroom preparing for bed. Tom heard her brushing her teeth; the bathroom door was slightly ajar. Tom yelled, "Beth, that was Thor. His friend Joe Brown is coming in three or four days."

"Tom, what's Joe Brown going to do for you?" asked Beth as he watched her walk out of the bathroom and into the bedroom. The bedroom was dark, with only one lamp lit.

"He is going to find out if we're being watched," said Tom as he jumped up off the bed, hurried over to Beth, and helped her take off her bathrobe.

"Tom, answer me honestly," said Beth as she stood next to the bed in her pajamas. "Do you think the person watching is the same person who sent the flowers and that awful drawing?"

"Honey, I can't be sure, but my gut feels like it's the same person," said Tom as he pulled back the bedspread for Beth. He waited until she climbed into the bed, then he ran around to the other side of the bed and climbed in. They sat with their backs up against the bed's headboard. The room was dark with the exception of the one lamp sitting on the nightstand on Tom's side of the bed. "Are you ready for me to turn off the light?" asked Tom as he reached toward the nightstand.

"Can we talk in the dark?" she asked, smiling.

"We can do more than talk in the dark," joked Tom as he turned the lamp off.

"Tom, I'm serious," she continued. "Is it because we are wealthy that we got threatened?" They both sat in the dark bedroom wondering about that question.

"Yes, Beth, it is because of our wealth and all the publicity that draws the weirdos and kooks out from under their rocks," explained Tom as he reached for Beth's hand.

"Let's just try to get a good night's sleep," Beth whispered, "and maybe tomorrow things will look better."

"Okay, Beth," replied Tom as he leaned over and kissed her. "Good night," he whispered.

They slid down under the bedspread and proceeded to fall asleep, but Tom just lay there as time passed. He did not want Beth to know just how worried he actually was. He believed that the threats justified his gut feelings about being watched. In the morning he would talk to Thornton about getting additional security staff to stay with his family.

Eventually, Tom drifted off to sleep, but it was a disturbed and restless kind of sleep which made him toss and turn until he woke and had to go to the bathroom for a glass of fresh, cool, water.

After he drank the water, he quietly went to his children's rooms to check on them. He was genuinely worried about his family's safety. Lastly, he went into Danny's room. The boy had restlessly kicked off his covers. Tom covered Danny, leaned over, and gently kissed him on top of his curly, red-haired head. "Good night, my lovely little boy," whispered Tom as he tightly tucked the covers around Danny's shoulders.

Tom returned to his bedroom and carefully and quietly climbed back into their bed. And he rested until sunrise.

Chapter Three

Tuesday, Day Two

That Tuesday morning at the Cleveland bungalow, the Murphy family members were all sitting around the kitchen table eating their breakfast. Tom looked at young Danny, his ten-year-old son, and he asked, "Danny, what do you think about school today?" Tom knew his wife, Beth, would not let the children go to school today because she would want them all to go shopping for new clothes for that evening's special occasion. "Danny, what do you think?"

"I think we should all stay home today and get ready for your award tonight," said Danny.

Tom smiled at Danny then he looked at Jenny, his thirteen-year-old daughter, and he asked, "Jenny, what do you think?"

"I agree with Danny," said Jenny. "We'll need all day to prepare. We all want to look our best tonight."

Tom looked at his oldest son, Tommy, who was tall for his age of fourteen, and he asked, "Tommy, do you agree with your sister and younger brother?"

Tom watched as Tommy finished drinking his orange juice and then with a big grin he eagerly said, "I definitely think we should skip school today."

Tom laughed and said, "So among my three kids, it is unanimous. What does my lovely wife say?" He watched as Beth smiled at him and then nodded at him affirmatively.

"Tom, we're all going out for new clothes," said Beth proudly. "Each boy is getting a new suit."

"Can we both get navy blue suits?" asked Tommy.

Tom turned and looked at Beth, who said, "Yes. Tommy, navy blue suits would look great for tonight."

Tom stood up, saluted his wife, and said, "Then it is unanimous. No school today." He loved to play the comic with his family.

Beth stood up and copied her husband by saluting him. Tom listened as Beth continued, "I am taking the boys to get suits this morning, and then all of us are going to lunch, and afterwards Jenny and I are getting new dresses and a tour of duty at our favorite beauty parlor."

Tom grinned and said, "That sounds like a full day."

"Nothing is too good for the family of the man being honored as the Man of the Year at the famous City Club of Cleveland tonight," said Beth with a proud grin.

Tom reached down, picked up his half-filled coffee mug and finished drinking. "That all sounds great, but I can't join you. I have an appointment at the ranch site to discuss things with the contractor," said Tom as he set his coffee mug back down on the kitchen table. "Bill should be here anytime now."

"Is Thornton joining you?" asked Beth with a serious tone in her voice. "With those threats, he should stay at your side all the time."

"Ever since that wacko tried to shoot me last year," said Tom, "Thor goes everywhere with me." Tom walked away from the kitchen table, down the hallway, and into his bedroom. He was finishing dressing when he heard Danny shout that Bill and Thornton had arrived. As Tom finished dressing, he knew that Bill and Thornton would wait respectfully in the living room. "Good morning, boys," he said as he entered the living room.

"Good morning, boss," they replied in unison.

Tom was slipping on his suit coat as he said, "Bill, I have a ten o'clock appointment this morning with my general contractor at my ranch site in Bainbridge. We better leave right away." Tom gave Beth a kiss and wished her a happy day.

"Bye, Dad," the children all shouted.

Tom walked out the front door with both Bill and Thornton and headed for the shiny black Escalade, which was waiting in the driveway.

* * *

Tom watched as Bill drove away from his small bungalow. His mind was focused on the construction site of his new home, and he wanted to talk to Thornton about the home's security systems. While he collected his thoughts, he noticed the traffic seemed light for that time of the morning. Tom leaned forward from the backseat and said, "Thornton, while I meet with the general contractor, I want you to get together with the head of security. Remember, his name is Mr. Jamieson."

"Don't worry, Tom," said Thornton. "I remember Jamieson from before, and I will make sure all aspects of the security systems are up to your highest standard."

"Don't forget about our infrared outdoor systems," urged Tom as the car phone began ringing.

Tom watched as Bill picked up the phone. "Hold on, Leroy," shouted Bill. "Boss, it's Leroy, and he's upset as hell 'bout something." Bill handed the phone to Thornton, who safely passed the cordless phone back to Tom.

Tom grabbed the car phone and shouted, "What's wrong Leroy? Slow down, Leroy …" Tom listened for three minutes without uttering a single word. Next, Tom punched the button to turn off the phone, then he handed the phone up to Thornton. "Guys, somebody bombed my new house," said Tom as he looked up into the front seat. "There was an explosion and fire in the front of the house. You know the massive oak cathedral double doors I had? Well, they were blown out by a bomb, which then started a bad fire."

"Was anyone injured?" asked Thornton as he looked back at Tom, whose face was ashen.

"I don't know. Leroy didn't say," replied Tom. "Speed it up, Bill. Get me to the construction site as fast as you can." As Bill sped up, Tom wondered if the bomb was related to the threats he had received the day before. Thinking these things through, he concluded they had to be related to one person. But who? he wondered.

Twenty minutes later, Bill was driving up to the construction site. The fire trucks were wrapping up and preparing to leave. Tom was lucky to find the fire marshall just as he got out of the Escalade. He walked up to him and asked, "Fire Marshall Gordon, can you tell me what happened, and has anyone been injured?"

"Mr. Murphy, the bomb exploded before any of the crew reported to work, and so, thank God, no one was injured. The bomb was set inside the front entrance of the house, so the entire front of the house exploded outward, destroying the front entrance and the front of the house. Plus there was fire damage that was started by the bomb, which ignited flammable supplies. The bomb squad is investigating the scene," said Fire Marshall Gordon as he was finishing explained things to Tom. Then he added, "There was a warning spray-painted on the outer south wall of the house."

"What was the warning?"

"It said, 'For you, we are coming!'" said the fire marshall as he looked at Tom. "Does that mean anything to you, Mr. Murphy?"

"Yes. I've had several threats in the last two days. Each threat used that same phrase," explained Tom.

"Well, you better report that to the bomb squad, and they'll report it to the police, who will follow up on it with you later," explained the fire marshall as he put his helmet back on and proceeded to rejoin his men.

"Thanks, Fire Marshall Gordon," said Tom, then he and Thornton went to get a closer look at the extent of the damage. Tom walked up close, looked, and said, "Thor, the entire superstructure of the front of the house has been destroyed, and the massive oak cathedral doors have been reduced to millions of sprinters."

"Tom, this must have been a hell of a bomb to do all this damage," said Thornton. "But thank God no one got hurt." They walked around the mess as they examined the front of the home.

"That's the bright side," said Tom. "No one got hurt." Tom was thinking, while he walked through the rubble, that the explosion was related to the same man because of the same threat, and he was certain Thornton was having the same thoughts. "Thor, let's go inside. The general contractor, Mr. Marlowe, will be eager to see us," said Tom as he led Thornton through the rubble and into the inside of his huge, damaged, new home. Tom walked first through the foyer, then down the long hallway, which led to the grand room where Marlowe had set up the command center. In the middle of the grand room, a table was set up, where Marlowe kept the blueprints of the construction site. Once Tom entered the grand room, he immediately saw Marlowe standing and examining the blueprints of the house. Tom shouted, "Marlowe, what happened?" Marlowe was a tall, strong, formidable man, who looked up and saw Tom and Thornton walking toward him.

"Thomas, bad luck has bit you in the ass this morning," yelled Marlowe as he stood by the blueprints, which were spread over a sheet of plywood suspended over two worn-out wooden sawhorses.

"The last two days have been a stream of bad luck," Tom said as he reached Marlowe and vigorously shook his hand and glanced down at the spread-out blueprints.

Marlowe replied, "The bomb squad hasn't made it official yet, but Fire Marshall Gordon told me he knew it was a bomb, which was set to explode just before my crew showed up for work this morning."

Tom said, "Thank God, no one got hurt."

Marlowe raised two fingers and said, "Two things, Tom. You're gonna need armed guards to protect my crew, and you are gonna have to give me at least one, maybe two additional months for completion."

Thornton cleared his throat and said, "We'll need around-the-clock armed guards to protect his crew from any further complications."

Tom looked at Thornton and asked, "Can we get the men we need?" He was concerned that the needed men might not be immediately available. He also now remembered he would need additional security men to protect his family members.

"I can get all the men we'll need," replied Thornton.

"Good," Tom replied. Then he looked at Marlowe and asked, "Is Jamieson still on-site?" He knew Thornton had a morning appointment with the security expert.

"No," said Marlowe. "When he saw the damage, he left."

"Shit," said Thornton, "I had an appointment with Jamieson at eleven this morning."

"Bombs change things," said Marlowe with a big grin on his leathery tanned face. "Jamieson came to me this morning, and he told me he and his men weren't coming back until this site was safely guarded."

"Crap!" shouted Tom as he threw the ball cap he was wearing across the room. Whoever was doing these things were getting more severe as time passed, thought Tom. "Marlowe, what are your men saying?" He believed Marlowe tried to keep them working.

"They feel the same way," said Marlowe, "but they are willing to stay and clean up the mess in the front of the house until you can put together around-the-clock armed guards to protect them." Tom knew Marlowe had urged them to stay. Tom knew in order to keep the project moving ahead, he'd need a full around-the-clock staff of certified armed guards to both protect the men and also the home. He knew Thornton was already calculating the staff of armed personnel they would need.

"Marlowe, Thornton and I will get working immediately on the guard situation," said Tom as he nervously ran his fingers through his wavy copper-red hair. Thornton had gone to retrieve his boss's ball cap and was walking back when Tom said, "Thor, let's leave Marlowe to his job, while you and I start working on our new security needs." Thornton handed Tom his cap, then they both headed out of the grand room, back down the long hallway to the foyer, and then through and out the exploded cathedral front doors. Tom asked, "Thor, what do we need?" The bright sun hit them as they stepped outside. Tom shielded his face from the sunlight with his right hand. The clouds were gone and now it was bright and sunny.

Thornton replied, "Tom, we're gonna need at least five armed guards per shift with three shifts per day for as long as it takes."

"Thor, get on the phone," said Tom, "and make it happen." Tom adjusted his cap and said, "Let's go see where our psycho spray-painted the outer south wall." They started walking around to the south side of the ranch.

"Yeah. I'd like to see the paint job," said Thornton.

Once they reached the south wall, Tom became furious. The special designer brick that made up the exterior of the ranch was disfigured by big, bold, red, spray-painted letters composing the threat: For you, we are coming! Tom hoped that sandblasting could remove the red paint without disfiguring the shade of the bricks. But that job would be left for the construction crew, he thought. Thornton commented that the paint could possibly be removed without too much trouble, but his comment did not sooth Tom's anger much. "Thor, we gotta find this psychopath before he hurts someone," said Tom sternly.

"I agree, Tom. But how?"

Tom stood staring at the big red letters, and he hung his head until his chin touched his chest. "We gotta stop this guy!" said Tom prophetically.

Next, they turned and proceeded to walk back toward the front of the damaged ranch. Once Tom and Thornton reached the front of the ranch, Tom was approached by several members of the bomb squad and a Bainbridge police officer. They talked for over thirty minutes. First they talked about the bombing, then Tom gave them a full, detailed timeline of the threats starting with the phone call he received just before lunch yesterday and ending with the present bombing. "Mr. Murphy, we will be reporting all of this to the Cleveland police, who will be contacting you for further follow-up and to give you protection," explained the Bainbridge police officer.

"I would appreciate if you could apprehend his guy before he hurts someone in my family," said Tom as he shook hands with the police officer. Tom gave his business cards to each member of the bomb squad and one to the Bainbridge police officer. "You can always get me at my cell phone number," said Tom as he and Thornton prepared to leave. Tom walked side by side with Thornton until they reached Bill and the black Escalade. He watched as Bill jumped out of the vehicle and opened the back door for him. "Bill, let's get back to the facility." Tom grabbed his shiny laptop, as Bill and Thornton got into the vehicle.

Once Bill got under way, Tom saw Thornton turn in his seat to speak to him. "Tom, do you still have that interview with that newspaper reporter today?"

"Yes, Thor. Why?" asked Tom as he looked up from his laptop computer.

"I thought while you were involved with the reporter, then I'd go over to the university and drop in on my professor friend. I'm anxious to get his interpretation of the materials," explained Thornton.

"Thor, that'd be a perfect time to run that errand," said Tom, "because I'll be tied up with the reporter. And we both need that stuff professionally interpreted."

"Then I'll go while you're being interviewed," said Thornton as he turned back in his seat and stared out the front windshield.

Tom leaned forward and said, "Thor, take care of our security problems before you go to the university. Okay?"

"Absolutely, Tom."

Traffic was slow. While they rode, Tom tried to keep busy on his laptop making notes to himself regarding the upcoming interview that afternoon. Even though he tried to keep his mind busy, he still could not stop worrying about the threats that had come into his life. Who could be after them? he wondered. "Thor, I can't concentrate on the interview. These threats are freaking me out! What the f… is going on?" Tom's Irish Catholic upbringing kept him from outright saying that word, but the implied use of that superlative was as harsh as Tom could go, and it meant he was doggone serious. "Don't you agree the bombing of my house must be the ultimate threat?"

Thornton frowned and said, "I'd bet a dollar the threats are just getting started." Tom was discouraged as he listened to Thornton.

"I hope you'd loose that bet," Tom said firmly.

"Look on the positive side; maybe the bomb squad can trace the evidence back to the bomber," said Thornton, trying to look on the bright side.

"Is that possible?" asked Tom with a hint of surprise.

"It is rare, but it is possible."

Bill interrupted them when he said, "Boss, we'll be arriving in two minutes."

"Thanks, Bill."

"Tom, don't get discouraged," urged Thornton.

"Sorry, but I'm freaking out over this," said Tom as his ruddy Irish face flushed with anger.

"When we get back to the office, then I'll call the bomb squad. Okay, Tom?" asked Thornton, trying to give hope to Tom. "We'll see what evidence they've come up with."

"My wife is already freaking out about the other threats," expressed Tom. "Do you think she'll freak out when she hears about the bombing of our new home? Do you?" Tom was shouting angrily from the backseat of the Escalade.

Thornton turned back, facing Tom, and he urged him to calm down. "Tom, chill. You're gonna blow a gasket!"

"Chill? What's this guy gonna do next?" shouted Tom. "Who knows?" Tom angrily pounded his fists on the back of the front seats, then all of a sudden he laid back in his seat, crossed his arms across his chest, and remained silent until Bill drove the Escalade into the company garage. Bill pulled into Tom's reserved parking spot, then he announced they had arrived. For a moment, Tom remained silent, with his arms across his chest. Bill watched

Tom in the rearview mirror, until finally Tom quietly said, "Let's go in." Bill jumped out of the vehicle and ran to open the back door for Tom to get out. Once all of them were out of the Escalade, Tom said, "Bill, at noon I want you to drive Thor to the university. Stay around while he conducts his business, then drive him back here afterwards. It's eleven now, and so that gives you an hour to fetch lunch. Tom motioned for Bill to take off, which Bill did by hurrying into the building, heading for the coffee lounge and the vending machines. Tom and Thornton slowly walked out of the garage and into the building, heading toward Tom's personal office. Tom instructed Thornton when he said, "Thor, use this hour before noon to contact Lockhart Security and recruit the staff we're going to need to adequately protect the construction crew and my house."

"I'll call Mr. Lockhart personally. He'll know just the personnel to more than adequately protect our people and our property," said Thornton reassuringly. Tom reached his office door, which, as of yesterday's dead flowers and threats, he had started locking. Once they were in the office, Thornton asked, "Are you gonna prepare for your twelve o'clock interview?"

"First I've got to call and tell Beth about the bombing," explained Tom as he sat down at his large glass-top desk, and under his breath he briefly started to rehearse what he would say to his already upset wife. Thornton went to the far east end of the large office, where he had set up a small work area for himself. Tom heard Thornton talking on the telephone, and then he knew he could call his wife and not be overheard by Thornton. He dialed Beth's cell phone and listened as it rang, then when he heard Beth's sweet voice he chimed, "Hello, sweetheart!"

"Oh, hello, Tom," she replied. "How's your day going?"

"Not good, Beth."

"Why? More dead flowers?" she asked with a giggle. At least she had a sense of humor, he thought.

"No, nothing like that," said Tom. "Something worse!"

"Oh, my God," she uttered, "what could be worse than the threats we've been getting?" He could hear the strain in her scared feminine voice. He wanted to gently tell her about the bomb, but the only way was to be straight to the point. "You know the threats we've been receiving. Well, whoever sent those threats exploded a bomb in the front of our new house early this morning."

"Oh, my God!" she uttered, "was the entire house destroyed? Was anyone injured or killed?" He could hear the scared tone in her voice.

"The damage was just to the front of the house."

"Were my cathedral doors ruined?"

"Yes, but they can be replaced," Tom encouraged her.

"Was anyone injured?"

"No. The bomb exploded before the work crew arrived."

"Who is doing these things?" she asked nervously. "Tom, I'm scared. What if he hurts the kids?"

"I won't let anyone hurt you or the kids."

"Tom, I'm scared," pleaded Beth.

"Listen! The bomb squad is checking for evidence that may lead them to the man who planted the bomb. Once they do that they will catch the guy," explained Tom with a false optimism.

"Tom, the man who is doing these things is too smart to be caught," said Beth to her husband, who was trying to give her hope. "He has our address. He knew where to send the scary letter and that means he knows how to get to us. We need to get away from our home. Maybe we could stay at a hotel until the authorities caught him."

"That is a good idea," said Tom, who was trying to go along with his scared wife. "We'll move tonight after the City Club ceremonies." He was hoping she was still prepared for that night's celebration, where they were awarding him the status of Man of the Year.

"Aren't you canceling that under the circumstances?"

"I'm not canceling. We're still all going," said Tom. "This is important to me."

"Are you still going through with the newspaper interview today?" she asked hotly.

"Yes! The interview is in a few minutes," said Tom sternly. "I can't cancel that. They're waiting down the hall for me." He knew she was upset, and he shared her feelings. He was more than upset; he was scared because he did not know what was coming at them next.

"You should drop everything and come move your family," shouted Beth into the phone. "This maniac knows our address, which makes us sitting ducks." He knew she was right, but he wanted this interview and he wanted to be awarded Man of the Year!

"Listen, Beth, get everyone's clothes gathered up for tonight, and then go to your mom's house for the rest of today. I'll send Bill to drive you all to the City Club tonight," explained Tom, who was trying to be as accommodating as possible.

"Tom, we are all shopping. We aren't at home," said Beth with an irritated tone.

"When you are finished shopping then go to your mom's house and I'll have Bill pick you all up to go to the City Club for the award dinner," said Tom, hoping she'd go along with his instructions.

"I'll call Mom right away."

"Good! I'll see you and the kids tonight," said Tom. "I love you, Beth."

"I love you too," she said, then hung up the phone.

Tom placed his receiver back on its cradle, then he looked at the notes he had gathered in preparation for that afternoon's newspaper interview.

*   *   *

At exactly noon Tuesday, Tom finished reviewing his notes and was ready for the newspaper interview. He left his office and walked to the front desk, where his company welcomed visitors. He had made arrangements over the phone to meet with a journalist named Liz Walker and her photographer, Calvin. When he reached the front desk he saw a tall, well-groomed young woman, who he assumed was Liz Walker. He walked up to her, extended his hand to shake, and said, "Hello, I'm Tom Murphy, and you must be Ms. Liz Walker."

"It's nice to meet you, Mr. Murphy," said Liz, "this gentleman is Calvin, my photographer."

"Nice to meet you, Calvin," he said as he shook the photographer's hand. "Please, both of you, call me Tom."

"And, please, call me Liz," she said as she swept her long brunette bangs out of her sparkling green eyes.

"Liz, I thought we could do the interview in my office and then afterwards I could give you and Calvin a tour of my facility," he said as he guided them away from the front desk and down the hall toward his private office.

"The atmosphere here looks so cheerful," observed Liz.

"I want everyone's workday to be enjoyable," said Tom.

When they reached Tom's private office, the door was wide open and inviting. The overhead lights were on, and the windows, overlooking a manicured lawn, were open and letting in a cool fall breeze. As they walked into the office, Liz said, "Tom, I briefly spoke to the receptionist at your front desk, and she claims everyone here loves you."

"I doubt my children would agree," he said, laughing. "Liz why don't you sit on my couch so that you can spread out your notes and tape recorder on the coffee table." He watched as she gingerly worked her way between the coffee table and the long, white, leather couch. Calvin set up his camera equipment on the opposite side of the office. Tom stood leaning up against the front of his desk and tried to look casual. He watched as Liz arranged her material on the coffee table. "Is it all right if I record our conversation?" she asked pleasantly as she turned on the tape recorder, not waiting for a reply.

"Liz, that would be fine," replied Tom, who noticed she'd already turned it on. He hoped she was not going to be pushy and aggressive.

She smiled and started right out of the gate by asking, "Can we start with your background before you won the lottery?"

"Sure," he replied, wondering why.

"Tom, bear with me. Would it be accurate to portray you, before you won the lottery, as a thirty-two-year-old married man with a wife and three children, who was struggling financially to provide for his family?" asked Liz.

"Yes. I guess that would've been true. At the time, just before winning the lottery, my wife, Beth, and I were struggling to support our three children. I was a poor life insurance salesman, and so I supplemented our income by doing janitorial work at our parish and handyman work in our neighborhood," Tom explained as he uncomfortably remembered the tough times.

"So, things before the lottery were tough."

"Yes," replied Tom, not knowing where she was headed.

"Pardon me, but do you mind if I smoke?" asked Liz.

"I don't mind. There is an ashtray on the coffee table." While she lit up her cigarette, Tom's thoughts drifted away from the interview. His thoughts temporarily focused on his problems with the mystery man who was sending threats, bombing his home, and scaring the hell out of his poor wife.

His attention drifted, and Liz startled him when she said, "Tom, are you with us?"

"Sorry," he replied as he watched her exhale cigarette smoke out of her slim, long nose.

"When you won the lottery," stated Liz, "then I assume things instantly changed, didn't they?"

Tom shook his head, trying to refocus, and said, "What was that you said?" His thoughts were still on his problems.

Liz looked at Tom and said, "Tom, I assume when you won the lottery, things changed."

He picked up on her change of direction and he said, "Yes! Things changed. It was like bah-boom, I won the lottery, and everything changed for the better." He became animated and excited just thinking about the winnings.

"Describe how it was for you and your family."

"For us, it was great! Like we were walking on ultrabright moonbeams," explained Tom as he recalled his first few days after winning the lottery.

"Great description, Tom."

"Thank you," replied Tom, watching her take a quick drag off her lady's thin, long cigarette.

"Tom, I was in the audience the night you were awarded the lottery check," explained Liz, "and I heard you mention a surprise. Was that your idea to clean up the city? And had you had that idea prior to winning the lottery?"

"Yes, I did mention a surprise, and that was the idea to clean up the city of Cleveland," Tom said. "Actually, the idea came to me as a dream over a year before I won the lottery, and I'd been playing with the idea ever since."

"A dream?" asked Liz. "Can you describe it?"

"It was vague. I was directing men and women to pick up trash, and at the end of the dream the city of Cleveland sparkled," said Tom with animation.

"In the last two years you've made your dreams come true," said Liz. "You've hired two thousand workers to clean the city, and now the city shines because of you."

"I was lucky. I got to fulfill a dream," smiled Tom.

"And since the win you've put millions of dollars back into the city's economy. You're the most recognized and admired man in this area. Everyone knows and loves you. The mayor of Cleveland claims turning your lottery winnings into your crusade to clean up the city was totally unselfish and a touch of genius."

"Did the mayor say that?"

"Yes, and now everyone calls you the Prince of Cleveland," Liz said with a smile.

"I like that title," said Tom. "My kids like the title too." Calvin took a couple shots, catching Tom's big, Irish smile.

"How does all the notoriety feel?"

"It feels great, Liz."

"Let's talk about tonight. I was told you are going to the City Club of Cleveland to be awarded the honor of 'The Man of the Year.' Now there is no question you earned and deserve that title. Now, in a few words, tell my readers why people call you 'The Man of the Year,' and the other title, 'The Prince of Cleveland.'"

"Liz, I think the answer is simple. Two years ago I won the lottery, and since then I've taken my winnings and created good-paying jobs for men and women to clean up the trash and make the city of Cleveland the cleanest city in the country," explained Tom, proudly. "A real treasure."

"Is it just that simple?" asked Liz.

"Yes. I think so," replied Tom.

"No! I think there is a lot more to the story than just a guy spending his lottery fortune to clean up a city that he obviously loves. I think the story has much more to it. Bear with me a moment, Tom, while I tell my readers just how unselfish you are. That's the word the mayor used, wasn't it? 'Unselfish!' Let's back up a minute. How much money did your lottery fortune come to?"

"Fifty-eight million dollars," said Tom.

"Let's clarify that. It's fifty-eight million dollars after the taxes were taken out. Am I correct?" she asked.

"Yes!"

"And I hear from your friends you can't give it away fast enough. Your employees who pick up trash make twenty dollars an hour, with unlimited overtime and a full benefits package. This is generous, Tom. Isn't it?"

"There are a great many unemployed workers in our city. I wanted to help. I personally interviewed each and every employee, and what I am looking for are folks who love the city and who want it to sparkle. I want workers who are enthusiastic and excited about making the city of Cleveland beautiful."

Liz smiled and said, "Let me tell my readers how you have constructed your army. You have two thousand field workers, fifty field managers, and one overall supervisor, who is your business manager. You have an elaborate telephone branch where folks can call in and request a personal property cleanup for free. You have a communications branch, which tracks and dispatches with all your field workers, field managers, and vans and trucks. You have quite an army," said Liz. "At your two-acre facility you have a payroll and accounting department, a secretarial staff, the mailroom, a garage, and a small staff of mechanics and janitors and secretaries."

"It is not an army, Liz. It is a crusade, a mission."

"Tom, you are giving your fortune away."

"What a great reason," replied Tom.

"Your employees love you and call you 'The Prince of Cleveland,'" said Liz as she smiled while looking into Tom's bright blue eyes and ruddy Irish face.

"I guess so," smiled Tom. "My kids love the title."

"Tom, can we walk around your two-acre facility you've built and take some pictures for the newspaper article?" requested Liz as she stood up from the couch.

"Sure, what would you like to see first?" asked Tom as he helped Liz put her notes and her recorder back into her briefcase. "Would you like to see our telephone branch?"

Liz motioned to her photographer, Calvin, to prepare to take a lot of pictures, then the three of them walked out of Tom's office and proceeded down a short, cheerfully decorated hallway to the company's telephone branch. Tom introduced Liz Walker to Wanda, the head of the branch and coordinator of all the incoming calls at the facility.

After the phone branch, Tom took them to the communication center, where they met Leroy, the dispatcher. This area monitored all the activities of the field workers and field managers, all cell phones and vehicles—trucks and vans. That department had a whole wall with a large map of the city of Cleveland on it. Tom explained, while Leroy was on the horn, that in this area Leroy can communicate and GPS track all company vehicles, all fifty managers and the two thousand field workers along with a small collection of other important folks that work for the company. "Every employee has a trackable GPS functioning cell phone, which Leroy controls and communicates with. Again, Calvin quietly proceeded to take pictures in the dispatcher's area, as he had done in the telephone branch. Tom continued, showing them the payroll and accounting office, the loading docks, the mechanics working area, the janitorial working area, the secretarial pool, and the small shipping and receiving area and the mail room. There was a huge parking area where they kept vans and trucks. The last of the facility that Tom showed them was the huge auditorium, where Tom could address all his workers at one seating.

As they finished the tour, Liz smiled and said, "Tom, thank you for showing us your wonderful facility and your marvelous mission you are undertaking."

Tom replied, "It was fun talking with you and Calvin. Maybe the next time you can meet my wonderful wife and my three crazy kids."

"That would be nice, Tom," she said as she and Calvin shook Tom's hand. Then as she was concluding she said, "Good luck tonight at the City Club." They left by way of the front door of the facility, and Tom walked them out.

*   *   *

At noon Lukas was wearing his business suit and carrying a briefcase filled with ten thousand dollars, which he was using as bait to lure a client. He had a noon appointment. Dagmar would be accompanying him to Radio Station WKKID.

Lukas watched as Dagmar primped with her short, blonde, pixy haircut in the mirror of their motel room. "Finish up," said Lukas. "It's a noon appointment, and you know I insist on being punctual." He watched as she finished by putting on her red bolero jacket and grabbing her large purse, which held their surprise plastique bomb.

Lukas drove out of Willoughby and headed east on the freeway until he nearly reached the Pennsylvania border, then he doubled back southwest on a private dirt road until he reached the puny little community that was home to radio station WKKID.

When Lukas drove up to the building which housed the radio station, he was not impressed. The building was small and run down in its general appearance. The transmitting antenna was in back of the building along with the small heliport that housed the station's small two-man helicopter. In the front parking lot there were two older-model cars and a badly rusted pickup truck.

Lukas parked in the last parking spot. He looked at Dagmar and said, "Remember to act rich and confident. I will have the pilot show you the helicopter, and that is when I want you to plant the bomb. Remember, place the bomb in the interior and in the rear, out of sight."

"I totally understand," said Dagmar confidently as she reached for the van door handle, but out of respect she waited for any further instructions from Lukas.

"Let's do this," said Lukas as he popped the van door open and climbed out into the gravel driveway. He walked around and assisted Dagmar out of the van, and then they walked into the front door of the small building.

"Welcome to radio station WKKID in the boonies. My name is Mick Myerson and I am the owner and general manager," said the husky gentleman with a full white beard.

Lukas looked him straight in the eye, shook his hand, and said, "My name is William Gonnatake and this lovely lady is my assistant Linda Gotcha. Just call us Bill and Linda." Lukas saw that Dagmar was having a hard time not laughing, but he continued. "Mr. Myerson, we represent an anonymous benefactor who has selected you to help promote a charity event. To show you that my benefactor is one hundred percent on the up and up, he has authorized me to outright give you ten thousand dollars, which I have here in my briefcase." He lifted the briefcase, set it on the counter, and opened it.

"Wow! Is this a down payment of some kind?" asked Myerson as he touched the currency.

"No. This is no down payment," said Lukas. "This is an out and out gift from my benefactor."

"A gift?"

"Yes!" Lukas closed the briefcase and handed it to Myerson and said, "This is for you."

Lukas stood looking at Myerson, who was holding the case. "What kind of charity event is it?" asked Myerson.

"The charity event is a publicity stunt. We will need the use of your helicopter. Oh, and there is going to be tons of television exposure, which will be great for your radio station," said Lukas as he continued to tell his mark about the event.

"This all sounds great," said Myerson. "Let me introduce you and Linda to our DJ and our helicopter pilot. Folks, this is Talkin' Teddy, our DJ, and this other fellow is Grasshopper George, our helicopter pilot."

Lukas and Dagmar shook hands with the two fellows and Lukas said, "Linda is a helicopter pilot herself. Why doesn't George take her out back and show her your helicopter while I explain to you two gentlemen what all is involved in this charity event."

"That sounds great, Bill," said Myerson. "George, go show Linda our bird."

While George showed Dagmar the helicopter, Lukas explained all the details of the publicity stunt and charity event to Myerson and Talkin' Teddy. After the presentation Lukas knew they were both eager to participate in the event. He knew he had caught them hook, line, and sinker.

* * *

Dagmar made friendly small talk with George as they walked around to the rear of the property. When she reached the helicopter she said, "George, you've got a real pretty helicopter. I really like the way you have the radio station's call letters painted on the helicopter."

"Thanks, Linda," said George. "That was my idea."

"Can I climb in and look around inside?" asked Dagmar as she saw George nod his head, reach up and open the door; then she climbed inside, purse and all. Once inside, she took a quick look around before George could get in, and she found a small compartment in the far rear of the helicopter. Once she opened it, she found an onboard first aid kit. Luckily, there was enough spare room to slip in the bomb. The small compartment was located right next to the fuel tank. Just as she closed the compartment, George climbed in and almost caught her with the bomb, but she quickly said, "George, someday I'd love to go up with you."

"How 'bout now?" asked George with enthusiasm.

"Unfortunately I've got a headache, and flying would aggravate it, but you're on for another day," she said kindly. She had him show her the controls and all of the special features of his helicopter. She knew enough to ask the appropriate questions to convince him that she knew her helicopters. Afterwards, they walked back to the radio studio where Lukas was finalizing his sales pitch to the owner and his disc jockey.

When she and George entered the station, she could hear that Lukas was finished with these men, and so she said, "Bill, I hate to say it, but our next appointment is coming up soon." It had been a preplanned signal to get Lukas out of the station gracefully.

"Yes, Linda," said Lukas as he looked at his wristwatch. "We must be pushing off. Thank you Mr. Myerson."

"No, thank you, Bill," uttered Myerson as he energetically shook hands with Lukas. "We look forward to the event."

"I will call you tomorrow," said Lukas as Dagmar put her arm around his and walked him out of the building and back into the sunny afternoon. They went directly into the van and drove back to the Willoughby Travelodge. When the two of them arrived back at their room at the Travelodge they met with the remaining members of Team One, and they reported to them how the meeting went at the radio station.

"So everything is set in place for the first ransom exchange," said Boris eagerly.

"Yes Boris," said Lukas. "Everything is set."

* * *

While Tom was being interviewed by the newspaper reporter, Thornton went across town to the university to meet with Professor Crawford in the Psychology Department. Tom was not planning on using Bill or the Escalade, and so he told Bill to drive Thornton to the university.

As Bill drove, Thornton had thoughts about Tom. He knew Tom was preoccupied with the threats, and he worried how well Tom could handle the interview. But Thornton knew Tom was mentally tough, and he would probably handle the interview quite well.

Bill pulled up to the front entrance and let Thornton out. He walked into the building, and then he headed for the third floor. Without too much trouble, he found Dr. Crawford's office. The door was open, but he still politely knocked. "Come in, the doors open," said Crawford as he looked up from his work.

"Dr. Crawford," said Thornton as he entered.

"Mr. Williams, nice to see you." They shook hands. "Are you still looking after Tom Murphy?"

"Yes. In fact that is why I'm here, Doctor. Tom has gotten a series of threats in the last two days that concern me, along with some questionable materials sent to him."

"What type of material?" asked Dr. Crawford curiously.

"Let me show you," said Thornton as he pulled his cell phone out of his pants pocket. "Yesterday afternoon Tom received two dozen dead red roses with a dead red robin placed inside the flowers. Here is the photo of the roses and the robin." He showed the doctor the pictures in his cell phone. He waited and watched as Dr. Crawford viewed the pictures. "The last picture, as you can see, is the picture of the card with the threat written on it."

"For you, we are coming," read Dr. Crawford. "That is a strange way of expressing a threat."

"I thought so," replied Thornton, who then pulled the drawing from its envelope to show the doctor. "Then when we arrived at his home last night this drawing had been delivered. Would you look closely at the grotesque figures and hideous faces?"

He waited for a couple of minutes while Dr. Crawford analyzed the drawing. The doctor looked at it from various angles, then he took out a magnifying glass from his desk drawer and looked closer at the figures and faces, which were cleverly drawn in various colors and shades of crayon.

"Extraordinary details for a drawing done in crayons," said the doctor. "And look again. The same threat in the exact quote."

"Yesterday morning, before these item were delivered, Tom received an anonymous phone call. The caller asked for Tom specifically, then he twice repeated the quoted threat. On the drive home last night, he claimed he has had the feeling of being watched for the last few weeks," explained Thornton.

"Were there any deliveries today?" asked the doctor.

"This morning, on our way to the construction site of his new house in Bainbridge, the house was bombed," said Thornton as he showed the doctor another picture from his cell phone. "The picture is of the front of the bombed house."

"That bomb appears to have done a lot of damage," said Dr. Crawford as he handed the cell phone back to Thornton.

"Doctor, here is another picture," said Thornton as he adjusted the cell phone picture function and handed the phone back to the doctor. "This is spray paint on the south side of Tom's new home. As you can see, the bomber left the same threat: 'For you, we are coming.'"

"I can imagine that Mr. Murphy has got to be quite scared," speculated Dr. Crawford.

"Doctor, what do you see?" asked Thornton as he put the cell phone back into his pants pocket. "Overall, this material, what is your professional opinion?"

"I assume it is a male, and I'd say he is very angry. His attention to details leads me to believe he is very, very intelligent, maybe even at the genius level of IQ, and there are strong traits of persistence and determination, which is demonstrated by the severity of his acts," explained Dr. Crawford as he played with a pencil.

"Could you classify him?" asked Thornton as he watched the doctor intensively.

"If I were to profile this man based on the evidence, then I'd say you are dealing with a severely compulsive psychopath," said Dr. Crawford as he snapped his pencil. "He could be extremely dangerous, Thornton. Be careful. Have you and Tom contacted the authorities?"

"Tom dealt with both the bomb squad and the Bainbridge police this morning," said Thornton, "but I'm not sure how much he told them." He started putting the drawing back into its envelope, and then he prepared to leave. "I won't keep you any longer. I know how busy you are."

"Williams, nonsense," uttered Dr. Crawford. "I will always have time for one of my best students." They shook hands, and Thornton turned to leave. "Remember to warn Thomas about how dangerous this man may be."

"I will. Thank you, Doctor," said Thornton as he walked out of the office toward the stairway. He stepped outside and looked around for the Escalade that Bill was driving. At first he didn't see the Cadillac, but after a few minutes he saw that Bill had been driving in circles around the academic buildings. Bill pulled up in front of Thornton and told him to jump in. Once he was buckled in, Bill pulled away and headed back toward the facility.

"Thor, what'd the shrink say 'bout Tom's boogeyman?" asked Bill as he made his eyebrows go up and down.

Thornton looked sternly at Bill and said, "The doc says Tom's boogeyman is a bona fide psychopath."

"Oh, shit! That sounds bad."

"It is bad, Bill. Tom and his family are in grave danger," said Thornton as he played with the edge of the envelope that held the scary drawing. "I think the Murphy family should be moved to a safe house until this psychopath is apprehended."

"Can you convince Tom to do that?"

"Tom's mind is preoccupied on tonight's award ceremony," explained Thornton as he pulled out his cell phone, started to dial a number, then changed his mind and closed the phone.

"Who were you going to call?"

"Tom," said Thornton, "but I remembered he is busy with the newspaper folks."

"Thornton, you won't be able to get Tom to cancel tonight's event," said Bill. "He has been talking about this evening for weeks."

"I know, Bill, but I've got to get him to understand how much danger he and his family are in," he stressed.

Bill drove away from the university. "How was your visit with your professor?" asked Bill as he drove around University Circle.

"It was good," replied Thornton. "We're old friends, and it was good to see him, even if it had to be under these serious matters."

"Old friends are good to keep in touch with."

"Bill, I don't want to go back to the facility quite yet. Can you first drive me to the Lockhart Security Company?"

"Sure," Thornton. "Where is Lockhart Security?"

"It's in Beachwood. Head east on the freeway."

It took them thirty minutes to reach the security company. Thornton had worked for James Lockhart for many years; his latest assignment was that as Thomas Murphy's bodyguard. James Lockhart was like a father to Thornton, taking him straight from the Navy SEALS to training him in all aspects of commercial security. Thornton liked being a bodyguard; in fact, he thrived on it. He turned out to be one of Lockhart Security's top bodyguards. For the last year and a half Thornton had been assigned to Thomas Murphy full time.

When they arrived at the security company, Bill stayed in the black Escalade while Thornton went in to speak directly with the owner of the company, James Lockhart, who was waiting to see him. Thornton walked into the big front office, and Lockhart greeted him eagerly. "Hello. How are you, Thornton?" asked his boss as they shook hands. Thornton answered his boss, and then he sat down. They had talked briefly earlier, and Thornton had quickly told Lockhart about the events and threats that were plaguing Murphy. Lockhart asked Thornton to refresh his memory regarding the needs Thornton wanted for his client, Thomas Murphy.

"As we briefly discussed, Tom wants a bodyguard for each of his family members, which works out to be one for the wife, Beth, and three bodyguards for each of his three children," explained Thornton as he rubbed his clean-shaven bronze head. "Next, we need to discuss the security factors for his new under-construction home in Bainbridge. As we discussed, the front of the home was bombed earlier this morning, and now we need five armed guards 24/7 for as long as it takes to find the bomber. We still would need security even after the house was completely built."

"Thornton, the bodyguards we can easily handle," said Lockhart, "but that many armed guards is going to be a task to fill. We can, but it'll take some outsourcing," Lockhart said as he stroked his long gray beard. "Who is guarding Thomas while you are here?"

"He's in his private office right now preparing a speech. Tonight he is getting The Man of the Year award at the City Club," said Thornton.

"Do you want more bodies to protect the family tonight?" asked Lockhart as he adjusted his spectacles.

"I asked Tom, and he just wants to interview and select your people tomorrow morning," said Thornton as he stood up to go and adjusted his pants.

"So we'll all meet at Tom's facility at nine in the morning tomorrow." Lockhart stood up to walk him out.

"That's what Tom wants," said Thornton as he smiled. "I'd better get back. I don't want to leave him alone too long." The two men shook hands. Lockhart admired his young protégé and sent him on his way back to protect Murphy and the family.

*   *   *

Tom returned to his office after walking Liz and Calvin to their vehicle. It was 1:00 PM when he walked into his office. Tom decided to lie down on his long couch, hoping to relax and sort things out for a few minutes. He was worried about the threats. He realized the man making the threats had increased the stakes by bombing his house, and he wondered what would be next. Within minutes he unintentionally fell fast asleep. Half an hour later, Tom was startled awake when Thornton shook his shoulder. "What is it?" shouted Tom as he sprang into a sitting position.

"Tom, I'm back from the university," said Thornton as he stood over his boss.

"Okay!" said Tom as he stood up off the couch; then he walked over to and sat down behind his desk. He needed coffee to wake him from his short nap.

"How was the interview with the newspaper folks?"

"It was fun," said Tom. "Let's go get some coffee."

Tom led the way as they both walked down the hall to the company's coffee lounge. They helped themselves to the coffee. And as they stood sipping the coffee Thornton said, "Tom, we need to talk."

There were others in the coffee lounge, and Tom did not want to be overheard, so he looked at Thornton and said, "Not here, Thor. Let's go back to my office." Once they returned to Tom's office, they sat down next to each other on the couch. They each set their coffee cups on the glass-top coffee table. First, Tom asked, "Did your professor think we had a crazy man on our hands?"

"Dr. Crawford was concerned with what he saw," replied Thornton as he reached for his coffee cup and took a sip.

"How concerned?"

"Tom, Crawford profiled the man as a genius and as an extremely dangerous compulsive psychopath. He sees the man as a very angry individual, who has focused his anger on you," explained Thornton.

"Sounds serious."

"Dr. Crawford suggests we contact the authorities."

"I've already started that process," said Tom. "This morning when the guys with the bomb squad questioned me I told them about the threats and all the deliveries."

"Good," responded Thornton, drinking his coffee.

"Thor, this afternoon I've got to get ready for tonight's award ceremony, but after the ceremony we'll move my family to a safe hotel, and then first thing tomorrow morning we'll interview those bodyguards for my family." Tom took a drink of his coffee. "We can't wait for Joe Brown. We need more help right away. Don't you agree?"

"Yes, Tom," replied Thornton as he finished his coffee and put the empty cup back on the coffee table. "Tom, after seeing my professor, Bill drove me over to Lockhart Security. I met with James Lockhart directly, and I explained what has happened so far, and he is concerned, as I am, about the seriousness of the threats. I set up a meeting for nine o'clock tomorrow morning to interview bodyguards for the family, and armed guards for the security at your new home."

"That sound great, Thor," replied Tom. He got up off the couch, took his coffee and walked back behind his desk. Tom sat down at his desk, looked at Thornton, who was still sitting on the couch, and said, "These threats are interfering with my ability to practice my acceptance speech for tonight's ceremony at the City Club." Tom felt impatient.

"I know all about it, Tom," said Thornton. "Do you want me to help you practice your acceptance speech?"

"No! Katelyn is going to help me," said Tom as he finished drinking his coffee. "I'd like you to call Beth on her cell phone and ask her if she and the kids have made it to her mother's house yet?"

"What if she hasn't yet gone to her mother's?"

"Tell her to hurry up," said Tom, "and tell her to stay away from our bungalow." Tom rubbed his chin nervously. Next, Tom dialed his phone, talked to Katelyn, and asked her to come help him practice his speech. He hung up the phone, looked at Thornton, and said, "She'll be here in a couple of minutes."

"Tom, do you want me to get lost for an hour or so?" asked Thornton as he stood up off the couch.

"Don't go too far …" Tom stopped talking just as his desk phone started to ring. He looked at Thornton and pointed for him to wait while Tom took the incoming call. "Just Clean It Up. Tom Murphy speaking. How may I help you?"

"Thomas Murphy?"

"Yes. This is Thomas Murphy."

"For you, we are coming!"

"What'd you say?" shouted Tom as he waved at Thornton and whispered, "It's him."

Tom listened as the caller said, "Thomas, for you, we are coming!"

Tom screamed, "Who are you? What is your name?"

"Thomas, soon we are coming!"

"Who are you?" he yelled. Next, Tom heard the phone go dead. Thornton rushed to Tom's side. "He hung up, Thor." Tom, who was standing, fell back into the chair behind his desk and said, "Thor, he said he was coming soon."

"Tom, did you recognize the voice? What exactly did he say?" asked Thornton just as Tom saw Katelyn enter the office.

"Good afternoon, guys," chimed Katelyn. "We're going to work on your speech, Tom?" He watched her as she walked up to his desk.

Tom felt anxious as he looked at her and said, "Katelyn, something just came up. Could you give Thor and me thirty minutes, then come back?" He nervously ran his hands through his red hair.

"Sure, Tom," she replied, "is thirty minutes long enough?"

"Yeah. Sure," uttered Tom. "See you later." He watched her leave the office, closing the door as she left. "Thor, this guy said 'soon, he is coming soon,'" said Tom, whose stomach felt like knots. "Thor, this guy is getting under my skin. He is freaking me out!"

"Tom, maybe you should cancel tonight's activities and take your family into hiding," suggested Thornton. "What do you think?"

"After the presentation," said Tom stubbornly. "We'll move into hiding after the ceremony." He had looked forward to being awarded Man of the Year for months. "My family will be safe in that crowd, don't you agree, Thor?"

Tom watched Thornton rub his shaven head and reply, "I don't think this guy is a crackpot."

"We'll move my family after the City Club," said Tom, who pulled out his speech and reread it several times, practicing until Katelyn returned to help him.

* * *

That afternoon the mission of Teams One and Two were to find, follow, and tag with GPS tracking devices all of Tom's personal vehicles, which included his Cadillac Escalade, his Lincoln Navigator, his family leisure van, his BMW sedan, his wife's SUV, and her Cadillac touring car.

Lukas had tagged Tom's Cadillac Escalade several days earlier and had been tracking its movements since then. The Lincoln Navigator was harder to tag because it remained in Tom's guarded facility parking lot and it did not come out until his Cadillac Escalade was either down for general maintenance or down for repair. The Lincoln Navigator was Tom's second car.

Boris and Stephan from Team One were stationed outside the facility parking lot. They were hoping and waiting for the family's leisure van to be driven off the property for a wash job or for fuel in preparation for that night's award ceremony. They sat just off the exit of the facility after hours of waiting. Stephan was the driver while Boris was second in command of Team One. Out of boredom, Stephan asked, "Boris, how long have you known Lukas?"

Boris did not answer right away. He sat and thought back to when he first met Lukas Krueger. "Stephan, I've known Lukas for almost fifteen years. I knew him before he'd started his string of kidnappings. He's changed a lot since those early days," said Boris as he looked at Stephan sitting behind the wheel.

"The rumors say Krueger is very rich," uttered Stephan with envy as he drummed his fingers nervously on the steering wheel.

"Well, I've been on all of his five kidnappings and he pulled each one of them off miraculously. He's made me a lot of money," said Boris as he lit a cigarette.

"They say this is his last kidnapping. Is that true?"

Boris blew smoke and said, "He's going for a perfect record. He only kidnaps the ultrarich Americans. And yes it's true he wants to retire after this gig." Boris looked at Stephan, who had a strange look on his face. "What is it, Stephan?" asked Boris as he blew smoke out of his nose.

"Honestly? He scares me," confessed Stephan.

"Why? Because he killed Alex?"

"Yeah, and because of other things."

"He's less tolerant than he used to be," said Boris as he took another drag on his cigarette. "He won't hurt you. He wants more perfection as he grows older."

"Just between you and me, sometimes he gives me the creeps," admitted the young driver.

"Don't let him get you spooked," advised Boris. He took out a piece of paper from his coat pocket. "Stephan, according to this list that Lukas gave me, all the vehicles, including the two that the wife uses, are already tagged with GPS tracking devices except for Tom's Lincoln Navigator and the family leisure van, which we are watching for this afternoon," said Boris as he took another drag of his cigarette.

"When do we get to have lunch?" asked the naïve and younger Stephan. Boris started to laugh at him.

"We don't leave until we tag that van."

Boris watched as Stephan leaned back behind the steering wheel, pulled his black ball cap down over his face, and mumbled, "Wake me when you see the van!" Boris flicked his cigarette stub out the window and proceeded to light up yet another one. While Stephan napped, Boris pretty much chain-smoked. Boris yearned for his beautiful Europe, and he yearned for his now middle-aged siblings who were preparing to retire and spoil their toddling grandchildren, but he was not yet ready to retire even if Lukas Krueger was.

At two, Boris reached over and nudged Stephan. "There is the van! Wake up. See, there is that black leisure van. Hurry, start the engine!" Boris watched the van as it drove off the property and headed down the road.

"Okay! Okay! I see it," shouted Stephan as Boris watched him follow the black leisure van. They followed it for fifteen minutes; finally it pulled into a car wash, where they hoped they may be able to tag it. "Where should I go, Boris?"

"Don't get in line," shouted Boris. "Pull into the parking lot, Stephan." Boris kept his eye on the black leisure van as it got into line to enter the car wash. He sat and watched as the long, black van entered and disappeared into the car wash building. Once they lost sight of the van, Boris shouted, "Stephan, drive around front so we can see when the van comes out of the car wash." Stephan proceeded to drive around to the front, then he put the car in park and waited. After about ten minutes the van rolled out the front of the car wash. The black van sparkled after having been cleaned and then towel dried. "We'll stay with the van and hopefully it'll stop again, which will give us another opportunity to tag it," said Boris as he urged Stephan to follow the moving black van. After tailing the van for five minutes, it suddenly stopped at a Burger King. Boris watched as the driver of the van parked and went into the restaurant, leaving the van totally unattended. "This is our chance to tag the van," said Boris as he reached back and grabbed his GPS tracking device. "Stephan, go in and keep him busy until I've had time to finish." Boris and Stephan got out of their car. Boris hurried over to the black van, while Stephan went into the Burger King. Boris slid himself under the van and started to attach the GPS equipment to the undercarriage.

* * *

Stephan entered the Burger King and walked up behind the driver of the van. They both proceeded to advance in line toward the order taker and cashier. The line moved along quite quickly, and before long the driver of the van was speaking to the order taker. Next, the driver was paying the cashier, while Stephan ordered a cola and moved forward to the cashier. They both stood waiting for their orders, which both came at once. The driver took his tray to the condiment stand while Stephan watched him grab a couple of napkins and a straw. Next they both walked over to the drink stand, where they both got colas. Stephan nonchalantly watched the driver as he headed for the exit. Stephan ran to the window to check on Boris, who was still under the van. He dropped his cola in the trash receptacle on his way out and headed toward the driver of the van. Stephan stepped out into the parking lot and shouted, "Stop! Stop!" He saw the driver of the van turn and look at who was shouting. Stephan walked up to the driver just as he neared the van, and he started shouting in French something about how unlucky the driver was to be a babbling baby baboon breathing bully. Of course, the driver of the van did not understand a word of French, but it gave Boris just enough time to finish and slide out, unseen, from under the black van. The driver of the van stood just outside his van trying to explain to Stephan that he did not understand him. Stephan switched back to English and shouted, "Never mind, my good man. I am an idiot!" He turned and walked away from the driver and the now GPS-equipped van. He walked around the parking lot until he knew the driver of the van had lost sight of him, and then he returned to his car and his team leader, Boris, who was laughing after having heard what Stephan had uttered to the van driver. "Quit laughing, Boris," said Stephan. "I bought you the time you needed, didn't I?" "Yes! You were quite resourceful, my friend."

Stephan drove them back to the Willoughby Travelodge to rendezvous with Lukas and the rest of Team One.

* * *

Lukas was sitting in his motel room waiting for Boris and Stephan to return from their task of equipping the family van with its GPS tracking device. Lukas was sitting with Dagmar and Hooter, the fifth member of Team One. Hooter was a strange character, but Lukas liked him. He was not a superstitious man, yet he felt that Hooter brought him good luck. Hooter was not his real name, but Lukas had no trouble referring to him by his nickname. Hooter was a tall tree trunk size of a German, who wore his head clean shaven and could stare you down with his large crystal-blue eyes.

Lukas heard the door open; he looked up and saw both Boris and Stephan enter. "Well, did you do it?" he asked as he stood up near the small kitchen table.

"We tagged the black van," boasted Stephan as he took off his black ball cap and sat down onto a stuffed chair.

"How'd it go, Boris?" asked Lukas as he walked to the center of the room where he planned on having his meeting.

"At first, the driver went to a car wash," said Boris, "and we couldn't get him there, but, afterwards, he stopped at a Burger King, and we tagged the van there."

"Good … good … let's have a team meeting," said Lukas. "Everyone gather around me." He sat down in a stuffed chair in front of a small coffee table in the center of the motel room. Dagmar sat next to him, then Hooter, Boris and Stephan.

"Then we did good, Lukas?" pleaded Stephan as he searched for praise.

"Stephan, you and Boris did real good," admitted Lukas. "The tagging of that van was paramount to the success of our kidnapping plans. You see, tonight the Murphy family will use that van for the entire evening, and we will need to follow their whereabouts throughout the night. While the Murphy family is at the City Club we will enter their house and set them up for a shock. After they return to their home, they won't want to stay there that evening, and that is when we will need to track them to their next destination," explained Lukas.

"Why won't they want to stay at their home?" asked the naïve Stephan as he lit a cigarette and waited for an answer from Lukas.

"They won't want to stay at their home because I am going to scare the hell out of them," replied Lukas as he stared back penetratingly into Stephan's eyes.

"Can I ask, how are you going to scare the hell out of them, Mr. Krueger?" asked Stephan nervously.

"I'll tell you what, Stephan. You can come along with Dagmar and me tonight, and you can see first hand how I scare folks," said Lukas as he deliberately struck a match and lit a long, thin cigar. "Boris and Hooter can stay at the farmhouse this evening and keep track of the family van. Team Two set up all the tracking equipment at the farmhouse this morning, and so everything is set to go."

Boris asked, "What is Team Two doing this evening?"

Lukas took a puff of his cigar and replied, "They are staying at the farmhouse to track Tom's several other vehicles." Lukas stood up and stretched his arms over his head.

Dagmar, who was drinking hot coffee, looked at Lukas and she said, "My Lukas will scare the pee right out of the Murphy family tonight."

Everyone laughed at Dagmar's statement. Lukas also laughed at her little humor, but he knew underneath her humor he was deadly serious about the haunting he was applying to Thomas Murphy.

* * *

The Murphy family had arrived at the City Club of Cleveland without the patriarchal leader of the family, who was also the recipient of the evening's award. Beth Murphy was hiding her anger, as she and her three children were seated. "Your Dad is late," she whispered to her children. They were seated at a large, round table to the right of the stage. Thomas and Thornton were late, and Beth was upset and a little more than angry at their tardiness.

"Don't be mad, Mom," said Jenny, sipping her cola.

"Yeah," chimed her two sons in unison.

"The least he could do is be here on time," complained Beth as she took a sip of her glass of white wine.

The restaurant was filled to its capacity. A murmur of conversation floated through the room, along with the constant clinking of china and the faint, smooth sound of piped-in music. The room held many dignitaries, celebrities and many important local and regional citizens. Even the mayor of Cleveland and his beautiful wife were in attendance for the occasion.

Beth looked across the room at the entrance, and she saw both her husband and his tall black bodyguard standing in the doorway. She could tell they were scanning the room trying to locate her and the three children. Tommy stood up and waved both his hands over his head, attempting to gain his father's attention.

* * *

"There they are," said Tom as he nudged Thornton and pointed next to the podium where his wife and children were seated. He and Thornton quickly worked their way through the crowd until they reached the Murphy table. "Sorry I'm late. I got caught straightening out some business problems," said Tom as he leaned over and kissed his wife, hoping she was not too angry with his tardiness.

"Tom, I didn't want to be sitting here alone among all these important people," whispered Beth, kissing him back.

"I'm sorry," he said as he sat down at their table. "Ya'll look great in your new clothes. Boys, your blue suits look jamming." Thornton asked Tom if he wanted anything from the bar. He requested a gin and Squirt, while Thornton wanted a cold beer. While Thornton was gone, Tom again apologized to his wife for being late, and he got the feeling she was all right now that he was there. He looked around the crowded room and was surprised at the large crowd. "Your Mom and I used to watch the City Club on television when we were young, but we never imagined someday we'd actually be here. And getting an award," explained Tom to his three children. Tom took notice of the muffled conversations and the clinking sounds of silverware against fine china. Tom scanned the vast room, and he wondered how he and his family had gotten to the City Club in just two short years.

Tom slowly looked around his table. He saw Beth and Jenny were wearing matching blue dresses, and then he looked at his two sons, who were wearing matching blue suits. He was proud of them. He thought they certainly cleaned up nice. Tom was wearing a black tuxedo, which highlighted his bright, copper-red hair and freckled, ruddy face. Tom's bodyguard, Thornton was wearing a jet-black, suit, which was highlighted by his shiny, shaven, black scalp. Tom was always proud to have his handsome bodyguard at his side, and tonight was no exception. Everyone had already eaten. Tom and Thornton had gotten there too late to enjoy the dinner, but Tom was glad because he was too nervous to hold anything on his stomach. Tom greeted Thornton as he returned with a beer in one hand and a gin and Squirt in the other hand. "Thanks, Thor," said Tom as he took his drink and took a big swig to settle his nervousness.

Tom watched and listened as the master of ceremonies stepped up to the podium, adjusted the microphone, and cleared his throat. "Ladies and gentlemen," he started. "Good evening and welcome to the City Club of Cleveland. Tonight we are presenting the Man of the Year Award. This year's award goes to one of our own native sons. This year's recipient won the Ohio lottery two years ago and has since turned his fortune back into the community by creating over two thousand good-paying jobs. And he has also turned his fortune to unselfishly revitalizing the city of Cleveland. His employees and the many grateful people of this city joyfully call him the Prince of Cleveland. Let me introduce to you, Thomas Murphy, the owner and operator of the now famous local business entitled 'Just Clean It Up.'"

Tom stood up; the audience applauded, and he tipped his head, acknowledging the crowd. Next he leaned over, kissed Beth, and proceeded to walk to the stage. Once upon the stage, he shook hands with the master of ceremonies, who then handed the plaque to him. Tom thanked him, and then stepped up to the podium. He briefly looked over the crowd, then said, "Thank you! Thank you, everyone." He again paused while the audience continued to applaud. When they quieted down, he continued, "I want to personally thank each and every one of you for coming tonight and for awarding me with this wonderful plaque. I was just a lucky guy who turned his lottery winnings into a good idea." The audience roared with clapping and cheers. "Bear with me. I would like to thank a few important friends, if I may. First, I'd like to thank God, who made this all possible. I'd like to thank my wonderful parents, who raised me to follow the Irish Catholic way of life. Next, I'd like to thank my lovely wife, Beth, who supports and loves me every day, and also my three fine kids, Tommy, Jenny, and Danny, who really do believe I am the Prince of Cleveland." Tom paused as the audience tapped their water glasses with their spoons as if they wanted newlyweds to kiss. Once the audience stopped, Tom said, "Thank you. Thank you. I'd like to thank the folks at Just Clean It Up. First, I'd like to thank my overall supervisor and manager, Mike Max, who along with his management team has created and streamlined our company. I'd like to thank the fifty field managers and the two thousand field workers, who make the company work. Lastly, I'd like to thank the various departments—the phone branch, where folks call in requesting cleanups; the dispatcher's department, where all company communication takes place; the accounting and payroll department. Then there are the many folks like the mechanics, the janitors, the secretaries, and all the rest that I may have overlooked. Thank you all." Tom then stepped back from the podium, waved to the audience, and again shook hands with and handed the microphone back to the master of ceremonies, who said, "On behalf of the City Club of Cleveland, it is my honor to award Thomas Murphy our Man of the Year Award for the year of 2009." Tom remained on the stage while the audience applauded him.

After the ceremony, Tom returned to the table where his family and bodyguard were waiting for him. "Thor, how'd I sound?" asked Tom as he kissed Beth, rubbed Danny's head of red hair, and sat down at his spot. He chugged his glass of gin and Squirt and again asked, "How'd I sound?"

"You sounded strong," replied Thornton.

"Really, Thor?" he asked again, then he showed everyone at the table his plaque. "Doesn't it look cool?"

Thornton stood up, reached over, and took Tom's empty glass. "Tom, I'll get you another."

"Thanks, Thor," replied Tom as he passed the plaque to Beth. "What do you think, honey?" asked Tom as his smile beamed across his ruddy Irish face.

"It's beautiful, Tom," said Beth as she held it up in order to get a good look. "We'll hang it in your study at the new house." Tom could tell by the look in her deep blue eyes she was proud of him and proud of his accomplishments. Tom watched Beth hand the plaque to each child. Each child made his or her own observation, and Tom could tell they were each proud as hell of their dad. Thornton returned with Tom's drink just as the master of ceremonies approached Tom's table. He told Tom that people in the audience wanted to stop at his table and meet him personally. During the next hour, people from the community did stop by to meet him and his family.

At the end of the hour, the mayor of Cleveland and his pretty wife stopped to introduce themselves. When they reached the table, Tom jumped to his feet and said, "Mr. Mayor, it is nice that you stopped by our table."

The mayor introduced his wife, as did Tom, then the two men shook hands while the mayor's cameraman snapped several shots of them. "Thomas, I can't even begin to tell you how wonderful you've made the city look. All your efforts have helped raise our city's image," said the mayor. Tom looked over, and the two wives were talking.

"Mr. Mayor, we have plans on hiring another five hundred field workers next spring, whose sole job would be to come behind our cleanup workers and plant wildflowers to even further beautify the city," said Tom as he sipped the fourth gin and Squirt that Thornton had brought him.

"Tom, how would that work?" asked the mayor.

"Well, sir, our flower plan is two-pronged. Our first plantings would be targeted for older sites that we had previously cleaned, and our second plantings would be targeted toward our newer cleanup sites," said Tom as he continued to sip his gin and Squirt.

"Perhaps I may be able to funnel some federal grant moneys your way to augment your flower plantings. I can only imagine how fast your efforts are eating up your money," added the mayor.

"If you could help with federal dollars it would sure help," admitted Tom, who was starting to feel the effects of the gin.

Tom watched as the mayor pulled a business card out of his wallet and proceeded to write on the back of the card. "Here is my personal business card. Call me anytime you need anything. On the back of the card I've written a Mrs. Royal's name and phone number. I want you to contact her. She can help get federal funding through my administration." Tom had not expected financial assistance, especially federal dollars. But he was extremely grateful. The mayor and his wife politely said goodnight and returned to their table. Tom looked over at Beth, and he realized she had overheard what the mayor had offered.

At the end of the evening, Tom, his family, and Thornton thanked and shook hands as they worked their way toward the exit. Once at the front door, Thornton ran outside to find Billy and the family van, while Tom and his family waited. Within a few minutes, Thornton returned and said, "Tom, Billy is waiting right outside." The family headed out the door, led by Tom, with Thornton bringing up the rear making sure there were no stragglers.

It was a cool autumn evening with a brisk north wind blowing in across Lake Erie onto Ohio's north coast. The family van was setting in front under a large canopy. Bill had run around to the passenger side to assist Beth and the children into their backseats. Tom climbed in next to Beth, and Thornton got in up front next to Bill, who was behind the wheel. "Are we headed home, boss?" asked Bill as he put the van into drive and pulled out from under the large canopy.

"Yes, Bill, straight home, please."

"It's a pretty night. How about once through the park?" asked Bill as he pulled out onto the street.

Beth looked at Tom and said, "The kids are tired."

"No Bill, just straight home," slurred Tom as the gin was clouding his mind. He listened to his three children chatter among themselves. Driving away from the restaurant, Tom thought about all the wonderful things that had happened to him and his family since winning the lottery two years earlier. Tom's thoughts were interrupted when his youngest son, Danny, shouted, "Dad, you were cool tonight."

"Yeah, you were cool in front of all those people," yelled Tommy, Tom's oldest son, who had wavy red hair and sparkling blue eyes just like his father.

"Your dad is certainly cool," urged Beth. "Your dad is the Man of the Year."

"He looked distinguished this evening," added Jenny.

While Bill drove out of downtown Cleveland, the Murphy family rejoiced at their many good fortunes, one of which was their new home, being built in Bainbridge. Tommy asked, "Dad, how soon are we moving into our new home?"

Tom paused. He did not want to tell the family about the bombing, which had occurred earlier that morning, and so he said, "Kids, the big house will be ready soon."

Twenty minutes later Bill drove onto Tom's street. He looked at his house as Bill approached it, and he quickly sobered and said, "Bill, don't pull in the drive. Just pull up in front of my neighbor's house." Tom took a deep breath and whispered, "Thor, my front door is wide open, and the lights are on. I know they weren't left that way."

Beth whispered, "Tom, I know I locked up the house when we left this morning."

Tom leaned to open the van door but first said, "Bill, stay with my family and call the police. Thor, let's go check out the house."

Thornton quietly opened his van door and climbed out along with Tom. Tom stood momentarily wondering whether it was a kid's prank, a real burglary, or the work of the man making the threats. Somehow he knew this break-in was done by the man making all the threats. As they both moved toward the house Beth whispered, "You guys be careful."

As they approached the front steps, Thornton placed his hand on Tom's shoulder and said, "Tom, let me go first." He stopped and let Thornton start up the steps. As Thornton reached the top step, he drew his weapon from behind his suit coat. Tom watched Thornton as he grabbed the front door, which was flapping in the evening breeze. They entered the house, and Tom followed behind Thornton as he swept the house, room by room, until the entire upstairs and main floor were clean. Next, there was the basement to sweep.

As they approached the basement stairs, Tom heard police sirens outside the house. They slowly descended the stairs, knowing the Cleveland police were entering the house. When Tom and Thornton reached the bottom of the stairs, Tom sensed something was wrong. He held Thornton's arm and said, "Thor, let's wait for the police to catch up with us." They waited while the police checked the first and second floors, then Tom heard them coming down the basement stairs. Tom looked up the stairs as two police officers were coming down toward him. "Officers, I'm Thomas Murphy, the home owner, and this gentleman is Thornton Williams, my personal bodyguard."

The older police officer said, "Mr. Murphy, I am Officer Kelso and this is my partner, Officer Milton. We have checked the two upper floors, and now we'd like to check your basement." Tom stepped back and gave the two officers access to first the laundry room and then the family room. "Have you been in the family room, yet?" asked Kelso.

"No, just to the bottom of the stairs," said Thornton, who had holstered his gun before the officers entered the basement. Tom did not want that to be an issue.

Kelso motioned for them to stay back, then he said, "Milton, follow me." Tom watched as Kelso slowly opened the door to the family room and stepped into the room.

Tom touched Thornton and said, "The lights were off when we left. Now they are on."

From the stairs Tom heard Kelso shout, "Oh, shit! Don't touch it, Milton."

Tom rushed to the doorway and shouted, "What is it?" He looked into the family room but could not see what the two officers were looking at in front of the fireplace.

Tom saw Kelso turn toward him and say, "Mr. Murphy, it's your dog. It is dead." Tom and Thornton both rushed into the room. "Stay back, guys. It might be booby-trapped," whispered Kelso as he approached the German shepherd, which had been executed by hanging it from a noose that was nailed to the top of the fireplace, with its intestines cut up and dripping down onto the foot of the fireplace.

"Duke," shouted Tom, who saw blood everywhere at the foot of the fireplace. "Who killed my dog?" shouted Tom as Thornton tried to hold Tom back from reaching the dead animal. Tom gasped and whispered, "Oh, my God!"

Next, Tom felt Thornton's hand on his chest. "Don't move! It may be booby-trapped," whispered Thornton as Kelso carefully examined the dog for a bomb. Tom stood still while Kelso checked for a bomb. After several minutes Kelso declared it all clear.

Tom stood in his family room staring at his pet dog, Duke, as it hung from a noose, which was nailed above the fireplace, with blood and guts pooling on the floor. "What sick bastard would break into my house and hang my family's pet German shepherd?" asked Tom.

Kelso said, "Mr. Murphy, there is a note."

"I know, it says, 'For you, we are coming!'" interrupted Tom, who looked at Kelso, "I've been getting that same threat for two days now." He looked at Thornton and said, "Thor, I loved that dog. What am I gonna tell my kids?" Thornton patted Tom reassuringly on his shoulder.

"What do you mean, 'you've been getting that same threat for two days?'" asked Kelso.

Tom looked at Thornton and said, "We have a problem! Why did they hang my dog?" He angrily ran his fingers through his wavy red hair. "What do they want?"

"They want your attention," suggested Thornton.

"Then they've got my attention," snapped Tom.

Kelso said, "Don't touch anything. We're getting our lab techs out here to process the evidence."

"We won't touched the crime scene," said Thornton.

Tom watched as Kelso looked closely at the dog and the threat. "Mr. Murphy, can you tell us about the other threats."

"Yes."

"Have you already reported these other threats?"

"Officer Kelso, this episode has me upset," explained Tom as he rubbed his ruddy face with his opened palms. "I want to check on my wife and kids. Thornton can answer all your questions." Tom walked out of the family room.

Thornton motioned to Kelso to wait, then he followed Tom into the laundry room adjacent to the stairs leading to the first floor. Tom turned and faced Thornton and said, "This is far too close. This guy has stepped over the line. I'm moving my family tonight, and I'm never bringing them back here again. I want more security on my family."

Thornton again placed his hand on Tom's shoulder reassuringly and said, "First thing tomorrow morning we're scheduled to meet with a full staff of bodyguards."

"I know, but it's not soon enough."

"Nine AM at your facility."

"Good. Would you fill Kelso in on the things that have been happening? Remember I reported this to the bomb squad and the Bainbridge police this morning," said Tom as he started to walk up the stairs.

* * *

Thornton watched Tom ascend the stairs until he was out of sight, then he turned and walked back into the family room where Officer Kelso was studying the dog. "Don't touch," Thornton joked as he stepped to the center of the room.

"No … No …" replied Kelso. He was startled by the bodyguard's humor and timing. "Mr. Williams can you start at the beginning?"

"Please, just call me Thor," said the tall black man.

"Okay, Thor, can you start at the beginning?"

"First of all, you must understand Tom gets a lot of notoriety, which pulls all kinds of weirdoes out from under their rocks," explained Thornton.

"Well, he is the Prince of Cleveland, after all."

"Yeah," said Thornton, who smiled and added, "and that is why this case should be given a high priority."

"It will be given a high priority. Now tell me about the other threats and all that has gone on," Kelso replied as he sat down on a worn-out couch next to the bloody fireplace. Thornton sat down on an overstuffed chair across from Kelso as Kelso lit a cigarette and pulled a small note pad and pen from his shirt pocket.

"Let me start by telling you that Tom Murphy is mentally tough, and he has a courageous spirit, but these series of events have him and his wife scared," said Thornton as he rubbed his shaven head. "It all started yesterday.

Monday before lunch he got what we thought was a prank call. The caller asked for him specifically, then gave the threat, 'For you, we are coming!'"

Kelso interrupted, "That's the phrase on the dog."

"Yeah," confirmed Thornton, who went on to describe the dead flowers, the dead robin, the card, then the terrible drawing, and Tuesday's bombing of Tom's new home, with the threat spray-painted on the south wall of the house, and the reporting all of this to the bomb squad and the Bainbridge police. Thornton stopped while Kelso searched for an ashtray. Thornton found an empty soda can, which served Kelso's needs. Thornton got up off the chair and walked a bit to stretch his legs. Thornton said, "The drawing came addressed to the Prince of Cleveland; but here is the scary part, it came addressed to their home address. So you see this creep knows where they live, which was proven by tonight's break-in."

Kelso had a few questions, which Thornton answered, then Thornton explained his psychology professor's interpretation of the material. Kelso replied, "Your professor profiled this guy as a psychopath?"

"Yes. Aggressive and dangerous psychopath," clarified Thornton as he sat back down and waited while Kelso caught up with his notes.

"He keeps repeating the same threat, 'For you, we are coming!'" clarified Kelso as he wrote and blew cigarette smoke into the family room. Kelso, who was sitting on the edge of the couch, took the last drag on his cigarette, then he dropped the stub into the soda can.

"What did Tom say when you told him about your professor's interpretation?" asked Kelso.

"I talked to him about the profile, and he seemed to understand, and he seemed to be seriously concerned. I ordered bodyguards for his family and a bunch of armed guards for the homesite. We are going to interview and hire them all tomorrow at 9:00 AM at Tom's facility," explained Thornton.

"Why not this afternoon?"

"Because Tom's afternoon was preoccupied with preparations for tonight's awards ceremony at the City Club. Tom was being awarded the Man of the Year Award."

"Is that where you guys just came from?"

"Yes, and we arrived here maybe ten minutes before you did," said Thornton as he wondered how Tom was doing talking to Beth.

Officer Kelso continued to write down notes.

* * *

While Thornton was in the basement with Officer Kelso, Tom sat on the front steps trying to think things through. He wondered how this man had gotten so close, so fast, and he wondered how he could fight or stay ahead of him. He could not imagine what would be next.

He looked up into the sky, and he saw millions of stars tinkling across the horizon. For a brief moment he wished he could stay watching the stars, but he knew he had to talk to Beth. He got up off the front steps and walked across the lawn to the van. As he walked toward the van, he wondered how he could keep his family safe. Tom approached the van, opened the front door, and thanked Bill for watching his family. He turned to look at Beth and said, "Beth, let's go for a short walk." He got out of the front seat and came around and opened the side door, letting Beth out onto the neighbor's tree lawn. He held her hand as they walked over to the sidewalk. "We had a little break-in," he said as they walked along the sidewalk.

"How little of a break-in?" asked Beth impatiently.

"Calm down."

"Was the house trashed?" she asked apprehensively.

"No. Nothing like that," said Tom as he put his arm around Beth's shoulder.

She stopped defiantly and asked, "What happened?"

"The intruder killed Duke," he said flatly.

She sobbed, and he hugged her. Then she said, "Was it the same man with the flowers and drawing?"

"Yes. It was the same man."

"How do you know for sure?" she asked.

"He left the same note."

He continued to hold her as she cried. After several minutes, she collected herself, and they walked back to the van just as he saw Kelso and Thornton walking out the front door. He stepped away from the van, walked over to Kelso as he approached, and asked, "Officer Kelso, what is happening?"

"We're bringing in our lab unit. Is there a possibility that your family could stay with relatives overnight?" asked Kelso.

"I'm taking them to a safe hotel," replied Tom.

"Mr. Williams and I both agree that it may not be safe to stay at your home until we check everything out."

"We can stay at a hotel for a couple of days," said Tom as he looked Kelso in the eye. "Who do you feel is doing this?"

"It is far too early to know," said Kelso. "I can see you are upset, Mr. Murphy."

"Sure, I'm upset! Somebody is after us. I have to protect my family, and I have to tell them about the dog," Tom said emotionally. Tom was upset, but he had to pull it together, so he looked at Thornton and said, "Thor, you stay and deal with the authorities while I take care of my family."

"You going to a hotel?" asked Thornton.

"Yes. I'll never bring my family back to this house again," said Tom as he shook hands with Thornton. "I'll call you from the motel, and give you our location." He turned, walked back to the van and climbed into the front seat. He looked at his wife, then at each of his children. "Bill, I'm going to need you for a few more hours. Beth, kids, we are all going to spend tonight at a motel."

Danny looking worried said, "Dad, what about Duke? Is he coming to the motel with us?"

"Son, I need you to listen to me, and I want you to be a brave boy. Can you be brave?" asked Tom as tears swelled in his wounded deep-blue eyes.

"Is it about Duke?" asked Danny, the youngest.

"Yes, son."

Tommy quietly whispered, "Is Duke dead?"

"Tommy!" snapped Tom, sternly showing his displeasure at his oldest son's insensitivity. "Kids, some bad person broke in, hurt Duke, and killed him." Tom watched as Danny buried his face in his mother's lap and sobbed. "I'm sorry, Danny. Really, I am!"

Tom looked at Beth, hoping for her support, but she just stared back at him with almost disbelief. "What?" she asked, as if she expected something from him.

Tom shook his head, then said, "We're spending the night at a motel."

"Can we go in and grab some clothes?" asked Beth.

"I'll go check with the officer," replied Tom as he quickly climbed out of the front seat of the van and walked to the squad car that was parked behind the family van. Next to the squad car stood Thornton and Kelso. As Tom approached them he asked, "Kelso, can my wife and I go into the house to get some clothes for overnight?"

Kelso paused then said, "I'd rather not have you going into your home until after our lab has a chance to dust for prints."

"How about we stay out of the family room? We just need access to the bedrooms," said Tom, who was trying to accommodate the officer and his wife.

"All right, but don't touch the front door or the door knob," explained Kelso.

"Thanks, Officer Kelso," said Tom, who turned and walked back to his van. Tom took Beth back into the house. They went directly upstairs to the bedrooms, and they collected just the clothes they would need for that night.

Tom brought Beth down the front steps, and Thornton ran up to them and asked, "Are you ready to go to the motel?"

"Yes. Thor, thanks for your help tonight," replied Tom as he walked Beth toward the van and the children. "My family is upset. It's been a big night, and we need to get away from here to someplace safe and tranquil."

"Tom, I'll stay here with the authorities. The lab boys just pulled up," Thornton explained. "Call me later with your location, and I'll be there."

"Okay," replied Tom as he reached out and shook Thornton's hand. Then he helped Beth into the van. The three children had many questions, which Tom urged them to wait on while he spoke briefly with Bill. He gave his driver the instructions to the motel, and the Murphy family drove away from their home. Tom was scared. For the first time in his life, someone scary was after him and his family, and he did not like the feeling. Who is he, or who are they? he wondered. What would they do next?

* * *

At Lukas's farmhouse in Lake County, Boris was tracking the sudden movement of Tom Murphy's family van. It had been setting at the Cleveland home for several hours, but now it was moving west out of town. Boris was drinking hot coffee and watching the movement of the vehicle when Lukas, Dagmar, and Stephan walked into the front of the farmhouse.

"Boris, is it on the move?" asked Lukas as he slipped his jacket off and smiled at Dagmar, whom he had been teasing all evening.

"Yes, Lukas, the Murphy van is moving west out of town," replied Boris as he sipped on his hot coffee.

Stephan went into the kitchen to get a cold beer from the refrigerator; when he returned to the living room he said, "Boris, you should have been with us. Early this evening, we broke into the Murphy house. Lukas scared the shit out of the Murphys by hanging their dog."

Boris was listening to young Stephan, and he wondered what kind of lasting impression Lukas had made on the young man. He finished his mug of hot coffee and continued to track the family van. "Lukas, where do you think Tom will take his family?" asked Boris as he stood up and went into the kitchen to get a fresh mug of coffee.

When Boris returned from the kitchen, Lukas said, "I do believe Tom Murphy will settle his family at a motel near the airport for tonight."

Boris smiled and said, "You know this man well. He has just stopped at the motel adjacent to the airport." He was impressed at how Lukas knew his subject.

Lukas pulled out his cell phone and dialed information. "Operator, may I have the front desk of the motel across from Hopkins Airport." He waited, and when the operator came back onto the line, Lukas quickly wrote down the telephone number. "Thank you, operator." After he had obtained the front desk number of the motel, he called and requested the telephone numbers to those two rooms. Afterwards, Lukas shouted, "We are all set to scare them again. Shall I inquire about the health of their poor dog?"

Dagmar whispered, "Go for it, Daddy!"

* * *

Tom had Bill drive to Hopkins International Airport, where he paid for two connecting double motel rooms. Tom did not know that Lukas Krueger had placed a tracking device onto the family's van. Actually, all of Tom's vehicles were equipped with Krueger's tracking devices, and so Krueger's teams one and two were taking shifts tracking all of Tom's activities. Tom also did not know that Team Two had followed him and his family to the airport motel.

After Tom paid for the rooms, he walked out of the motel office and climbed into the front passenger seat of the family's van. "Bill, pull around the corner to rooms 200 and 201, where I've reserved rooms for tonight."

Bill drove through the parking lot to the rooms, and then he helped Tom unload his family. Everyone got out of the van and waited as Tom unlocked the doors. Tom opened the doors, and Beth and the kids rushed into the connecting rooms. "These are nice rooms," said Beth as she checked the bathrooms. "Kids, check the beds. Are they firm?" asked Beth as she lay down on the bed that she and Tom would share that night.

Tom placed his hand on Bill's shoulder and said, "Bill, will you call Thornton and give him our location? And have him get over here as soon as possible."

"Sure, Tom," said Bill. "I'll do it from the van."

Tom watched Bill leave the room just as he saw Danny running between rooms shouting, "Where am I gonna sleep?" Apparently Danny had forgotten about the dog, thought Tom as he continued to watch his son hurry room to room.

Tom sat and relaxed momentarily in an overstuffed chair. Beth came into the room. "What do you think of the rooms, Beth?" asked Tom as she walked up to him and sat down on the arm of his chair.

"The rooms are very nice, Mr. Murphy," she said kindly. "Thank you very much!" He looked up at her just as she kissed him on the lips.

After she kissed him, he said, "Why thank you, Mrs. Murphy." Just then the telephone, next to Tom's chair, rang. He picked it up thinking it would be Thornton calling. "Hello," Tom said into the phone.

"Mr. Murphy?" asked the caller.

"Thornton, where are you?" asked Tom.

"No. Thomas, this is not your bodyguard."

"Who is this?" shouted Tom, jumping to his feet.

"My name is not important, but what is important is 'For you, we are coming,'" whispered the caller.

"Who is this?" shouted Tom, "How'd you find us?"

"How I found you was easy," said the caller quietly. "What I want to know is how is your dog?"

"What's your name?" screamed Tom angrily. Tom heard the phone being hung up, but before he slammed the receiver onto its cradle he shouted, "You coward!"

"Tom, who was that?" asked Beth, who was also on her feet. "What'd he say to upset you so?"

"It was just some jerk," replied Tom hotly.

"Tom, what'd he say?" demanded Beth as she grabbed Tom's arm.

"He said, 'For you, we are coming,'" said Tom flatly.

"That was on the flowers and the drawing," said Beth as she followed Tom across the room.

"And on the dog," whispered Tom.

Beth shouted, "What do you mean?"

"There was a note on Duke's back that had that same threat—'For you, we are coming,'" said Tom as he sat down on the bed and placed his face into his hands.

Beth sat down next to him, put her arm around his waist and asked, "What's happening, Tom?"

"Someone is trying to scare us."

"It's working. I'm scared," confessed Beth. "How'd he know we were here?"

Tom jumped up off the bed, kissed his wife, then walked to the door. "I'm going to get some ice. Don't answer the door or the phone," he said as he started to open the door. He mumbled something as he walked out of the door. As he walked to the vending machines for ice he was thinking aloud. "How'd they find us? We've only been here less than an hour and they're already calling. How can I protect my family? Where is Thornton?" He got his ice and was walking back to the rooms when he heard Thornton's voice. He looked up and saw Thornton and Bill standing outside the family's van talking to each other. He started to run toward them as he shouted, "Thornton. I've got to talk to you!"

"Thomas!" he shouted back.

Tom ran up to Thornton, and he shouted, "They've already found us, Thor. They called me on the phone in the rooms."

"How is that possible? You just got here," said Thornton as he started walking with Tom and Bill back to the rooms.

Tom said, "The caller didn't identify himself, but he used the same threat, and he asked how was the dog."

"The bastard," uttered Thornton. "Tom, we're gonna need more men. At least one man for each family member, and we gotta move your family somewhere else."

"How'd he find us?" asked Tom as they reached the door to the rooms. "We just got here, Thor." He turned away from the door, indicating that he wanted to talk some more with Thornton before they went into the rooms. "Who is he? He has an accent. Thor, who is he?" asked Tom as he set his ice on the doorstep.

"You said he has an accent," said Thornton. "What kind of an accent, Tom?"

"His accent sounded European. Maybe German."

"If the police get any fingerprints, then we could check with Interpol and check European criminals," said Thornton as he rubbed his bronze, shaven head. "Let's make plans. Tomorrow morning you and I will go and hire half a dozen extra men for security, then we'll come back here, and move your family to a more secure location."

"We'll do that first thing in the morning," said Tom as he picked up his ice. "My family is too tired to move again tonight."

"I'll call tonight and have the men meet us at your headquarters," said Thornton as he opened the door for Tom.

"That sounds great, Thor," said Tom as he carried his ice into the motel rooms. "Beth, Thornton is here, and we've got a plan to protect the family."

"Great! Let's hear the plan," said Beth, who had changed into her pajamas and robe.

"Tonight I'm going to call the security company I work for, and I'm going to interview half a dozen men to meet us at your company headquarters; then I'll hire five bodyguards to protect each one of your family members. We'll all come back here so we can move the family to a safe house in the morning," explained Thornton. "Beth, if you don't have any questions, then Bill and I are going to go back out to the van and hurry to make those security calls."

"Thornton, I'm too upset to ask any questions."

"Okay, Beth, then Bill and I will see you first thing in the morning," said Thornton as he and Bill walked out of the motel room.

After Thornton and Bill left, Tom and Beth put the children to bed. It was near midnight. Tommy and Jenny each took a double bed in the first room, while Danny, who was already fast asleep, was in the second room with his parents.

Tom turned off the television that Danny had been watching until he fell asleep. Tom wanted to talk with Beth about the bombing. He had not told her much of the details, and he felt uncomfortable, as if it were a lie by omission. He took the ice and went to the mini-bar to get a small bottle of gin. He made himself a drink to steady his nerves, which were frayed and raw.

Beth, do you want a drink?" he whispered, trying not to wake Danny, whose bed was next to theirs.

"No, Tom," she whispered. She was sitting in the little sitting area at the foot of their bed. Tom came over to her, and he sat down. It was the first time they had relaxed all day long.

"My God, Tom, what is this man going to do to us?" whispered Beth. "He knows we're here. What does he want?"

"We'll get more men in the morning, and move the family to a safer location where this guy can't get at us," whispered Tom reassuringly.

"Won't this man just follow us like he did tonight?"

"No! Thor's security agency has a safe house we can use," said Tom as he took a long swig of his glass of gin.

"How does that work? How does that keep this man away?" she asked with a tone of fear in her voice.

"I'm not sure how it works, but if Thor says it is safe, then I trust him," he said, taking another swig of gin.

"Tom, I'm scared."

"I'll protect you and the kids," he reassured her. "I have always protected you, Beth."

"So far you haven't stopped anything he has done," she said bitterly as she got up and stomped into the bathroom crying.

"Wait, Beth," uttered Tom as he first finished his gin with one large gulp then ran to the bathroom, which he found locked. He quietly tapped on the bathroom door, trying not to wake little Danny. He whispered, "Honey, let me in, please." He waited as he heard her crying. He pleaded with her; then she came out. "Let's not play the blame game. We need to stick together."

"I'm so sorry Tom, but I'm just so scared."

"I understand," said Tom. "Just come sit down. We need to talk," He took her by her arm, and he guided her back over to the sitting area at the end of their bed. He quickly mixed himself another gin and Squirt and sat down next to Beth. "Our new house wasn't damaged as much as you may have guessed. Only the front entrance was damaged, but the bomb caused a fire which did further damage. The general contractor said it would add maybe a month or two to the completion date. But here is the big problem. He and his crew won't resume work until Thor and I have provided around-the-clock armed guards to protect the site and the work crew." Tom stopped to take a large swig of his gin. He sensed his drinking was starting to annoy Beth. "Here is the itinerary for tomorrow. Thor and I will go to my facility to meet and select bodyguards for the family. After that has been accomplished, then Thor and I and the bodyguards will all return back here to the motel rooms, introduce everyone, and then move the family to the safe house. After everyone has moved and are settled in, then Thor and I will go to the security agency and hire the staff of guards to protect our new home. Beth, do you have any questions?" he asked as he took another drink of his cool gin.

"You're gonna be busy tomorrow. So maybe you should slow down on the gin. Just an observation," said Beth.

"You're probably right," he said draining his glass.

It was late, and they were tired. They climbed into bed and kissed each other good night. Beth quickly fell asleep, but Tom lay flat on his back staring at the ceiling. The room was dark and silent. Tom needed to sleep so that he would be fresh in the morning, but he was worried. How could the man find them, he wondered, and what would the man do next?

*   *   *

After Lukas placed the receiver back onto the telephone cradle, he joined Dagmar on their bed. He looked into her eyes and whispered, "Tomorrow Thomas will take a beating and lose his family. And there is nothing he can do to prevent it."

Dagmar stared into his eyes and cooed, "I love you."

"Of course you do, my darling," he whispered.

Chapter Four

Wednesday, Day Three

At 6:00 AM Wednesday the telephone rang next to Tom's head, and as he grabbed the receiver he mumbled something. It was the front desk with the wake-up call Tom had arranged the night before. "Thank you, operator," mumbled Tom as he fumbled to replace the receiver onto the telephone cradle.

"Who was that?" asked Beth, just waking.

"It was the front desk," said Tom. "It's time for me to get up." He stumbled out of bed, walked to the bathroom and turned on the light fixture, which cast a beam of light into the dark bedroom. By six thirty, Tom walked back into the bedroom showered, shaved, and dressed. "Wake up, Beth," he whispered, shaking her shoulder. "I gotta go, honey," he again whispered, trying not to wake young Danny, who lay in the next bed.

"Tom, where are you taking us?" asked Beth as she rubbed the sleep from her foggy eyes.

"Thornton has worked all that out," whispered Tom. "I gotta go; they're waiting for me outside. I'll be back in an hour. Order room service for breakfast."

Tom slipped on his suit jacket and hurried for the door. Once outside, he immediately saw his black Escalade parked in front of his room with Bill behind the wheel and Thornton seated next to him. Tom saw Bill jump out, run around the vehicle, and open the side door for Tom. "Good morning, boss," said Bill as he helped Tom climb into the rear of the Escalade.

"Good morning, boys. Did either of you get any sleep last night?" asked Tom as Bill started the engine.

"We got some sleep," said Bill as he pulled out of the parking space, drove out of the motel parking lot, and headed east toward Tom's company headquarters.

Thornton turned toward the backseat and said, "Tom, I talked with Lockhart Security Company last night. They have four bodyguards waiting at the facility and a list of one dozen armed guards to start. Mr. Lockhart assured me they have a secured safe house for your family."

"Great, Thor, I feel better knowing that," said Tom, who was leaning forward from the backseat. "Can we start with the guards for the new homesite right away?"

Thornton hesitated, then said, "We're still working out the details. We should have it staffed by tonight."

"Good," replied Tom as he sat back.

As Bill continued to drive to Just Clean It Up headquarters it began to slowly drizzle, and by the time they got close to the facility it was raining steadily. The usual route from the Cleveland bungalow to his downtown office took fifteen to twenty minutes depending on traffic, but today they were starting out from the motel near the airport, and so it took longer. It was a crisp, rainy autumn morning, and the windshield wipers were vigorously clapping across the windshield. Tom sat back and started thinking about what he wanted to accomplish that morning. He was anxious to get to his facility and meet the security people; then he wanted to get back to his family to take them to the intended safe house. He was trying to prioritize his thoughts. "Thor, do you know where the security company's safe house is located?" asked Tom as he looked forward at his bodyguard.

"It's a secret. The agency won't even let us use our own vehicles to move your family," explained Thornton as he looked back at Tom sitting in the backseat.

"How will we know where they are?"

"We'll all go in their vehicles to the safe house, and then afterwards they'll bring us back to our vehicles."

"I hope this works," said Tom as he looked out the side window at the downpour of rain. After a while, time had gotten away from Tom, and he looked up front and shouted, "How soon, Bill?"

"Two minutes, boss," replied Bill as he suddenly stopped short at an intersection to let a woman with a baby carriage cross the street in front them. Tom noticed it was raining harder, and because of the rain the woman started running. She got halfway through the intersection when she tripped and fell forward, losing hold of her baby carriage.

From the backseat Tom shouted, "Thor, help that lady." Tom leaned forward and put both hands on the top of the two front seats.

Thornton shouted, "I'm on it, boss."

Tom watched as his bodyguard popped open his door, swung out into the street, and ran to help the fallen lady. Thornton reached her just as two loud gunshots crackled, and Thornton fell down onto the pavement. Tom screamed Bill's name just as a bullet shattered the glass of Bill's driver-side window. The bullet entered the left side of the Bill's skull and exited out the right side with blood and brains spraying all over the front seats. Bill fell forward, dead before his skull hit the steering wheel. Tom screamed as blood oozed down the passenger side window. Almost instantly, Tom saw both backseat windows shatter inwardly as men on both sides of the Escalade reached in and popped the locks. The back doors swung open as men grabbed and dragged Tom out of the Escalade. Once out of the Escalade, a hood was slipped over Tom's head. Moments later, after hearing men speaking Spanish, something hit Tom's skull, and he became unconscious.

*   *   *

After Tom left the motel room, Beth first woke Danny, who was in the bed next to hers, then she walked into the connecting room and woke both Jenny and Tommy. Once everybody was awake, she called the front desk and ordered a pot of hot coffee and four continental breakfasts. While she waited for the room service, she took a quick shower and fixed her long red hair. Danny was in his room watching cartoons, while Jenny and Tommy were in their room watching a scary movie on pay-per-view. Beth was anxious to get the hot coffee from room service to help her wake up. She listened to Danny as he complained about staying in the boring motel. "Be quiet, Danny, room service is bringing us our breakfast anytime now," Beth explained to her cranky youngest son.

"I ain't hungry," complained Danny. "I want to go to school this morning. I got a test!"

"Sorry, Danny, your father knows best," said Beth as she heard a loud knock on the motel room door. "Quiet, Danny. Here is room service," said Beth as she jumped up off of the bed and hurried to the door.

"But I ain't hungry," squealed Danny.

"Shush," scolded Beth as she started to opened the door. Suddenly the door was forcefully pushed open, causing her to fall backwards onto the carpeted floor. She looked up from her vulnerable position, and she saw a large man standing over her. "What are you doing?" she instinctually screamed. Next, she saw Tommy, her fourteen-year-old son, run into the room and lunge into the big man. "Leave him alone," she screamed as she saw the big man toss Tommy across the room; he landed on one of the beds. The big man reached down, grabbed Beth's hand and lifted her to her feet. "What are you doing?" she continued to scream.

"Calm down, Mrs. Murphy," said the big man as she looked him over from top to bottom. She saw he was a white man dressed in all black. Next, she looked behind him and saw three other big men all dressed in black.

"Who are you people," demanded Beth, "and what do you want?" She saw all the men were large and threatening.

"We've already told your husband what we want," said Otto, the team leader. "We want thirty million dollars."

"Are you crazy?" screamed Beth just as she started to realize these men were serious.

"Your husband had the same response. It was unproductive and not very businesslike," said the team leader. "Mrs. Murphy, I am Otto, the leader of Team Two. The leader of Team One has already abducted your husband. We are serious. We had to kill his driver and bodyguard in order to capture Mr. Murphy. We want thirty million dollars. When we get the money, we will release you and Mr. Murphy."

"Is Tom all right?" she asked as she started to cry in the dark motel room. Jenny entered the room, and now all three children were in Beth's motel room.

"Yes. Tom is being cared for," he replied. "Calm down, Mrs. Murphy. This is just business."

"Can you take me to him?" she practically begged.

"That may be possible," replied Otto. "Can you give us the thirty million American dollars?"

"I can't do that!" she screamed hysterically.

"Why not?" asked Otto.

"Tom controls all the money," said Beth.

"We are going to keep you and the children until we get the money," said Otto, as she watched him motion to the other three men. He grabbed Beth by her arm, pushed her, and maliciously said, "Get your purse."

Beth watched as Tommy climbed off the bed and prepared to attack Otto again, but he saw the boy, and he shouted, "Tommy, don't try that again. I'd hate to have to hurt your brother or sister."

"You touch them and my dad will tear you apart," Tommy shouted as he ran toward Otto with his fists clenched. Otto stepped up to Tommy, pushed him backwards, and said, "Don't be stupid, kid!" Then he turned to his three men and said, "Leave everything where it lay. Just take the mother, the kids, and the purse." Beth watched as Otto's team members grabbed the purse and forcefully shoved it into her hands. They then walked the family out of the motel room and into a waiting van that was parked just outside their rooms. Once everyone was securely in the van, Otto told the driver to head for the East Seventy-first Street area in Slavic Village and the abandoned building where the Murphy family would spend the night. Mrs. Murphy was nearly frozen with fear.

*   *   *

Otto sat in the front passenger's seat next to the van driver. Otto felt the Murphy family was too scared to speak, which he thought was good. The money would certainly be coming soon. The rain had changed from the early-morning drizzle to a much harder downpour now. Team two approached East Seventy-first Street. Otto knew they were driving through Cleveland's well-known Slavic Village as they reached the foreclosure which would serve as Team Two's first hideaway for Beth and her three children.

Otto knew this place was just temporary; Lukas and Team One would relieve him and his team in the morning. Otto also knew that Lukas would leave a teasing clue for Tom to find, but first he would take Beth and the children to the second hideaway out in Lake County at his dilapidated farmhouse. Just as they approached the first hideaway, Otto placed a call to Lukas. Once the call went through, Otto said, "We have them, but she won't give us the money. What about Mr. Murphy? Will he give you the money?" Otto paused to listen. "No! Okay." He put away his cell phone and instructed his driver to drive directly to the first hideaway. When they arrived at their destination, the four men escorted the Murphy family into the abandoned two-story house that had a big sign over the front door, which proclaimed it as a foreclosure. Once inside, the men separated Mrs. Murphy from her three scared children. Separating her from her children was meant to upset Beth, and it did. Otto watched as Beth started to cry and demand her children. "Mrs. Murphy, will you give us the money?" asked Otto as he took her purse from her and set it off to the side.

"Even if I wanted to give you the money, which I don't, I can't because my husband controls it," she said, sniffling.

"Very well," uttered Otto angrily.

Otto left Beth in the living room, and he walked to the kitchen where she could not hear him. He used his cell phone to call Lukas. Once the call went through, Otto said, "The misses claims she can't get the money because Tom has all the control of the money. What do you think, Lukas?"

Lukas replied, "Keep her separated from her children for now. We'll let her and Tom talk later. I'll get back to you real soon. Otto, stay available."

Otto closed his cell phone. He wondered how long it would take to get the ransom money and get out of Cleveland and the country and the continent and back to his beloved Europe.

Otto went back into the living room to check on Mrs. Murphy. She was seated on an old wooden chair when he entered the room. "Can I see my children, Otto?"

"Not until you convince your husband to pay us the thirty million American dollars," said Otto forcefully.

"How can I possibly do that?"

Otto wanted to intimidate her, and so he walked up close to her and said, "If you want to keep your children from being hurt, then when we call your husband you'll tell him to pay us the money." Otto reached over, grabbed her by the back of her hair and twisted her head back. "Do you understand, Mrs. Murphy?"

"Yes," she squealed.

Otto released her and watched as she started to sob. "Save your tears for Mr. Murphy," said Otto as he walked out of the living room, down the hallway, and into the master bedroom. He was mentally preparing a speech to tell the three children. He opened the bedroom door and walked into the room. The three children were all sitting on the bare wooden floor. "What are you kids doing?" Otto asked sharply.

"Absolutely nothing," barked Tommy.

Otto closed the door so that their mother could not hear them. "We aren't going to let you see your mother until she convinces your father to pay us," explained Otto.

"My dad will never pay you lousy guys," threatened Tommy as he shook his fist at Otto, who started to laugh. Next, Otto promised to tie them if they caused him any trouble. Then he turned to leave, and Tommy shouted, "You stink." Otto laughed louder as he left the bedroom, locking the door behind him.

Otto walked back to the small kitchen where his other three men were sitting, drinking coffee and quietly talking. He walked to the stove, grabbed a coffee mug and poured himself some hot coffee. "If the three kids give us any trouble, then we're going to tie them up," whispered Otto, so Beth did not hear him, as he sat down at the small kitchen table with the others. None of Otto's teammates replied to his statement about tying up the children, and so he remained silent. He sipped his hot coffee and dreamed momentarily about his cut of the grand prize of thirty million dollars. He fantasized what he could do with the money. Perhaps he would buy a small condo in London. Yes, perhaps he would do that.

*   *   *

Several minutes after Tom had been abducted, a police squad car arrived at the intersection where Tom's SUV had been attacked. Thornton Williams slowly opened his eyes as raindrops fell. It had been raining, and he was wet. He shook his head and found himself lying on the ground in the intersection a few streets from the Just Clean It Up headquarters. As he looked up and shook his head, an older police officer barked, "What happened here?"

"I was shot in the chest, but I was wearing a vest. I was stunned and unconscious for a while. My name is Thornton Williams, and I'm a bodyguard for Mr. Thomas Murphy," said Thornton soberly as he continued to shake the cobwebs of unconsciousness out of his skull.

"The Prince of Cleveland?" asked the policeman with astonishment.

"Yes," he replied as he climbed up off the pavement and instantly thought to check on Tom and Bill. "Where are Tom and the driver?" shouted Thornton as he looked toward the front of the black Escalade. He saw a younger police officer standing near the driver's door.

The younger police officer looked into the front seat of the Escalade, and he shouted, "The driver's dead. One clean shot, close range to the skull," the police officer reported as he beamed a flashlight into the interior of the front seat of the bloodied Escalade.

Thornton and the older police officer walked over to the Escalade, where the younger police officer said, "There is quite a mess in there."

"Watch it! Bill was my friend," growled Thornton, who was still groggy and a bit shaky as he walked toward the Escalade.

"Take it easy fellow," advised the older police office. "Can you tell us what happened?"

"Yeah, we stopped in the intersection. There was a lady with a baby carriage. She slipped and fell, and I rushed to help her; then there were shots, and I was hit. By the look of things, Tom has been kidnapped."

"What is your name, again?" asked the older officer.

"My name is Thornton Williams," said Thornton as he pulled his wallet from his back pants pocket. "Here is my license. I am Thomas Murphy's bodyguard." He watched as the older police officer read his license.

"From the beginning, what do you remember?" asked the older police officer as he wrote notes on his notepad.

"We were driving to Tom's company headquarters."

"Who was in the vehicle?"

"Tom was in the back seat. I was in the front, and Bill was driving. Bill stopped at this intersection because a woman was crossing the street pushing her baby carriage."

"Was it raining?" asked the older police officer.

"Yes. It was raining, and she slipped on the wet pavement and lost control of the baby carriage," said Thornton.

"What happened then?"

"Tom told me to help the lady. So I jumped out of the Escalade and rushed into the intersection. I was wearing my vest under my suit coat, and so when I felt the bullets they just knocked me down," explained Thornton.

"What happened next?" asked the younger police officer as he turned off his flashlight.

"I was knocked out. I was unconscious," replied Thornton. "Afterwards, I assume they shot Bill and then took Tom. Most likely a kidnap for ransom!"

"We responded immediately," said the older police officer, "so if it is a kidnapping they have not had time enough to call in their demands."

After talking to the officers for about fifteen minutes, Thornton realized there were now multiple police cruisers. He watched as the crime lab team and the coroner's van arrived.

The EMS techs wanted Thornton to go to the emergency room, but he refused. Instead, he told the police how important it was to check on Beth and the children. "The Murphy family had been receiving threats, so they spent last night at the airport motel. Cleveland Police Officer Kelso took the full report last night at Tom's Cleveland home. You need to check on Mrs. Murphy and her three kids at the airport motel right away," stressed Thornton.

"We'll check the motel right away," said the older police officer as he spoke into his two-way radio. While Thornton listened to the police officer talking to police headquarters, he sudden felt as if the buildings were swaying. He leaned and steadied himself against the front of Tom's Escalade. He suddenly collapsed onto the wet pavement and became unconscious.

Thornton woke up hours later in an emergency room. He lay on a gurney, and at his feet stood a big black doctor reading his chart. He sat up suddenly, and the doctor rushed to his side and said, "Steady, Mr. Williams. Take it easy."

"Where am I? What happened?" he wanted to know.

"You're at Metro's ER. I am Doctor Boyer. You passed out on the street from a combination of conditions—trauma from the gunshots, dehydration, and low blood sugar. We are running an IV to hydrate you and to bring up your sugar levels. All in all, you are going to be fine in an hour or so," said the good doctor. "You have a visitor," said Doctor Boyer with a smile as he pulled back the privacy curtain.

He saw that on the other side of the curtain stood Mike Max, Tom's top supervisor. "Mike!" shouted Thornton as Mike rushed up next to the gurney and hugged him. "It's good to see you, Mike."

"How are you, Thor?" asked Mike Max as they held each other in a buddy's bear hug. "Your doc told me you were wearing your vest, thank God."

"I'm good, Mike," he said. "Thanks for coming."

"I came as soon as I heard. We've got to find Tom."

"How are Beth and the kids? Are they all right?" asked Thornton as he fussed with the IV in his arm.

"Sorry Thor, but Beth and the kids are also missing," said Mike Max as he stepped back from the gurney.

"Any ransom calls?"

"Not yet."

"How many hours has it been?"

"Six hours. The Cleveland police and the FBI are setting up in the phone branch as we speak," said Mike Max.

"They've been missing for six hours," repeated Thornton as he sat upright in his gurney.

"The FBI claims Tom and his family were taken at approximately the same time," said Mike Max as he helped steady Thornton, who appeared weak and shaky.

Doctor Boyer said, "Steady there, Thornton." He stepped next to the gurney, took Thornton's wrist and began to check his pulse.

"Doc, I appreciate what you've done for me, but now I really need to be going," said Thornton as he pulled out the IV from his arm.

"Mr. Williams, you should stay and finish the treatment," advised Doctor Boyer as he applied a wad of cotton to the bloody IV site.

"Doc, I've got to rescue Tom Murphy and his family," said Thornton as he tried to convince Doctor Boyer. Mike Max and the doctor tried to help steady Thornton as he jumped off the gurney and proceeded to dress.

"Are you sure you're ready to go?" asked Mike Max.

"I'm okay, Mike," declared Thornton. "Doctor Boyer, I appreciate all that you've done for me. Do I need to sign a release?"

"Yes. I'll go get the forms," said the good doctor.

While the doctor was gone, Thornton finished dressing. He showed Mike Max his bulletproof vest where the two bullets had hit. "If I'd not worn this vest this morning then I'd have surely been murdered," said Thornton as he pulled his pants up around his hips. Next he put the vest back on, then he pulled his sweater over his head and down around the vest. Finally, Mike Max helped Thornton slip on his suit jacket. Just as Thornton finished dressing,

Doctor Boyer walked back into the small emergency room cubicle. "Where do I sign, Doctor Boyer?" asked Thornton as he pulled a pen from within his breast pocket. The doctor showed him where to sign. After signing, Thornton shook the doctor's hand and said, "Thanks again, Doctor Boyer." Thornton and Mike Max left the small cubicle and made their way out to the hospital's parking garage. "Mike, Bill picked me up this morning, and so my car is still parked at my apartment. Can you drop me there so I can get my car?" asked Thornton.

"Sure," said Mike Max as he unlocked his car. "Are you going to head for phone branch?"

"No," said Thornton. "I've got to go to Lockhart Security and straighten out Tom's security needs." He fastened his seat belt and Mike Max started his car's engine.

"Thor, I've got some family matters to take care of," said Mike Max as he drove out of the hospital's parking garage. "We've both got things to do. So let's meet at ten tonight at our favorite spot, Mr. Bill's Tavern on East Ninth Street, then we can discuss the situation. We need to make a plan how to help Tom."

"I have some good ideas," replied Thornton as he adjusted his seat belt.

As Mike drove, he looked over at Thornton and said, "So, is ten good for you?"

"That's good with me, Mike," agreed Thornton.

* * *

Thirty minutes later, Mike dropped Thornton at his apartment. Thornton unlocked his car and drove directly to Lockhart Security Company. Thornton had worked for James Lockhart for many years; his latest assignment was Thomas Murphy. Lockhart was like a father to Thornton. Within minutes, Thornton was sitting in James Lockhart's office discussing the Murphy kidnapping with Mr. Lockhart.

"Tell me what happened, from the beginning," said Lockhart as they sat in overstuffed wingback chairs arranged to face each other.

"Well, James, after I visited with you yesterday in the early afternoon, I reported to Tom about what my professor friend and you advised. Tom asked me to spend the rest of the afternoon recruiting armed guards for his new homesite as well as bodyguards for his family," explained Thornton as he looked at his advisor, employer, and dear friend, who was starting to show his years. James Lockhart was a tall, lean gentleman with gray hair and beard. He wore gunmetal black spectacles on the end of his long, slim nose.

"What was Tom doing during the time you were recruiting your security staff?" asked Lockhart as he stroked his long gray beard.

"Tom was rehearsing his speech for the City Club's presentation of Man of the Year Award," Thornton informed Lockhart, whose wrinkled face showed Thornton just how on in years his mentor was getting.

"Oh yes, you were at the City Club last evening," said Lockhart. "Now I remember you telling me that."

"Now, here is where things get dicey," said Thornton. "When Tom and his family and I arrived home from the presentation, the house had been broken into. Tom and I and two Cleveland police officers searched the house and found, in the basement's family room, the family pet dog hanging by a noose from the fireplace mantle with its guts ripped open and pouring down onto the floor."

"Gee, how gruesome," speculated Lockhart.

"We know it was the same guy who had made the prior threats because on the dead dog was the same note, 'For you, we are coming,'" explained Thornton, whose bright bronze head shone under the light that fell from the above windows. "It's always the same threat."

Lockhart, whose eyes sparkled with curiosity, said, "Where did they stay last night? I can't imagine them staying in their house."

"You're correct," affirmed Thornton, "and here is the strange thing. The entire family went to the airport motel, and within thirty minutes of their arrival a man with a European accent called Tom in his room and asked how was the dog doing; then he recited the same threat, 'For you, we are coming.'"

"My God, this guy is two steps ahead of Murphy and you," said Lockhart as he reached over and slapped Thornton on his knee as he sat across from Lockhart. "That's enough about last night. Thor, tell me what's happened since early this morning."

"Bill and I picked up Tom at his room at the airport. We were on our way to Tom's facility to meet with you, the bodyguards, and the armed guards," he said with stress in his voice.

"Take it easy, Thor," advised Lockhart, who saw Thornton's difficulties.

"We stopped at an intersection three or four streets from the facility when Bill allowed a woman with a baby carriage to cross. I remember it was raining hard this morning and the lady slipped and fell, losing control of the carriage. Tom shouted for me to help the lady, and so I ran to help. By the time I got to her, two shots rang out. I was hit in my vest, knocking me out," said Thornton, stopping to collect himself.

"What did you remember when you woke up?" asked Lockhart as he patted Thornton on his knee again, reassuring him.

"When I first came to, I remember, the rain was hitting my face, and I looked up to see a police officer talking to me," said Thornton as he rubbed his face with his large hands.

"What was going on at that moment?"

"I climbed to my feet, and I instantly looked around for Tom. He wasn't there; next, I looked for Bill. There was a second police officer standing looking into the driver's window. He shouted something about Bill being shot dead," said Thornton. "Can we get some coffee?"

"Sure, Thor," said Lockhart as he got up, walked to his desk, and used his intercom to order two coffees. "What happened after you realized Bill had been shot and Tom was missing?"

"I guess I was a little out of touch because things started happening fast. The number of police cruisers increased rapidly, then the lab guys and the coroner were suddenly there," said Thornton as he nervously rubbed his shaven head.

"What happened next?"

"I passed out and woke up hours later in Metro's ER with an IV stuck in my arm," said Thornton. They continued to talk about the events at the hospital. He told Lockhart about how he had signed himself out against the doctor's advise. Next, he told him about how Mike Max drove him to his apartment to get his car. By the time Thornton finished, Lockhart's secretary entered the office carrying a tray with a carafe of hot coffee and two mugs.

"Thanks, Molly," said Lockhart to his secretary. "You are always so thoughtful."

"Thank you, Mr. Lockhart. It is my pleasure," said Molly as she poured the two mugs of coffee. She knew Lockhart took his coffee with one sugar and two creams. "Mr. Williams how do you take your coffee?"

"Black, Molly. Thank you."

After she prepared the coffees, she handed them to each man, then moved the tray out of their way. Molly asked, "Are you ready for Mr. Roberts? He is waiting in the outer office, sir." Mr. Roberts was Mr. Lockhart's personnel coordinator and the second man in charge of the security company. "Send him in," said Lockhart as Molly opened the door to leave. She motioned for Mr. Roberts to enter. When he entered the room, Thornton set down his coffee and turned to shake hands with the personnel coordinator.

"Hello, Thornton," said Roberts as they shook hands. "Sorry to hear about the kidnapping."

"Yeah, it's been quite a shock," replied Thornton as he sat back down and picked up his coffee mug.

Lockhart cleared his throat and said, "Roberts, pull up a chair and have a seat with us. You've heard Tom Murphy and his family have been kidnapped."

"Has there been a ransom call, yet?" asked Roberts.

"Not yet," Thornton struggled to say. "The Cleveland Police have already brought in the FBI. They're setting up a command center in Tom's phone branch."

"That sounds logical," said Roberts. "If there is anything I or the company can do, don't hesitate to ask."

"Thanks, Roberts," replied Thornton.

"So Thor, let's talk about your staffing needs."

"I obviously won't need the bodyguards to protect the family members now that they have been kidnapped," explained Thornton, "but I will definitely need those armed guards to protect Tom's new homesite and the workers."

"Thor, however we can help," said Roberts.

"Yes, Thor, however we can help," added Lockhart.

"I'll still need five armed guards for a three-shift day for as long as this thing goes on," said Thornton.

Roberts said, "I'll set it up. Is it okay if they start first thing in the morning?" Roberts looked a little overwhelmed by the chore.

"Roberts, first thing in the morning will work just fine," Thornton reassured him. Roberts got up, nodded his head and walked out of Lockhart's office.

Lockhart waited for the door to close then he said, "That is a pretty big order for him to fill on such short notice. He is just a little overwhelmed, but he'll pull it all together. I promise, Thor. You can count on Lockhart Security every time." Lockhart sipped his coffee.

"James, I know that to be true," said Thornton, "and Tom and I appreciate that." He also sipped his coffee.

"Thor, I want you to know how terrible bad I feel that Tom and his family are missing and I want you to know that Lockhart Security will do whatever is necessary to help get them safely back," said Lockhart as he finished his coffee, then gave a grin of reassurance.

"Thank you, James," replied Thornton, "I feel so unprofessional. They snatched Tom right from under me."

"Thor, these guys are professional too, and all you need to focus on now is getting them back. Wait for the ransom call and be prepared to act," advised Lockhart.

"Thank you, James, that's good advice," said Thornton. He left, feeling as if he finally had someone in his corner.

* * *

By noon, Tom woke for the first time since he had been abducted. His skull hurt from where it had been struck, and he could not see because he still had the hood over his sore head. He sensed he was indoors, in a building of some kind. As he listened, he heard men speaking in the distance, but this time they spoke English rather than the Spanish he had heard earlier. He flexed his muscles and felt the restraints as he realized his hands were both tied behind him. He tried to move his legs, but he realized they were also tied. The ropes were tight, painfully tight, he thought.

He tried to listen to the men talking in the distance, but even though they were speaking English, he still could not make out what they were saying. He felt alone and unwatched. So again, he tried to wiggle out of the ropes, but they were too tight. He gave up for the moment, and again he tried to hear the men. He could tell there were more than three men speaking, and one man seemed to be giving the orders, maybe the boss man, he thought. The room was cold and everything sounded muffled from the hood that was around his head. He felt the couch he sat on.

After several minutes of concentrated listening, Tom started to mumble to himself. He was startled when he heard a male voice whisper, "It's not polite to mumble, Mr. Murphy."

"Who's there?" shouted Tom as he suddenly realized he had been watched all along. He recognized the accented voice speaking as the man who had made the phone call last night to the motel room. "You're the man who called us last night." He knew he would remember that accented voice for the remainder of his life.

"Mr. Murphy, I want to have a civilized conversation with you," requested the accented man.

"You killed my driver and my bodyguard," roared Tom, "and you want civility."

"Those boys were a bit of unfortunate collateral damage," he said. "You need to look beyond them."

"How do I look beyond two dead men?" asked Tom as he fiercely bit at the hood over his face and head.

"Quit biting the hood and focus, Thomas! Focus!" he whispered. "Your very life may depend on your ability to focus, Thomas."

"Are you threatening me, again?"

"Of course I am threatening you, Thomas," he said. "I am threatening to kill you if you do not pay me."

"Why should I pay you?" asked Tom. "I don't even know your damn name."

"I will tell you my name. It is Lukas Krueger, and I am a famous Austrian, who is well known all across greater Europe," he bragged.

"Well, this ain't Europe. So why should I pay you, Krueger?" asked Tom as he again bit and tugged at the hood.

"You owe me for three months of surveillance. My time is very expensive. I figure ten million dollars a month; that is thirty million American dollars. I have many expenses. I brought ten men from Europe to ensure your safety and the safety of your beautiful wife and your three wonderful redheaded children," said Lukas.

"What does my wife and kids have to do with this?" Tom asked angrily. "Krueger, this is between you and me."

"When Team One picked you up, then Team Two picked up your family, as well."

"You've taken my family?" Tom shouted.

"I have taken your family for insurance."

"You better not hurt my family!"

"You have already cost me greatly," stated Lukas as he grabbed the top of the hood and Tom's scalp, and yanked his head backwards viciously. "I want thirty million American dollars," shouted Lukas. "Focus!"

"Let go!" yelled Tom.

"Let go? That'll cost you thirty million dollars, Thomas Murphy," said the man with the thick accent.

"Thirty million?" repeated Tom.

"Yes, Mr. Murphy. Thirty million dollars and all this can end right now," said Lukas. "This is strictly business, my good man. This is strictly business. What do you say, my good man?"

"Is this strictly business? Oh, hell, no!" shouted Tom. "I'm not paying a maniac like you anything." He waited for a reply, but there was only silence. Tom thought he may have upset the man by using the word maniac. He continued to wait, then suddenly Tom felt Lukas grab him by the front of his jacket and pull him down off the couch he had been sitting on. Next, Tom felt himself fall to the floor. He felt his face explode as the bottom of Lukas's boot come crushing down hard on the left side of Tom's hooded face. His mouth was instantly split and bleeding. The left cheek was split and bleeding as his nose and left eye swelled and bled profusely.

As he lay on the floor bleeding, he heard the muffled sound of Lukas chuckling. Tom slowly faded into unconsciousness.

* * *

Boris was watching the others as they played blackjack. He sat drinking hot coffee. He looked at his wristwatch, and he saw it was three in the afternoon and his turn to question Thomas. He got up from the card table and went into the kitchen where Lukas and Dagmar were sitting at the kitchen table.

"Lukas, it's time I question Thomas. Do you think he'll give us the money?" asked Boris as he refilled his coffee mug from the large metal coffeepot.

"Boris, to be honest, I don't feel he'll give us the money until after he has been released, and we put the screws to his lovely wife and those three sparkling kids," said Lukas as he got up from his seat at the kitchen table, walked over to the coffeepot and got himself a refill of hot coffee.

"If you don't believe he'll give in until he is released, then why keep questioning him?" asked Boris as he took a swig of his coffee. "What's the point?"

Lukas finished filling his coffee cup and returned to his seat at the kitchen table. "What is the point?" he repeated. "The point is we are slowly breaking him down psychologically. We must do the process to break him down. Don't you see, Boris?" asked Lukas as he reached over and squeezed Dagmar's hand and winked at her as if he were looking for support.

"What should I do?" asked Boris.

"Keep asking for the money and rough him up, but don't overdo it," warned Lukas as he stared at Boris.

"Okay, Lukas," said Boris as he set his coffee down on the kitchen table. He got up and walked into the far room, where they were keeping Tom. He looked at how uncomfortable Tom must have been in his restricted position. "Wake up, Murphy," shouted Boris as he walked up close to Tom and kicked his shoes.

"Who's there?" shouted Tom as he was startled out of his semiconscious state.

Boris grabbed Tom by the front of his jacket, pulled him up off the floor, and sat him back onto the old dirty couch. "Lukas wants his money," Boris whispered. "What do you say?"

"No," Tom whispered back.

Boris pulled back his right arm and let loose with a vicious punch to the center of Tom's face. He heard the dull crunch as Tom's nose broke.

When Boris hit Tom, Tom's head bounced backwards and then ricocheted forward. After several rabbit punches, Boris whispered, "Can we have the thirty million?"

Tom's head wobbled back and forth in the blood-soaked hood as he slowly whispered, "Screw you!"

Boris pushed Tom from the sitting position onto his back, lying on the dirty couch. He mumbled under his breath, "Then screw you, Murphy."

As Boris went back into the kitchen, Lukas asked, "Is Thomas giving us the money?"

Boris replied, "No! I damn near beat the bloody pulp out of that stubborn Irishman, and he wouldn't even budge a bloody inch." He sat back down and picked up his mug of coffee he had left. "He's a tough booger!"

"Like I said earlier, 'he'll break when he's loose, and we put the screws to the wife and kiddies,'" explained Lukas as he looked Boris in the eye and further explained, "It's a psychological process I've developed over the years. I've had total success with the process."

Dagmar interrupted, "He's a bloody five for five."

"You can't argue with success," boasted Lukas as he took a sip of his coffee and lit a short, stubby cigar. "The next time we question Thomas, later this evening, we'll have him talk to his wife."

"Is that part of the process?" asked Boris.

"Affirmative," replied Lukas as he took a puff.

* * *

It was three thirty in the afternoon when Tom woke from the beating he had taken from Boris. His entire body screamed with pain. He was on his back facing the ceiling, but he was still wearing the blood-soaked hood. Boris had rabbit punched him until he passed out from the staggering pain. He was now awake, and he knew his nose was broken. His nostrils were full of blood, which caused him to breath through his mouth. His upper and lower lips were cut open and bleeding. The left side of his face was throbbing with pain. He yelled, "Damn you!" Then he listened, but no one came to check on him, and so again he yelled and again no one came. His arms and legs were numb from being tied and restricted. He drifted off and slept for an undetermined amount of time. When he woke, he was uncertain how long he had slept. He lost track of time. He was starting to feel delirious and disorientated, as he babbled for his wife and kids. Tom kept trying to speak, but his left jaw and face were swollen, bloodied, and stuck to the hood. He tried to take a deep breath, but the bloody hood impaired his breathing and speech. He started babbling, "Krueger, do you want my money? Do you, Krueger?" When no one answered, Tom started quietly sobbing to himself as if his spirit was on the brink of breaking under the stress and pain. He could no longer tolerate the excruciating pain.

Tom drifted back into unconsciousness, and his body's automatic breathing mechanism tried to breathe for him. Boris's rabbit punches had broken Tom's nose, further impairing his breathing ability.

But as he drifted through levels of unconsciousness he dreamt about his family. He dreamt they were all falling, and as they fell he was trying to catch them. He felt them slipping away as he grasped for their hands and fingertips, but it was hopeless as he called their names. He suddenly was awakened by the sounds of his own muffled voice.

* * *

Stephan wanted to help Lukas get his money, and so when no one was watching, he snuck into the far room where Tom was being held. First, he peeked into the room, then he tiptoed in and quietly closed the door. With an exciting spring in his step, he gently walked over to the couch where Tom was lying. Looking down at Tom, Stephan was filled with anxiousness to please Lukas by getting Tom to cough up the cash. Stephan looked down at the sleeping victim. He saw the bloody hood, and he knew he would not touch the blood. He slowly reached down, grasped Tom's kneecap and nervously shook it. Tom was startled awake, and he murmured, "Who's there?"

Stephan jumped back as if he had aroused a poisonous snake. "Thomas Murphy," he whispered as he again grasped the kneecap and shook it. "Give us the money." When there was no reply, Stephan bravely reached for the front of Tom's jacket and pulled him up into the sitting position and whispered, "Murphy, give us the money."

"Take off the hood," mumbled Tom through the bloody hood, which was stuck to his bruised and battered face.

"I can't do that," replied Stephan, who stepped back.

"Take off the hood."

"I can't do that."

"I need water bad!" slurred Tom.

"What about the thirty million dollars?"

"Screw the money," Tom tried to shout.

Stephan stepped closer to Tom and he pushed him onto his back. He got close to Tom, pulled off Tom's tie and ripped open the front of Tom's white dress shirt, exposing Tom's red-haired chest. Next, Stephan took out his cigarette lighter and again whispered, "I hate burning you, but I gotta get the money." He leaned closer, lit his lighter and maliciously placed the burning end of the lighter onto Tom's exposed chest. Tom screamed in excruciating pain. At first, Stephan could smell the long, curly, red hair on Tom's exposed chest burning, and then he could smell the flesh burning. Tom again screamed. Stephan pulled the lighter away and whispered, "What about the money?" Tom did not answer; he just moaned. "I'll have to do it again, Mr. Murphy," Stephan again lit his lighter and placed the burning flame back onto Tom's chest. Stephan did not hear the door open, and he did not hear Lukas walk up behind him, but he suddenly felt Lukas grab him and throw him across the small room. He fell helplessly into a small bundle in the corner of the room. As he tried to scramble to his feet, Lukas placed a hand on Stephan's chest and forced him back up against the wall. He saw Lukas draw his weapon and place the barrel of the gun up against Stephan's forehead.

"Are you crazy?" screamed Lukas as he cocked his gun.

"Lukas, I was trying to get the money for you," yelled Stephan as he squirmed under the gun that was still pressed against his now sweating forehead. He could see the rage in his boss's eyes and he could feel the trembling in his boss's gun hand as he tried not to discharge the weapon. He wondered, would the gun go off or would Lukas spare him? "I was trying to help," shouted Stephan as he breathed heavily under Lukas's scrutiny and anger. "Really, I was just trying to help," screamed Stephan, who was now panic stricken and desperate to save his life.

"Are you crazy?" again screamed Lukas.

"Yes, sir," pleaded Stephan trying to save his life.

Stephan watched as Dagmar and Boris both ran into the room. Lukas shouted, "Dagmar, attend to his burns."

"Please don't shoot the boy, Lukas," begged Dagmar, as she checked Murphy's burns.

"Stephan, I should kill you where you stand," whispered Lukas as Stephan watched his boss tremble with anger. Dagmar ran out of the room, just to return moments later with a bottle of cold water, which she immediately poured onto Tom's scalded chest. Tom screamed when the water hit the burns. Stephan saw Dagmar turn away from Tom, look at Lukas and ask him to spare Stephan. Lukas shouted, "Why should I spare this fool?"

"I swear, I meant to help," uttered Stephan as he slid down the wall once Lukas removed his hand from Stephan's chest and the gun from his head. "I'm sorry, Lukas," whimpered Stephan as he watched Lukas walk away from him and walk toward Tom. Stephan got up off the floor as he cautiously watched Lukas inspect Tom's burns.

Stephan stopped apologizing when Dagmar said, "Shut up, and go retrieve the first aid kit out from the kitchen." First, Stephan walked slowly to the doorway; once he reached the doorway, he quickly ran out of the room and headed for the kitchen. In the kitchen, he searched for the first aid kit, but he could not find it. He turned around suddenly, and Dagmar was standing in front of him. "The first aid kit is in the brown travel bag next to the sink," she informed him.

"Thanks. I didn't know where to look," he said.

"This certainly isn't your day," she replied as she walked over to the travel bag and retrieved the kit. He watched as she walked out of the kitchen. Stephan felt stupid. He sat down at the kitchen table and put his head in his hands. He thought he was just trying to be helpful and make Lukas happy.

* * *

Outside Mr. Bill's Tavern it was still raining. Inside the tavern it was dark and smoke filled with jazz playing in the background. Thornton drank beer while Mike Max drank hard scotch on the rocks. "It seems like nothing is being done, and I feel useless," said Thornton as he took a drink of his cold beer.

"Much is being done. I authorized Wanda to have the phone branch on full throttle, and the police and the FBI are working feverishly to set up their kidnap hotline," said Mike as he sipped his scotch.

"We should be there in order to take action if the call comes through tonight," said Thornton as he took a big bite out of the cheeseburger he had ordered.

"The FBI agent I spoke with predicts the call won't come through until morning," replied Mike.

"How do they know?" asked Thornton.

"They handle hundreds of these kidnappings, and there are protocols they follow, which predicts a morning call," said Mike, who took another sip of his scotch.

"If that's true, we should get some sleep so we can be prepared to handle tomorrow's action," said Thornton as he looked at his wristwatch. "Mike, it's already eleven. I wonder what condition Tom's in tonight."

"I hope the wife and kids are being treated well. I can't imagine what's happening," speculated Mike as he finished the club sandwich he had been nibbling at for the last hour.

"I hope Tom's all right. I feel so responsible for letting them get him," said Thornton, "I wish I could have saved Bill."

"Thor, you're lucky to be alive!" said Mike as he took a drink then continued. "There was nothing you could have done under the circumstances."

"I still feel lousy. Why did they need to kill Bill?" asked Thornton. "It was excessive. It was not necessary. They could have abducted Tom without killing Bill."

"Thor, I agree," Mike said, shaking his head.

"It just shows us how extreme and brutal they are prepared to be." He took another bite of his cheeseburger.

"I agree," said Mike, "and that worries me. How extreme are they going to be with Tom and his family?" He took the final swig of his scotch. "Listen, not to change the subject, but how early tomorrow morning are you gonna show up at the phone branch?"

"I'd like to be there by dawn, but I've got to check on security. I've got to arrange for guards to protect Tom's new homesite," explained Thornton as he finished his cheeseburger. "I've gotta take care of that first thing in the morning. So I won't make the phone branch by dawn."

"Oh, yeah, the bombing," said Mike, "I'd forgotten about the bombing. How many armed guards you gonna need?"

"Five armed guards per shift and three shifts a day," said Thornton with a grimace. "Let's get out of here." He raised his hand and waved for their waitress.

Their waitress came to the table and asked, "Was everything all right?" She took away their empty plates and asked, "Would you like the bill?"

"Yes," replied Thornton. She handed him the bill, which he paid along with a twenty-dollar tip. He and Mike got up to go. When they were outside it was still raining. "We better make a run for our cars," shouted Thornton, "I'll see you in the morning, Mike." Thornton saw Mike run for his car, as Thornton ran for his. He had gotten revitalized by talking with Mike. He planned on going straight home and get some quality sleep if possible under the prevailing circumstances.

* * *

It was early evening when Tom woke up. He could hear the rain steadily hitting window panes. The back of his head hurt from where he had been struck earlier outside the Escalade. His face hurt worst than before from the boot stomping he had received during his conversation with Lukas Krueger and the rabbit punching he had received from Boris. The hood was stuck to his bloody face and the ropes were painful as they dug into his flesh. The burn on his chest had hurt terribly at first, but the salve the girl had applied helped ease the pain. He was getting pretty angry, as he floated in and out of consciousness.

Tom listened as the men grumbled in the distance. He could hardly breathe lying on the couch. Suddenly someone grab him and sat him upright on the couch. He mumbled, "Who is it?"

"Lukas!" shouted the Austrian as he casually slapped Tom on his bloody, hooded face.

"Quit doing that," snapped Tom as he turned his head away from Lukas.

"Thomas, you must understand this is only business. Have you decided to give us the thirty million dollars?" asked Lukas as he kicked Tom's feet. "Remember, we have Beth and your three kids. Do you want to change your thoughts about the money?"

"You better not hurt my family, you maniac," shouted Tom through the bloody hood, "or I'll hunt you down like a common street mongrel dog."

"You're not in any position to make threats," Lukas reminded him forcefully.

Tom heard Lukas walk away, and he shouted, "Don't you hurt them!" He listened for a response, but heard nothing. His body was cramping up due to the restraints of his hands and legs. Periodically he shouted, but no one answered. He tried to sleep, but that was difficult. He was worried about his wife and children. He considered his options: give up or hold tight. He chose the latter. It seemed as if hours had gone by. Then he heard Lukas talking to Boris in the not-so-far distance. Lukas said, "Boris, Murphy called me a mongrel dog. Damn! We'll see who turns out to be the mongrel, won't we?" Then he heard the two men walking toward him; before he knew what was happening, he was being shaken by Lukas. "We are going. Do you want to pay us?"

"No."

Tom knew Lukas was standing over him. Then Lukas said, "Otto, put Mrs. Murphy on the phone." He waited, then Lukas said, "Mrs. Murphy, I have your husband. Would you like to talk to him?" Tom imagined she was anxious to talk to him.

Tom felt Lukas hold the phone next to his hooded head and Lukas sternly said, "Speak to you wife, Thomas."

"Beth?" Tom mumbled through his bloody hood.

"Tom, are you hurt?" she asked as she sobbed.

"Beth, I am all right," he uttered. "Are you and the kids okay? Has he hurt you?" Tom felt Lukas pull the phone away and shout, "Beth, tell Tom to pay me. Do you understand? Tell Tom to pay me, or I'll hurt your kids." Lukas didn't wait for her to answer. Instead, Lukas immediately held to phone next to Tom's hooded ear and shouted, "Listen to Beth! Tom, listen to her."

"Tom, he wants you to pay him, or he'll hurt the kids," he heard her say.

Again he felt Lukas jerk the phone away from his ear and scream, "Will you pay the thirty million dollars?"

"Screw you, Krueger!" he shouted through the muffled hooded.

Tom did not know Lukas had signaled Boris. Boris struck him again in his hooded face. Tom heard Lukas say, "Beth, Tom said no to you and your children." Tom knew Lukas had hung up the phone. He heard Lukas as he said, "Boris, roll him onto his stomach so maybe he'll suffocate overnight."

Tom felt his face smothered down into the cushions of the dirty, smelly couch. Tom tried to roll onto his back, but could not move because of the tight ropes. Tom listened. "Boris, get everyone into the van. We'll go back to the Travelodge and get some sleep," As they were preparing to leave, Tom did not know that Lukas was smiling at the thought of the thirty million dollars that was just out of his greedy reach.

Tom knew he was fading in and out of consciousness. He heard the men leave, and he felt helpless. After he heard them leave, he soon fell asleep. He dreamed of being trapped in a steel cage. He woke periodically throughout the night. Everything was silent with the exception of the busy street traffic that sounded not far from the building. It was still raining. He heard the raindrops hitting the building's window panes.

With his bloody, hooded face shoved onto the dirty old couch cushions, it was a struggle for Tom to breathe. He finally fell into a deep sleep.

He dreamt about his family, who were on winding train tracks in a snowy mountain setting. He dreamt his family was hopelessly screaming for his help as they were in a train caboose running out of control down the mountainside. His family was calling for him to rescue them, and he was running down the train tracks trying to catch them. The faster he ran, the farther away went the caboose. He awoke screaming for his family, with the noise of a big Harley motorcycle revving its engine just outside the building.

Chapter Five

Thursday, Day Four

By seven o'clock Thursday morning, Wanda, the supervisor of the phone branch, opened the phone lines. The incoming calls were scarce that early, so she was available to assist the special units that were being set up to handle the ransom calls. She was helping Cleveland Police Officers Mattingly and Polo set up the equipment for the Cleveland Police Special Kidnap Unit. At the same time she was also helping FBI Special Agents Barlow and Coffee set up their equipment for the FBI Kidnap Command Center. Wanda knew that Mattingly was senior to Polo and that Barlow was senior to Coffee, and she knew to address them accordingly. She helped the two authorities set up. They went straight to work, and by eight the kidnap hotline was up and running, which surprised Wanda.

Shortly after eight, Wanda had returned to her desk in the phone branch. After a few minutes, she looked up and saw Mike Max enter the phone branch. She rose from her chair and walked over to meet him. "Good morning, Mike," she said as she greeted him at the double doors of the phone branch.

"Morning, Wanda. Have we heard anything yet?"

"No. The kidnap hotline has just gone online within the last few minutes," said Wanda as her deep-brown eyes twinkled from the strong morning coffee. She looked at Mike and noticed how pensive he appeared. "How are you holding up, Mike?" she asked as she took him by his arm and guided him toward the Kidnap Command Center, where she introduced him to Officers Mattingly and Polo and Agents Barlow and Coffee.

"Agent Barlow, how soon do you think we'll get a ransom call?" asked Mike as he shuffled his feet.

"Typically, these ransom calls come shortly after the kidnapping. These guys want to get the ball rolling right away," said Agent Barlow as he glanced at the clipboard he was holding. "The call should come in any time now."

"Mike, come with me," said Wanda as she walked him back to her desk. When they reached her desk, she looked at him seriously and asked, "When is Thornton coming in?"

"He should be here soon," said Mike. "He had to arrange for the security at Tom's new home." Mike pulled up a chair and sat down next to Wanda's desk.

Wanda checked the calls that were coming in to the phone branch. After she finished her phone check, she looked at Mike and asked, "Do you know for sure when Thornton will be available?" She glanced at her phone monitor to again check the incoming calls.

"I'm not certain. Why?" replied Mike.

"Because I know Tom would want him here when the ransom call comes in," said Wanda as she sipped her mug of hot coffee and checked yesterday's messages.

"I know you're right about that," said Mike. "I can't imagine Tom being kidnapped. Nor can I imagine Bill being dead and Thor almost dead if not for his vest."

They discussed the situation for ten minutes or more, then Agent Barlow walked up to Wanda's desk and asked, "Wanda, is there anyway you folks could send up coffee for my people?"

"Certainly, Agent Barlow. I'll call our coffee lounge and have that sent right up for you and your folks. Anything else?"

"No. Just coffee would be greatly appreciated."

"Agent Barlow, I'll get right on it."

"Thanks," said Barlow as he turned and walked back to the Kidnap Command Center and the hotline.

Wanda dialed the company's coffee lounge and said, "Hello, Martha, this is Wanda in the phone branch. We have a group of police officers and FBI agents setting up a kidnap hotline for Tom, and these guys are asking for coffee. Can you set them up with a pitcher of coffee and mugs?" She listened to Martha, who was anxious to help, then she replied, "Thanks, Martha. I'll tell them it's on its way." As she hung up, she looked out the windows of the phone branch and saw it was still raining, cloudy, and dreadfully dark.

While Wanda was making the arrangements for the coffee, Mike tried to contact Thornton, but after three attempts Mike said, "Wanda, Thor is not answering his cell phone. I'll try again later."

Fifteen minutes later, the double doors to the phone branch swung open, and the coffee tray was wheeled into the room. Wanda yelled, "Martha! By the police officers." The tray was wheeled over to the Kidnap Command Center, where the officers and agents all dove into the much-appreciated hot coffee.

As the minutes ticked by, the anxiety mounted for the much-anticipated ransom call. It was approaching 8:30 AM, and everyone's nerves were on edge.

Wanda was aware that the phone branch was quiet that morning, which made her happy because she wanted to pay less attention to her incoming calls and pay more attention to the specially dedicated hotline the FBI had established.

By 8:45 AM, Cleveland Police Officers Mattingly and Polo were working with FBI Special Agents Barlow and Coffee, who were anxiously waiting for the ransom call. They were anxious to hear the kidnapper's demands, which would hopefully free Mr. Murphy and his wife and children.

By exactly 9:00 AM, the hotline buzzed an incoming call, and immediately the FBI started their recording and tracing machines, as Wanda took the call. Wanda said, "Just Clean It Up. This is Wanda. How may I assist you?"

"Who am I talking to?" asked the deep-voiced caller.

"My name is Wanda. Who is calling?"

"Wanda, listen carefully. We have abducted Thomas Murphy and his wife and his children. We want thirty million dollars. We do not want to harm any of the family, and so in a show of good faith we are releasing Thomas. We are releasing him so that he can arrange for the payment of the thirty million dollars." The accented caller paused.

Wanda waited, then asked, "Are you still there?"

"Yes, I am still here. Listen carefully. Thomas is located in an abandoned house in Ohio City. The location of the abandoned house is somewhere near the intersection of Franklin Avenue and West Twenty-fifth Street, just past the famous Westside Market. Do not test our resolve. We are serious. We want exactly thirty million American dollars," explained the caller, then he hung up the telephone.

Wanda stood stunned, holding the receiver.

Agent Barlow shouted, "Wanda, hang it up!"

She was startled but hung up the receiver, and she immediately proceeded to write down the location of the abandoned house where the caller claimed Tom was located. Her plan was to take Tom's location to Leroy, the company dispatcher, who would notify all of Tom's employees.

Barlow shouted, "Coffee, did you get the trace?"

Coffee shouted, "Nah! Too short!"

Barlow replied, "Damn! Let's go."

Wanda watched as the police and the FBI agents all rushed out of the Kidnap Command Center to rescue Tom. Wanda looked at her staff and shouted, "Hold down the fort, gang. I'll be right back." She grabbed the pad of paper with the information of Tom's location, then she ran out of the phone branch and headed down the hall toward the communications center. As she hurried down the hall, she wondered what condition Tom would be in when help finally did arrive. She knew Tom to be a tough and determined individual, but she knew his abductors were killers. They had killed Bill and attempted to kill Thornton. As she ran down the hall, she offered up a quick prayer. As she entered the communications center, she shouted, "Leroy, where are you?" She looked around and did not see him until he popped out from behind a large wall partition.

"Wanda, what's up?" asked Leroy, the communication center's dispatcher.

"Leroy, the ransom call just came through. The caller is releasing Tom. Here is his location," said Wanda as she handed Leroy the paper with the location on it. "Leroy, can you dispatch that information out to all our field workers and managers?"

Wanda watched Leroy quickly read the short note. "Sure! We'll find Tom in a quick minute," said Leroy as he headed for his radio equipment.

"Leroy, the kidnapper wants thirty million dollars for Beth and the children," said Wanda, as she watched the dispatcher prepare to send out his message to all of Tom's employees. "Leroy, you're a gem," she said, as she listened to him broadcast the message. She knew it would be a foot race between Tom's people, the Cleveland Police and the FBI. Her money was on Tom's people to find and rescue him first.

As Leroy finished dispatching the information, he added, "Folks, hurry and fetch our boss ..." Wanda thanked Leroy, who replied, "They want thirty million. That'll wipe Tom out."

"Tom's family is priceless," said Wanda.

"I know that, Wanda."

Wanda patted Leroy's shoulder, again thanked him, and said, "call me when you hear anything." She left the communication center and headed back down the hall toward the phone branch. She believed it would only take minutes to find Tom, but she wondered how long it would take to find and rescue his family.

When Wanda got back to the phone branch she found that both Cleveland Police Officers Mattingly and Polo and FBI Agents Barlow and Coffee had left the phone branch in pursuit of Tom Murphy's location. They left no one to man the hotline, which infuriated Wanda, as she witnessed their incompetence.

There were few incoming calls, and so the staff of the phone branch was just standing waiting to hear from Wanda. After she checked the hotline, she returned to her desk and looked at her phone staff and shouted, "Leroy has sent out Tom's location to all our field workers and field managers. So hopefully our people will get to him as soon as possible." She smiled as she heard her staff cheering for Tom. "I'll let you all know when they find Tom. Until then, keep taking calls." Standing by her desk, she saw Mike walking around the phone branch placing cell calls to Thornton. "Mike," she yelled as she waved her hand over her head. Mike saw her and came running to her desk.

"Wanda, I've been calling Thor, but there is no answer," complained Mike as he sat down next to her desk. "I should go to the hospital. Which one do you think they'll take Tom to?" he asked. "It will most likely be Metro ER, wouldn't you think?"

"Ohio City is where they located Tom, and that is close to Metro ER, so they'll probably take him there," agreed Wanda. "You can have Thornton meet you there."

"If he ever answers his phone," criticized Mike.

"You head for Metro," said Wanda, "and I'll call Leroy and have him radio Thornton's car phone and tell him to meet you at the hospital. Okay, Mike?"

"Thanks, Wanda," said Mike as he ran out of the phone branch and drove to the hospital to meet up with Tom Murphy when they brought him in.

* * *

At 10:00 AM Charles "Checkers" Mulroney, one of Tom's field workers, a tall, slender, light-skinned black man with a face speckled with freckles was driving his work van down Franklin Avenue when the alert came over the radio. He immediately responded by making a U turn in the middle of Franklin Avenue and headed straight for the intersection of Franklin Avenue and West Twenty-fifth Street, just past the Westside Market in the famous Ohio City area of Cleveland. He drove but a short distance when he spotted and pulled up in front of what appeared to be a boarded-up old bungalow. He turned off the engine, then ran up the walk to the front door. He tried to enter the house, but the front door was locked. He ran to the side door, but he found the same problem. He spotted a small basement window, which he immediately kicked in. Then he snaked his slim body through the small basement window and slid into the dark, dusty basement.

Once in the dark basement, looking for the steps, he started shouting for his boss. He quickly found the steps. At the top of the stairs, he tried to flip the light switch, but the house remained dark without electricity. He heard sirens in the distance and continued to look frantically for Tom Murphy. As he ran into the living room he spotted an old dirty couch with a twisted up body lying face down with hands pulled behind and securely bound with ropes. "Mr. Murphy," Checkers shouted as he rushed to Tom's side. "I got you, Tom. You're all right now," whispered Checkers as he slowly and carefully rolled his boss off his stomach and onto his back. He was not even sure if his boss was awake, unconscious, or dead. "Easy does it," repeated Checkers as he helped him sit up. "Easy does it." He looked at the dried, blood-soaked hood that was stuck over Tom's head. "Easy does it, Tom." Checkers took a bottle of drinking water he had been carrying on his belt, and he gingerly poured the water onto the hood. The bloody dried hood had stuck onto the left side of Tom's face. He continued to pour the water, and it slowly loosened the hood. Tom had not yet spoken, and Checkers had not seen him move his limbs. Next, Checkers slowly wiggled the water-soaked bloody hood up and off of Tom's head. He kept repeating himself, "Easy does it, Tom. Easy does it … " Once he got the hood off of Tom's head, he then saw how badly Tom had been beaten. Tom's nose was obviously broken. He had a deep gash over his left cheekbone, his left eye was nearly swollen shut and the left side of his face was bruised, bloodied, and swollen. "Can you hear me, Tom?" whispered Checkers as he poured some more water directly onto Tom's face. "Can you hear me?" He pulled a clean handkerchief out of his back pants pocket, wet it with water, and tried to wipe the blood from around Tom's swollen mouth. "Can you hear me?" whispered Checkers, who was not certain if his boss was alive.

He saw Tom slowly open his eyes and murmur, "Thanks."

"Tom, are you all right?" whispered Checkers, wondering if his boss recognized him as an employee.

"I'm all cramped up," uttered Tom. "Cut me loose!"

"Okay, boss." He pulled his pocketknife out of his pants pocket and again rolled Tom onto his side so that the ropes were exposed. "Hold on, Tom. I'm gonna cut your hands free first." Checkers carefully sawed at the ropes. Suddenly, the knife cut through the biting ropes, and he heard Tom moan as his hands and arms sprang free from the agonizing position he had been forced to tolerate for nearly twenty-four hours.

"Oh, God, that hurts," moaned Tom as he brought his arms back around to the front of his body. "God. Thank you, Checkers." It was apparent, at that point, that Tom did recognize Checkers, and that made Checkers feel good.

He helped Tom sit back up, then he started cutting the ropes that bound Tom's feet. In less than two minutes, Checkers had Tom's feet free. The sirens he had heard earlier were now quite close, and he knew the authorities would be arriving any minute.

"Checkers, they got my wife and kids," said Tom, "and they've killed Bill and Thor to get to me."

"Thornton was wearing his vest," he said. "Thor is alive!" He watched as Tom reached up, grabbed him, and gave him a big hug.

"Thor is alive?"

"Yes. Thor is looking for you, also."

"Checkers, thank God you've found me," whispered Tom, who was dehydrated, cramped up, and breathing shallowly from being restrained in an awful position for such a long time.

"Lay back, Tom," whispered Checkers. "You've been through a lot. Take it easy." Checkers saw Tom was doing poorly.

"Easy," moaned Tom, "I'm hurting real bad."

"Hear the sirens? The cops are on their way," said Checkers with excitement.

"They've got my wife," said Tom, "but Thor is alive."

"Yes." Checkers thought maybe Tom was disoriented.

"Checkers, he's got my kids."

"I know, but we'll get them back, boss!"

Just then he heard the police pounding on the front door. "Hold on! Hold on!" he shouted as he jumped up, ran to the front door, and unlocked it from the inside. As the door swung open, men rushed into the living room.

"Over there," shouted Checkers as he directed them to Tom's side. The Cleveland police, the FBI and an EMS unit stormed into the room. Immediately, Checkers backed up in order to make way for the EMS to attend to Tom, who looked quite poorly. "He needs water bad," said Checkers as he watched the attendants carefully place an oxygen mask over Tom's badly bruised and bloody face. "Be careful fellows. My boss has a broken nose, and his face hurts." He noticed the three attendants ignore him, but he did not care as long as they treated Tom with the best care they could provide. He continued watching them as one tried to clean up Tom's bloody face, while another guy tried to start an IV line in Tom's arm. He could see all three attendants were working feverishly to help Tom.

Checkers noticed one attendant appeared to be older, and he was giving orders to the other two, so Checkers assumed that he was the one in charge. He listened as the older attendant said, "Guys, he's doing poorly. He's been tied up so long he is having trouble ventilating. We need to transport him to the hospital."

"I've got the IV started," shouted one attendant.

"Good job," said the man in charge. "Let's get him on the gurney." Checkers wanted to assist them, but he was afraid he would get in their way. He watched them move and secure Tom onto the cart.

Barlow, the FBI agent in charge, asked, "Can we talk to Mr. Murphy?"

In unison, the three attendants shouted, "No!"

Checkers stepped back and watched as the EMS attendants lifted the gurney and proceeded to wheel it out the front door. Checkers followed behind them down the front steps and out to the ambulance. As they were lifting Tom into the ambulance, Checkers shouted, "Tom, I'll follow you to the hospital." He saw them close the back doors, then he rushed to his work van and started to follow them to the Metro Health Medical Center emergency room.

Checkers switched on his two-way radio equipment, and he shouted, "Leroy ... Leroy ... Pick up, Leroy! This is Checkers."

"Checkers, this is Leroy. Talk to me ..."

"I found Tom Murphy. He's in bad shape. The EMS has taken him to Metro emergency room. I'm following them."

"How bad is he?" asked Leroy.

"Leroy, he's barely alive!"

"Checkers, call me back when you arrive at Metro."

"Will do, Leroy!"

Checkers continued to stay on the ambulance's bumper.

*   *   *

Leroy shut down his radio connection with Checkers. He stood and ran down the hall to the phone branch. As he raced through the double doors, he saw that the Kidnap Command Center was unmanned. He saw Wanda, who was sitting at her desk, so he ran up to her and said, "Wanda, Checkers found Tom. He's in bad shape! They're taking him to Metro emergency room." Leroy stammered as be panted for breath.

"How bad is Tom?" asked Wanda anxiously.

Leroy took a deep breath and said, "Checkers just said Tom is alive." Leroy took another deep breath and said, "Checkers wasn't very encouraging. Sorry! He did promise to call me when they got to Metro. So I gotta get back to my radio. Oh, also, I touched base with Thornton, and he is on his way to meet Mike Max at the emergency room."

Wanda stood up from her desk and said, "Leroy, keep me informed." Leroy nodded his head and ran back to the communications center.

* * *

Wanda grabbed her branch intercom microphone, and she shouted, "They've rescued Tom! He is alive!"

The twenty-member phone branch staff all stood up, pulled off their headsets and yelled while simultaneously applauding the rescue of their boss. Pandemonium broke out as they cheered, whistled, and celebrated. All the staff members were running around hugging each other and screaming joyfully. While her staff continued to celebrate, she looked over at the empty Kidnap Command Center and wondered why they had not gotten more agents to man the hotline. What if the kidnappers called before the agents returned? She knew she could take the call, but what would she say? It appeared that the FBI was incompetent.

After ten minutes Wanda said, "Go back to manning your phones, and I'll keep all of you advised as I learn more about his status."

After Wanda's workers returned to their work stations, she placed a phone call to the parking garage. She intended to talk to Tom's mechanic, and when he answered the phone she said, "Garry, this is Wanda from the phone branch. Mike Max was here earlier, and he instructed me to call you regarding Tom's Lincoln Navigator. Mike wants you to get it ready for Tom to use in replacement of his Cadillac Escalade, which the police's crime scene unit has for the moment."

"Wanda, I can have it gassed and ready within the hour," replied Garry, the company mechanic.

"Wonderful, Garry."

"Has Mr. Murphy been found?" asked Garry.

"Yes. He has been taken to Metro ER," she replied.

"I'll get the Lincoln ready."

"Thanks," she said as she hung up the telephone. Then she checked the phone board to see who of her staff were taking incoming calls and who were not taking calls. As she checked on her staff, she could not get her fears for Tom's condition out of her thoughts. When Leroy reported Checker's version of Tom's condition, he was not at all optimistic. She was scared Tom would not survive, but then she remembered the ransom caller said they were releasing Tom so that he could get the money for them. If that were true, then they would most likely want to keep him safe and able-bodied. That rationale gave her comfort and optimism.

As she sat sipping her hot coffee, she remembered back to when she first met Thomas Murphy. Her interview was in the early morning, and she remembered being very nervous. She had just received her associate degree from the Cuyahoga Community College. She had no practical work experience with the exception of several part-time jobs flipping burgers. She had three teenagers at home and an absentee husband, but she did have enthusiasm and an eagerness to prove herself. She remembered that morning of her initial interview with Tom went very well. He took a liking to her right away. He told her that he saw great potential in her, and he asked her if she felt like she could be a supervisor and lead people. She recalled smiling at him and answering with a big yes. He discussed the phone branch and how it worked. She recalled showing an interest, then he told her how it needed to be supervised. An hour later, she was making thirty thousand a year with a full benefit package, which included a college reimbursement package for her three kids.

She remembered becoming a professional that morning. She also remembered how scared she was on her first day as the supervisor of Tom's phone branch. After the first day, she felt the job fit like a finely crafted pair of gloves. Wanda recalled six months after she started the job, Tom gave her what he considered a well-earned bonus and raise. That day she asked him why he hired her, and he told her it was because she kept talking about her three teenage children. He was a family man, and he liked that about her. She knew because of Tom her life changed, and she was grateful.

Just then, one of Wanda's workers approached her desk, and instantly her mind was back on her job.

*   *   *

Checkers knew the time from the abandoned foreclosure to Metro emergency room was less than ten minutes. He stayed right on the ambulance's rear bumper, and when they were within four blocks from the ER they suddenly turned on its siren and flashing lights—as if Tom's condition had worsened. Checkers saw the ambulance speeding away from him, as the vehicle was now racing to Metro. He was breaking the speed limit in order to stay close behind the racing ambulance. As he turned the corner, he looked beyond the speeding ambulance as it pulled into the emergency room parking lot and under the canopy of the ER entrance. Checkers slammed on his brakes and watched as the EMS guys ran around to the back of the ambulance. He saw them spring the doors open and quickly pull out the stretcher. He saw them rush Tom through the electric doors as they automatically sprang open.

Checkers put his van in reverse just as the cars of the police and FBI pulled up into the parking lot. He blared his horn, and then he pulled into a parking space. While he watched the police and agents run into the ER,

he got on his radio and called Leroy's communication center. "Leroy ... Leroy ... This is Checkers."

"Checkers, are you at Metro?" squawked Leroy.

"Yeah, Leroy, I'm at Metro," yelled Checkers as he shook nervously.

"How is Tom? Talk to me," demanded Leroy.

"They were racing with their sirens blaring and their lights flashing. Maybe he got worse," proclaimed Checkers as he turned off his radio and ran into the emergency room. He ran past the police officers and the FBI agents and rushed up to the front desk. "Nurse, can you direct me to where they are keeping Thomas Murphy?" uttered Checkers as he shuffled his feet anxiously.

"What is your name, sir?" the nurse asked flatly.

"I work for Mr. Murphy. My name is Charles Mulroney."

"Mr. Mulroney, you'll have to take a seat in our waiting room," said the nurse, "Mr. Murphy has just arrived and the doctors are doing their initial assessments."

Checkers turned away from the front desk and he bumped chest to chest into Agent Barlow. "Sorry, guy," he uttered as he backed up, "the nurse won't tell you anything." He walked around the group of law enforcers and proceeded to the waiting room. Just as he sat down facing the front double electric doors, in rushed Thornton and Mike Max. He jumped up and ran to them. "Guys, they won't tell me anything. The nurse said they're assessing Tom," said Checkers as he anxiously shook hands with both the men.

"Calm down, Checkers," urged Mike, his supervisor, as they finished shaking hands. "We'll get some information." Checkers followed both men as the three of them walked back to the front desk and found the same nurse who had told Checkers to wait. As they stopped and leaned against the front desk, Mike said, "Nurse, I'd like to check on Thomas Murphy."

"I'll tell you what I told the FBI. Go wait in the waiting room," snarled the front desk nurse.

"That's what she told me," confessed Checkers.

Mike recognized FBI Agent Barlow standing in the hallway along with Agent Coffee and Cleveland Police Officers Mattingly and Polo. Mike walked over to them and said, "Who's manning the Kidnap Command Center, Agent Barlow?"

"Additional agents should be reporting as we speak," replied Barlow as he tried to cover his embarrassment.

"You saw Tom as the EMS worked on him right in the abandoned house," said Mike. "What did you see? How bad were Tom's injuries?"

Barlow replied, "Better you ask your man there. He found and attended to Tom right before we or the EMS arrived," said Barlow as he pointed at Checkers.

Mike turned to face Checkers, and he said, "Is it true, Checkers? Did you arrive first and did you attend to Tom before the EMS arrived?" Mike and Thornton were both surprised to discover their man was the first to discover and attempt to rescue Tom.

Checkers said, "When I found Tom he was wearing a blood-soaked hood, which had dried blood stuck to his injured face. I had a bottle of water, and I poured the water onto the hood to loosen it. After a moment or two, I was able to gently wiggled the hood off his head. When I got the hood off, I found Tom had a broken nose. The left side of his face was bloody, swollen, and badly bruised. He had a deep cut on his left cheekbone just below his left eye. The left eye was almost swollen shut."

"Was he conscious?" asked Thornton.

"He was barely conscious," replied Checkers.

"Could he talk?" asked Thornton.

"Again, barely," said Checkers. "He could barely talk for two reasons. His face was terrible swollen, and his jaw was injured. The big problem was his restricted position. He was tied up, and his face was shoved into the dirty old cushions of an old sofa. Tom was having a real hard time breathing."

Mike said, "It seems they worked him over pretty bad, doesn't it?" Mike ran his hand through his hair.

"Tom thanked me," said Checkers. "He thought Thor was killed along with Bill, but I told him you were wearing your vest and that you were alive. Then he asked about his wife and kids. He somehow knew the kidnappers had taken them also."

"How did he know his wife and kids were also kidnapped?" asked Thornton as he rubbed his shiny bronze head.

"I'm sure the kidnapper told him," suggested Mike.

Checkers asked, "Mike, can I use your cell phone?" Mike pulled his cell phone from its side belt holster and handed it to Checkers, who quickly dialed a memorized number. "Hello, Wanda, this is Checkers. Thor, Mike and I are at Metro ER, and the doctors are evaluating Tom. What's that?" He paused to listen to what Wanda had to say, then he said, "Tom was able to speak to me. He is conscious, but he was beaten pretty bad. Wanda, I'll call you back as soon as we hear anything. What's that? Sure." Checkers lowered the cell phone from his ear and looked at Mike and said, "Mike, she wants to talk to you." He handed the cell phone back to Mike, then he turned to

Thornton and said, "She is extremely worried." Checkers nervously stroked his pencil-thin moustache.

"We all are, Checkers," replied Thornton. "Tom asked about me?"

"Yeah," said Checkers. "He thought you had been killed along with Bill. Tom thinks highly of you, Thor." Checkers started walking down the hall back toward the waiting room, and Thornton and Mike automatically followed him without saying a word. Mike Max was still listening to Wanda on his cell phone. As soon as Mike finished talking to Wanda, he put his cell phone back into his side belt holster. Checkers looked at Mike and asked, "What did Wanda want, Mike?" Mike grabbed Checkers by the arm and stopped him from walking any closer to the waiting room.

"Checkers, she wanted me to get Agent Barlow to get some agents to man their hotline," explained Mike.

"There's no one there?" asked both Checkers and Thornton.

Checkers led the way as the three men headed back up the hall away from the waiting room and toward the front desk, where the FBI agents were congregating. "Hey Agent Barlow," shouted Checkers. Mike rushed in front of Checkers and also shouted the agent's name. He informed him that the hotline in the Kidnap Command Center was still unmanned.

Both Agents Barlow and Coffee were embarrassed. Agent Barlow puffed his chest out and shouted, "Agents are on their way to man the hotline."

"Sloppy ... sloppy ... sloppy ..." shouted Checkers as Thornton grabbed him and held him back from charging the two agents.

"You are jeopardizing Tom's family," shouted Mike. "What if the kidnappers call back and no one is there?"

* * *

Tom remembered his ambulance ride just up until he slipped into unconsciousness a few streets before the ambulance reached Metro ER, and when he awoke his stretcher was being rushed through the entrance and down the hall past the front desk. At that time, to Tom everything seemed vague and dreamlike. The first thing he heard was an attending doctor shout, "Mr. Murphy, can you hear me?" He tried to reply to the doctor but was unable. He knew he was in an examining room. The big, bright, overhead lights hurt his eyes. He sensed there were many doctors and nurses rushing around him. His face and head ached. His face felt like a pumpkin that had been battered by a baseball bat. He felt the room spinning, then everything went dark.

An hour later. "Thomas ... Thomas ... My name is Dr. Stern. You've been sleeping for the last hour while we attended to your wounds," said the good doctor.

"Dr. Stern," Tom mumbled as he slowly rolled his head from side to side. "What happened?"

"Don't you remember, Thomas?"

"What?" he said groggily.

"You were kidnapped and beaten about the face and head," said Dr. Stern, who was examining Tom's eyes.

"Yes …" he replied slowly. "Yes."

"While you were sleeping we cared for you, Thomas."

"Yes …" he again replied slowly.

"You do not have a concussion. There are no broken bones in your skull except for your nose. We have splinted your nose and stuffed gauze in your nostrils," the doctor started to explain.

"Yes. Thank you, doctor," said Tom slowly as he breathed through his mouth because of the plugged nose.

"You must breathe through your mouth until tonight when you may remove the gauze from your nose. We have just taken you off a breathing machine, which helped restore your natural breathing rhythm and oxygen level," said Dr. Stern, who did not want to explain things too quickly and possibly confuse his patient.

"Thank you, doctor. What else?" asked Tom as he reached up to touch his face.

Dr. Stern grabbed Tom's hand and said, "Don't touch your face. It's extremely sore. We've cleaned all your facial wounds, and the cut under your left eye at the cheekbone required ten stitches to close it. None of your teeth have been affected. I'd like to put you back on the breathing machine and admit you overnight, Mr. Murphy. If you feel better tomorrow we can discuss discharging you.

"Doctor Stern, I need to find my family," he said with determination as he slipped into unconsciousness.

Then the respiratory therapist assisted the doctors by attaching Tom to the breathing machine. They gave Tom an injection to help him sleep for a short time while he got his breathing treatment.

Several hours later, Tom was resting comfortably in a little exam room. By 2:00 PM, Dr. Stern returned to check on Tom's progress. When the doctor entered the room, Tom was resting with the lights dimmed and his eyes closed. He heard Dr. Stern step in from behind the yellow curtain. "How are you feeling now, Thomas?" asked Dr. Stern as Tom watched him approach the small bed.

"Much better. Thank you, Doctor Stern," said Tom.

"Good! I am glad to hear that," replied Dr. Stern as he took hold of Tom's left wrist to check his pulse. "You have several friends outside waiting to see you. Are you ready for company?"

"Yes," replied Tom. "I need to be discharged."

"Your pulse is a little fast," observed the doctor.

"Is it?" asked Tom as he tried to look around the curtain to see if he could spot his friends.

"How are you breathing? Can you breathe with ease?" asked the doctor as he used his stethoscope.

"Yes. I'm much better. The machine helped."

"I'm concerned about your pulse," said Doctor Stern.

"That is because I'm anxious to get out."

The doctor looked at Tom and said, "Before your pals come in, the FBI have some questions they want to ask you."

"Send them in," said Tom. "And get the discharge papers ready, doctor."

"Okay, Tom," replied Dr. Stern, "if that is what you want to do." The doctor walked out of the small cubicle.

Tom watched three FBI agents enter his little cubicle. "Mr. Thomas Murphy?" asked the agent.

"Yes. I am Thomas Murphy."

"My name is Agent John Barlow," said the agent. "It looks like you had a rough go of it, Mr. Murphy." Tom watched as Agent Barlow stepped closer.

"I'm all right," said Tom. "I'm worried about my family. Agent Barlow, you do know they were kidnapped, don't you?"

"Yes, of course. I need to ask some questions. Dr. Stern said you were up to it. We are trying to get your wife and kids back."

"That's my priority," said Tom.

"Did you see your kidnappers?"

"I was hooded the whole time."

"Were there any distinguishing traits?"

"The kidnapper gave me his name!"

"He did? What name did he give you?"

"Lukas Krueger."

"Did you say, 'Lukas Krueger'?" asked Barlow.

"Yes. He is an Austrian," replied Tom as he watched the other two agents repeat the name under their breath.

"Mr. Murphy, if this is Lukas Krueger, then this is a very serious matter. We've been trying to catch him for well over ten years."

"I'm sure it is Krueger," said Tom.

"Did he have a thick European accent?" asked Barlow.

"Yes," replied Tom confidently. "I just mentioned Krueger is an Austrian."

"May I use your bedside telephone?" asked Barlow, who did not wait for an answer, but just walked over to the nightstand and started dialing the telephone.

"Who are you calling?" asked Tom.

"I'm calling my partner. He is at your phone branch manning the Kidnap Command Center hotline. I want to advise him that Lukas Krueger has surfaced again," said Barlow with an excited tone in his voice.

"Go ahead, Barlow," said Tom as he watched Barlow finish dialing the number.

Tom listened as Barlow said, "Agent Coffee, you're not going to believe this, but Thomas Murphy has identified the kidnapper as no other than our elusive Lukas Krueger." Tom waited while Barlow listened to Agent Coffee, then Barlow said, "I want you to call the director, and apprise him of our discovery. Then I want Senior Special Agent Donald Kellogg flown here directly from Quantico ASAP." He watched as Barlow hung up the telephone, turned, and said, "This is quite an event."

"I assume Krueger is something special," said Tom.

"Senior Special Agent Donald Kellogg has made a career chasing and attempting to capture Mr. Lukas Krueger," said Barlow. "We will fly him in today to advise and assist us in the apprehension of this dangerous fellow."

"Look Barlow, I don't want my family exposed to this guy if he is that dangerous," shouted Tom.

"We don't have much of a choice. Krueger already has your family, but we are going to do everything we can to get your family back, Tom," said Barlow. "Are you going to be admitted today?"

"No. I'm being discharged," said Tom. "Why?"

"We can all meet at your phone branch," said Barlow, "and then we can brainstorm our strategy. I'll go tell Dr. Stern about the development and hurry him along with your discharge."

Tom watched as Barlow motioned to his two other agents, then the three of them left. Ten minutes later, Dr. Stern entered Tom's private exam room and said, "Tom, I just spoke with Agent Barlow. He claims he needs you back at your place. Are you ready to be discharged? Do you feel up to it?"

"Surprisingly, I feel much better," said Tom. "Thank you, Dr. Stern."

"Good, Thomas. I'm getting the paperwork ready and in the meantime I'll get a nurse to come pull out your IV line," said Dr. Stern as he reached and shook Tom's hand. "Oh, yes, Thomas, because you are a public figure, the hospital requires me and the hospital's public relations people to make a statement on your condition to the media," added Dr. Stern formally.

"I understand, doctor," said Tom as Dr. Stern pulled back the privacy curtain so that Tom could see his friends—Checkers, Thornton, and Mike—standing in the hallway waiting to see him. Tom waved at his three friends.

"You visit with your friends while I get your paperwork done," said the doctor as Tom watched him walk away.

Tom turned to face Checkers, Thornton, and Mike as they all rushed to his bedside. Tom shook Checkers's hand and sincerely said, "Thanks for saving me, Checkers."

"Boss, it was my golden opportunity."

Tom motioned to Thornton to come closer, and as they bear-hugged he said, "God, Thor, I thought I lost you." Tom hesitated to let go of his close friend and bodyguard. "Thor, he's got my family," said Tom with a grimace.

"We'll catch his sorry ass!" whispered Thornton into Tom's ear as they continued to hold each other.

"Thank you, Thor," said Tom as he released him and laughed. "Yes, we will catch his sorry ass."

Tom felt his feet being touched; he looked at the end of the bed and saw Mike playing with his feet. "Mike, my main man," said Tom quietly. "How are things at Just Clean It Up?" asked Tom with a renewed smile.

"Good, boss!" said Mike. "Good to see you."

Tom looked back at Thornton and said, "Thor, Checkers told me you wore your vest yesterday morning. Why?"

"I guess talking to Joe Brown made me think of safety, and so I just slipped it on, and it saved my life," Thornton said as he scratched his chin comically.

"I guess we won't need Joe Brown to find out who we are dealing with," said Tom, "because the kidnapper told me his name. It's Lukas Krueger, and the FBI thinks he is a real big deal kidnapper from Europe."

"Lukas Krueger," repeated Thornton.

"Yeah," confirmed Tom, "Agent Barlow told me the FBI has been chasing him for over ten years."

He tried to sit up straighter in his hospital bed and Thornton said, "Take it easy, Tom. This Krueger guy really worked you over."

"I look worse than I feel," suggested Tom as he fiddled with his nose splint.

"Tom, you may feel all right at the moment, but when your pain meds wears off you're going to feel shitty," explained Thornton, who was helping Tom sit up straighter. "Sorry to be the bearer of such bad news."

"I know, Thor," said Tom as he thought about his wife and three children and wondered how they were faring.

Mike squeezed Tom's toes affectionately and said, "Boss, you better get a pain script to take home with you, or you're going to be worthless to search for Beth and the kids." Tom did not respond. He was thinking about his family and hoping they were not being mistreated "Tom, you there? Hello … Hello …"

"Sorry, Mike," he replied, "I was thinking about my family. You guys don't think Krueger would hurt them?"

Checkers shouted, "Not a woman nor kids."

Tom smiled and said, "Thanks, Checkers."

Tom appreciated his visit with his three friends. He was relieved that he had been rescued from the kidnappers, but he was worried sick over the kidnapping of his wife and his children. He looked at his friends, and he asked, "Who heard the ransom call?"

"The FBI recorded the call so you can hear it verbatim later, but for now I can tell you the call consisted of basically two parts. He gave us instructions where to find you, and, secondly, he asked for the thirty million dollars," explained Thornton.

"Yeah, when he had me tied up he just kept talking about the thirty million I owe him," said Tom as he fiddled with his nose splint.

"What do you mean by 'you owe him'?" asked Thornton.

Tom said, "He seems delusional. He claims to have spent three months doing surveillance of me and my family. So now I owe him for his time."

"He is delusional," said Thornton.

Just then a young, black, female nurse came into the room, and she proceeded to remove Tom's IV line from his right arm. She looked at Tom and said, "Mr. Murphy, it's an honor to meet you, sir."

"Thank you," said Tom. "What is your name?"

"My name is Janet," said the young nurse. "May I ask a favor, sir?"

"Call me Tom. What is your favor?"

"My auntie is a huge fan of yours. She loves the way you've beautified the city of Cleveland. Well, I've got her autograph book, and she would love to have you sign it," explained Janet as she pulled the book from her uniform waist pocket.

"Janet, I'd be glad to sign it for your auntie. What is her name?" asked Tom as he took the book.

"Her name is Miss Pearl," said Janet.

He recited as he wrote. "Dear Miss Pearl, My Best Regards, Thomas Murphy."

He started to hand the book back when Janet said, "Would you add under your name the Prince Of Cleveland?"

"Certainly, Janet," said Tom as he added the postscript. "You tell your auntie to keep her chin up!"

"She is ninety-one years old," added the pretty, chocolate-colored Janet with a giggle.

"Good for her," said Tom, smiling as he handed back the book to the young nurse. "Thank you for taking out my IV." He watched her as she gathered up her equipment, thanked him again, smiled, and left the room.

Thornton smiled and said, "Wow, she is a real cutie!"

Tom snapped his fingers and said, "Focus! Where do ya'll think Krueger has my family?"

"We gotta look for clues," urged Thornton.

"I'm gonna give him the money," declared Tom as Thornton helped guide him off the hospital bed, then he helped him pull off his hospital gown. Checkers reached for Tom's clothes, which were folded and setting on top of his nightstand next to his bed. "Help me with my pants, guys!"

As Mike held his pants, Tom put one leg into the pants, and Mike said, "You better wait on giving this creep your money. See what the police and the FBI have in store for him." He helped Tom with the other pant leg, and then Tom pulled the pants up over his hips.

After Tom finished dressing, in came Dr. Stern, who said, "Tom, sign these papers, and you are a free man."

Tom took the papers, leaned on the mattress, and signed the forms. "Thanks, Doc," said Tom as he shook hands with his physician.

As Dr. Stern shook Tom's hand he said, "Go see your regular doctor in a few days and have him check those facial wounds. We do not want to see those wounds become infected. Oh, here is a prescription for some antibiotics and a prescription for a helpful painkiller, which should keep you comfortable without fogging your mind."

"Thank you, Dr. Stern."

"Tom, here is a bottle of painkillers you can use until you can fill those scripts," said the doctor.

Tom took the scripts and the small bottle of painkillers just as Thornton helped him pull on his suit jacket and said, "Thanks for everything, Doctor Stern." He motioned to his three friends, and they left the room and walked down the hall toward the waiting room, where the media was waiting to ask Tom all sorts of questions.

Tom and the others all sneaked down the back hallway. They walked passed the waiting room. Thornton grabbed Tom by his arm, and Tom was rushed out into the cold, wet afternoon where the four of them avoided the nosey media. They briskly walked through the parking lot. "I'll drive, Tom," said Thornton as they reached his car.

"Let's head straight back to the facility. I can change clothes there and clean up," said Tom as Thornton drove through the afternoon rain.

* * *

By 4:00 PM, Dr. Stern stepped through the emergency room's electronic doors to get a bit of fresh air. He stood under the huge canopy, where the ambulances pulled in and parked. The afternoon air was cool and moist because of the falling rain. After five minutes, the doctor felt rejuvenated by the cool, moist afternoon air. He did not smoke, but he saw several nurses and orderlies standing by the doors smoking near the big sand-filled ashtrays. Two ambulances pulled in while he was standing there, and he had an urge to help, but the attendants seemed to be able to handle the situation. So Dr. Stern walked back into the emergency room, and then he headed for the hospital's public relations studio, where he hoped to find Miss Bye, the hospital's public relations officer. When he reached the studio, he found Miss Bye preparing to meet the public. "Miss Bye, are you ready?" asked Dr. Stern as he approached her. When he looked at her, he saw a young lady in a woman's professional business suit with brown hair worn in a bun on top of her head. She had a pleasant face but with a bit too much makeup on it.

"I am ready," she replied confidently.

Dr. Stern stepped up next to her on the small platform in front of the podium and said, "I'm also ready."

He scanned the audience and spotted several Cleveland Police officers, several agents from the FBI, and reporters from the *Plain Dealer*, the *News Herald*, *USA Today*, along with television reporters from channels 3, 5, and 8, and some people from several area radio stations. He knew Thomas Murphy was big news, and the kidnapping of his family was even bigger news.

Dr. Stern stepped up to the podium next to Miss Bye, who started her address when she said, "Good afternoon, ladies and gentlemen. My name is Miss Bye, I am the public relations officer for the Cleveland Metro Hospital. With me today is our esteemed director of the emergency room, Dr. Stern." Then she paused to clear her throat. "Mr. Thomas Murphy, popularly called the Prince of Cleveland, came into our emergency room approximately four hours ago and has been attended to by Dr. Stern for a variety of medical needs. Dr. Stern has a statement. Please go ahead, Dr. Stern."

Dr. Stern adjusted the microphone and said, "Thank you, Miss Bye, and good afternoon, ladies and gentlemen. I have been attending to Thomas Murphy's medical needs for the last four hours. When he initially came into our ER, he was in a fairly poor condition. As you all must know by now, Thomas was the victim of a kidnapping. His captors beat him, causing extreme trauma to his face and skull. We ruled out a concussion right from the very beginning. X-rays showed there were no broken skull or facial bones, with the exception of a broken nose, which we treated. We cleaned all his facial wounds and stitched a severe cut under his left eye, which was located on his left cheekbone. He was extremely dehydrated, so we ran an IV to replenish both his fluids and his blood sugar levels. His breathing was diminished due to his being in a restrictive position for the better part of twenty-four hours. We used an IPPB machine to restore his regular breathing as well as his oxygen level.

A reporter shouted, "Doc, what does IPPB mean?"

"That stands for intermittent positive pressure breathing machine, which helped Thomas get his breathing back to where it should be."

"Will Mr. Murphy be admitted?" asked another reporter.

"No. He was discharged thirty minutes ago," said Dr. Stern as he pointed toward the next reporter.

Dr. Stern continued to take questions for about half an hour then said, "Thanks for your time." Then he stepped back away from the microphone, thanked Miss Bye and left the studio.

* * *

It was 4:00 PM at the FBI headquarters in Quantico, Virginia, and Senior Special Agent Donald Kellogg was working in his small, cluttered office in the Behavioral Science Department. Kellogg had just finished talking with Agent John Coffee, who was in Cleveland working on a kidnapping case. Once he hung up with Agent Coffee, he set his pipe on the ceramic ashtray his granddaughter had made for him in her art class. He was suddenly filled with renewed excitement. He would soon be back on the hot trail of a "supercriminal" who he had been pursuing for over ten years. Still sitting alone at his desk, he spoke, "Lukas Krueger, I'm back on your trail." He stood up, crisply clapped his hands and shouted, "Hot damn!"

Kellogg left his small office and walked down the hall to his supervisor's office. The door was shut, and so Agent Kellogg knocked gently on the door frame. "Come on in," he heard Special Agent Singer reply. He opened the door and eagerly stepped into his supervisor's office. "What's on your mind, Kellogg?"

"Agents Barlow and Coffee are working in Cleveland on a high-profile kidnapping case," explained Kellogg.

"What makes it a high-profile case?" asked Agent Singer as Kellogg watched him stand up and walk around to the front of his desk.

"Two things make this case high profile," explained Agent Kellogg with exuberance. "The kidnapper has abducted the locally famous Thomas Murphy and his wife and kids. And are you ready for this? The kidnapper is our boy, Lukas Krueger. He has again surfaced. I must go and assist them with his capture. Certainly, you understand, boss," Kellogg said as if he were a student pleading with his principal.

"Agent Kellogg, I understand your position and your eagerness," said Agent Singer. "I will make a deal with you. I understand you have pursued Lukas Krueger for the last twelve years, and your dossier on him is several inches thick. I will authorize you to leave immediately today to aid and assist Agents Barlow and Coffee, but our director has a departmental meeting tomorrow, Friday, morning, in which your presence is crucial. So, Kellogg, you can go to Cleveland today to advise, but be back by Friday for the meeting. Then you can return on Saturday to finish helping Agents Barlow and Coffee capture Krueger."

Kellogg smiled and said, "Thanks, boss. I'll be back tomorrow morning for the meeting."

Agent Singer looked confidently at Kellogg and said, "Have my secretary get you a flight to Cleveland, then have Barlow send one of his junior agents to pick you up at the airport. I don't want you getting lost in Cleveland with a rental car trying to find your way around that town on your own," said Agent Singer firmly.

"Okay. Again, thanks," said Agent Kellogg. He shook hands with Agent Singer, then headed out of the office and went straight for the secretary's desk. He knew he had to gather his dossier on Krueger and some other pertinent material, but he would coordinate flight instructions with Singer's secretary first.

He walked up to the secretary's desk and said, "Hey, Sharon, Agent Singer wants you to arrange a flight for today for me to Cleveland." He went on and told her his itinerary for the next three days. He watched her write everything down as he dictated it to her.

"What's in Cleveland?" asked Sharon.

"The infamous kidnapper Lukas Krueger," he replied.

"Haven't you been chasing him, like, forever?"

"Yes. Now, this time I'll get him, dead center."

She smiled at him, believing he would get his man.

Next, he returned to his small office. He gathered his necessary material, then he placed a direct call to the kidnap hotline, where he briefly informed Agent Coffee about his assignment and tentative arrival time.

Before long Agent Kellogg was on a direct flight to Cleveland, the home of the world champion Cleveland Browns football team.

When Kellogg arrived in Cleveland, he entered the terminal and saw a young gentleman wearing a cheap polyester suit and holding a cardboard sign with the bold letters "Kellogg" scribbled on it. Agent Kellogg approached the young agent, and he said, "Agent Johnson, I assume!"

"Special Senior Agent Donald Kellogg?" asked the young agent as he clumsily dropped his sign and shook hands.

"I'm Kellogg."

"I'm Johnson."

"Good. Where is your car, Johnson?"

"Follow me, sir."

*   *   *

By four o'clock Thursday afternoon, Tom and Thornton entered Tom's office, where Tom needed to shower, clean up, and change into a fresh set of clothes. Thornton helped Tom take a seat in a wingback chair adjacent to his desk. After Thornton eased Tom into the chair he asked, "Tom, are you sure you shouldn't rethink staying in the hospital just overnight?"

"Thor, I'll be okay after I get a shower and clean up," reassured Tom to his bodyguard, who was concerned for his boss's well-being. "The hot shower will loosen my tight muscles."

Tom was having difficulty breathing. His nostrils were still packed with bloody gauze, so he was still breathing through his mouth. The breathing machine he used at the hospital had helped regulate the pace of his breaths, but now he needed to remove the gauze and breathe through his nose again. As Tom sat, he appreciated the fact that he had a private bathroom and shower in his office. There was a knock at the office door, which Thornton answered. "It's the coffee we ordered," said Thornton as he helped Martha, the coffee lounge helper, wheel the coffee cart into the office.

"Thanks, Martha," said Tom.

"How are you, darling?" asked the matronly Martha as she helped Thornton wheel the coffee cart over to Tom's desk. "Let me prepare your coffee, Tom, darling."

He sat breathing heavily with his mouth wide open as he waited for Martha to give him his coffee. "Are you all right, Tom?" asked Thornton just as Martha handed Tom his coffee.

"Thanks, Martha," said Tom in a nasally tone as he tried to swallow his coffee while still breathing through his mouth.

"You're quite welcome, Tom, darling," said Martha as she returned to the coffee cart to fix Thornton his coffee. "How do you take your coffee?" she asked as she looked at Thornton.

"Black with one sugar, Martha."

After Martha prepared coffee for the two men, she then left quietly. Once Tom finished his coffee, he stood up, walked to the coffee cart, and put his coffee cup back onto the cart. "Help me, Thor," said Tom as he painfully tried to remove his soiled and torn suit coat. As Tom struggled with the suit coat, Thornton rushed to his aid.

"Are you sure you don't need to be in the hospital?" asked Thornton as he slipped Tom's suit coat off of him.

"Thor, I'll be okay after the warm shower loosens my cramped muscles," said Tom as he moved toward the bathroom and the inviting shower. Thornton followed Tom. Tom carefully sat on a stool in front of the full-length bathroom mirror. "Thor, get the tweezers out of my shaving kit," said Tom. "I need to have you help me pull these plugs of gauze out of my nose."

"Aren't you afraid you'll start bleeding again?" asked Thornton as he searched through the shaving kit for the tweezers. "Here they are," proclaimed Thornton.

"I'll have to take that chance," said Tom. "I sure as hell can't keep breathing through my mouth." He leaned his head back so that Thornton could get a closer look at the plugged nostrils. Thornton got closer. He used the shiny tweezers to first remove the gauze that plugged Tom's right nostril. As he pulled the first plug, Tom grimaced as it came out. Thornton dropped the bloody gauze into the bathroom sink. "What a relief, Thor," muttered Tom. "Pull the left one, Thor." Tom held his breath while Thornton took a deep breath, reached in with the tweezers, and pulled the left plug out of Tom's bloody nose.

"Are you all right?" asked Thornton as Tom pushed his bodyguard away so he could lean over the sink and drain globs of thick blood out of his nose. While still leaning over the sink, he thanked Thornton. Next, Tom rinsed out his nose with cold water. After several minutes, he was breathing quite easily through his nose.

Thornton adjusted the shower temperature while Tom continued to undress. Tom carefully removed the splint from his nose. He did not want to ruin the splint in the shower. Tom's intention was to replace the splint after his shower. After a ten-minute hot shower, Tom felt refreshed and flexible. He blow-dried his red hair, then he carefully shaved his injured face. His suit was ruined, so he dropped it in the trashcan in the bathroom. He went to the clothes he had set aside in his office, and he quickly dressed. He put on a Notre Dame sweatshirt, jeans, and a denim jacket, then he walked into his office from the bathroom. He opened his safe and took out his pistol license and his holster and weapon. He assembled everything and closed his belt after winding the holster through the belt. Next, he checked his weapon for bullets and found it was fully loaded. "Thor, I might need this if I get close to Krueger," said Tom, looking for reassurance.

"Tom, I'm carrying; you might as well be too."

"Let's go check on the feds," added Tom with a smile.

While Tom was cleaning up, Checkers went back to work and Mike Max went to the phone branch where the Cleveland Police and FBI were adjusting the hotline equipment for receiving, recording, and tracing the incoming calls from the kidnappers.

Once Tom walked into the phone branch, he first glanced at the Kidnap Command Center and its hotline, then he walked over to Wanda's phone branch control desk, where she was monitoring the incoming company calls. "Hello, Wanda," said Tom as he reached to give her a hug.

"Good to see you, Tom," said Wanda, taking off her headset and embracing him. "I'm sorry about your family."

"We'll get them back!" said Tom sharply as he hugged Wanda. "Thanks for holding down the fort. It meant a lot to me."

"I want to thank the phone branch staff," said Tom as he walked away from Wanda's desk and proceeded to mingle with the twenty phone branch members. He took time to visit and thank each and every one of them. Next, he returned to Wanda's desk and said, "I need to talk to Agent Barlow. I'll talk to you later, Wanda." He walked to the phone branch area where the FBI had set up their equipment. "Agent Barlow," said Tom getting the agent's attention.

"Yes. Tom, how are you feeling?" asked Barlow as he turned to Tom. "I thought they'd admit you."

"I'm feeling ready for bear," snapped Tom, who wanted to discuss kidnap business. "When is your expert on Lukas Krueger arriving?" asked Tom.

"Senior Special Agent Donald Kellogg will be arriving this evening and briefing us tonight, " said Barlow. "Tomorrow morning he must return to FBI headquarters to attend a departmental meeting with the director, then he'll return early Saturday to continue assisting us in the capture of Lukas Krueger."

"From what you've said, I assume Agent Kellogg is quite the expert on Lukas Krueger," said Tom as he frowned at Barlow, who was smoking a stinky cigar.

Barlow took another puff on his stubby cigar and said, "Agent Kellogg is the quintessential expert on Krueger."

"If Kellogg is so good, why hasn't he caught Lukas Krueger?" asked Tom as he waved the cigar smoke away.

"You'll find out that Krueger is a genius," said Barlow. "He's hard to find and even harder to catch."

Just then the hotline rang, and Agent Coffee shouted, "We got a hot call! It rang a second time, and Tom rushed to the phone as earlier planned. He lifted the receiver and calmly said, "Good afternoon. Just Clean It Up. How can I assist you?"

"Well, Thomas is that you speaking?"

"Yes, it's me, Lukas."

"Good!"

"Lukas, why did you let me go and not my family?"

"Isn't that obvious? So you can get me my money. Remember, I still want my thirty million American dollars. I'm now giving you time to gather up the money. I want the total amount by tomorrow."

"I'll give you the thirty million," stated Tom, "but I want assurance that you will return my family unharmed."

"Thomas, I'm not a barbarian. You give me the money, and I'll give you your lovely family," said Lukas.

"Unharmed," demanded Tom as he trembled.

"Of course, they'll be unharmed," guaranteed Lukas. "I'll call at noon tomorrow with the instructions. I'll only talk to you, Thomas, and there must not be police or FBI at the exchange. That is a definite. Do you understand, Thomas?"

"Yes, of course," uttered Tom. "I understand."

"Then we do have an agreement?" asked Lukas.

"Yes."

"I'll talk to you tomorrow, Thomas."

"Lukas! Why must we wait?" he pleaded.

There was a click, and Lukas was gone.

"Barlow, he hung up," shouted Tom as he placed the receiver back onto its cradle.

Agent Coffee shouted, "The connection was too short, we were unable to get a fix on a location."

Tom saw Barlow walking toward him with an angry look on his face as he vigorously puffed on his stubby cigar. Tom prepared himself for a long lecture from the FBI agent.

"Tom, we gotta talk," said Barlow as if he were going to talk to Tom like a Dutch uncle. "We really don't care what you promised Krueger. You must understand, here at our Kidnap Command Center, we have a certain set of FBI kidnap protocols, which we must follow. These protocols have been established through many years of actual applications in the field. Tomorrow, we won't be giving Krueger your actual thirty million. Instead, we will be giving him fake FBI currency with a hidden tracking device placed in the bundle."

"Fake FBI currency," repeated Tom for clarity.

"Yes. And when you promised that you alone would make the exchange, well, that is just not gonna happen," explained Barlow. "First, you are not going to be at the exchange. You will be miles away in a safe environment, while the FBI kidnap control teams execute the actual exchange. This is to ensure your family's safety."

"Barlow, I gave my word," shouted Tom.

"You can't bargain with a madman," insisted Barlow.

Tom thought for a moment. Should Barlow take over the exchange? he wondered. What was best for his family? Would Lukas Krueger keep his word if he paid the money as agreed? Could he trust Krueger? Could he trust Barlow? Finally, he decided the safest move would be to keep his promise to Krueger.

"Agent Barlow, my gut tells me the safest way to keep my family unharmed is for me to go alone to the exchange with the money," explained Tom, who immediately recognized that Barlow did not like his decision by the angry and anxious way he suddenly started chewing the end of his cigar.

"I can't allow you to do that," said Barlow, who put his hands on his hips and stood his ground.

"What do you mean, you can't allow me?" Tom responded angrily. "You can't stop me! It's my family!"

"Tom, kidnapping is a federal crime, and this is a federal investigation," said Barlow as he pulled the cigar out of his mouth so he could speak clearer. "Tom, I don't want to be a hard-ass, but if you interfere, I'll simply have you arrested and put on ice until we clean up this kidnapping."

"You can't have me arrested."

"I can and I will have you arrested," warned Agent Barlow as he crushed his cigar into an ashtray and smiled sinisterly. "I will have things done my way."

"Screw you, Barlow," shouted Tom as he turned and hurried out of the Kidnap Command Center. He walked directly toward Wanda's desk, where both Thornton and Mike were waiting for him. "Those guys suck," he shouted once he reached Wanda's desk.

Tom saw the sudden frightened look on Wanda's face as she asked, "What's wrong, Tom?"

"Nothing is wrong that a good old-fashioned baseball bat wouldn't cure," Tom said to Wanda as he motioned to his two best pals—Thornton and Mike. "Guys, follow me to my office. I wanna kick around some ideas." He led the way across the phone branch, past the Kidnap Command Center, and through the double doors out into the hall which lead to his private office. Once in his office, Tom looked at Thornton and said, "Close the door, Thor, I don't want anyone hearing us." Next, Tom looked at his two best friends and asked, "Who does Agent Barlow think he is?"

"What did he do, Tom?" asked Thornton.

"Yeah. What happened, Tom?" asked Mike.

"He threatened to arrest me," shouted Tom.

"What?" his friends asked in unison.

"Yeah. I made a promise to Krueger. No cops and I'd pay him the thirty million in exchange for my family's safe return. Barlow said he won't let me keep my promise," explained Tom.

"When does the part about arresting you come in?" Mike asked as he lit a cigarette and took a seat.

"Barlow claims this is a federal crime, and he doesn't want me interfering," said Tom as he stood in front of his desk and stretched back. "He claims the FBI has kidnap protocols they must follow, which excludes me and my money. They use only agents at the exchange, and they use fake currency with a tracking device hidden inside the bundle."

"Not to disagree Tom, but that sounds safe," said Mike as he puffed on his cigarette.

"Yeah. But Krueger specified no police or FBI at the exchange. Only I bring the money," said Tom.

Mike stood up, took a drag on his cigarette and said, "Tom, I understand how you feel, but the FBI has been doing these sort of things for years. They've handled thousands of these types of kidnappings." Tom watched Mike walk anxiously around the office.

"Yeah. Mike, I understand. But for some reason I don't trust Barlow. He seems too arrogant," said Tom as he stretched his arms over his head and then carefully touched his injured face. "My gut is telling me not to trust him. He seems overconfident, and maybe that causes incompetence."

Thornton rubbed his shaven bronze head and reluctantly said, "I got the same vibe from Agent Barlow. He is too confident, a know-it-all. Those kind of guys always screw up." Tom watched Thornton pace the room.

"Tom, I don't want to upset you," said Mike as he puffed on his cigarette, "but I think you should follow Barlow's procedures. At least, give him the benefit of the doubt for now."

Tom looked Mike in the eye and said, "Mike, I admire your courage to disagree, but what if Barlow doesn't catch Krueger in the exchange? What if he slips away? Then I'm screwed. What if, in Krueger's mind, he believes I've betrayed him. Then, in his mind, he won't have to keep his promise to release my family unharmed." Tom wondered if Mike understood what he meant.

Mike extinguished his cigarette in an ashtray and carefully said, "I see your point, but you should not base your decision on what-ifs. There are too many what-if scenarios, Tom. Do you understand? Too many things could still go wrong even if you handled it."

"I guess you're right, Mike," Tom agreed. "Maybe we should let Barlow go ahead with the exchange, and, in the meantime, we should prepare for a fallback plan in the event he fails."

"There you go, Tom," said Mike. "Now you're on the right track."

"Yeah. Tom, I like that," said Thornton. "It's something we can all get our fingers into."

"A fallback plan," repeated Tom as he stepped away from his desk and started pacing the office. "What can be our fallback plan?"

"If Barlow fails," started Thornton, "then we take over the next exchange."

"No. Agent Barlow isn't going to let go of the kidnapping," said Mike as he lit another cigarette.

"He's right, Thor. Barlow is never going to let go. We need a strategy." Tom paced and said, "What kind of strategy can we develop, guys?" He walked behind his desk and opened the drawer to his credenza and pulled out a big piece of bubblegum. He got a wad and put it in his mouth, chewed it until it was soft, then he tucked it in the right side of his mouth. The purpose of the bubblegum was to loosen his tight jaw.

Mike laughed at Tom's protruding jaw and said, "What are our strong points?"

Thornton said, "We've got a big workforce, over two thousand bodies. How could we use them?"

Tom pointed his finger into the air and stated, "If we had a tip where they're holding them, we could put together a search party." Tom did not know just how prophetic his statement was.

"A search party sounds good," said Mike, "but where do we search?" Mike slowly inhaled his cigarette.

"Like Tom said, 'we'd need a tip,'" said Thornton as he paced enthusiastically. "What kind of tip could we get? We need some way to narrow the search area."

"Yeah. We need a tip," said Tom as he smiled and chewed his bubblegum on the right side of his mouth. The left side of his face was too sore to move the gum there. As he chewed his bubblegum he continued to think of ways to rescue his family. "Maybe Krueger has my family near where I was held. Or, maybe Krueger will leave a clue when he calls tomorrow at noon."

Mike inhaled on his cigarette and said, "Just like there were too many what-ifs, now there are too many maybes." He flicked his cigarette ash into the nearest ashtray and kept pacing and brainstorming for good ideas.

"You're right, Mike," uttered Tom. "We're not getting anywhere. We need to just outright help Agent Barlow. After all, the main goal is to rescue Beth and the kids."

"Okay. How can we help Agent Barlow?" asked Thornton.

"I can start by being at the hotline at noon tomorrow," said Tom as he attempted to blow a bubblegum bubble, but the left side of his face was too sore and his pain medication was wearing off. His pain level was rising, but he would not mention it to his friends.

"And be alert, rested, refreshed, and ready to go," shouted Thornton as he clinched his fist and waved it vigorously in the air, showing enthusiasm.

"Let me suggest a good night's sleep tonight so you can be your best tomorrow. You should take an afternoon nap so you can be ready for the special FBI agent who will be lecturing this evening," said Mike, who always seemed to have the right thing to say.

Thornton agreed. "Why don't you take a nap. You've been on overdrive for almost thirty-six hours, my friend."

"Yes. Tom, lie down on your couch," said Mike, "and, Thornton, help me draw those blinds." He crushed his cigarette in the ashtray and rushed to help Thornton, who was already pulling the blinds. While they closed the office blinds, Tom walked over to the couch and comfortably stretched out, putting a decorative pillow under his head. "You can get a couple good hours of sleep before that briefing," said Mike as he turned out the lamps in the office.

As Tom reclined onto his long white couch, he took the bubblegum out of his mouth and placed the gum into the ashtray that set on the coffee table in front of the couch. Tom closed his eyes, and he said, "Thanks guys. I'm pretty tired and sore. Thor, when I wake up, remind me to take my medications."

"Tom, why don't you take one of your pain pills before you fall asleep?" asked Thornton, who waited for an answer.

"Thornton, he's already asleep," whispered Mike.

In Tom's sleep, he almost heard his two friends as they quietly left the office, shutting the door as they exited. Within the next few minutes, he fell into a deep sleep, which took him to a faraway place. He could see his family drifting on an iceberg. They were floating away from him as he called to them. He could only whisper. As he quietly whispered, they floated farther and farther away.

*　　　　*　　　　*

By three o'clock Thursday afternoon, the weather was still wet. As Lukas drove, he noticed it was still darkly overcast, and there was a slow but constant drizzling of rain. Lukas drove Team One through Slavic Village toward the foreclosure where they were to relieve Team Two, who were holding Beth and the three kids. He pulled Team One's van in front of the abandoned house and parked. Within minutes, Lukas, Dagmar and the rest of Team One were out of the van and stepping into the first hideaway for Tom Murphy's family. As Lukas stepped through the doorway, he said, "Otto, we've come to take over. Has Mrs. Murphy decided to give us the thirty million?"

"She remains fixed on the belief that only her husband has access to the money," whispered Otto, just as Lukas saw Beth Murphy sleeping on the couch in the living room, where she had been drugged to sleep.

"Are the three kids also asleep in the bedroom?"

"Yes. Lukas, we've drugged the entire family in order to control them," explained Otto, the leader of Team Two, as he slipped on his jacket. "Lukas, is it still raining?"

"Yes. Otto, before you leave, have your men wake the misses and the kids," requested Lukas, who approached the kitchen along with Dagmar. "Is there hot coffee?" While Team Two woke the Murphy family, Lukas, Dagmar, and the rest of Team One put their belongings on the kitchen table. Lukas scanned the contents and said, "Dagmar, you left their breakfast in the van. Stephan, go fetch the breakfast in a bag." Lukas heard Team Two waking Beth and the three kids. He wondered if they would be groggy from the sedatives they were given. The sedatives were Otto's idea. They were meant to control the mother and her kids between the time they were abducted through most of the second day, Thursday. Now, Lukas and Team One were ready to move the family to the second hideaway, which was Lukas's abandoned farmhouse eight miles east of the Willoughby Travelodge. Team One took over guarding Beth on the couch while the rest guarded the three children in the bedroom. Team Two prepared to leave when Lukas said, "Otto, you and your men go get some much-needed sleep." After Team Two left, Lukas looked at his team members and said, "I want to move them right away." After he made that statement, Boris and the other members of Team One went into the bedroom to hurry along the children, while Lukas had a conversation with Beth in the living room. "Mrs. Murphy, or should I call you Beth?"

"Either one. It doesn't matter to me."

"Okay then I'll call you Beth. My name is Lukas Krueger, and I'm the leader of the group who have captured your husband and your family." He untied her hands, which had been bound since the night before.

"Thank you for untying my hands," said Beth. "They were awfully tight."

"I'm sorry, Beth. Any other concerns?"

"Yes. My children and I are cold."

"I'm sorry. This old abandoned house has no utilities, and so it is chilly. We did buy your family breakfast. That should warm your bellies," said Lukas as he rubbed her sore wrists. "This morning I freed your husband and now he is back at the Just Clean It Up headquarters."

"How is Tom?" she pleaded.

"Tom is just fine," lied Lukas, "and he is looking forward to seeing you and the kids soon. First, he must get the thirty million American dollars."

"He'll never do that," she snapped.

"He has already agreed to give me the money," Lukas said confidently, then he stopped rubbing her wrists. He stood up and said, "Would you like to see your children?"

"Yes. Please let me see them," she said, as she jumped up off the couch.

"All right. Sit back down on the couch, and I will go get them and bring them to you," explained Lukas as he walked out of the living room and down the short dark hallway that led to the bedroom where Tommy, Jenny, and Danny had been kept. Once in the bedroom, Lukas looked at Boris and said, "Bring the three of them into the living room, where their mother is waiting." He watched while Boris and the others herded the children out of the bedroom, down the dark hallway, and finally into the living room. Lukas was amused as he watched Beth embrace her three children.

Minutes after the reunion, Lukas walked over to Beth and put his arm on her shoulder, preparing to speak, but Tommy, her fourteen-year-old son, jumped up and shouted, "Let go of her, you jerk!"

"You must be Tommy," said Lukas. "I've heard so much about you, son." He let go of Beth, stepped toward Tommy, and raised his hand as if he intended to hit the boy.

"Don't you touch him!" cried Beth as she put herself between Tommy and Lukas. "Don't hit him!"

"Beth, I wouldn't hurt any of your children," he said as he lowered his striking hand and laughed. Next, he turned and pointed at Dagmar. "This lady is my Dagmar, and she has brought you and your children breakfast from our local McDonald's restaurant. Please bring your family to the kitchen." He watched as Beth gathered her children and walked from the dark, cold living room to the small utility kitchen at the rear of the house.

* * *

Dagmar walked into the kitchen as Beth and the three children followed. "Sit down. Please sit down," Dagmar requested. "The bag on the table has your breakfast in it. Please enjoy." She pulled up a seat and sat down with them. Dagmar tried to be friendly with Beth and the children, which is exactly as Lukas had instructed her to do. She helped them unpack the two big bags of breakfast food and the hot coffee. As they started eating, Dagmar asked, "Did you all sleep well?"

Beth swallowed and said, "It was cold!"

"I am sorry for that," she replied, trying to appear sincere. "Don't be scared. Lukas won't let any harm come to you or your youngsters."

"I'd like to believe that," said Beth as she anxiously sipped her hot coffee.

"Trust me," again replied Dagmar as she reached over and helped Danny with the wrapper around his morning croissant. "He won't hurt a fly."

"He almost struck my boy," said Beth defensively.

"He didn't mean anything by that," said Dagmar. "You must be worried about your husband. No?"

"Yes! How is Tom? Is he hurt?"

"No harm has come to Mr. Murphy. He is fine. Lukas had him captured, but now he has been set free. No harm came to him," lied Dagmar as she sipped coffee along with Beth and the three children, trying to be friendly.

"Tom has been set free?" asked Beth, "where is he?"

"Where is he?" she repeated. "Hopefully, at his bank getting the money so that you all can go free."

"To the bank," stammered Beth.

"I also want your children to go free. You have such pretty children, Beth." Dagmar reached out and held Beth's trembling hands. "Don't be scared. You will go free soon."

"Thank you, Dagmar," said Beth. "You seem to care."

"I do care, Beth," said Dagmar. "Will he get the money so you and the children can go free?"

"I don't know what he'll do," cried Beth.

"Mom, stay strong," urged Tommy.

"Yeah, Mom," said Jenny. "Dad will come get us."

"You should urge Tom to pay Lukas so everyone can go home," said Dagmar as she casually sipped her coffee.

"I can't even talk to Tom."

"Lukas will let you talk with your husband."

"When?" asked Beth anxiously.

"Soon," encouraged Dagmar. "Will he pay?"

"I think he will."

"Then you must tell him so," urged Dagmar like an anxious bill or tax collector. "You must, for your beautiful children." She tried to sound sincere and passionate then there was quiet while the family ate their breakfast and drank the warm coffee. While time passed, Dagmar remained smiling at the family.

* * *

While they ate their breakfast, Lukas stood outside the kitchen door, and he listened as Dagmar's voice cooed reassurance. Then Lukas walked into the kitchen and said, "Beth, has my girl, Dagmar, been visiting with you?"

"Yes. We've become good friends."

"I'm so glad to hear that," said Lukas as he smiled. "If you are done, Beth, then come with me. Oh, and bring your purse to the living room." He helped her out of her chair, guided her out of the kitchen and into the living room, where he asked to see her purse. Once she gave him her purse, he then produced a large plastic garbage bag from his pants pocket. After pulling Beth's cell phone from the purse, he emptied everything else into the garbage bag. After the purse was emptied, he pulled a matchbook from his shirt pocket and laid the matchbook in the purse, followed by Beth's cell phone. After arranging the two items in the purse, Lukas set the purse on top of the fireplace mantel.

Lukas turned from the mantel, looked at Beth, and said, "Your husband can follow you here by using the GPS tracking system in your cell phone, but you and your wonderful children are being moved to a more comfortable location."

"Then how can Tom find us if we move to another location?" asked Beth incredulously.

"I've planted an intriguing clue for him to follow," said Lukas as he gently patted Beth on her shoulder. "Come, let's gather up the children." He took her back to the kitchen and gave her the garbage bag filled with the items removed from her purse. "Boris, help the Murphys to the van. Careful, it is raining and slippery."

He escorted everyone into the black, windowless van parked in front of the house. Lukas sat up front and Stephan drove. Dagmar and the rest of Team One sat in the back of the van along with the Murphy family. As it drizzled, Stephan pulled away and started to drive to Lake County.

Stephan, who was trying to regain Lukas's better feeling, asked, "Lukas, what was the purpose for leaving the purse?" Stephan continued to drive while he listened for Lukas's reply.

"Beth's purse contains her GPS-equipped cell phone. Thomas can track the phone, then he'll find the abandoned foreclosure and the purse. Stephan, I'm playing a cat-and-mouse game with my prey. Once he finds the purse, he'll find a matchbook advertising the Willoughby Travelodge. We'll see how smart my adversary actually is."

"What if he spots us?" Stephan asked incredulously.

"Thomas has never seen any of our faces," Lukas pointed out. "So, even if he sees our faces, he won't know who we are. I enjoy teasing my victims. It's great sport." Lukas gave Stephan a sinister smile.

*   *   *

After the long drive out of Slavic Village and into Lake County, Tommy had positioned himself so that he could see out of the front windshield. He carefully watched where they were going; once into Willoughby he knew where they were. Tommy's Boy Scout training was very valuable.

Tommy watched as Stephan pulled off the freeway and exited into Willoughby. He watched as Stephan pulled into the Willoughby Travelodge, turned off the engine, and Lukas got out. He watched as Lukas ran passed the front office and continued toward the rooms. He lost sight of Lukas as he watched him go into a particular set of units. Approximately fifteen minutes later, Tommy spotted Lukas come out of a room and run back to the van.

Tommy anticipated that from the Travelodge Stephan would then drive to their new and final location. His Boy Scout training helped him count the minutes traveled in each direction; east, west, south or north.

He tracked the left and right turns, the distance in minutes between turns, and all the directions to and fro. Finally, he saw that the van had entered an area that looked like farmland, and then Stephan turned into a long driveway. They approached an old, worn-down, clapboard farmhouse. Stephan circled in front of the building and turned off the engine. Tommy determined this was their final destination when Lukas shouted, "Everyone out!"

*   *   *

At four thirty Thursday afternoon, Tom woke refreshed from his quick, short, afternoon nap. He jumped up off the couch, hurried to his desk, and dialed Leroy in the communication center. He had Leroy page Thornton and Mike, who were somewhere in the building. Five minutes later, both men returned to Tom's office.

"How was your nap?" they both asked in unison.

"Guys, I've got an idea," said Tom as he rubbed the sleep from his eyes. "It came to me while I was sleeping. It's kind of a long shot." Tom ran his fingers through his wavy, coppery-red hair then shook his head, hoping the nap had not given him a bed-head.

"What's the long shot?" asked Thornton curiously.

"I can't believe I didn't think of it sooner," said Tom as he stretched his arms over his head, trying to shake the sleep from his muscles.

"What is it, Tom?" shouted Mike anxiously.

"Okay. If Beth has her purse, which she usually does, then her cell phone is in it. Her cell phone, like all our company phones, has the GPS technology. Leroy should be able to triangulate the location of the phone, and, hopefully, her location and the kids," Tom explained to his two friends.

"Tom, that's so obvious," said Thornton. "I can't believe we didn't think of that sooner."

"Yeah. It's been right under our noses all the time," said Mike as he lit a cigarette.

Tom was giddy with excitement as he dialed his dispatcher, Leroy, in the company's communications center. "Leroy? It's me again. Listen, I want you to use my wife's GPS feature of her cell phone to locate her, or, at best, her cell phone. Come to my office as soon as you have that location. Thanks, Leroy." Tom hung up the phone on his desk, then he smiled at Thornton and Mike. "Guys, when Leroy brings us the location we're not going to tell Agent Barlow. Instead, we'll all go investigate on our own. Are you both with me?" Both Thornton and Mike nodded affirmatively. Tom sat at his desk waiting for his dispatcher, while Thornton paced and Mike sat smoking his cigarette.

Within ten minutes, Leroy came rushing into the office shouting, "I've triangulated the GPS signal and found the location. It's in Slavic Village. I can take you there." He waved a sheet of paper with the location scribbled on it. "The address is on East Fifty-fifth Street in Slavic Village."

"We do that routinely to locate the field managers," said Mike as he reminded Tom of how things worked.

"Uh huh, I do that daily," said Leroy, "but I never thought about Beth's cell phone till just now."

Tom was ecstatic as he rushed his employee. "Let's all four of us head for Slavic Village," shouted Tom as he reached for his denim jacket, which was hanging on the back of his desk chair. As he slipped on the jacket, he said, "You've done great, Leroy." Tom placed his right hand on the man's left shoulder and shook him vigorously with appreciation. "Who is going to drive?"

"I'll drive," shouted Leroy, "Garry, our mechanic, has your black Lincoln Navigator ready for you, Tom."

"Great!" shouted Tom. "Then, Leroy, you drive."

Thor shouted, "Let's go."

"Are you armed, Thor?" asked Tom as a reminder as he headed for the office door.

"Yes. And I have my backup," said Thor as he tapped his shoulder holster. Thornton had qualified Tom as an excellent marksman and had him licensed to carry a gun if a situation ever arose when he had need to be armed.

"Maybe we'll need them," said Tom, who was now filled with new hope.

"We'll take my Lincoln," said Tom. "Let's check on the cops in the phone branch." Tom led the way to the phone branch, where the police and FBI were waiting just in case an earlier ransom call would come in with their demands and instructions. "How are you guys doing?" asked Tom to the handful of coffee-drinking and donut-eating law enforcers.

"The phones are quiet," said Agent Coffee. "Tom, we need to talk about a plan to drop the money and trap these bad guys."

Barlow puffed on his stubby cigar and said, "Tom, I know you promised Lukas the money, but we can't let that happen. Our FBI guidelines provide our own fake money, which we'll use tomorrow." Barlow took another long pull on his cigar and then added, "We can't let you be there. It is too dangerous. We'll have our standard team in place. Krueger is a blatant killer, and we plan to catch him and ultimately save your family."

"Work something up and get it to me," said Tom, "but remember they have my family." Tom stomped out of the room followed by Thornton, Mike, and Leroy.

* * *

By 5:00 PM Tom's black Lincoln Navigator was parked quietly in a street near the house where the GPS signal was coming from, and so Tom and the three men carefully approached the house. Thornton walked up to the house first and looked around, then he returned to where Tom, Mike, and Leroy were waiting. "Tom, there are no cars and the house looks empty," said Thornton just as he returned from surveying the abandoned, foreclosed, empty house.

"Let's just bust in and check it out," said Tom. As they walked up the driveway, everything looked abandoned. "Looks like a foreclosure," speculated Tom as he watched as Thornton jimmied the side door lock. "Are we in?"

"Yep!" whispered Thornton as the door popped open. Thornton drew his gun and led the men into the house, which was a true run-down fixer-upper. After a quick check of the interior rooms, Thornton declared it empty. "There is fast food in the kitchen. Looks like whoever was here is now gone," said Thornton as Tom watched him move. "I found Beth's purse," called Thornton from the empty living room.

Tom ran from the kitchen and shouted, "Where's the damn purse?"

"Tom, wait! It might be booby-trapped." Tom watched as Thornton pointed at the purse lying on the floor in front of a closed-off fireplace. "Wait! Careful," whispered Thornton as he gently examined the outside of the purse. Tom watched Thornton pull a small pocketknife from his pant's pocket and use it to carefully pry open the latch on the purse. "Good! No wires," whispered Thornton.

Tom watched as Thornton slowly opened the purse and then announced, "There is her cell phone." He watched as Thornton gently picked up the purse; then he removed the cell phone, and he handed it to Tom, who examined it and verified it was his wife's phone. Next, Thornton reached into the purse and removed a matchbook. "The purse has been emptied except for the cell phone and this matchbook, which advertises the Willoughby Travelodge. Why the matchbook?" asked Thornton. "Why?"

"Is the matchbook a clue?" asked Tom as he examined the matchbook.

"Tom, I have a hunch this Austrian fellow is teasing us. It's probably a false lead. A dead end," said Thornton as he held the empty purse.

"I know where the Willoughby Travelodge is," said Leroy as he stood with his nervous hands in his pants pockets. "I can drive us there in ten minutes if ya'll want to check it out. What do you want to do, boss?"

"Let's give it a shot," said Tom. "What do you say?"

"We gotta check it out!" said Thornton as he handed Beth's purse to Tom.

"Yeah," agreed Mike as he stood in the center of the empty living room. All four men left the empty house by way of the side door. Tom had put the contents of the purse back in it and headed for the Lincoln.

Leroy started the Navigator, drove away from the empty house, and headed for the Willoughby Travelodge. Tom hoped the matchbook would lead to either Lukas Krueger or to his family.

*   *   *

By 5:30 PM, the Navigator exited the freeway and drove into the parking lot of the Willoughby Travelodge. It was drizzling when Leroy parked the Navigator. From the backseat, Tom waited for Leroy to turn off the engine, then he said, "Let me and Thor go in first and ask a few questions. Leroy, you and Mike wait here in the Lincoln, but keep an eye open." Tom anxiously opened the car door.

"I sure better go with you," shouted Thornton as he followed Tom out of the SUV and into the parking lot. They walked through the light rain, hoping they were not wasting their time on a wild goose chase.

"I don't know what we're looking for," said Tom.

"Just keep your eyes and ears open," replied Thornton as they reached the front door of the lobby. Tom opened the door and held it while Thornton thanked him as they both shook off the rain. Tom stood inside the door and scanned the lobby. He heard soft overhead music playing, and he commented to Thornton on how nice everything looked as they casually walked across the small lobby toward the front desk. He noticed the lobby was empty with the exception of one customer standing at the front desk talking to the clerk behind the front desk.

"Let's question the clerk," said Tom as he and Thornton walked in that direction. Once they reached the front desk, they waited for the clerk to finish with his present customer.

The clerk said, "Sorry sir, but we just don't have any more rooms available."

"This is strictly business, my good man," said the thick-Austrian-accented man, who was trying to bully his way with the passive clerk.

Tom instantly recognized that phrase, the Austrian accent, and the voice. He had heard those same words when he had been hooded in the abandoned house. Once he heard those familiar words, he looked over at the man standing next to him, and a surge of adrenaline rushed through him. He instantly knew the man was the kidnapper. He screamed for Thor and lunged onto the man's back, wrapping his arms around him in a bear hug.

The accented man instantly raised his foot and stomped down hard onto Tom's toes, which buckled him in pain. As Tom stumbled backwards, the man hit him in the throat, causing him to fall backwards onto the floor. Lukas instantly recognized Tom, pulled his revolver and aimed at Tom's bodyguard, sensing he would be armed.

Thornton had already drawn his gun, and he was half a second faster as he uninhibitedly shot the Austrian in his upper right shoulder, causing him to drop his weapon, fall backwards against the front desk, and then slide down onto the floor.

Within seconds, while Tom was choking, he scrambled to his feet and grabbed Lukas's gun, which lay on the floor. "Thor, that's Lukas Krueger." He pointed the gun at Lukas and screamed, "Where are you keeping my family?"

"You're crazy," shouted Lukas as he winced with pain.

Thornton pushed himself between Tom and the Austrian then shouted, "You, behind the desk, call 911. We need an ambulance right away and the police."

"He's the man, Thor," shouted Tom just as Thornton gently took the revolver from him. "He's the kidnapper. I recognize his accent. He knows where they're keeping my family." Tom rubbed his sore Adam's apple as he stumbled backwards, slightly disoriented from the assault to his throat.

Thornton leaned down, checking the wound and verifying whether the Austrian was conscious. The man grunted when Thornton asked, "What's your name? Where are you keeping the Murphy family?" Still, the man did not answer; so Thornton pushed his fist into the wound, and the man screamed in pain. "He's conscious!" replied Thornton.

"Make him tell you where my family is," ordered Tom as he pressed to get closer to the wounded man.

* * *

By 5:45 PM, Leroy and Mike had heard the gunshot and had raced into the lobby to see what was happening. As they stepped through the lobby doors, Tom looked toward them and shouted, "Mike and Leroy, get over here!" He watched as they ran to where he was standing and to where Thornton was guarding the downed kidnapper, whose gun was setting on the front desk.

"What's happening?" asked Mike as he reached Tom.

"Yeah. What's going on?" asked Leroy.

Tom hugged both men as they reached him, and he said, "We've captured Lukas Krueger, the kidnapper. He won't say a word. Thor stopped me from forcing the truth out of him." Tom was overexcited, almost irrational with emotions.

Thornton looked at the three men and said, "The police will be here any moment, and I'd prefer they not see us torturing the man. We'll get to the bottom of things. Tom, he'll tell us where he's keeping your family."

Just then, in rushed the local sheriffs as Tom shouted, "Over here! Over here!"

"What is going on here?" asked the older sheriff.

"This man has kidnapped my family," said Tom. "His name is Lukas Krueger. He's an international criminal."

"Slow down, sir," said the older sheriff. "What is your name, and did you shoot the man on the floor?"

"My name is Thomas Murphy, the owner of Just Clean It Up, and here is my bodyguard, Thornton Williams, who shot Krueger while defending me from Krueger's attempt to shoot me," Tom explained.

"Mr. Murphy, I am very familiar with the kidnapping case," said the older sheriff. "Our department has been alerted to the particulars of the case." The sheriff waved the EMS into the lobby to attend to Krueger's injury. He asked for Thornton's license, and, after verifying it, he returned it to the bodyguard. While the EMS attended to Krueger, the sheriff asked to see Tom's license for his sidearm. Everything checked out, and Tom's license was returned to him. The EMS attendants determined that the bullet had only grazed and not entered Krueger's shoulder, and so after they attended to Krueger, they put him on a gurney, strapped him down, and moved him to their ambulance. The older sheriff told Tom and his three friends to follow the ambulance and his squad car to the local hospital.

Once at the hospital, while Krueger was being examined, Tom told the two local sheriffs about the Kidnap Command Center set up at Tom's company. "Sheriff, please contact FBI Agent John Barlow at the kidnap hotline so that he can immediately come and handle the capture of Lukas Krueger," Tom explained as he stood with his three friends in the emergency room lobby.

"Mr. Murphy, I'll call your FBI agent as soon as I check on Krueger and establish adequate security for him," said the older sheriff as he walked away from Tom and up the hallway toward the room where Krueger was being held.

Tom and his friends watched the sheriff walk away. Tom looked around the lobby until he spotted a pay phone. He immediately placed a call to the kidnap hotline. He waited as it rang twice, then he heard Wanda answer. "Wanda, it's me, Tom. Let me talk directly with Agent Barlow," said Tom, almost out of breath from anticipation.

"Thomas?" shouted Agent Barlow.

"Yeah. Listen. We're at the Willoughby Travelodge."

"Stop. Who all are we talking about?" interrupted Agent Barlow stubbornly.

"Me and Thor, my bodyguard, and two employees, but that isn't the point," stressed Tom anxiously.

"I just like to keep the facts straight. Now, who were the other two employees?"

"That doesn't matter," screamed Tom.

"I need the facts."

"Listen to me," shouted Tom. "We've captured Lukas Krueger at the

Willoughby Travelodge. Lukas tried to shoot me, but my bodyguard shot him first. The sheriffs brought him to Lake Hospital System in Willoughby." Tom shuffled his feet.

"Why didn't you just tell me that in the first place?" argued Agent Barlow as he chewed on his cigar and flicked the ash obstinately.

"Barlow, I don't have much confidence in the local sheriffs, so get yourself out here, pronto," urged Tom as he hung up the phone, not allowing the FBI agent to have the last word. He looked at Thornton and said, "Agent Barlow is a putz, who can't stay on point." He and the others walked into the waiting room, sat down, and waited.

From inside the waiting room, Tom saw the sheriffs talking to the administrators. He jumped up and ran out of the waiting room and walked up to the senior sheriff and asked, "Who is guarding Krueger?"

"One of our sheriffs is standing guard outside Krueger's hospital room," said the senior sheriff.

"Have you questioned him?" asked Tom anxiously.

"Not yet."

"Can you get him to tell you where he is keeping my family?" He looked at the sheriff sternly.

The sheriff replied, "We're waiting for the FBI to arrive, and then they'll question Krueger. In the meantime, you and your three pals go to the hospital cafeteria. We have a lot to do."

Tom looked sternly at the sheriff and said, "I want to be here when Agent Barlow arrives."

"Go get some coffee, and when the FBI arrives I'll send someone for you," replied the senior sheriff gruffly.

Tom's friends had followed him from the waiting room, out into the hallway, and down the hallway where Tom and the senior sheriff were talking. "Come on, guys," said Tom flatly, "let's get some coffee." They walked through the ER to the elevator, then headed for the hospital's cafeteria.

*   *   *

By 6:00 PM, Tom, Thornton, Mike, and Leroy were waiting in the hospital cafeteria for Barlow to arrive. "I hope these local sheriffs keep a good guard on Krueger," said Tom. "Even after they spoke with agent Barlow, they still didn't appear to see the seriousness of the situation."

Thornton said, "Let's get some coffee and sit down."

Tom walked with Thornton, Mike, and Leroy up to the coffee pots, poured themselves some hot coffee, and, after paying, they headed for an empty table. After they sat down Tom said, "I got a shaky feeling about those sheriffs. They seemed not to take my family's kidnapping seriously." He sipped his hot coffee and looked around the cafeteria for a clock.

Thornton replied, "Tom, I've got the same feeling, but Barlow and his men will be here real soon. So try to relax and enjoy your coffee." Tom watched Thornton smile reassuringly.

"The cavalry, meaning the FBI, can't get here fast enough to suit me," said Tom. "Maybe we should go back to the ER and help them guard Krueger. But from a distance."

Thornton took again sip of his coffee and said, "Let's first finish our coffee, Tom."

Tom sat quietly. He stared at Thornton, Mike, and Leroy as they enjoyed the hot coffee, and he hoped Krueger would soon reveal where he was keeping Beth and the kids.

* * *

By 6:30 PM, Team One pulled into the emergency room parking lot. Stephan drove a black Hummer, which he and Hooter had stolen moments earlier. Dagmar and Boris sat in the backseats while Hooter sat shotgun up front. Stephan parked the Hummer, and Dagmar whispered, "Hooter, listen! Don't speak to anyone. Don't make eye contact with anyone. Just walk casually a few paces behind me. Once I spot the guard standing outside Lukas's examining room, you know what we rehearsed!"

Hooter grunted affirmatively.

Dagmar and Hooter walked through the emergency room doors. She saw that this emergency room was like most emergency rooms, typically hectic and overcrowded, which she knew would work to their and Lukas's advantage. As she approached the nurse at the front desk, she looked down toward the floor and walked on like an invisible ghost.

After passing the front desk, Dagmar continued walking. As she glanced down the hall, she saw that the third examining room was being guarded by a police officer.

They walked nonchalantly toward the examining room. Dagmar and Hooter had rehearsed what they would do to disarm the officer, and so they proceeded casually. He followed behind her, as planned, and as she reached the guard she smiled at him seductively. When she stepped a few feet beyond the guard, she intentionally tripped and fell flat on the floor. Immediately, the guard rushed to her aid, and as he tried to help her, from behind Hooter fatally stuck a dagger into the guard's back. Hooter grabbed the officer as he collapsed. Dagmar helped him drag the body into Lukas's cubicle, behind the privacy curtain. When she saw Lukas sitting with a large bandage on his right shoulder, she rushed to him, threw her arms around him, and kissed him passionately. "Does it hurt, love?" she asked as she watched Hooter lay the dead officer onto the floor.

"It's only a scratch, Dagmar. I'll be fine," reassured Lukas. "Let's get out of here." He jumped off the gurney. "Do we have wheels?"

"We snatched a black Hummer," said Dagmar, "and the rest of Team One is waiting for us just outside the front doors." She helped him finish putting on his shirt, then the three of them casually walked out of his examining room. She saw that the hallway from the examining room to the front doors was free of police, and so they proceeded to walk confidently to the exit. She knew not to make eye contact with anyone, but to keep walking briskly, even if anyone spoke to them.

Just as they passed the front desk, the nurse shouted, "Mr. Krueger, where are you going?"

He stopped, looked at her, and shouted, "Out!"

Dagmar grabbed Lukas by his arm, pulled, and whispered, "Come on, Lukas! We gotta go!" She started running, and both Lukas and Hooter followed. The automatic doors swung open, and just outside the doors the stolen black Hummer was waiting for them. "Come on, boys," shouted Dagmar as the three of them climbed into the Hummer. Stephan stepped on the accelerator, and the Hummer took off away from the entrance of the emergency room.

The Hummer was trying to get out of the hospital parking lot, but it stopped because there was a vehicle blocking the way. Agent Barlow was driving the cruiser, which had stopped dead in the entrance to the hospital parking lot. When the two vehicles came head to head at the entrance, Dagmar screamed, "Ram them!" Stephan obeyed by ramming the front end of Barlow's cruiser. The big front-end grill of the Hummer rolled up to the front end of the cruiser, made contact, and then proceeded to push the cruiser backwards out of the entrance. The front end of the cruiser started to smoke, and the hood started to bend in half, just as the tires were smoking. "Stephan, ram them!" screamed Dagmar. She wanted to make a statement, and she wanted to get Lukas to safety. Stephan accelerated, and the big Hummer pushed the cruiser back out into the street from where it had been. Then the Hummer sped away down the road, away from the long arm of the law. "Let's hear it for Team One," shouted Dagmar from the backseat of the Hummer. She sat in the back with Lukas and Boris, where they all three laughed vigorously while Stephan drove; next to him was Hooter running shotgun.

As they sped away, Barlow and his other agents in the cruiser were all disoriented from the head-on crash from the stolen Hummer.

As they sped away, Dagmar looked back and saw the destroyed, smoking cruiser. She watched from a distance as the FBI agents poured out of the burning vehicle. She started to laugh hysterically, then Lukas joined in.

*   *   *

It was 7:00 PM, when Barlow and his other agents climbed out of their destroyed cruiser, smoke billowing out from under the front end. The tires were ruined and smoking. Barlow forced open his side door as he attempted to exit the burning cruiser. He stumbled away from the car, coughing and gagging from the fumes and smoke. He and his two other agents crawled on their hands and knees to a safe distance from the burning car. They lay on the grass just as the local fire truck arrived to put out the fire.

"Who the hell were they?" asked Barlow just as three sheriffs came running up to the three agents.

"That was Krueger and his gang," shouted a sheriff as he reached down and offered Barlow a hand up, which he refused indignantly.

The emergency room doctor ran up behind the sheriffs, and he shouted, "You three stay down until we've gotten a chance to check you for injuries." The next twenty minutes the doctor checked Barlow and his two other agents for burns, cuts, and smoke inhalation. After the doctor established that none of the men had any serious injuries, they were moved into the emergency room for more extensive care. While the medical team attended to the three agents, Barlow sat while a doctor sutured a nasty cut on his forehead, and he listened to the senior sheriff. "Krueger's gang sneaked in, killed our guard, and escaped in a stolen black Hummer."

"Can you be a little more specific?" asked Barlow.

"Yes. The front desk girl said a large man seemed to be following the woman. The next thing, about five minutes later, the women, the large man, and Krueger came strolling down the hall, headed to the exit. After they left, we found a dead sheriff in Krueger's room with a fatal knife wound in his back," said the senior sheriff.

Barlow was furious with the sheriff's incompetence and general stupidity. Barlow wanted to control his anger because he knew he would need the sheriff's assistance. "Sheriff, when you called and told me you had Lukas Krueger, I tried to tell you how important he was to both the FBI and to Interpol," said Barlow earnestly.

"Well, we underestimated him," said the sheriff. "We thought he was flying solo, and we didn't figure he had a gang with him," said the senior sheriff in his own defense.

"I told you he was dangerous," said Barlow, trying not to raise his voice accusatorially.

The sheriff shouted, "Now I know, and it cost me a damn good man, and I'll now have to tell his wife and kids!"

"I warned you, sheriff," shouted Barlow, returning the insensitivity. Barlow was losing patience with this man.

"A lot of good that does me now," moaned the sheriff.

Barlow planned on arresting whoever remained of Krueger's gang at the Willoughby Travelodge, and he knew he would need the local sheriffs to aid and assist him. So he needed to mend fences with this county sheriff.

"Sheriff, I am sorry you lost a good man, but we still need to apprehend Krueger and as much of his gang as possible," pleaded Barlow sincerely. "Can I count on you and your men?" He hoped he had not offended the man and lost his support.

"Agent Barlow, you can count on me and my men," replied the senior sheriff as he shook hands with Barlow.

Barlow made two calls. One call was to the command center at Just Clean It Up, and the second call was to FBI headquarters in the federal building in downtown Cleveland. He told Agent Coffee what had happened, and he requested that Coffee join him in Lake County with a cruiser and more men. Then Barlow called downtown, requesting more men and warrants for no-knock searches and arrest warrants.

* * *

Tom and the others were finishing their second cup of coffee when a hospital orderly hurried into the cafeteria, ran up to the cashier, and shouted, "A sheriff was just killed in the emergency room."

Tom jumped up from where he was sitting. He ran over to the orderly, grabbed him by his shirt, and shouted, "What happened?"

"Let go of me," insisted the orderly.

"What happened?" repeated Tom angrily.

"A sheriff was stabbed. Let me go."

Tom pushed the orderly back toward the cashier, then he turned to his three associates and shouted, "Krueger is loose. Let's go." Thornton, Mike, and Leroy all jumped up and run with Tom to the elevator. Once in the emergency room, Tom shouted, "Where is Agent Barlow?"

As he looked around for the agents, a nurse rushed up to him and said, "The agents are in exam rooms. There has been a terrible car accident."

"What do you mean, a car accident?" asked Tom with a sense of confusion. "What do you mean?" He suspected that Krueger had escaped but did not want to believe it.

The nurse, who was still standing in front of Tom, said, "A man and a woman helped Krueger escape after killing a sheriff. They drove out of the parking lot and crashed into the FBI's car. Our staff is in the exam rooms attending to their wounds."

"Did Krueger get away?"

"Yes, I believe so," replied the nurse as Tom ran toward the exam rooms, followed by Thornton, Mike, and Leroy. Tom burst through the electronic doors and proceeded to run toward the exam rooms. Before he could reach the medical care area, several hospital security guards stopped him and turned him back into the emergency room, where he and his three friends waited to talk to someone who knew exactly what happened.

Tom waited, sitting in the emergency room waiting room, while the hospital personnel finished the FBI agents' medical care. Tom sat with Thornton, Mike, and Leroy, patiently waiting to talk either with Agent Barlow or one of the county sheriffs. Thirty minutes went by, and no one had yet been available to talk with Tom. He went back to the front desk and looked at the intake person and said, "Please, isn't there anyone I can talk to?"

"I know you've been waiting," said the lady behind the bulletproof window. "Let me try something." Tom watched as the lady dialed her phone and talked to someone. After several minutes of conversation, the lady leaned up to the window and said, "Our chief of security is going to be right down to talk to you, Mr. Murphy."

"Thank you, ma'am," responded Tom as he walked back to his seat next to Thornton and Leroy. He looked at them and said, "Chief of security is coming." In the next couple of minutes, he saw an elderly, tall, large security guard approach the front desk and ask the lady something. Tom instantly knew the guard was the chief of security and he stood up just as the guard approached him and said, "Chief, I am Tom Murphy."

"Mr. Murphy, I'm Chief John Stone."

"Chief Stone, I'm trying to find out what happened an hour ago to Lukas Krueger. My bodyguard and I captured Krueger several hours ago, and the county sheriffs brought him here for medical care," explained Tom.

"Mr. Murphy …"

"Chief, call me Tom."

"Tom, this entire afternoon has been botched. The county sheriffs left only one guard on Krueger, who is known as an international high-profile criminal, and he should have had several armed guards," said Chief Stone as his big eyes flared and his thick grey eyebrows raised. While freeing him, his associates killed the lone guard, then they tore out of our parking lot in a stolen Hummer, which crushed the FBI's cruiser just as it entered our parking entrance. They damn near killed the agents, who were damn lucky to get out of their burning vehicle."

"Krueger has my family, and we had him," shouted Tom,

whose jaw was locked tight with anger.

"I know, Tom," said Chief Stone. "It was piss-poor police work."

"Did anyone get a license number?" asked Tom.

"The stolen Hummer was found a half hour ago, abandoned two miles up the road," explained Chief Stone.

"So we got nothin'," said Tom, with discouragement written all over his face. "We're going back to the Kidnap Command Center and start from scratch. Thank you for your help, Chief Stone, you've been of great help to me."

"Tom, good luck and God's speed getting your family back," urged Chief Stone as he shook Tom's hand.

Tom finished shaking hands, looked over at Thornton and the others and said, "Come on, guys. We got lots of work to do." Tom led them through the electronic doors and out into the parking lot. The Lincoln Navigator was waiting for them. Next, Tom and the others were headed back to Tom's headquarters. Once Tom got back to the Just Clean It Up headquarters, he immediately went to the phone branch, which was operating an overnight shift just in case a hotline call came through. Tom went straight to Wanda, the phone branch director and asked, "Are things quiet, Wanda?"

"Tom, look at the Kidnap Command Center. There are only two agents posted," explained Wanda, whose coffee-colored complexion looked worried.

"Wanda, Agents Barlow and Coffee and the others are all in Lake County issuing arrest warrants for part of Krueger's team," uttered Tom as he looked at the two sleepy FBI agents holding down the Kidnap Command Center.

Tom looked at Leroy and said, "You need not stay. Go home and get some rest, Leroy."

Tom shook his hand. "Call me if you need me. Otherwise I'll be back in the early morning," said Leroy as he walked out of the phone branch.

Tom looked at Wanda and said, "Hold down the fort while I take Thornton and Mike to my office to help me do some thinking." Tom, Thornton, and Mike left the phone branch.

* * *

By eight o'clock Thursday evening, Agent Barlow had everything he needed to apprehend whoever remained of Krueger's gang at the Willoughby Travelodge. He had talked extensively with the staff of the Travelodge, and they had informed him that Krueger appeared to have two groups of workers. One group would leave and go somewhere while the other group would eat, rest, and sleep.

Agents Barlow and Coffee had ten FBI agents set to sweep the two rooms where half of Krueger's group were sleeping. Barlow did not know he was about to arrest Team Two of Krueger's group, and he did not know he was about to arrest Otto, the leader of Team Two, and his three other members. Barlow knew these men would be extremely dangerous because Lukas Krueger hired only the best and most dangerous of people from the criminal pool in Europe.

It was planned that Barlow and five other agents would attack room 300, and Coffee and five other agents would attack room 301, where they hoped to find half of Krueger's group of kidnappers and assassins. There was no need to bust down doors because the agents had keys to each room, and so once the doors were unlocked the agents simply rushed in on the sleeping Europeans.

Agent Barlow unlocked the door to room 300, and he and five other FBI agents quickly but quietly rushed into the room. The room was dark, with the windows covered so that the men could sleep during the daytime. The agents had flashlights, which they trained on the Europeans just as the agents woke them. Barlow stood by the door, and he tripped the switch to the overhead lights. Once the overhead lights came on Barlow shouted, "Don't move or we'll shoot! Don't move!" The other five agents searched the room and the men for weapons, which they found in abundance. Once the weapons were secured, the agents stood the kidnappers up against the wall and proceeded to immediately read them their rights. Then Barlow looked at Otto and asked, "What is your name?"

"My name is Otto, and I'm the leader of Team Two."

"Where is Lukas Krueger?" asked Barlow, not expecting an answer of any value.

"My name is Otto," is all he replied.

"All right. Once we take your fingerprints, we'll run them through our data base, and then we'll know who each and every one of you are," said Barlow roughly.

The agents confiscated all the weapons, and then they let the men dress before they took them all to the FBI headquarters in the federal building in downtown Cleveland, where they would be processed, questioned, and jailed.

While they were dressing, Barlow stepped outside the rooms and spoke with Agent Coffee. "Anyone gonna confess?" asked Barlow as he lit a cigarette.

"Mine won't say a thing," replied Coffee as he looked into the night. "Once we get them downtown maybe they'll talk. What do you think, John?"

"They're seasoned pros, they won't talk," said Barlow.

"Yeah. You're right," agreed Coffee.

Barlow took a long drag on his cigarette and said, "We gotta get these guys downtown so we can get back to our Command Center to meet with Senior Special Agent Kellogg."

"Yeah, it's going on nine," said Coffee. "We better hurry." They stood in the rain smoking.

Barlow instructed his other ten agents to take Otto and the others back to FBI headquarters in Cleveland. He explained that he and Coffee had to meet Agent Kellogg for a late-night briefing. And so Agents Barlow and Coffee returned to their established Kidnap Command Center, located at Tom Murphy's business center.

* * *

As his plane landed and taxied toward the airport terminal, Senior Special Agent Donald Kellogg saw the raindrops bouncing off the tarmac like millions of Ping-Pong balls bouncing up off a tennis table. Kellogg had only been in Cleveland once before, and he remembered it had been raining then too. He had heard about the lovely autumns on the shores of Lake Erie, but he knew he was not here to enjoy the seasons. He was here to capture his longtime nemesis, Lukas Krueger, and rescue Tom Murphy's family.

As Kellogg stepped off the plane he saw a young man holding a sign, which had "Kellogg" printed on it in bold letters. The young agent was tall, lean, and wearing a cheap polyester suit. He walked up to the young agent and said, "Hello. Are you Agent Johnson?"

"Yes. Are you Senior Special Agent Donald Kellogg?"

They shook hands and Kellogg said, "Thanks for being on time, Agent Johnson."

"It's an honor to meet you, sir," said Johnson as he nervously fumbled to discard his sign into a trash receptacle. "Do you have luggage?" They walked down the terminal.

"No. Just these two carry-ons," replied Kellogg, who had a large briefcase and a fresh suit in a garment bag.

"How was your flight, Senior Special Agent Kellogg?" asked Johnson, who was nervously looking for something to say to this phenomenal FBI agent.

"Johnson, it was a good flight," said Kellogg. "It was a direct flight. You'd be surprised how fast a flight from Virginia to Ohio actually is. Oh, and by the way, stow all that Senior Special Agent stuff and just call me Kellogg." He smiled at the young agent as they continued down the walkway. "Where did you park?"

"Not far. I just parked in a garage near the airport terminal's front doors," explained Johnson. "Can I help carry your garment bag?"

"No, Johnson, I'm fine. Thanks. How is the kidnap investigation going," asked Kellogg as the two of them reached the front doors, which slid open automatically as they walked through them.

"There are big developments. Tom Murphy and his bodyguard, while in Lake County, temporarily captured Lukas Krueger."

"Krueger has been captured?" shouted Kellogg as he came to a standstill in the middle of the street. Johnson grabbed him by his arm and hurried him across the street.

"No. Let me explain," said Johnson once they were safely across the street. "Krueger had been injured and was taken to the local hospital for medical care. Meanwhile, Agent Barlow and other agents were on their way from the Kidnap Command Center to the hospital. Krueger's gang walked into the hospital, killed the sheriff guarding him, and escaped."

"Damn! Krueger was apprehended and was allowed to escape?" yelled Kellogg just outside the door to the parking garage.

"Senior Agent Kellogg, it gets worse."

"How could it get worse?"

"When Krueger and his associates escaped in a stolen Hummer, they exited out of the hospital parking lot through the entrance and crashed into Agent Barlow and other agents," said Johnson. Kellogg could see the young agent was scared.

"Settle down, Johnson," urged Kellogg. "Was Barlow or any other agent injured?"

"Yes. The Hummer rammed the FBI cruiser and pushed it back out of the entrance and into the street. Barlow's cruiser exploded and caught on fire," explained Johnson. "Agent Barlow and the others suffered from cuts, burns, and smoke inhalation."

"How bad are they?"

"Not as bad as it sounds, sir," replied Johnson. "The Hummer was found abandoned a couple of miles from the hospital." Johnson opened the door to the parking garage for Kellogg. They entered and started walking toward

Johnson's car. As Kellogg followed Johnson to the car, he could not believe that Krueger had been under police guard and had escaped.

"Were the agents admitted to the hospital?"

"No. In fact, Agent Coffee met up with Agent Barlow, and, together with other agents, they went back to the Willoughby Travelodge and captured Team Two of Krueger's group," said Johnson reaching his car.

"Krueger usually works with two teams," said Kellogg. "Where did Barlow take Team Two?"

"Team Two has been taken to our local FBI headquarters in the federal building in downtown Cleveland," explained Johnson as he unlocked his car and helped Kellogg put his luggage in the backseat. They entered the car, and Johnson proceeded to drive out of the parking garage. "We hope to get quite a bit of information from these men."

"Don't be disappointed, but Krueger only gives enough information to each man to carry out his own function," said Kellogg, "and he, himself, is always in Team One. So the men of Team Two actually know even less than the men of Team One. That is how he controls his men. None of them know enough to betray him. Krueger is compulsive when it comes to having control over his men as well as the kidnap scenario. He craves control, and if someone in his group threatens his control, he will simple kill them or have them killed, which also tests the man he has assigned to do the killing."

"Krueger sounds ruthless," stated Johnson.

"Krueger is ruthless," replied Kellogg. "He'll kill without conscience or concern for his victim." They pulled up to the parking lot booth, paid the parking fee, and drove off the airport property.

Once on the highway, Agent Johnson said, "Sir, we'll be at the Kidnap Command Center in less than thirty minutes."

"When I spoke to Agent Coffee over the phone, he told me that our Kidnap Command Center is located inside Tom Murphy's company. Is that a good location?" asked Kellogg as he looked from the freeway to downtown Cleveland.

"Mr. Murphy's company is the perfect location for our Kidnap Command Center because it is in his phone branch. Since the kidnapping, he is leaving it open 24 / 7," explained Johnson as he merged into traffic.

"Murphy is an interesting individual," said Kellogg. "He has used his lottery winnings to clean up his beloved city. Not many guys would do something so altruistic."

"Barlow tells me that it was Murphy's publicity that got him on Krueger's radar screen," said Johnson as he pulled off the freeway and onto a city street, where he would drive to the Just Clean It Up facility.

"Barlow is most likely correct about that," agreed Kellogg. "High profile and the ultra rich are the requirements for Krueger. Unfortunately, the thirty-million-dollar ransom will just about wipe out Murphy's relatively small lottery fortune. The five prior Krueger ransoms were from what I truly call the ultra rich. Those millionaires had great wealth and could easily afford to pay Krueger and still maintain their wealthy lifestyle."

"I hadn't thought about it like that, sir," replied Johnson with a bit of sadness.

"Sir, why do you think Krueger has murdered his last two out of five kidnapping victims?" asked Johnson as he stopped at a stoplight.

"Well, Johnson, you'll agree it is a given that Krueger is a classic psychopath."

"Okay."

"Now in Krueger's case, he has a compulsiveness to his overall behavior. When added to his fear of losing control, this manifests itself in anger, which he translates into violence. The light's green, Johnson."

Johnson drove through the intersection and replied, "I'm not sure what that means, but I think he is an angry man."

"In the last three kidnappings, the ransom money wasn't enough. He had to have the ultimate control over the kidnap victims. He executed them ritually, which, within itself, shows another form of control. Do you understand?" asked Kellogg as they drove closer to the facility.

"Yes sir, I understand. Do you think he'll kill the Murphy family?" asked Johnson as he turned a corner.

"My guess is he'll keep on his same behavioral pattern, but we'll have to put our heads together and try somehow to stop him. We will have to use his mental illness against him. Tell me about the Murphy family, starting with Tom."

"Tom is a unique man …"

"I guess to use your lottery winnings the way he did, then he'd have to be unique," interrupted Kellogg.

"They are all Irish Catholics. All five have bright red hair."

"Tell me about the kids."

"Tommy is the oldest, at fourteen. Jenny is next, at thirteen; then there is Danny, who is ten. They are all extremely loyal to one another," explained Johnson.

"Johnson, let's change the direction of our conversation a bit. What do you say?" asked Kellogg as he smiled at Johnson.

"What is on your mind, sir?"

"How is your career track with the FBI going?"

"I was going to ask for your advice on the best way to keep moving upward, careerwise, in the bureau," said the young Johnson anxiously.

"The best way to keep on a good career track with the bureau is to look for a good man whom you admire and trust and who can advise you as you move along," said Kellogg.

"How about Agent Barlow?"

"I wouldn't suggest Barlow. He has FBI tunnel vision and an ability to only see his point of view," said Kellogg just as they pulled onto the grounds of Tom's facility.

Kellogg looked at the building and the grounds of the facility, and he was impressed. "Nice-looking building."

"It is a green building," said Johnson.

"No, it is brown," Kellogg corrected.

"No. I mean ecologically," said Johnson. "The roof is all solar paneled."

"Oh, I got you. Green, ecologically."

"Yes, sir." Johnson pulled into the parking garage, looked for a parking spot, and pulled in.

"I'm impressed. Murphy's facility is easily accessible to the airport and yet close to downtown," observed Kellogg as they got out of the car. Johnson helped Kellogg get his luggage out from the backseat. Johnson led the way out of the parking garage and into the building. They entered into the hallway that led directly to the phone branch. As they walked through the double doors of the phone branch, Kellogg said, "This is an attractive facility."

"Yes. Mr. Murphy put a lot of energy into designing a productive and enjoyable work environment. Or so I've been told," explained the junior agent. "Over here is our Kidnap Command Center." Johnson directed Kellogg over to the hotline, where no one was manning the equipment.

"Johnson, no one is manning the command center. Where are our agents?" demanded Kellogg with irritation. He looked up, and an attractive black woman walked into the command center.

"I am Wanda, the supervisor of our phone branch, and I wanted you to know that the sole agent manning the hotline presently is on a potty break," she giggled.

"Well, it is nice to meet you, Wanda. My name is Agent Kellogg," he said as he shook her hand graciously.

Wanda smiled and replied, "Senior Special Agent Donald Kellogg, we have been anxiously waiting for your arrival with great anticipation this evening."

"Why, aren't you quite the darling, Wanda," said Kellogg still holding her tiny hand in his big paw. Once he released her hand, he pushed his spectacles up his nose as he puffed on his pipe. "Johnson, go find our delinquent agent, would you please?"

"Yes, sir," obeyed Johnson as he scurried out of the command center in search of the agent who was supposed to be manning the center.

Kellogg put his luggage on an available chair and scanned the command center, which was filled with all sorts of electrical equipment used for recording, editing, and tracing incoming calls. "Wanda, where is Tom Murphy?"

"He just returned from east of here," explained Wanda, "and he is cleaning up in his office." Kellogg liked what he saw when he looked at Wanda. She was well dressed and appeared professional. Kellogg could tell a lot about a man by the class of people with whom he associates, and Wanda made Tom Murphy look classy. "Can I get you anything, Agent Kellogg?"

"No, thank you," he replied. "I'll just help myself to some of this coffee."

As he walked toward the coffee urn, she ran over to assist him and said, "Here, let me help you." She poured him a Styrofoam cup of hot coffee and asked, "How do you take your coffee, sir?"

"One sugar, black," replied Kellogg as he puffed on his pipe. "Thank you, Wanda." He was grateful for her help.

"Is there anything else I can get you, Agent Kellogg?" she asked as she handed him the coffee.

"No. I'm going to get ready for my briefing," he said as he opened his thick briefcase and proceeded to pull files out of it. "When Agent Johnson returns I'll have him go fetch Tom Murphy. If that is okay?"

"That is fine," she agreed. "If there is anything you need during you stay with us, please call on me."

"Thank you, Wanda."

* * *

By nine o'clock Thursday evening, Tom was sitting at his desk in his office talking to Thornton and Mike Max. Tom was listening to Thornton as he ranted on about the county sheriff's incompetence. "He never should have had only one guard," said Thornton as Tom frowned.

Tom looked at his two friends and said, "Guys, Krueger has already had my family for thirty-six hours. I've got to do something." He heard a knock at the door. He started to answer the door when the others rose. He motioned for them to stay seated, and he said, "I'll get it, boys." He opened the door and found Agent Johnson, a subordinate of Agent Barlow. "Agent

Johnson, what can I do for you?" asked Tom as he backed away from the door in order to allow the young agent to enter the office.

"Mr. Murphy, I just returned from the airport, where I picked up Senior Special Agent Donald Kellogg. Agents Barlow and Coffee have not yet returned from the federal building downtown, but Agent Kellogg is waiting for you in the Kidnap Command Center," explained Agent Johnson nervously.

Tom pointed at the young agent and said, "Relax Johnson, we don't bite." He walked back behind his desk, where his denim jacket was hanging on the back of his chair. He slipped on the jacket and said, "You two come with me." Tom pointed at Thornton and Mike. "I want all of us to greet and meet Agent Kellogg." Agent Johnson led the three men out of Tom's office and down the hall toward the phone branch and the Kidnap Command Center.

As they were walking down the hall, Agent Johnson said, "Kellogg is the definitive expert on Lukas Krueger."

Mike asked, "What makes him quite the expert?"

"He has been studying and chasing Lukas Krueger for the last twelve years," explained Agent Johnson as he led the way toward the phone branch. "Kellogg has a four-inch-thick dossier on Krueger." They finally reached the double doors to the phone branch and entered.

Once in the phone branch, Tom and the others went directly to the Kidnap Command Center, where Tom saw Senior Special Agent Donald Kellogg sitting puffing on his pipe. Agent Johnson walked up to Kellogg and said, "Senior Special Agent Kellogg, I'd like you to meet Mr. Tom Murphy."

Tom stepped forward and said, "Agent Kellogg." Tom shook the older man's hand.

"Mr. Murphy," said Kellogg.

"Please, just call me Tom."

"Good enough, Tom. Then drop the senior special agent stuff and just call me Kellogg," replied the agent as he continued to puff on his pipe.

"Kellogg, I'd like you to meet Thornton Williams, my bodyguard and close friend, and Mike Max, again a close friend, who manages my company," said Tom, pausing while the three men shook hands with one another. Everyone pulled up chairs and sat down. "Agents Barlow and Coffee will be back soon," said Tom.

"Yes. Agent Johnson tells me they are at the local FBI center in the federal building in downtown Cleveland, and that they have apprehended Team Two of Krueger's group," said Kellogg as he primed his pipe with his penknife. "Tom, before we get started, I'd like to say from the bureau and directly from the director, that we are all sorry you and your family had to go through this, and that the entire efforts of the FBI will be used to solve this kidnapping and to bring your dear family back to you," said Kellogg sincerely.

"Thank you, sir," replied Tom, slightly moved by the small speech. "Can we get started with your briefing?"

"I'd rather wait until Barlow and Coffee arrive before we start," said Kellogg. "In the interim, may I answer any questions you may have?"

"Yes, Agent Kellogg," started Tom. "I understand you've been pursuing Krueger for nearly twelve years."

"That is correct. Ever since his first kidnapping, twelve years ago, of the Lewis family in 1997 in New York City," said Kellogg as he rubbed his long jowls.

"My question is, sir," said Tom, "have you developed a strategy over the twelve years to capture Lukas Krueger?"

Kellogg leaned over and took a four-inch-thick folder from his brown leather briefcase. "Gentlemen, this is my own personal dossier on Lukas Krueger."

Tom smiled and said, "Johnson told us about that file."

Kellogg placed the file on the table next to him. "Tom, before we get started and before Barlow and Coffee get back, let me ask you how you happened to run into Krueger," said Agent Kellogg as he waited for Barlow and Coffee.

Tom sat for a moment thinking about what he would say, then he said, "We got this idea. My communications dispatcher checked the GPS tracking feature on my wife's cell phone, and he got a fix on her location. And so, the four of us drove to the location."

Kellogg interrupted, "Who were the four?"

Tom paused, then said, "Me, Thornton, Mike, here, and my dispatcher, Leroy, who drove my Lincoln. We followed the fixed location to an abandoned house in Slavic Village. We broke in to find an empty house with the exception of Beth's purse."

Kellogg interrupted again when he asked "Who is Beth, your wife?"

"Yes! We found her purse, and all that was in the purse was her cell phone and a matchbook advertising the Willoughby Travelodge."

Kellogg continued to interrupt when he asked, "Where is Willoughby?"

"The city of Willoughby is eighteen miles east of the city of Cleveland in Lake County," said Tom, who was excited to tell the story to the senior agent. "The four of us drove from Slavic Village to the Travelodge in Willoughby to just see if there was a connection. To just look around, to see what we could find." Tom's eyes widened with excitement.

"Krueger is known to tease his victims by placing clues, to play a game of cat and mouse," said Kellogg, who was equally as excited about the story as was Tom.

"What happened next is I believe Krueger had not actually expected us. We entered the lobby and proceeded to approach the front desk, where Krueger was trying to conduct business. When I was being held captive, Krueger gave me his name, but he never took off the hood. So, I never saw his face. When Thor and I walked up to the front desk, I instantly recognized the European accent. I looked at him, shouted Thor's name, lunged, and wrapped by arms around Krueger in a bear hug," Tom explained with a glow in his eyes.

"How did Krueger react?" asked Kellogg.

"He reacted gracefully," said Tom with a grin on his ruddy face.

"Gracefully?"

"Yeah. He gracefully lifted his foot then viciously stomped down hard onto the toes of my foot. As I stepped back he karate-chopped me in the throat. As I stumbled backwards, Krueger saw my bodyguard draw his weapon and instantly Krueger responded by drawing his weapon. Thor had a slight edge, fired first, and struck Krueger in the uppermost fleshy part of his right shoulder. Krueger fell back against the front desk and then slid down onto the carpeted floor."

"So your bodyguard shot Krueger, and he was hospitalized?" asked Kellogg, not quite comprehending the severity of the wound.

"The wound was not much more than a bad scratch, which only required a bandage. While recuperating in the emergency room and being guarded by a county sheriff, Krueger was busted out by a woman and a man, who killed the sheriff in order to escape," explained Tom.

"The woman would be Dagmar, his closest associate, and the man would probably be Otto, his second closest associate. She is his lover," said Kellogg.

"The sheriff was killed?"

"Yes. He was stabbed from behind."

"That sounds like Otto," said Kellogg. "That would be Team One." Kellogg could not believe Krueger got away.

Tom smiled and said, "Well, Team One escaped in a stolen black Hummer, which crashed into Agent Barlow's car as he was entering the hospital parking lot just as Krueger was exiting through the entrance."

"They crashed?"

"Yes. Then the Hummer pushed the car back out into the street, crushing the car and setting it on fire," said Tom. "Agent Barlow and the other agents in the car suffered minimal cuts, burns, and smoke inhalation, but Barlow was released, and he and Agent Coffee interviewed the staff at the Travelodge regarding Krueger's people. They raided two rooms and arrested Team Two," said Tom as he nervously ran his hands through his wavy coppery-red hair. "Agent Kellogg, we had a hell of an afternoon."

Thornton, who was still sore about the competence of the county sheriffs, said, "They should have guarded Krueger better. We told them he was dangerous."

Kellogg looked over at Thornton and said, "You are absolutely correct. No one has ever taken Krueger into custody, and they let him slip away." Tom could see the anger in Kellogg's eyes. "I'm outraged! These local authorities don't even seem to understand what they have allowed to happen. I'm outraged! I've spent twelve years chasing this maniac, and they let him go."

"How do you think I feel?" asked Tom. "I could have had rescued my family." He held his head in his hands in sorrow.

"Hold on, Tom," urged Kellogg. "We'll get another chance to capture Krueger and rescue your lovely family."

At that moment, Agents Barlow and Coffee entered through the double doors of the phone branch, talking loudly like celebrities. Barlow, in his bombastic voice, shouted, "Good to see you, Senior Special Agent Donald Kellogg. I am glad the director could spare you for our crucial briefing. It is good to see you again after such a long time." Tom watched as Barlow vigorously shook Kellogg's hand. "How long has it been?" Tom heard him ask.

Tom glanced at Kellogg, who seemed embarrassed, and suddenly Tom realized that Kellogg was not that close of a friend to Barlow. "It's been about two years since we last spoke," replied Kellogg as he returned to his seat.

"It is an honor to meet you, sir. I'm Agent John Coffee," said the junior agent as Kellogg stood back up to shake Coffee's hand. "Agent Barlow tells me you are an FBI legend, and you are the definitive expert on the Austrian-born Lukas Krueger."

Tom looked at Thornton and Mike Max, who both acknowledged they also sensed Barlow's self-importance. He watched as everyone sat in preparation for Kellogg's briefing.

Tom heard Barlow clear his throat and say, "Senior Special Agent, we have Krueger's Team Two in custody. We arrested them in the Willoughby Travelodge. We feel Krueger can't be far from that location." Barlow said, smiling proudly.

"Good work, Agent Barlow," replied Kellogg as he returned the smile.

Barlow said, "We have the men of Team Two in custody in the federal building at our own FBI center. We are going to sweat the truth out of those men. It won't be long before we know where to pick up Krueger."

Kellogg frowned at Barlow and said, "Those men know very little about the kidnapping details. Krueger tells his men just their jobs. Team Two knows even less because Krueger himself is always in Team One. Even Dagmar doesn't know all the details of each kidnapping. Pressuring the men at the federal building would be a waste of resources and effort and energy."

"Are you saying it would be useless to interrogate the men of Team Two?" asked Agent Barlow, frowning.

"Barlow, that is exactly what I'm telling you," said Kellogg, who was arranging papers for his presentation. "My time is limited, and, so, let me start my briefing."

"As most of you have heard, I work in the Behavioral Science Department at the FBI headquarters in Quantico, Virginia, where we primarily deal with serial killers and criminals who have behavioral and mental problems. Over twelve years ago, I began tracking and studying the behavioral crimes of Lukas Krueger, a classic psychopath." Kellogg paused. "Krueger was born in Austria and his operation is based in Europe."

Agent Coffee asked, "How old is Krueger?"

"His exact age is not known, but we estimate him to be in his mid- to late fifties," said Kellogg as he referred to his notes and then continued. "Abroad, they call him the European soldier of fortune, which is misleading because all of his kidnappings have occurred in America. He only kidnaps the American ultrarich. Tom, your notoriety and the publicity about the lottery money and the publicity regarding your attempt to clean up the city of Cleveland is what put you on Krueger's radar screen and got your family kidnapped."

Tom wanted to know everything that Kellogg knew. He was anxious and asked, "Can you tell us about all five of Krueger's American kidnappings? The details of each."

"Certainly. In the last twelve years, Krueger has kidnapped five excellently controlled victims. The first three were in New York, Miami, and Los Angeles. In that order. All three victims in these three cities were returned unharmed and alive. The last two cities were Chicago and New York. In that order. Both of these kidnapping victims were murdered," explained Kellogg as he puffed on his pipe and paused for a moment so the information could be absorbed.

"The last two kidnappings resulted in murders?" asked Tom, who, with a sense of anger, jumped to his feet, walked over to the coffee urn, and poured himself a hot cup of coffee. "Why the last two?"

Kellogg thought for a moment then said, "Krueger is a shrewd and complicated man. He is a genius. He scores over 200 on the I.Q. scale, but don't let that fool you. Lukas Krueger is a sociopath, and, although he is smart, at the same time he is truly insane by all of our standards. He is dangerous. He kills without conscience."

"If he kills without conscience, will he kill my family?" asked Tom as he slowly sipped his hot coffee.

"Tom, before I answer your question about your family, let me explain something to you. Lukas Krueger is emotionally spiraling down, like a tire losing air. I have a European informant who knows Krueger intimately, and he confirms to me that Krueger is losing control of his mind. He has developed a severe facial tick, which acts like a barometer gauging his struggle to control his mind and his behavior."

"So, he's losing his mind," said Tom. "Will he kill my family?" Tom crushed the Styrofoam cup in his hand and coffee spilled out over his bare hand. "Damn!" he shouted. Near the coffee urn, Thornton grabbed a roll of paper towels and helped Tom clean up the spilled coffee.

"We'll have to catch him, Tom, before he kills," said Kellogg quite bluntly. "It's that simple."

Tom grabbed another cup and poured himself another cup of coffee. Tom looked at Kellogg's face, whose jowls hung like the face of an old, worn-out bloodhound in search of an elusive scent.

"Krueger has a four-phase approach to his kidnappings. "Lukas first watches his victim for weeks. During this surveillance, he studies the subject and grows to hate the subject. After he knows the subject's schedule and his family's daily routine, he starts with harassment. In your case, the dead flowers, the bird with the note, the drawing and the warning, the bomb at your construction site, the noose on the dog , the note, and the threatening phone calls. That was his haunting phase. First the watching, then the haunting, then the snatching, and, finally, the collecting of the ransom money."

"Four phases," replied Tom as he thought through the problem. "Why did he let me go after kidnapping me?"

"He attacked your convoy, kidnapped you, beat you, then he released you. And, also, he kidnapped your family. He is trying to break you down, psychologically, while playing a high-stakes cat-and-mouse game," clearly explained Agent Kellogg. "You must remember, he is a genius and insane, all at the same time."

"Then, how do you predict his behavior?" asked Tom.

"I don't believe his behavior can be predicted," said Agent Kellogg, "I believe we can anticipate his behavior and use his intelligence against him."

"How do you do that?" asked Tom.

"That is our job to figure out," said Kellogg, "isn't it, Tom?"

"Yes! And before he kills my family."

"Yes, Tom," replied the older agent. "Let's stretch our legs and take a five-minute break." While everyone was taking a break, Tom stood watching as younger Agent Johnson helped Agent Kellogg set up for a PowerPoint presentation on a laptop computer. After ten minutes, Kellogg cleared his throat, clapped his hands and said, "Let me show you some pictures of some of the folks involved with Lukas Krueger. The first several are of Dagmar. She is Swedish, blond, short, slim, muscular, and she is extremely deadly." Tom watched as Kellogg showed several pictures of a younger Dagmar. "These pictures are of Lukas's girlfriend, Dagmar. They share a sadomasochistic relationship. She likes to be beaten, and he likes to beat her. She adores him and is always at his side. They have a relationship where their violence is sexually arousing. But these shots are about eight years old. She'd look older now," said Agent Kellogg as he adjusted his metal spectacles.

"Hold on, Agent Kellogg," interrupted Tom. "I saw that woman in the lobby of the Travelodge. She wasn't with Krueger."

"No! She was off to the side looking out the window," added Thornton, "but the woman was definitely Dagmar."

"Yeah. And after the shooting, she ran out into the parking lot," said Tom, who excitedly set down his coffee cup and jumped to his feet. "That must've been Dagmar!"

"That is probably how his team knew to come rescue him," stated Agent Kellogg. "Krueger's team must've just followed the ambulance to the hospital."

"Well, that answers quite a lot," added Tom as he sat back down, picked up his cup of coffee, and took a big swig. "Don't you have any pictures of Krueger?" he asked naively.

"No! No one has ever taken a picture of Lukas Krueger," stated Agent Kellogg. "My European informant has seen him, and he has verbally described him to me."

"I got a good look at him," declared Tom.

"Tell us what you saw," requested Agent Kellogg.

"Okay," agreed Tom. "He is about my height and of similar structure. His face is pulled tight and his facial skin looks like cheap plastic."

Agent Kellogg interrupted, "That look is from many plastic surgeries to disguise his facial appearance. He had his nose and eyes done several times in order to confuse us."

"He was wearing a trimmed beard," added Tom as he finished his coffee.

"Tom, describe the beard," said Agent Kellogg.

"It was a trim beard, which ran down from his ears down along the bottom of his jawbone and met at his chin, where he had longer chin whiskers like a Billy goat, and his upper lip was shaven clean," described Tom. "He wore no mustache."

"You've described him to a tee," reassured Agent Kellogg as he clapped his hands. "He always wears that same style of beard."

"It seems strange that you've never seen a picture of him, Agent Kellogg," speculated Tom.

Agent Kellogg frowned and said, "Krueger is very elusive. He refuses to have his picture taken, and he hates the FBI and Interpol. He will go out of his way to embarrass and humiliate us. Agent Barlow, be careful at each and every ransom exchange, because he'll literally make them blow up in your face," Kellogg prophesized. "Let's move on. I still have a few more pictures," said Agent Kellogg as he clicked the remote and advanced to the next picture. "This is a shot of a man named Otto. He is Krueger's second-hand man. These two men are extremely close."

"I have Otto locked up in the federal building," bragged Agent Barlow. "He claimed to be the leader of Team Two and gave us his name without a problem."

"I thought he'd be in Team One," said Kellogg, "but it makes sense that he'd be in charge of Team Two."

Agent Barlow smiled and eagerly said, "I'll notify our interrogation team immediately and have him spilling the beans within the night."

"Otto won't give you any information," claimed Agent Kellogg. "He is fiercely loyal to Lukas and won't say a single thing. It's a waste of time!"

"We gotta try," blurted Agent Barlow like a chastised child. Tom saw the desperation in Agent Barlow's eyes. "We gotta try!" Agent Barlow repeated.

"Give it a go, Barlow," said Agent Kellogg, "but you'll get nowhere, I promise you. But I would like to speak to Otto personally when I return on Saturday."

"I'll make those arrangements," said Barlow. "Kellogg has to go back to Quantico tonight, but he will return in two days. He wants to be in on the capture of Lukas, or at least the postcapture for questioning and ultimately to study him."

Tom said, "Thank you for all this useful information. May I ask, how would you suggest we capture him?"

Kellogg said, "Use his intelligence against him and somehow trick him."

Tom asked, "How can I read that tick?"

"When he becomes stressed or trapped, his tick increases in speed," explained Kellogg as he puffed on his pipe.

Tom said, "You're telling me he is dangerous."

"Yes, he kills almost on impulse," said Kellogg. "Back to my European informant, he has suggested Krueger may be on his last kidnapping. The totals of the first five kidnappings come to about one hundred million dollars. That total has been confirmed by my European informant. I am certain he has invested that amount, and that the true amount must be quite larger."

Kellogg puffed on his pipe and said, "It is rumored by my informant that Krueger is on his last kidnapping. Once completed, he and Dagmar will retire to a life in the Caribbean. That is based on what my informant tells me, and he has always been incredibly accurate."

After the presentation, Agent John Barlow had concerns. "Senior Agent Kellogg, Krueger's last call told Tom he'd call back at noon tomorrow and at that time he would give us his instructions for the money and hostage exchange. I've explained to Tom that the FBI has kidnapping team protocols that need to be followed." said Barlow, who had not posed a question.

"Agent Barlow, what are you asking?" said Kellogg.

"Tell Murphy he can't be there and we use only FBI fake currency," urged Barlow, who was showing his insecurity.

"Tom, I'm only here as an advisory consultant," said Kellogg, who felt sorry for Tom. "Agent John Barlow is in charge of this case totally and we must do it his way. But, he is correct about using FBI protocols."

"Kellogg, Agent Barlow threatened to have me arrested if I interfered," explained Tom, who was worried about his wife and children, not some rigid protocols.

"Well, that is a little harsh, John," said Kellogg.

"I was just making a point," said John Barlow.

Tom saw Agent Johnson stand, look at his wristwatch and say, "Pardon me, gentlemen, I must get Senior Special Agent Kellogg back to the airport in order to catch his return flight back to headquarters. He must be there for the director's morning departmental meeting, where he is addressing the department heads." Tom was impressed the young agent could remember all that.

"You are correct Agent Johnson," agreed Kellogg. "It was nice meeting with all of you. I wish you all the best of luck apprehending Lukas Krueger, and I will return Saturday in order to further assist you." Tom watched Kellogg gather a small pile of papers and say, "I have a handout from a prior presentation. I only have three copies, so I'll give Tom one copy to share with his staff, then I'll give Agent Barlow the last two copies to share among his people. This handout will explain further the doings of Lukas Krueger."

After Kellogg finished handing out his material, he gathered up his material and prepared to leave. Kellogg walked over to Tom, thanked him, and shook his hand.

Tom, Thornton and Mike walked out of the Kidnap Command Center and went over to Wanda's desk. "Mike, why don't you go home and get some rest? We will need you to get back here early. I will need both you and Thor fresh tomorrow," explained Tom.

"Okay Tom," replied Mike as he reassuringly patted Tom on his back and prepared to leave.

"Thor, take me home, then go home and rest," said Tom.

"Tom, you need protection," urged Thornton.

"Thor, I appreciate your concern, but I need to be alone for a few hours in order to think and rest," said Tom, "so drop me off at my bungalow and then go home."

"If that is what you really want," said Thornton.

"Yeah. That is what I really want," said Tom with a tired grin on his face. "I really need to be in my home tonight for some reason." Tom playfully pushed Thornton out of Wanda's office and headed them toward the big double doors of the phone branch. "Tomorrow is going to be a big day for all of us," said Tom as he let Thornton and Mike open the double doors.

*   *   *

By midnight it had stopped raining, and Tom was back at his Cleveland bungalow. He was impressed by the meeting with Senior Special Agent Donald Kellogg. He was glad that Thornton went back to his apartment and had not argued with Tom about needing protection. Tom truly wanted to be alone in his family's home, where he could smell the scents of his family. When he first stepped into the front room, he momentarily stood in the dark. He listened to the empty sounds of the house. It was quiet. It was scary. After turning on the lights, he walked upstairs and into the bedroom, where he changed into his sweats. Next, he walked from their bedroom into the bathroom just down the upstairs hallway. He stepped into the bathroom, closed the door, and in the dark bathroom he took Beth's bathrobe off the hook. Tom placed her bathrobe over his face, and he inhaled, smelling his wife's pleasant scents. His olfactory senses were stimulated, and he felt her near him momentarily. He fell to the floor, privately sobbing. After ten minutes, he dried his eyes and wiped his tears away. He placed the bathrobe back on the hook and went back downstairs to the kitchen. Out of habit, he started to call his dog, but he quickly remembered the dog was dead. Having forgotten about the dog's death made Tom feel stupid. He walked to the refrigerator and grabbed a bottle of Squirt soft drink, then he went to the kitchen cabinet and grabbed a bottle of Gordon's gin. Getting a tall glass, he poured half Squirt, half gin.

He walked into the living room, where he built a small fire in the fireplace. The house was cold, but the small fire helped comfort him.

He wondered how Beth and the kids were doing. He sat down on their small sofa and set his drink on the coffee table. He took the picture frame off the end table and looked at his family photograph. They all looked so sweet. He took a big swig of his drink and reflected over what Agent Kellogg had told him earlier in the evening. Kellogg had painted the image of Lukas Krueger as a brutal killer. Tom had tangled with him and believed he was a killer, but Tom told himself he was not going to let Krueger hurt his family. He would stop him even if it meant he would have to kill Krueger. Tom looked at his half-finished drink and took a big gulp finishing it.

He sat back on the sofa and tried to relax. Next, he closed his eyes. He slipped into sleep. Thirty minutes floated by, then he started to dream. In his mind, he heard the Austrian-accented deep voice of Lukas Krueger. "For you, we are coming ..." Tom jumped up off the sofa, sweating and startled.

He went back into the kitchen and made himself another drink, and this time he finished it in one large gulp. The gin tasted good, and it soothed his aching mind. After the drink, he walked back into the living room, sat down, and decided to pray. First, he said the Our Father followed by several Hail Mary's. After the prayers, he stared at the family photograph for a long time. He felt desperate, and kept crossing himself. "Dear God, I need your help," whispered Tom. "Please protect my Beth and our three kids. Would you please send Saint Michael, the Archangel to watch over and protect my family? Do this for me, and then I'll forever be in your debt."

Tom stared for the longest time, in a stupor, at the burning logs in the small living room fireplace. Suddenly, the telephone rang, startling him.

It was after midnight and the Murphy family were sleeping on the second floor of Lukas's farmhouse. Beth and Jenny were on one mattress on the center of the floor, while Tommy and Danny were sleeping on the second mattress next to their mother. Tommy played opossum by faking sleep until he was certain his younger brother, Danny, was absolutely asleep. Tommy rose slowly and checked on his mother and sister. Once he was sure they were asleep, he quietly walked with stocking feet toward the steps leading to the downstairs. Before he descended the stairs, he looked down toward the landing to see if the guard was there. Tommy did not see any guards, and so he carefully started to descend the creaky steps. In his stocking feet, he was able to quietly move down one step at a time until he reached the landing. Next, he looked from the landing into the various rooms of the first floor. In the living room, he saw two guards sleeping on the worn-out, dirty sofa. Once he stepped quietly into the living room, he saw no more guards sleeping on the opposite side of the room. He looked out the front window and saw the third and last guard, Boris, standing guard in the driveway. He was armed, as were the others. Quietly, Tommy walked into the kitchen. He had seen a wall phone next to the doorway to the pantry. He did not know if it was in service. He had not seen any of the guards use it, but he was going to give it a try. His plan was to first call his father at the family home in Cleveland. If his father was not there, he would call the business phone branch. The kitchen and the downstairs had no lights on, but the bright, full, autumn moonlight shone in through the kitchen windows, so Tommy could see well enough to dial the phone if it worked. He slowly crept across the old, yellowed linoleum of the large country kitchen, and as he reached the wall phone he heard one of the guards in the living room speak. He froze every muscle in his young body. He listened, and within a few minutes Tommy realized the guard was just talking in his sleep. Tommy waited until the speaking had stopped, then he reached for the receiver. He put it to his ear, listened, and smiled as he heard a dial tone. A wave of excitement traveled through Tommy's body like a young, eager colt running freely for the first time. He held the receiver to his ear, ready to dial. Suddenly, he realized the old telephone was not the quiet push-button style but was the old, noisy, rotary-style phone. He knew that each time he dialed a selected number, the phone would spin the rotary dial back to its original place. He feared the noise of the old phone might awaken and alert the guards. He knew he had to try, no matter what happened. He decided to place his palm over the spinning dial as it returned to its original position. He dialed the first number of his father's area code. The first number was a two, then a one, and then a six. He had dialed the area code and none of the guards had heard him. Next, Tommy carefully dialed the seven-digit house phone number, then he waited as it rang. Tommy counted six rings, then he heard, "Hello." It was his father's voice.

"Dad, it's me Tommy," the boy whispered.

"Tommy, is that you?" asked Tom in an intoxicated fog.

"Yes, the guards are asleep. So I sneaked a call."

"Are you okay? How are your Mom and Jenny and Danny?"

"We're all good!"

"Tommy! Where are you?"

"Dad, listen carefully. We are eight minutes east from the Willoughby Travelodge in a rundown farmhouse. I can hear the freeway, but I can't see it," whispered his son, who stood in the moonlight that filtered through the grimy, old, kitchen windows.

"I'll come get you, son," said Tom as he shook the drunken cobwebs from his foggy mind.

"There are five armed guards," said Tommy stoically.

"Tommy, repeat your location," requested his father.

Tommy repeated the location, then Tom said, "We'll find you in the morning. All my men will be searching. Don't fight with these men. Keep your mom, sister, and brother safe. I'll be there soon. I love you, son!"

"I just heard someone. I gotta go, Dad," whispered Tommy as he gingerly placed the receiver back onto its cradle and crouched down so as not to be seen. He heard the front door open, as Boris came into the living room to be relieved by one of his comrades.

"Wake! It's my turn to sleep," shouted Boris, who had just come in from the cold outside.

Tommy ran behind the shadows, then he scampered up the steps to the safety of the second floor. His heart was thumping rapidly as he barely escaped the guard's sight. He softly bounced onto the mattress next to Danny and cuddled up to him for comfort.

Chapter Six

Friday, Day Five

Once Tom heard the phone go dead, he wished he could have talked longer with his son; but he had a general location, and that was enough to sober him up. He ran to the kitchen sink, splashed cold water on his numb face and looked at the kitchen wall clock, which read one o'clock Friday morning. Next, he ran to the phone and called Thornton. The phone rang several times before it was answered. "Thor, it's me, Tom. Wake up! I got a call from Tommy, and he gave me his location. Get yourself back to headquarters. We've got work to do." Next he called Mike, the company's supervisor, and gave him the same instructions. Tom cleaned up, shaved and dressed back in the clothes he had been wearing earlier. When he ran to his car it was raining again, and the sky was quite overcast. It felt quite chilly to him.

By one thirty, Tom arrived at the phone branch where he found Wanda, who was still working with a skeleton crew. Thornton and Mike arrived just as Tom was telling Wanda about his call from Tommy. "I have a general idea where my family is located. Later this morning, with the help of our staff, I want to put together a search party. I intend to find my family. In the next hour, I want the four of us to call all fifty field managers. I want all fifty field managers to call their designated field workers, and have all staff report to our auditorium by 6:00 AM. There Mike and I will tell everyone about the call from Tommy, the location, and the plan. We will start our search at the Willoughby Travelodge and all points east. Any questions?"

"We're gonna need to call Leroy," said Wanda.

"Yes. Leroy can radio all the field managers and their field workers simultaneously from our communications center," added Mike.

"Right," said Tom. "I hadn't thought of that, Mike."

"That'll save a lot of phone calls," said Thornton.

"Mike, would you personally call and inform Leroy of our current developments? And ask him to beat feet in here to radio all our employees," said Tom as he rubbed the sore left side of his face.

Tom looked over the skeleton crew working the phone branch. Seeing everyone at his own computer work station made Tom proud. He worried about Wanda, who had been working around the clock since Beth and the children had been kidnapped. He knew she took short naps in the company coffee lounge in order to rest when she needed it.

It was near 2:00 AM, and Tom was anxiously waiting for Leroy to arrive. He knew once his dispatcher arrived he would immediately radio all the company staff. Tom figured if Leroy could send the radio alert to the staff at approximately 2:00 AM, then the staff would have nearly four hours to gather their belongings and report to the company's auditorium by 6:00 AM. Tom thought was a workable timetable. As Tom waited for Leroy, he thought about his army of field managers and field workers, approximately two thousand workers.

Tom sat near Wanda's work area and waited for Leroy. He quietly sipped hot coffee. He was startled when Mike tapped him on the shoulder and said, "I just spoke to Leroy. He understands the situation and will be here in fifteen minutes."

"Thanks Mike," replied Tom. "I'll be relieved once we have the word out to the staff."

"I understand, Tom."

Mike had work to do, so he left Tom to sip his coffee and to contemplate the situation. Tom sat thinking about his family. He felt let down by the FBI, and he figured his two-thousand-man search party was his best bet in finding Beth and his children.

By two thirty, Mike rushed Leroy into the big double doors of the phone branch. "Here he is," shouted Mike as he and Leroy ran past the FBI Kidnap Command Center and over to Wanda's work area, where Tom was sitting.

"Leroy, am I glad to see you," said Tom as he stood up from his seat and shook the dispatcher's hand. "Did Mike explain everything to you?"

"Yes Tom. He has even written down what I should say over the radio," said Leroy as he handed the written script to Tom.

Tom quietly read the radio address that Mike had written, then he said, "This sounds good. Leroy read this word for word. Okay?"

"Yes, Tom," replied the anxious communications expert.

Tom led Leroy, Thornton, and Mike out of the phone branch and down the hall to the company's communications center. Once inside, Tom watched and listened as Leroy proceeded to radio the very urgent message to the staff. "First, I'm sending out an alarm, which will get their attention. Now, I'm sending out the message, 'Attention employees of Just Clean It Up. A mandatory meeting is scheduled for Friday morning at six o'clock in the company's auditorium. Tom Murphy has a general location where his family is being held, and he requests your participation in an all-out search party commencing after our meeting. Again, a mandatory meeting is scheduled for Friday morning at six o'clock in the auditorium.'"

"Leroy, that was great," cheered Tom as they shook hands, and they both smiled.

"Did I do good?" asked Leroy and danced a little jig.

*   *   *

By 5:30 AM, Tom along with Thornton and Mike all sat on the stage of an empty auditorium. The sun had not yet risen, the staff had not yet arrived, and it was just going on 6:00 AM. Tom and the other two were drinking coffee. None of them had slept since Tommy had called at midnight, and, yet, they were not tired. Tom had mixed feelings. He was worried about his family, and, yet, he had confidence that his staff had the ability to find Beth and the three children.

"Tom, you look tired," remarked Mike.

"I'm okay! My son's phone call is the break we needed," replied Tom as he took a sip of his hot coffee and tried to look in charge. "Soon, we'll find my family."

"That was great information," said Thornton as he tried to boost his boss's morale.

The far door of the auditorium opened and several staff members entered. Within thirty minutes, the entire room was full to capacity and many extra staff were forced to stand. The enthusiasm the men and women displayed was wonderful, thought Tom.

The dispatcher, Leroy, tested the microphone and had it operating just as Tom was ready to make his address to the men and women.

Tom stood up, walked around the long table that was set up on the auditorium stage and raised the microphone. "Good morning, everyone," he started. He put his right hand over his eyes to protect them from the glare of the lights and asked, "Can everyone hear me?" The audience murmured affirmatively, and so Tom continued. "I appreciate that all you fine folks came in at this early hour in order to help me and my family," he said, then cleared his throat. "As you all know, my family has been kidnapped and are being held for a thirty-million-dollar ransom. Now, let me be clear. I have the money, and I am willing to pay it to the kidnappers, but the FBI experts tell me that if I pay, my family will most likely be killed anyway. Now, that does not sound very promising!" He stopped, stepped back to the table behind him and took a quick drink of water. "I do have better news. Last night, I returned home to do some brainstorming. I did not get very far, but miraculously, my oldest boy, Tommy, called me from where the kidnappers are holding my family. The guards fell asleep, and my boy was able to place the call. We only spoke briefly, but he told me they were being held in a rundown farmhouse, eight minutes east of the Willoughby Travelodge. One more important thing, he said he could hear but not see the freeway from the farmhouse. Another thing, they are not masked, which means my family can identify the kidnappers. So they would probably be murdered after the kidnappers collect the ransom."

Mike hurried from behind the conference table, took the microphone from Tom and said, "We all can help! Tom needs our help! After all he has done for us, we all need to take this opportunity and search for his family. When you all entered this auditorium this morning, you were each given a search party handout, which gives you all the information we have. We are asking all field workers to meet up with your particular field manager, who will drive you to the search area. As you leave this morning, get a walkie-talkie and keep in touch with headquarters. Are there any questions?" Mike stood waiting.

There were many questions and it took half an hour to answer all the questions. Just as Mike was ready to release everyone, Tom jumped up and took the microphone. "One last thing," interrupted Tom. "We all need a cover story as to why you are searching. Let's say you lost your dog, Trooper, a mix between a German shepherd and a greyhound. Call for Trooper. That is our cover story."

Once the group coordinated with the field managers, they started to drive to the search area, which was Willoughby and points east.

*   *   *

It was day five. Ten o'clock Friday morning, and Tom's search party was well on its way to Willoughby and points east. Tom could not yet join the search party because he had to be at the Kidnap Command Center to take Krueger's call at noon to discuss the exchange details.

Tom figured he could use the time from ten to noon to visit his pastor for some spiritual guidance, and so Thornton drove Tom to his parish, Saint

Malachi. Tom had called ahead and made an appointment with his pastor, Father John Gallagher, who was waiting for him in the rectory.

The rain from the day before was now gone, but the weather was still overcast and chilly. Tom was dressed in outdoor clothes because he intended to join the search party later in the day. He was wearing jeans, boots, and a Notre Dame sweatshirt underneath a denim jacket.

Thornton let Tom out of the Lincoln Navigator in the church parking lot, and Tom walked up to the rectory. When he knocked, Mrs. O'Malley, the house mother, answered the door. "Good morning, Mrs. O'Malley," said Tom as she let him enter the quiet vestibule.

"Dear Thomas, I've been praying for your dear family," she said as she held his hands sympathetically.

"Thank you, Mrs. O'Malley," uttered Tom. "Your kind prayers are deeply appreciated." He patted her hands, and then she led him down the hall to Father Gallagher's office. When they reached the Father's office, the door was open. She knocked gently and said, "Father John, Thomas is here to see you."

"Thank you, Mrs. O'Malley," responded the priest. "Come in, Thomas. I wish this visit could be under better circumstances." The priest stepped out from behind his desk, walked up to Tom, and shook his hand.

The room could have been from the 1920s. While everything appeared clean, things were worn out and threadbare. While Tom had donated substantially to this historic church, the pastor spent no money improving or updating the parish house. Father Gallagher liked the surroundings, and he felt comfortable there.

"Father, I also wish this visit could be under better circumstances," replied Tom as the priest motioned him to sit down.

"Tom, this morning's Mass was dedicated to the safe return of your family."

"Thank you, Father. That means a lot to me."

"Let us pray together," suggested the priest.

"First, let me confess my sins," urged Tom. "Will you hear my confession?"

"Go ahead, my son," said the priest as he prepared to give the sacrament of confession to Tom.

"Bless me, Father, for I have sinned," whispered Tom. "It has been two weeks since my last confession."

"Go on, my son," encouraged Father Gallagher.

Tom's voice grew gruff as he whispered, "I confess to almighty God I did nothing to stop the devil from taking my precious family from me." Tom suddenly dropped his face into his open hands, broke down, and sobbed hopelessly.

Father Gallagher rushed to him and placed his hands on Tom's head. "My good man, you've committed no sin. It was not your fault your family was kidnapped."

"But it feels like I let them down, Father."

"Thomas, you've not let them down," said the priest. "The sin is on the man who took them."

"The man who took them is named Lukas Krueger and he is a known killer," explained Tom as he lifted his head and wiped his wet eyes.

"Has this man killed before?" asked the priest.

"Yes! He has killed many times," said Tom, "and he runs with men who kill."

"Thomas, what are your plans and what are you prepared to do?" asked Father Gallagher with a serious look on his ruddy Irish face.

"Krueger wants thirty million dollars."

"I'll ask you again. What are you prepared to do?"

Tom wiped his right hand down his face and said, "I'm prepared to give him the money! But God forgive me, if he hurts my family. God as my witness, I'll kill the mongrel!"

"Thomas, God is on your side no matter what you're forced to do," reassured his priest, who looked into Tom's eyes and saw the reflection of an angry man.

"Even if I must become a killer?"

"You're being forced to protect the innocent, my son," said Father Gallagher. "Let us pray." They both got on their knees and prayed for twenty minutes, then the priest gave Tom his blessing.

They both stood up. Tom thanked his priest and said, "I must go now and save my family." Tom shook hands with Father Gallagher.

"Go with God, Thomas."

Father Gallagher walked Tom to the front door. They said good-bye once again and Tom walked to the vehicle where Thornton was waiting. It was still overcast and very cool. When Tom reached the Lincoln Navigator, Thornton was reading a book and was startled when Tom jumped into the front passenger seat. "You're quite the bodyguard. You never saw me coming," teased Tom.

"How was your visit with your priest?" asked Thornton.

"It was good," said Tom. "My priest gives me spiritual strength."

"Good. Let's go get the bad guys," smiled Thornton as he started the engine and proceeded to drive back to the phone branch where the police and FBI were waiting for the next ransom call.

* * *

Near noon, Tom and Thornton and Mike were in the company's communication center. They were talking over the radio to Leroy, who had set up the search party's temporary communication center in an empty parking lot across the street from the Willoughby Travelodge. While Mike scanned a map of the Willoughby general area, Tom talked to Leroy over the radio. "Leroy, how is the search going?"

"We didn't get the search started until nine this morning, which has given us four hours so far," explained Leroy. "Has Krueger called yet, Tom?"

"Not yet, but it is just going on twelve," said Tom. "I'd better get over to the FBI's phone hotline." He turned off the radio, turned to Thornton and said, "Let's get some coffee before we head to the hotline." Both men filled coffee mugs from the coffee urn in the communication center. They headed for the phone branch near the FBI Kidnapper Communication Center and phone hotline. As Tom entered the phone branch, he saw Wanda talking to the Cleveland Police and to FBI Agents Barlow and Coffee.

"Pardon me, Wanda," interrupted Tom. "I need to talk with Agent John Barlow for a moment."

"Sure," said Wanda. "I'll get back to our phones."

"Wanda, wait! How are our calls coming?"

"Our incoming calls have been slow but steady," said Wanda. "The callers are all mostly expressing their prayers for your family."

"That's nice of folks," said Tom as he sipped his coffee. "Wanda, keep up the good work." He walked toward the FBI center and guided Agent Barlow away from the crowd, and he proceeded to explain, "John, I received a call last night at about midnight from my son Tommy."

"Tommy? How'd he get a call out?" asked Barlow.

"He caught the guards asleep."

"Did he tell you his location?"

"Yes, in a vague way," said Tom, who then proceeded to explain to Agent Barlow what his son told him.

Barlow replied, "That is too vague, Tom. I'd need a couple thousand agents to sweep that big of a plot of ground." Agent Barlow looked down at Tom condescendingly.

"Yes. I understand," said Tom, "but I already have two thousand men sweeping that location right now."

"Good. You go sweep that area while we go out and capture Krueger with our proven FBI methods," said Agent Barlow as Tom watched him walk back to the command center.

As Tom stood there, Thornton came over to speak with him. "What'd he say about Tommy's call?"

Tom looked at Thornton angrily and said, "He basically blew me off." Tom put his hand on Thornton's shoulders as he shook his head in frustration.

"What do you mean, he blew you off?"

"He's got an ego problem, I guess."

Just then the alarm from the FBI's phone hotline rang, and Agent Barlow shouted, "Tom, you're up! It's Krueger."

It rang as Tom rushed to the receiver. Once he reached the phone, Agent Coffee had counted three rings. Tom picked up the receiver and said, "Yes, this is Tom Murphy."

"Thomas, good to hear your voice," uttered Lukas.

"Krueger, is that you?"

"Thomas, please, first names. It's Lukas."

"Okay, Lukas."

"That's better, Thomas."

"Lukas, how are my wife and children, and when do I get them back?" asked Tom as he tried to disguise his anger.

"Tom, they are eager to come home. Do you have my money?"

"I have all the money ready," said Tom urgently.

"Good. I was getting anxious and had even considered selling your youngest boy, Danny, to a fat, rich, Mexican man-boy-lover, who was salivating at the thought of buying your tender little boy. How does that strike you, Thomas?"

"You're a sick bastard," shouted Tom as he tried to restrain himself.

"Now ... Now ... I don't much care for Mexicans, so when do we exchange your lovely family for my thirty million American dollars?"

"Is that what you think my family is worth?" asked Tom, followed by a long pause.

"Your family's worth exceeds your grasp, Thomas, but thirty million American dollars will do," chuckled Lukas.

"I have all the money ready for you, Lukas."

"That's the spirit, Thomas," boasted Lukas, "and I've taken quite good care of your loved ones. Here are the details. First and foremost, there are to be no police or FBI at the exchange. If they are there, I will not only abort the exchange, but such a betrayal will definitely put your family in further peril." Tom heard a long pause.

"Are you still there, Lukas?"

"Thomas, I'm still here."

"When and where?" asked Tom, avoiding the threat of further peril.

"Thomas, no police and no FBI," Lukas explained.

"Just tell me where and when," replied Tom as he motioned at Barlow to hurry up and trace the call.

"Today at 4:00 PM, I want two blue gym bags filled with fifteen million dollars in each bag brought to the fifty-yard line of the Browns' stadium. We will exchange there."

"How can we make the exchange in the stadium?"

"Be creative. Magic can happen," said Lukas as his laugh resembled a wild hyena.

Agent Barlow motioned for more time and so Tom said, "I need more time."

"Time to plot against me?" Lukas's tone of voice suddenly sounded angry, thought Tom.

"There's no plot!" responded Tom.

"Today at 4:00 PM," yelled Lukas and hung up.

Tom glanced at Barlow and shouted, "Did you get a location?"

Barlow looked at Coffee. Coffee replied, "It's a pay phone in a deli on West 115th Street."

Barlow threw up his hands and shouted, "Someone get the layout of the Browns' stadium!" Tom watched Barlow walk over to the table where they kept the hot coffee, and he proceeded to pour himself a fresh cup of coffee.

"Aren't you going to check it out?" Tom asked as he watched as no one seemed interested in checking out the deli where Lukas had called from.

"I am sure he is long gone by now," said Barlow. "Lukas is too smart to play in his own backyard."

"What does that mean?" asked Tom.

Thornton walked over to Tom and said, "He's right. Lukas wouldn't call from anywhere near his hideout."

Tom watched as Barlow gathered all his agents around him and whispered several commands, then after a couple of minutes he shouted, "Come on, ya'll know the drill!"

Tom watched as agents scattered everywhere. He then looked at his bodyguard and asked, "Thor, what's going on?"

"They're planning their trap," said Thornton. "They are doing it by the book, Tom."

Tom angrily crushed an empty paper coffee cup that was near him and tossed it into a nearby trash can. He then stomped over to where Barlow was giving out directions to his agents. He waited while Barlow finished talking, then he interrupted by shouting, "Barlow, can we talk?"

"Tom, I'm pretty busy right now," said Barlow as he signed his name to a document one of his underlings put under his nose. "Who is getting me the layout of the Browns' stadium?"

"I don't like the plan," said Tom definitely. "How is Lukas going to exchange my family out in the open field in the Browns' Stadium?"

"The Browns' Stadium has been conducting public tours all month," said Agent Coffee, "and that is most likely how Lukas plans to make the exchange."

Tom stood in the middle of the command center as everyone around him scurried in all directions. "Lukas doesn't want you FBI guys there," shouted Tom to whoever was listening.

"Every kidnapper says that they don't want the FBI there. It's a standard line," said Agent Barlow.

Thornton stepped forward and said, "Tom is right. You can't protect Beth and the kids in an open football stadium."

"We'll have a ton of agents as well as several sharpshooters. Lukas doesn't stand a chance," boasted Agent Barlow as he lit a cigarette and smiled.

Tom did not like the arrangements. He feared for the safety of his family. "I don't like it!" shouted Tom.

"Calm down Tom. We are the FBI. We are experts at this, for Christ sake," said Agent Barlow reassuringly.

Tom poured himself another coffee and drank it, buying time, and then said, "In my gut, this feels all wrong."

"Can you get me some armed agents to protect me with the thirty million?" asked Tom, who wanted to deliver the money as he had been told by Lukas.

Barlow frowned and said, "As I already told you, we aren't using your real money, and you're not delivering the fake money." Barlow took a long drag on his cigarette.

"Why not me?" asked Tom just as Barlow started to walk away from him. "Don't walk away from me, Barlow!"

"We are using our fake money, and you are going to stay here with the phones while we spring our standard-procedure trap on Krueger. It has been used and perfected," said Barlow as he again tried to walk away from Tom.

"Lukas was specific. No FBI!" shouted Tom as he grabbed Barlow's arm in order to stop him from walking away.

"Let go of me," snarled Barlow as he pulled his arm free from Tom's grasp. "All kidnappers say no FBI."

"What's your plan?" asked Tom as Thornton held his arms in order to reassure Barlow that Tom was not going to grab him again. "What's your trap?"

We'll have the stadium surrounded. He won't be able to escape once he tries to make the exchange," boasted Barlow as he smiled with a sense of self-assurance.

"That's stupid, Barlow. He's not going to put himself in a spot to be trapped," said Tom with a tone of despair. "There is no way out of the stadium."

"And that is why the stadium is the perfect place to trap Krueger," said Barlow, confidently.

Tom thought Barlow was making a big mistake. "Let me give him the money. If he doesn't see me, he may know it's a trap and hurt or even kill my family."

"Bullshit, Murphy. You're interfering with a federal investigation. Now, go join your silly search party, or I'll have you arrested," shouted Barlow as he stepped up to Tom and pushed him backwards. Thornton grabbed Tom and restrained him from striking the agent and urged him to leave the phone branch.

Agent Barlow looked directly at Tom and shouted, "Tom, go join your search party, and in the meantime let us do our jobs. We will bring your family home tonight for dinner."

Thornton dragged Tom out of the command center and then out through the double doors of the phone branch. Once in the hallway, Tom looked at Thornton and said, "Somehow Lukas is going to make a fool out of Barlow. He is not going to allow himself to be trapped in that stadium."

Thornton said, "I don't know what'll happen, but I agree with you, Lukas is not going to allow himself to be trapped." Tom and Thornton walked down the hallway toward Tom's personal office. "Let's take Barlow's advice and join the search party. We can catch up with Leroy and see what progress the men have made. What do you say, Tom?"

"Thor, I'm just worried that Barlow is putting my family at risk," said Tom as they reached his office door.

"Tom, I think Lukas won't even have your family at the exchange, just to embarrass the FBI," said Thornton as Tom unlocked his office door.

Upon entering the office Tom replied, "I bet you are right. I bet Lukas will embarrass the FBI somehow. Okay, Thornton, let's go join the search party."

* * *

By twelve thirty, Agent Barlow was assured that Tom and Thornton had gone to join the search party. He gathered all the agents and all the police officers. "Now that I have your attention, let me be clear. We want to capture, but not kill, Lukas Krueger. He is valuable to us alive not dead. We are using **FBI SWAT** teams, but under no circumstances are they to shoot to kill."

Agent Coffee raised his hand and said, "Agent Kellogg will be returning tomorrow morning, and he very much wants to study Krueger."

Barlow said, "The FBI wants to thank the assistance we are getting from our local police officers." He gave a little salute while looking in their direction, then he walked to the laptop computer. He turned the computer on and looked at the image. "Here we have the layout of the stadium," he said as he pointed at the image. "Here is the fifty-yard line where Lukas wants to make the exchange at 4:00 PM, and where we'll be prepared to trap him. A show of force is important, but we must not endanger the hostages or Krueger." Barlow looked at some papers that were next to the computer and he said, "We arrested Team Two of Krueger's gang, but so far Krueger does not know. So Krueger may show up either by himself or with other men. We don't know. We must be ready for either contingency." Everyone studied the image on the computer.

Agent Barlow continued to brief all the agents and officers on the plan that would be used to carefully capture and arrest hopefully not only Lukas Krueger, but also all of the remaining members of Team One.

After an hour briefing, Agent Barlow left the responsibility of the Kidnap Command Center and the hotline to Wanda, the director of the phone branch. Agent Barlow thanked Wanda before she had a chance to say no, and then he explained that he needed every agent and officer at the stadium. Agent Barlow he said, "Besides Wanda, no one will call because they'll all be at the stadium." He finished by shaking her hand, then he rushed out of the phone branch and through the double doors.

* * *

By two o'clock Friday afternoon, Lukas Krueger had telephoned Mick Myerson at radio station WKKID, and they had gone over all the last-minute details of the publicity stunt and charity fund-raiser at the stadium. "Well Mick, I'm sure everything will go smooth this afternoon at the stadium, and I'll be seeing you first thing in the morning with the remainder of your money," confirmed Lukas as he smiled and lied. "Have a good afternoon, Mick," finished Lukas as he hung up the wall phone in the farmhouse kitchen. He looked at Dagmar, who was sitting at the kitchen table, and he said, "We'll leave as soon as I speak to Mrs. Murphy." He walked out of the kitchen and proceeded to walk up the stairs to the second floor. Once he reached the landing, he saw Beth sitting in the wooden chair by the front windows. "Mrs. Murphy, we must talk." She started to stand up, but he shouted, "Stay seated!" He approached her, then glanced to see where the children were located.

She recognized why he was scanning the room, and she instantly whispered, "They're all asleep on the mattresses."

"I see," said Lukas, acknowledging that they were all three asleep, then he came closer to Beth. He knelt down next to her at the window. "We will be leaving soon to get the thirty million dollars from your husband. If he gives us the money, then you all will go home this afternoon, but if it is a trap, I'll return angry!" Lukas paused to let his statement sink in, then he said, "Pray we are given the money, Mrs. Murphy!" Lukas stood up, looked down at her, then he turned and stomped to the landing. He looked back sternly at Beth, then he descended the stairs.

Once back downstairs, Lukas looked at Boris and said, "Keep them safe. Dagmar and I will return soon." He grabbed Dagmar by her arm and dragged her to the front door. "We must go now," he said as he opened the door and left the farmhouse.

They drove the black panel van to downtown Cleveland, then they headed for the stadium parking lot, where they parked the van and waited for the helicopter.

*   *   *

By three o'clock Friday afternoon, Special Agent John Barlow was busy finishing the final details of the 4:00 PM kidnap exchange.

Barlow was anxious to finally have a chance to capture Lukas Krueger and the men of Team One.

He was glad that Tom had joined the search party and was out of Barlow's hair, at least for the time being.

He had great confidence in the bags stuffed with fake FBI currency and a tracking device. He knew Krueger was smart, but he believed Krueger's greed would be greater.

Finally, Barlow heard from the agents who had checked out the phone booth that Lukas had called from. "We've got tire tracks and fingerprints. It will take a couple of hours to collect evidence," said the outside agent.

"Forget that! We've got a four o'clock kidnapping exchange, and I need all your men back here immediately," shouted Barlow into the phone.

While Barlow and Coffee waited for all the field agents to report to the Kidnap Command Center, they prepared for all the final details. They checked the gym bags and continued to guzzle as much hot coffee as possible. They were hyped and ready.

After all the agents reported, Barlow assigned each man a specific job and assigned position in the stadium. Agents were assigned in the various tunnels. The sharpshooters were assigned positions in the bleachers, the Dawg Pound, regular seats, and field boxes. Barlow and Coffee controlled everyone via radio. Barlow demanded total operational control. He and Coffee sat at the fifty-yard line and half way up the seats.

By 3:00 PM, everyone was in position and prepared. By 4:00 PM, Barlow realized his men were getting overanxious and perhaps a little bored. He kept scanning the entrances and the exits of the stadium. Public tours were being conducted, which he did not dare cancel. It was just past four when he heard the loud hum of a motor from above. Next, he saw a small helicopter hover above the stadium. Over his radio, to all his agents, he shouted, "What the hell is that?" His radio dispatch warned all the agents, who were already aware of the helicopter.

As Barlow watched, he saw the small helicopter hovering over the football field. He noticed on the side of the suspicious helicopter the letters WKKID, which represented a small radio station far east of Cleveland. Agent Barlow shouted, "Agent Coffee, do you see the letters on the helicopter?"

"Yeah. Is that a radio station?" asked Agent Coffee.

"I think so," replied Agent Barlow as he raised his radio to his lips and shouted, "Stand by, men!"

Next, Barlow saw the small two-man helicopter descend onto the football field near the fifty-yard line. "What are they doing?" he screamed at Agent Coffee, who was sitting right next to him. "What are they doing?" He watched as the helicopter tried to land. The winds were fierce over the football field. The helicopter landed then popped back up in the air, swerving viciously, and landed again. Barlow saw the door open and a man climb out. He saw the man was dressed in a bright, colorful clown's suit. He continued to watch the man as he jumped up and down, comically acting like a fool. He had big clown feet, which Barlow watched as the clown comically walked toward the two big blue gym bags. "Agent Coffee, is this a joke?" asked Agent Barlow. They both continued to watch as the clown walked closer to the gym bags. Once the clown reached the gym bags, he raised his arms in the air, acting surprised to find the bags. He bent down and jiggled his body as he picked up one bag in each arm.

"Barlow, is that clown Krueger?" asked Agent Coffee as he looked closer at the clown's face by using his binoculars. "His face is painted," shouted Coffee, "I can't tell if it's Krueger."

Barlow watched as the clown turned and started walking toward the helicopter with a gym bag in each hand. Next, Barlow shouted into his bullhorn, "Grab that fool!" Instantly, Barlow watched as his agents ran from all over the field and started shooting at the clown's big feet. He raised the bullhorn, and he shouted, "Hold your fire! Hold your fire!" The clown ran as bullets hit the ground around his path to the helicopter. He dropped the two gym bags as he ran straight to the helicopter. Barlow shouted, "Drop to the ground!" Suddenly, the rifled agents attempted to swarm the clown, but the clown climbed up into the small helicopter. Next, Barlow shouted, "land the helicopter. Land the helicopter." The pilot appeared to panic. Instead of obeying, he ascended up high above the football field even as agents pointed their rifles at the helicopter. It just continued to rise. Barlow again shouted, "Stop firing. Stop firing!" The helicopter kept ascending above the football field.

* * *

From the parking lot of the Browns' Stadium, Lukas saw the small helicopter just as it popped above the stadium's rooftop. The helicopter swerved in the turbulent winds coming from Lake Erie. He laughed hideously as he saw the small helicopter bobbing up and down, trying to control itself while hovering over the football field. Lukas savored the moment as he got out of his van and prepared to punish the hated FBI. He thought punishing the FBI would be sweeter than grasping the Murphy ransom. He hated the famous FBI, who had hounded, chased him, and made his life miserable for the past twelve years. Now, he would get a measure of revenge.

Lukas pointed his electronic detonator at the helicopter and said, "I demand there be no FBI." He watched with joy as the small helicopter exploded into a huge fireball and came down, crashing onto the football field, exploding again as it hit the ground, and splattering fiery debris everywhere. Lukas Krueger smiled with revenge as he saw the black smoke rise up from the burning football field. He put the detonator back into his coat pocket and then he climbed back into the black van. Once in the van, he smiled at Dagmar and said, "The FBI will never laugh at me!"

* * *

Barlow cringed as he watched the helicopter explode into a fireball and descend onto the football field. As he saw it tumble down, he saw several agents, who were unable to scramble to get out from under the fiery ball. When it hit the ground, fiery fragments of the helicopter sprayed in all directions.

Agents Barlow and Coffee hurried down onto the field, where two agents were trapped under the burning helicopter and three other agents were out from under the helicopter but were afire and screaming in agony. As Agents John Barlow and John Coffee ran, Barlow looked at Coffee and shouted, "John, go call the fire department to put out these fires." Coffee ran back toward the FBI's temporary command center and proceeded to call the Cleveland Fire Department.

Barlow and other agents ran to the burning agents, and they tried rolling them to extinguish the burning clothing. Stadium employees came running out from the tunnels with large fire extinguishers to spray the burning agents, which helped save their lives. Unfortunately, the two agents trapped under the helicopter did not survive.

Agent Barlow shouted directions to the other agents, and he knew the fire department would be onsite soon to handle the fires.

As soon as things were somewhat under control, Barlow headed for the temporary command center, located inside one of the tunnels. As he entered the command center, he found Agent Coffee sitting in a chair, next to the telephone, sobbing.

"John, get a hold of yourself," encouraged Barlow.

Coffee took a deep breath, looked up, and shouted, "John, we've got two dead agents and three burned beyond recognition." Coffee buried his face into his hands and resumed sobbing uncontrollably.

Barlow grabbed Coffee by his scalp, pulled his face out of his hands, and shouted, "Get a grip! I need your help, John. The ambulances are here. Come help me!"

After the ambulances transported the burned agents and the fire department put out the helicopter fires, then Agents Barlow and Coffee got together in a tunnel where the temporary command center had been set up. It had been an hour. Near 5:00 PM, Mick Myerson had arrived at the stadium to explain why his radio station's helicopter had been involved in a high-profile kidnapping case. Agent Barlow introduced himself and Agent Coffee to Mick Myerson, then Barlow said, "Myerson, why was your company helicopter involved in our kidnap case today at the stadium?" Barlow lit a cigarette and looked sternly at Myerson.

"I was led to believe it would be a publicity stunt for charity," replied Myerson who was shocked by the event.

"A publicity stunt!" shouted Coffee, who was still not in self-control as his eyes looked red and puffy from crying.

"Hold on, John," said Barlow. "Myerson, what do you mean when you tell me it was a publicity stunt?"

"Listen here! I want answers; my pilot and disc jockey are dead, and my helicopter has been destroyed," screamed Myerson. "I want to know what is going on!"

"Shut up, you sniffling hick!" shouted Coffee defiantly as he stood up and leaned over Myerson.

"Listen Myerson, we took a loss too," said Barlow, who crushed his cigarette in an ashtray. "We've got two dead agents and three who are badly burned and on their way to the burn unit at Metro Hospital."

Just then, an FBI supervisor from the Cleveland office walked onto the scene. "Agents Barlow and Coffee, I'm taking over the interrogation of Mr. Myerson. Mr. Myerson, I'm taking you to the federal building for a discussion, which will hopefully explain this mess," said the FBI supervisor. "Agents Barlow and Coffee, you're ordered to return to your Kidnap Command Center and to maintain the hotline, which will hopefully result in a new contact from Lukas Krueger."

* * *

Tom was with Thornton, Mike Max, Leroy, and a few other members of his company. They were coordinating the search party from the empty lot south of the Willoughby Travelodge. It was 5:00 PM, and Tom was anxious to hear from Agents Barlow and Coffee regarding the attempted hostage exchange that had been scheduled for 4:00 PM.

"We should have heard something by now," said Tom.

"Yes. It has been an hour," agreed Thornton as he walked over to Leroy and asked, "Will you call the phone branch and ask Wanda if the agents are back?"

Tom watched as Leroy followed Thornton's request. Meanwhile, Tom was starting to worry because he had not heard anything yet. He listened while Leroy spoke to Wanda. "Tom," Leroy shouted, "Wanda has been listening to the radio, and she said there are reports of an explosion at the Browns' Stadium."

"Leroy, give me the phone," shouted Tom, who frantically grabbed the receiver from Leroy and shouted, "Wanda, what have you heard?" He stood still while Wanda basically repeated what she had told Leroy, which was not very informative or helpful. Tom hung up the phone, handed it back to his dispatcher, and motioned to Thornton and Mike to head for the car. "We're going back to headquarters!" he shouted as he walked to the car.

Tom drove fast as he made his way back to his company's headquarters. Thornton turned on the radio, as Tom drove, hoping to hear some additional information about the explosion. Only sketchy details were being reported. To Tom, it seemed to take forever to get back to his company, but he actually arrived in under twenty minutes.

As Tom drove into his parking lot, he saw the agents' vehicles. Tom, Thornton, and Mike all rushed into the building directly to the phone branch where the agents were at their command center. As they entered the phone branch, Tom immediately saw Wanda talking with both agents Barlow and Coffee. In the corner of the agents' command center, Tom saw Senior Special Agent Kellogg, who had returned early from the FBI headquarters in Quantico, Virginia. Tom wondered when Kellogg had returned.

Tom ran up to Agent Barlow, grabbed his arm and screamed, "Barlow, what happened? Was my family hurt? Talk to me!" Thornton pulled Tom off of Agent Barlow to prevent a fight. As Tom stepped back away from Agent Barlow he shouted, "You could have gotten people killed."

"Your family was nowhere near the stadium," stressed Agent Barlow. "Lukas tried to stage a publicity stunt and then exploded a bomb onboard a small helicopter. Four people were killed today because of your family," shouted Barlow, who was trying to hurt Tom's feelings.

"You damn thug!" shouted Tom as he sucker-punched the arrogant agent who had accused Tom's family of four deaths. Chaos broke out as Agent Barlow attempted to strike Tom, but Thornton got in the middle and he protected his boss. "You dirty thug," screamed Tom as Thornton carried him out of the Kidnap Command Center and over to Wanda's work desk. Once in Wanda's work area, she poured Tom a hot cup of coffee, and Thornton had Tom take his pain medication. Then Wanda gave him a kind ear. "He accused my family of those four deaths," said Tom who was visually upset and still terribly worried about his wife and kids.

"Tom, I think he is just mourning the loss of his agents," explained Wanda as she rubbed Tom's tense neck muscles and tried to help him relax.

Mike had been talking to Agents Coffee and Kellogg, and he had gotten the information about the terrible scene at the stadium. After speaking with the agents, he returned to Wanda's work area. "Tom, it's the general consensus that Krueger planned and executed this disaster at the stadium to embarrass the FBI, which he hates," Mike explained as he placed his hand on Tom's shoulder in a sign of reassurance. "Your family was not there and were never in any danger," said Mike.

"Thanks, Mike," said Tom with a smile of relief.

Just as they began talking, the hostage phone hotline rang. It is Lukas, thought Tom as he ran over to the Kidnap Command Center and picked up the receiver from its cradle and confidently said, "Hello, Lukas."

"Thomas. I am extremely disappointed. I said no law enforcement, and yet the stadium was crawling with those nasty little critters."

"They took control away from me," said Tom apologetically. "I tried to do it your way, Lukas." The bottom of Tom's belly felt empty as he searched for the right words to say to the kidnapper. "Let's try again," he pleaded.

"How can I trust you, Thomas?"

"You must trust me," he urged. "That is the only way we can get this done. Lukas, I have all the money ready."

"All right. We will try again tomorrow at 9:00 AM at the bear exhibit at the zoo. Come alone with the two gym bags as before, and we'll exchange your family for my money. This time, come alone. Do you have any questions?"

"Lukas, don't hurt my family."

"Then come alone." Lukas hung up.

Tom calmly set the receiver back onto its cradle, looked angrily at Agent Barlow, and sternly said, "This time, I go alone." Tom stared defiantly at Barlow.

Tom watched as Barlow raised his hands over his head and said, "Tom, we still have to play it by the FBI book."

"John Barlow, we're gonna go round and round on this," shouted Tom as he started toward the agent; again Thornton grabbed him, preventing a scuffle.

Kellogg rushed between the two men, raised his hands, and shouted, "Wait … Wait … Wait just one minute. We've already gotten four men killed. We've got to be smart. We're dealing with a psychopathic killer and we need to outsmart him." Kellogg walked closer to Tom, put his arm on Tom's shoulder, and started to walk him away from the group of agents in the Kidnap Command Center. "Tom, lets talk," said Kellogg in a sage tone. After they walked away from the command center, Tom suggested they talk in his private office. He invited Thornton to join them. Once they reached Tom's office, the three of them relaxed by casually drinking coffee and listening to Kellogg's advice regarding the characteristics of Lukas Krueger. "Today's ransom exchange was never intended to involve your family. Krueger simply wanted to embarrass the FBI and the local law authorities." Kellogg proceeded to tell Tom and Thornton about the fake ransom exchange and the helicopter that was intended to explode, making a grand blunder by the authorities. Kellogg explained that Krueger's past kidnappings never had the hostages at the point of exchange, and that he was one hundred percent sure that Tom's family would not be at the bear exhibition at the zoo. After an hour of persuasion, Tom agreed to allow the FBI to coordinate the ransom exchange.

As the conversation was ending, Tom asked, "Agent Kellogg, did Agent Barlow tell you about the telephone call I received last night from my oldest son?"

"No, Tom. Agent Barlow has been pretty busy the last few days," said Kellogg as he finished drinking his second mug of coffee. "Was the call from where the hostages are being held?"

"Yes. Tommy caught the guards sleeping, and he quietly called my home phone. We only spoke briefly because the guards awoke, but he told me that they were being held eight minutes east of the Willoughby Travelodge, and that he could hear but not see the freeway, and that they were being held in an old, rundown farmhouse," said Tom. "My entire staff is searching that area today."

"How big is your staff?"

"Two thousand people," replied Tom, hoping Kellogg would want to join the search.

"Where is the Willoughby Travelodge from here?"

"Approximately eighteen miles east of here."

"Tom, your people may very well find Krueger's hideout before the ransom exchange at 9:00 AM tomorrow," said Agent Kellogg as he set his empty coffee mug down on the coffee table. Tom watched him as he stood up from the couch. "Guys, I can't sit this long. My old bones and joints lock up on me." He gingerly stepped out from behind the coffee table, which was positioned in front of the couch.

Tom, who remained standing throughout the conversation, said, "Maybe we ought to wander back to the command center and see what they are up to."

"It is going on six," said Thornton. "The sun will be setting soon, and, Tom, we should be ending the search party efforts for tonight."

"You're right, Thor. Time has slipped away from me. We better go talk to Mike and have him call Leroy," said Tom as he guided Agent Kellogg and Thornton out of his private office, turning out the lights as he locked up.

Tom and the two other men entered the big double doors of the phone branch. They immediately saw a commotion in the command center where all the agents were busy at work. Tom presumed their activities were in preparation for tomorrow's 9:00 AM ransom exchange. Tom walked past the command center and directly over to Wanda's work area. He approached her and said, "Where is Mike?"

Wanda looked up, slightly surprised, and she replied, "Mike is in our communication center talking with Leroy, who is at the search party center. Tom, where have you been?"

"Talking with Kellogg in my office," said Tom as he turned to go, but as an afterthought he shouted back, "Thanks, Wanda." As Tom walked past the command center he tapped Thornton and said, "Lets go, Thor." They exited the double doors as they left the phone branch and headed for the communication center. Once they reached the communication center, they found Mike, who was talking over the radio. Tom approached Mike and asked, "Are you talking to Leroy?"

"Yeah, Tom. Leroy says the sun is setting," shouted Mike, who could not hear because he was wearing headphones. "He wants to know what to do," again shouted Mike.

Tom motioned for Mike to give him the headphones and the microphone. Once Tom had adjusted the headphones he said, "Leroy, can you hear me? Good. Lets stop the search party for today. Send everyone back here to the auditorium for an end-of-day briefing. Do you understand? Good. See you soon." Tom turned off the radio, looked at Mike and

Thornton, then said, "By seven, we'll have a briefing in the auditorium. Do either of you have any questions?" Both men shook their heads no. Tom looked at Mike and said, "Mike, will you see to it that everything is a go in the auditorium for seven tonight?"

"Sure, Tom," replied Mike as he hurried out of the communication center and headed down the hall toward the auditorium to alert the staff who managed the auditorium. Thornton followed Tom as he returned to the FBI command center, where he invited Agent Kellogg to join him at the 7:00 PM search party briefing in the auditorium. "Thank you, Thomas, I'd appreciate participating in that briefing," replied Senior Special Agent Donald Kellogg.

In the meantime, Tom spend the next thirty minutes alone in his private office praying for the safekeeping of his family.

* * *

By 7:30 PM, Tom, who was lying on the couch, heard Thornton knocking on the office door. As he answered the door, Thornton rushed in and shouted, "You're late. The entire auditorium is full and Mike has been answering questions for the last twenty minutes."

"Thor, I was praying and fell asleep."

"God knows you need the rest," urged Thornton as he helped Tom put on his denim jacket, and they then headed for the auditorium. Tom and Thornton rushed in the side door, and as they ran up the steps to the stage, the audience exploded with applause. He knew his employees admired and loved him and his family. Next he heard the employees chanting his name, "Thomas ... Thomas ... Thomas."

He smiled then hurried over to the microphone and sheepishly said, "Thank you, everyone. I'm so grateful and proud of each and every one of you for your great efforts to find my family." Tom covered the microphone with the palm of his hand, bowed his head and said, "Will you all pray a moment for my family?" There was a full minute of silence. After the silent moment, Tom raised his voice and said, "Are you with me? Will you all return in the morning to continue where we left off?"

The audience roared, "We are with you, Tom!"

"Great! Then go home and get some rest and meet me back here at 6:00 AM to resume the search party," said Tom, who looked behind him at the long table on the stage where he saw Mike, Thornton, Leroy, and Agent Kellogg all sitting with full attention on what he was saying. "Folks, we've got to be close, and, with your help, we will find my family tomorrow," said Tom with a broad smile on his ruddy Irish face.

Again the audience started chanting, "Thomas ... Thomas ... Thomas ... Thomas."

"Please, go rest and be sharp tomorrow," he said.

The audience slowly exited the auditorium. Tom walked back to the long table where Thornton, Mike, Leroy, and Kellogg were seated, and he asked, "Did I miss much?"

Mike said, "I answered most of the important questions. You didn't miss much, Tom." Mike crushed the cigarette he was smoking into an ashtray in front of him, then he added, "You better take you medication and get some sleep."

"Yeah. Mike is right, Tom," agreed Thornton as he stood up and started to walk around the long table to join Tom. Thornton looked Tom in the eye and asked, "Where are you spending the night?"

"I'm gonna crash in my office," replied Tom.

Chapter Seven

Saturday, Day Six

It was 6:00 AM Saturday, day two of the search, and Tom was sitting alone on the stage in the auditorium. He was waiting for his staff. Adjacent to the stage, Tom's people had set up a table with fresh coffee and sweet rolls for the searchers. He was sitting alone, while Thornton and Mike were busy somewhere else in the building. While alone, he was organizing his thoughts and preparing what he would say to his staff of volunteer searchers that morning. Once the searchers started arriving, Tom began to mingle and talk with them. He tried to keep a personal relationship with each one of his employees; he considered them friends. Just before seven, Thornton and Mike returned to the auditorium, where they found Tom in the middle of the audience talking to several of his workers. From the middle of the audience, Tom saw Mike walk across the stage, approach the microphone, and shout, "Tom, it's time to get started." Tom thanked his employees for listening and he walked down the aisle and up onto the stage. Tom smiled at Mike and walked up to the microphone. "Good morning, folks. I hope you were all able to get some rest overnight. Our search yesterday covered quite a large bit of territory, which should leave us with a much smaller area to search this morning. As you all know, we are looking for that special farmhouse my son, Tommy, described. I do believe we will find that farmhouse sometime this morning. Unfortunately, the weather has definitely turned wet and cold. To help deal with the weather, I've rented two large buses. The first bus will be used as a communications center, and the second bus will be used for first aid and a place to get warm, dry, and fed. The buses will be located in the empty parking lot across from the Travelodge until we find the farmhouse, then we will move them near the farmhouse. Once we locate the farmhouse, then we'll all gather around it and give the kidnappers a show of solidarity. Good luck to all of you this morning, and, as always, my family and I deeply appreciate your efforts," said Tom as he saluted the audience and walked back to his seat.

Mike walked up to the microphone and said, "Are there any questions before we resume the search?" Apparently everyone knew where to go and what to do. There were no questions. The audience proceeded to leave the auditorium. By seven fifteen, Thornton was driving Mike and Tom in the black Lincoln Navigator as they joined the search.

*   *   *

By 8:00 AM, Lukas and Dagmar were standing across from the bear exhibition at the Cleveland Zoo. They were dressed similarly in lady's long winter coats. Lukas was wearing a long pageboy-style brunette wig, bold facial makeup, and a facial scarf, which covered the lower half of his face, his beard, and his chin whiskers. They were both using black umbrellas, as icy, cold, rain pellets were falling down and bouncing off their umbrellas.

The two of them were clutched arm in arm and pretended to be lesbian lovers, who were taking in the zoo attractions, unfortunately, on a terrible weather day. They walked past the bear exhibit to the north, then they retraced their way past the bear exhibit to the south. Lukas whispered, "Dagmar, there are agents hiding everywhere." He clung closer, knowing she was chilled.

She looked up into his eyes and whispered, "I see the man with the two gym bags. Is that Thomas Murphy?"

"It should be; let's go see," whispered Lukas. They turned back toward the bear exhibit and strolled along casually until they reached the closest spot to the exhibit. Lukas guided Dagmar up to the man, who was guarding the two big money-filled blue gym bags, and Lukas boldly said, "Pardon me, sir, but could you guide us to the reptile house?"

Agent John Barlow, who was the owner of the gym bags, looked directly into Lukas's gray eyes and said, "Ma'am, I believe the reptile house is about half a mile down that path." Lukas saw the agent smile and point to the north pathway. He instantly knew it was not the beaten and bruised face of Thomas Murphy.

Lukas guided Dagmar away from the bear exhibit, and once out of the agent's earshot, Lukas whispered, "Dagmar, that was not Thomas Murphy.

That was definitely an FBI stooge, who would be more than happy to arrest us."

"Lukas, you are very smart," uttered Dagmar. "Can we go now? I'm very cold."

"Yes my dear."

They hurried to the zoo exit.

* * *

By 9:00 AM, Lukas and Dagmar arrived back at the farmhouse where Boris, Stephan, and Hooter were impatiently waiting to see the thirty-million-dollar ransom. "Did you get the money?" asked Boris anxiously.

"Does it look like we're any richer, fool?" shouted Lukas as he angrily rushed into the living room still wearing facial makeup and angrily pulling off his woman's long wig.

"Lukas, was it a trap?" asked Stephan, who was still scared of his boss because of the way he had burned Tom.

Lukas looked sternly into Stephan's young face and said, "Yes, Stephan, it was a damn FBI trap." He walked into the kitchen and yelled for Boris, who came running. He told Boris to go get Mrs. Murphy and to bring her to the kitchen, where they could call the FBI hotline using his cell phone, which he believed was untraceable. While he waited for Tom's wife, he had Dagmar make him some hot coffee. He depended on her for everything. Once Boris brought Beth downstairs and into the kitchen, Lukas casually walked up to her and casually slapped her across the face. "Now that I have your attention, I'd like you to know that twice now the FBI has tried to trap me instead of giving me the ransom." He was furious, and he knew his behavior was scaring Beth. He took his cell phone out of his pocket, looked sternly at Beth, and said, "We are going to call the FBI kidnap hotline and you are to plead with your husband to quit the FBI and bring me the ransom himself. Do you understand?" He grabbed her by the back of her hair and repeated, "Do you understand?"

"Yes, I understand."

He quickly dialed the cell phone and on the third ring he heard, "This is Wanda at Just Clean It Up. How may I assist you?"

"Let me speak to Thomas Murphy."

"Mr. Murphy is not here at the moment," said Wanda, who knew that Lukas did not know that Tom and his people were combing the countryside looking for Tommy's described farmhouse.

"Wanda, who is in charge?"

"I'm the phone branch manager. May I assist you?"

"Wanda, I'm carrying dead weight."

"Sir, what are you referring to?"

"Listen to this," said Lukas as he switched the phone.

"Wanda, this is Beth Murphy." Her voice was so strained Wanda wondered if Lukas was holding a gun to her head.

"Beth, are you and the kids okay?" asked Wanda.

Lukas interrupted, "Wanda, if you ever want to see Beth alive again then you'll tell the FBI to stop interfering and tell Thomas he better get me my money." Lukas covered the phone, looked at Beth and said, "Tell her I will start killing your kids." Lukas handed Beth the phone instead of placing it at her ear as he had done before, giving her some freedom.

"Wanda, he's gonna kill my children. Help me," she pleaded as Lukas snatched the phone from her.

"Wanda, have Thomas there," demanded Lukas, "I'll call back in one hour, by 10:00 AM." He then ended the call.

* * *

By nine thirty, Beth returned to her three children on the second floor, which was an empty attic with no walls. Earlier, Beth and Jenny sat quietly on a dirty mattress in the center of the floor. From her mattress, she watched Danny stare out the upstairs front windows. Beth was terrified, but she tried not to show her fear to her children.

"Mom, what did he want?" asked Jenny as she shivered.

"Lukas wanted me to call your dad at the FBI."

"Did you talk to Dad?" Jenny asked anxiously.

"He wasn't there," said Beth, "He was probably searching for us." She hoped she was correct, but she was worried that Wanda would not be able to locate Tom within the hour when Lukas planned on calling back.

She got up off the mattress and walked over to where Danny was sitting staring out the upstairs front window. "What do you see, Danny?" she asked as she rubbed her hands on his arms to warm him.

"Mom, it's starting to snow," replied her youngest son. She could see he was also shivering. She looked at the empty fireplace and wished there was wood to burn to warm them. "Mom, when is Dad coming?"

Beth looked at her children. They were all just wearing light T-shirts and jeans, which was not keeping them warm enough. The cold winds were blowing in through the loose clapboards and chilling them all. "Danny, your dad will be here soon to take us home," promised his mother. She wondered when they would be rescued and how soon help would arrive. She was making herself crazy by wondering about facts out of her control. She was startled back into reality when her son Danny again asked, "When is Daddy coming, Mom?" She didn't know what to say to her son.

"Soon, Danny, real soon," she said, trying to reassure him.

"I don't want to spend another night here, Mom," complained Jenny as she wrung her hands in the small dirty blanket she was holding. "Is Daddy going to pay them the money?" she whimpered.

"I am sure your dad will come rescue us real soon, Jenny," replied Beth hoping her prediction would come true. "We all have to be brave and patient. Okay, kids?"

Tommy was sitting by the stairwell hoping to eavesdrop on the three guards, but they were either out of earshot or they were not speaking. Suddenly, Tommy sprang up off the floor where he had been sitting for the last hour, and he hurried over to his mother. "Mom, this would be a perfect time for me to escape out the window, to slide down the downspout, and to then run for help. Dad doesn't even know where we are," urged Tommy with a gleam of excitement in his eager eyes.

"Tommy, you said your dad wanted us to all stay together. That is what he told you when you spoke on the phone," explained Beth, who was torn between them staying together and Tommy making an attempt at sneaking out. She was as scared as she could be. She was scared for her kids, and she was scared Tom would not be able to find them. "No, Tommy. We might make them mad if they returned and found you missing," she rationalized. "We'd better stay together. We don't want to upset them."

"Mom, you're right," agreed Tommy, "but it is so hard waiting." She felt his impatience.

"I know, honey," said Beth as she wrapped her arms around her oldest son and tried to hold back her tears.

"It's okay, Mom. Dad will make the exchange soon," said Tommy, trying to be brave.

Beth kept wrapping her children in blankets because the building was cold. The outside cold wind came right through the leaky clapboards, chilling them severely. There were fireplaces on the first and second floors, but there was no firewood to be seen. A fire would be nice, she thought, as she clutched the covers up around Danny's neck and shoulders.

The weather had turned cold early that autumn and the rain was turning to early snow. The winds had picked up, creating a chill factor, which made things seem even colder than they actually were.

Tommy, being brave, gave up his blanket to his sister, and he stationed himself back at the front window where Danny had been. After an hour of staring out the window, Tommy shouted, "We need firewood!" Next, Beth heard one of the guards stomping up the stairs. What does he want? she wondered.

"What are you doing up here?" the guard demanded as he cleared the stairwell and stepped onto the second floor.

Tommy jumped up off the floor and shouted, "My mom and my brother and sister are cold. Make a fire. Bring me wood." Beth watched as the guard barked at her son and shoved him back down onto the floor.

"Don't hurt him," she pleaded as she stepped toward the guard. He slapped her, and she fell onto the mattress next to Danny and Jenny.

Tommy was incensed by the guard hitting his mother, and he charged the guard, who was twice his size. Once the boy made contact with the guard, he was thrown back, hitting his head hard on the windowsill frame and knocking him unconscious.

"You are a bully," shrieked Beth as she ran to her oldest son.

The guard snarled and mechanically said, "No fire."

Beth watched the guard turn and walk back downstairs. She cradled her son's head; his eyes were closed. How bad could it get? she worried.

*   *   *

By 9:15 AM Saturday, Agent Barlow was preparing to brief Wanda on Lukas's next call. The FBI hotline remained silent while Agent Barlow schemed and plotted his next move. He paged Wanda from her desk at the phone branch, and she quickly walked over to the FBI hotline, where Agent Barlow was waiting. "Hello, Wanda," said Agent Barlow as he pointed at the seat next to his desk. "Please have a seat. We need to talk."

"Have you heard from Tom?" she asked as she took the seat next to his desk.

"Yes. That is why I asked to talk to you. Tom called me a moment ago," lied Agent Barlow. "We've mutually agreed that he should deliver the ransom by himself without the help from the FBI." Agent Barlow knew he had not gotten a call from Tom Murphy. He knew Tom was still in Lake County searching with his staff, but Barlow had a devious plan, which required he lie to Wanda. Lying did not make Agent Barlow feel uncomfortable or guilty. It came easily to him. He pulled a pack of cigarettes out of his shirt pocket and offered one to Wanda, who smiled politely and shook her head, indicating no. He lit up and put the pack back into his shirt pocket. "Tom has informed me that he wants to give his thirty million himself without the FBI involved," explained Agent Barlow as he continued to lie to Wanda.

"Exactly what should I say to Krueger when he calls?" she asked suspiciously.

Agent Barlow proceeded to tell Wanda all the details of his big, bloated lie, and after she left the FBI unit, he set in motion the details of his plan. He knew he would be the man with the two gym bags with the fake currency and the GPS tracking device, not Tom Murphy. This time he would be dressed as a common street derelict, with a dozen other agents waiting nearby to assist him.

Agent Barlow knew that making an exchange at noon would give him plenty of time because Tom Murphy was in Lake County and would be there for the balance of the day. Agent Barlow considered Tom's search a hopeless cause, which he laughed at from the warm, dry confines of his FBI hotline unit.

* * *

Lukas looked at his wristwatch, saw it was 10:00 AM, and he dialed the FBI hotline. Wanda answered, "This is Wanda at Just Clean It Up. How may I assist you?"

"Wanda, this is Lukas Krueger. Let me talk to Tom Murphy," he said boldly.

"Mr. Krueger, Tom couldn't be here to take your call. He has fired the FBI, and he is waiting for you with his own personal thirty million dollars. He wants to exchange the money for his family."

"No FBI?" asked Lukas suspiciously.

"Correct! There will be no FBI."

"Wanda, if this is another trick I'll start killing those lovely redheaded children of his," threatened Lukas.

"That won't be necessary, Mr. Krueger," she stressed.

"Where and when?"

"Tom will be dressed like a bum in front of the Baricelli Restaurant on Cornell Road in Little Italy at noon," explained Wanda, who then held her breath, hoping this international kidnapper would not object to the arrangements. "Do you know the location?"

"Yes," replied Lukas. "And be there in two hours. High noon!" He hung up. He looked across the kitchen table at Dagmar and said, "I do not trust them! It better not be another deception."

* * *

At 11:45 AM, Lukas drove Dagmar into the community of Little Italy. As he parked on Murray Hill Road, he looked across the front seat of his black panel van and said, "Dagmar, this may be another trap! So keep your ears and eyes open." He reached over and ran his hand affectionately down her soft cheek. He instructed her to wait, then he climbed out of the van, locked the door, and ran around to her side of the van to help her get out. Even under stress, Lukas was still chivalrous. Together, while still wearing the same female costumes they wore earlier at the zoo, they walked hand in hand down Murray Hill Road, then they turned right onto Cornell Road. As they slowly walked down Cornell, they were on the lookout for suspicious-looking people, who could be undercover FBI agents. They walked half way down Cornell, then they looked across the road at the Baricelli Restaurant. Foot traffic in the area was quite heavy, and so Lukas had trouble distinguishing civilians from feds. They stood across from the restaurant at exactly twelve noon. "Dagmar, look! There is the bum that Wanda had promised," whispered Lukas as they stood out in their lesbian costumes like a fragile ice sculpture placed in the desert.

"Should we both walk over to see if the bum is Thomas?" asked Dagmar as the midday weather turned bitter.

"I'm not sure," whispered Lukas. "If it is the same agent from this morning at the zoo, then he may remember us." He stood contemplating.

"Lukas, what should we do?" she asked as she started shivering in the cold.

"I'll go by myself," whispered Lukas as he let go of their embrace, adjusted his black umbrella against the weather and stepped into the road. Traffic on Cornell was light so he had no trouble getting across to the front of the Baricelli Restaurant. The bum, while holding two gym bags, was standing to the right of the entrance of the restaurant. Lukas stopped at the restaurant's front doors; he checked his wristwatch, then he turned left and casually walked past the bum, who appeared not to notice him. Lukas looked for Thomas's left facial wounds, and when the bum appeared absent of such impairments, then he quickly knew the bum with the gym bags was not Thomas Murphy. Without breaking stride, Lukas continued down Cornell until he reached Circle Drive. He then doubled back to where he had left Dagmar, who was by then shivering quite severely. "It's not Thomas," he whispered when he reached Dagmar.

"Lets go home! I'm freezing," she uttered.

He wrapped his arms around her, and they hurried back to the van. Once in the van, Lukas immediately turned the heater up and said, "It was another trap by the same FBI agent. I recognized him from this morning at the zoo."

"You told me Thomas fired the FBI," she replied.

"Thomas may not have even known about this trap," said Lukas as he defended Tom Murphy.

* * *

By one o'clock Saturday afternoon, Checkers was walking into the wind with ice pellets hitting him in his face, but he was determined to push on in hopes that he'd be the one to find the farmhouse where the Murphy family was being kept. The next farmhouse he approached was a rundown clapboard building in need of a fresh coat of paint and much repair. As he walked up the long driveway, he wondered if this next property might be the one that held the Murphy family. He walked half way up the long gravel driveway, then started yelling, "Here, Trooper! Here, Trooper! Here, Trooper!"

As he reached the house, he was suddenly startled when an armed man stepped out of the wraparound open front porch. "What do you want?" shouted an armed man who swung a military rifle from his shoulder and aimed it straight at Checkers.

The hairs on the back of Checkers neck stood up, but he played it cool and replied, "Have you seen my dog, Trooper?" He looked at the military rifle and instantly suspected this was where the Murphys were being kept.

"Get out of here! There are no dogs around here," said the man mechanically.

"I think I saw my dog run up your driveway," said Checkers enthusiastically. He then stepped one foot closer toward the man, testing his resolve. "My dog escaped from a cache of crazy kennel coughing K-9s, and I just can't find him," said Checkers in a singsong sort of way. He loved to play with words, but perhaps this was not the best time.

The armed man swung his rifle in a fluid motion and smacked Checkers in the mouth, knocking him onto the ground. "Go away! This is private property," grunted the man.

"Hold on, buddy! I'm just looking for my dog."

"This is private property," the man snarled, "get off this property!"

Checkers raised his hands as if he were going to surrender, then he shouted, "Trooper! Trooper!" He cupped his hands around his mouth and yelled for his pretend dog. Checkers jumped up off the ground.

The armed man stepped forward and again with one smooth move he hit Checkers harder with the butt of the rifle. This time Checkers fell to the ground like a bag of wet laundry. As he collected himself, he wiped the blood from his mouth and shouted, "What'd you do that for?" The armed man stood over him, grunting. Then Checkers scrambled to his feet and ran down the driveway away from the dilapidated farmhouse. Once he reached the end of the driveway, he heard the armed man screaming something in a foreign language, which set off a signal in Checkers mind. This must be where they are keeping the Murphy family, thought Checkers as he continued to run for cover. He turned right and ran down the road; then he ducked into a thick wooded area where he knew he could not be seen. He had a holster strapped to his right leg; the holster held a strongly powered walkie-talkie for communicating back to the search headquarters. He called in and was patched directly to Tom Murphy's mobile radio.

"What is it, Checkers?" squawked Tom.

"I found them, Tom," whispered Checkers, trying not to be heard by anyone from the suspicious farmhouse. "I found an armed guard at a rundown farmhouse on Apple Trail Road. The man ran me off. What do we do?"

"Good work, Checkers," said Tom. "Give me that location again." Checkers repeated the information, described the area, and conversed with his boss for several minutes. Then Tom said, "Stand by. We'll get back to you in a few minutes."

"Okay, boss."

Checkers put his walkie-talkie on standby, and he sat down onto the cold, damp ground, keeping himself as minimal a target as possible. Adrenaline raced through his body. Could this be where Lukas was keeping his hostages? thought Checkers. Could we be this fortunate? wondered Checkers.

As Checkers sat in a little forest on the wet ground, sleety ice pellets dropped down on him. He felt the chill on the ground penetrate up through his legs and butt. As he sat on the ground among the trees, he watched as the ice pellets fell down through the trees. What had been a chilly, rainy autumn day had now become near freezing with big, dark, snowy-looking clouds dotting the skyline.

Checkers waited five minutes, then Tom radioed back and said, "Thornton and I don't trust the FBI because they keep screwing up. And so I want you to approach the armed man out front and tell him Murphy wants to pay them directly. Checkers, tell them I have the thirty million, and I will trade the money for my family, unharmed. Checkers, make them show you my wife and all three kids. Make sure they are unharmed. Do you have any questions, Checkers?"

Checkers finished talking to Tom, clicked off his walkie-talkie, and strapped it back on his right leg. He took a deep cleansing breath, climbed up off the cold, damp ground and proceeded to walk out of the wooded thicket. It took him a few minutes to walk back to the driveway, during which time he ratcheted up his courage. He walked confidently toward the farmhouse as ice pellets hit his face, chilling him. "I hope this is the right farmhouse," he thought. He raised his hands over his head and walked toward the armed man, who remained sitting on the front steps of the wraparound open front porch. He made it half way up the long driveway when suddenly the man noticed him and shouted, "Go away! Go away!"

The man raised his rifle and aimed at Checkers, who stopped short and shouted, "Good news! Mr. Murphy wants to pay you thirty million dollars."

The man slowly lowered his rifle and mechanically shouted, "Murphy, pay millions?"

"Yes. Pay millions!"

The man slowly waved Checkers forward, and when he reached the steps the man repeated, "Pay millions?"

"Yes. Pay millions!"

The man grabbed Checkers by his shoulder and walked him up the front steps and onto the front porch. Once they were on the front porch, the man shouted something in a foreign language, and, moments later, other armed men came onto the front porch from inside the farmhouse. "My name is Boris," uttered the first man, who continued to appear language challenged. He looked at the other man and said, "Murphy wants to pay us!"

The second of the two new men pushed Boris aside and said, "My name is Hooter. What are you telling me?"

Checkers took a deep breath and said, "Mr. Murphy wants to give you the money in exchange for his family, with no one getting hurt." Checkers held his breath, anxiously.

"Who are you?" asked Boris.

"My name is Checkers. I work for Murphy. He wants to bring the thirty million to Lukas."

"Lukas is not here," blurted Stephan. "My name is Stephan."

"Shut up!" shouted Boris, shoving Stephan for having given away information. Boris seemed to be in charge in Lukas's absence, thought Checkers.

"Where is Lukas?" asked Checkers.

"He'll be back," said Boris. "Where is Murphy?"

"Murphy is close. I can talk to him with my radio," said Checkers as he pointed at his walkie-talkie that was strapped to his leg.

Stephan stepped up to Checkers and pushed him down onto a couch that sat in the corner of the porch. Next, the three men stepped away from Checkers. They had a brief conversation, which Checkers understood to be that they wanted to get the money for themselves before Lukas could return. Checkers pretended not to hear. Finally, Stephan stepped over to Checkers and said, "Call Murphy. I will exchange the money for his beautiful family." Stephan reached down and pulled Checkers back to his feet.

As Checkers landed on his feet, he asked, "What's your name?" He was trying to get straight the names of the men.

"Stephan!"

"Okay, Stephan," said Checkers as he grabbed his walkie-talkie and proceeded to radio Murphy. Once they made contact Checkers said, "Tom, Lukas isn't here, but one of his men named Stephan wants to make the exchange of the money for your family."

Tom replied, "Make Stephan show you my family and prove they are safe."

Checkers radioed back, "Okay Tom, I will get back to you." He clicked off the radio, turned to Stephan, and said, "Show me the Murphy family."

The three men took Checkers into the living room of the farmhouse, then they took him upstairs, where he found Beth and the three children. The Murphys simultaneously shouted Checkers's name, and the youngest boy, Danny, jumped up off the ground and ran over to him. They were not hooded, which meant they had seen their captors. Checkers knew the Murphys were not meant to survive. Since the kidnappers had let Beth and the kids see their faces, they were disposable, thought Checkers as he hugged little Danny and embraced Beth, Tommy, and Jenny. He looked at Beth sympathetically and said, "Tom is coming to get you and the kids."

"Thank you, Checkers," said Beth as she hugged him.

Stephan stepped up and as he grabbed Checkers, he said, "Come! Call Murphy!" Stephan led Checkers back downstairs away from the other two men and the Murphy family.

Once downstairs, Checkers radioed Tom and told him that Beth and the kids were just fine and to proceed. After Checkers had communicated with Tom, Tom talked with Stephan, and all the details of the exchange were worked out between them. When Stephan went back upstairs to talk with the other two men, Checkers slipped out of the farmhouse unseen. He quickly ran to the two vehicles that were parked inside the big garage. He used his pocketknife to slash the rear tires. All the vehicles were backed in, facing out of the garage toward the farmhouse. Just as he finished, a small van drove up the driveway with Lukas behind the wheel and Dagmar at his side. He watched them park next to the two other vehicles while he hid in the garage. After Lukas and Dagmar had gone into the farmhouse, Checkers, who was hiding behind the last vehicle, scurried into the big garage. Being in the garage protected him from the wind and rain/snow mix. He walked to the back wall of the garage, hoping not to be heard, and he radioed Tom to tell him that Lukas had returned. While talking on the radio, Checkers heard three distinct gunshots. "Oh, shit, Tom! There are gunshots coming from within the farmhouse," he whispered.

"Stay hidden, Checkers," said Tom over the radio. "We will be there soon."

Checkers broke off radio contact, and he wondered why there were shots fired in the farmhouse. There were four Murphys but only three gunshot sounds. He wanted to investigate, without getting shot himself. He decided to strap the radio back on his leg, and then he cautiously hurried over to Lukas's black van and proceeded to slash the two rear tires. Then he returned to the rear of the garage. He was worried about the three shots, and he hoped that Tom and Thornton would be there soon. Hopefully, before there were any more gunshots.

* * *

By 2:00 PM, while Checkers was outside, Lukas and Dagmar entered the farmhouse and proceeded through the living room and into the kitchen where Lukas found Boris, Stephan, and Hooter all sitting at the kitchen table. Boris was strumming his finger tips nervously on the tabletop. "What happened at the exchange, Lukas?" asked Boris, who was trying to hide his nervousness.

Lukas, still wearing his female attire, looked suspiciously at Boris, Hooter, and Stephan, and said, "The exchange was another FBI trap, which we were able to avoid." He stood there as he removed his page boy wig, and he noticed his three teammates were acting nervously. "What is happening? You all seem apprehensive. What is going on?" asked Lukas as he wiped makeup off his face with a wet kitchen towel.

"Lukas, good news," declared Boris sheepishly. "One of Murphy's men came to the front door. All Murphy wants is his family. He is bringing the money here to us." Lukas could see that Boris was scared by the way his hands were shaking as he spoke.

"One of Murphy's men was here?" asked Lukas.

"Yes!" uttered Boris, "but all they want are the family members." Lukas could see the fear in Boris's big, brown eyes. "They were very friendly," added Boris, who appeared scared and apprehensive.

"Boris, did you ever consider they could trap us here at the farmhouse?" calmly asked Lukas as he took a deep breath and shouted,

"Boris! Come into the living room." He watched as Boris slowly got up from the kitchen table, and they walked into the living room together.

"Are the other men in agreement?" asked Lukas flatly.

"Yes, Lukas."

"Then go bring them here."

He saw Boris exhale anxiously. "I will bring the men," said Boris as he turned and hurried to the kitchen, where the other two men of Team One where still sitting.

While Lukas waited for the men to come, he looked at Dagmar and whispered, "They've tried to cheat us. We must now kill them."

Boris and the other two men came into the living room. Lukas looked sternly at his three men, then he looked at Boris scornfully and asked, "Why did you invite Murphy here where we can be trapped?"

"He only wants his family," said Boris fearfully.

"He may say that, but he will send the FBI in to arrest all of us," explained Lukas rationally.

"Lukas, they were very reassuring," pleaded Boris.

Lukas stared at the man, then replied, "Were you trying to take the money when I was away and cheat me?"

"Lukas, I would never cheat you!" begged Boris.

"I do not believe you," said Lukas as he drew his weapon, fired, and struck Boris between his eyes. He watched Boris fall backwards, hitting the floor. Instantly Dagmar backed up Lukas by fatally shooting the other two men. "Now only you and I will share the thirty million," said Lukas with a heinous smile on his deadly cold face. Lukas watched as Dagmar checked the bodies to make sure all three were dead. "Let's move the bodies to the pantry outside the kitchen," suggested Lukas as he reached down and started dragging Boris's corpse through the living room, into the kitchen, and then finally positioning him in the pantry. Dagmar helped him move the remaining two men to a spot next to Boris.

After they were finished hiding the three bodies, Lukas said, "I do not want the Murphy family to discover the bodies in the pantry."

"There is a blue tarp folded on a shelf in the pantry. Do you want me to cover them?" asked Dagmar helpfully.

"Yes." Lukas ran his hand down along her waist. "You always have such good ideas. Go cover them." He playfully spanked her on her tight, firm bottom.

He watched as she teasingly pranced into the kitchen as if nothing had happened, and then she disappeared into the pantry. He picked up a damp, dirty dish towel off the big sofa in the living room, and he tried wiping up the traces of blood that were on the throw rug, which was positioned in the center of the room. By the time he was finished, Dagmar walked in and asked, "Who else can we kill?" He laughed as she smiled teasingly.

"Don't make light of betrayers," said Lukas. "I hate traitors."

While they stood in the living room, he looked at Dagmar, and he said, "We'll leave with Beth and the children. Later, we'll call Thomas Murphy to establish a safer exchange place where we won't be trapped. Now, let's get the family moving."

*   *   *

While Lukas was executing the three men, Checkers was quietly slashing the rear tires of Lukas's vehicle. He went to the rear of the garage to hide and call Tom to tell him what was happening. Moments after he radioed Tom, he searched the back wall of the garage, where there were assorted tools hanging from a peg board. He quickly scanned the tools, looking for a weapon he could use against Lukas. He spotted a short-handled sledgehammer, which he quickly grabbed, and then he returned to the front of the garage to continue his lookout.

He heard them coming out on the front porch. He carefully watched as Lukas led Beth, and Dagmar led the three children at gunpoint down the front porch steps. "Hurry," shouted Lukas. Checkers watched from his hiding spot in the garage as the kidnappers awkwardly walked the Murphy family toward Lukas's awaiting van. May be Lukas shot Boris, Stephan, and Hooter, thought Checkers as he watched them approach Lukas's black-paneled van.

Lukas found the slashed rear tires. "Dagmar, the tires are flat. We'll take another vehicle," said Lukas as he and Dagmar walked the family toward the two other vehicles. Unfortunately, Lukas found that all the vehicles had flat rear tires. He was incensed. He was trapped with no vehicle in which to escape. "Hurry! Into the house," screamed Lukas as Checkers watched from the garage. How soon would Tom arrive? Checkers wondered.

*   *   *

At that moment, Tom pulled into the long, gravel and dirt driveway and raced toward the farmhouse, stopping short by about three car lengths. Once stopped, he and Thornton popped open their doors and crouched down, using their doors as shields. "Let them go, Lukas," Tom shouted as he aimed his weapon at Lukas. He saw his family and Lukas and Dagmar all grouped together in front of the shiny black van that had been backed into the four-bay garage. "Let them go," repeated Tom, just as he saw Lukas grab Beth and put his gun to her temple. At the same time, he saw Dagmar do the same thing to Jenny. Tom was frantic as he watched Lukas walk Beth backwards toward the farmhouse. "Let them go," shouted Tom. Neither he nor Thornton had a clear shot at them. How were they going to rescue his family? he wondered. He watched as Lukas walked himself and Beth backwards up the front porch steps. Tom realized that Lukas was using Beth as a human shield to protect himself from any shots he or Thornton might try to make.

"Where is my money?" asked Lukas in a stern voice.

"Lukas, I have your money," shouted Tom determinately.

Tom watched breathlessly as Checkers crept up behind the vehicles, away from the safety of his hiding place. Slowly, he sneaked closer and closer toward Lukas until he was just a few feet behind Lukas. Tom watched as Checkers stepped forward and, unfortunately, onto a dry pile of noisy autumn leaves, which snapped and crackled, giving away his presence. Lukas instantly spun around and fired a shot at Checkers. Fortunately, Tom saw Checkers duck as Lukas's shot went wild. Lukas dragged Beth farther up the porch steps, almost to the porch door, followed by Dagmar and Jenny. Tom saw that Danny and Tommy were standing alone, frozen in fright. Then he saw Checkers run up and scoop up little Danny and shout for Tommy to follow him. While Lukas and Beth were now at the porch door, unfortunately, Dagmar and Jenny were still standing out in the open, several feet away from the porch steps. "Where is my money?" screamed Lukas as he reached for the doorknob.

"Lukas, I have your money," again shouted Tom as he saw Lukas open the porch door and start to enter. Tom was watching from his Lincoln while Dagmar stood holding Jenny, now several feet from the steps. Suddenly, Tommy rushed up from behind and pushed Dagmar, causing her to fall forward, letting go of Jenny, and dropping her handgun onto the ground. Tommy hesitated momentarily, then Tom screamed, "Tommy, grab her gun!" He watched as his son responded.

Tommy sprang forward, grabbed Dagmar's handgun from the thinly snow-covered ground and shouted, "Don't move lady!" Tom's heart swelled with admiration for his son as he and Thornton slammed the Lincoln's doors shut and ran to help Tommy.

As the porch door closed, Lukas noticed Dagmar wasn't near him, and he desperately screamed, "Dagmar, get over here!" Tom saw his wife disappear behind the porch door.

As Tom hurried to help his son, he shouted, "Tommy, hold her!" When he reached his son, he quickly took the gun from him, looked at him with a grin of approval and said, "You did good, Tommy!" Tom reached down and helped Darmar to her feet. He turned Dagmar so she was facing the farmhouse and pushed her gun into the small of her back. He again looked at his son, and, with his free hand, he ruffled his son's red hair affectionately. "Tommy, you saved your sister. Way to go!" Tom saw that Checkers had both young Danny and his sister Jenny as they rushed up to Tom. "Checkers, take them to the bus. You did great, Checkers. I owe you big time," said Tom.

"Come on, boys," said Checkers as he carried Jenny and led the boys down the driveway, away from the farmhouse, and hopefully to the safety of the bus.

Tom and Thornton and Dagmar all followed Checkers down the driveway to the street, where they could get on the bus and get out of the worsening weather. The first big bus had just arrived and Checkers led the three children up the steps, followed by Tom, Thornton, and Dagmar. While Tom checked his children in the rear of the bus, Thornton restrained the lovely Dagmar. After spending some tender time with his children, Tom walked up front, looked at Thornton and said, "Lukas still has Beth."

"Yeah. But we have Dagmar to use as leverage," said Thornton as he rubbed his hands for warmth.

"That's right, boss," said Checkers, "Lukas is gonna want his girlfriend back real bad."

After Tom checked with Thornton, he went back to the rear of the bus to spend some time with his children. Tom hugged each one of his children, then asked about their mother. "She is real cold, Dad," explained Danny, the youngest of the three children.

"Danny, we're gonna go get her real soon," said Tom as he affectionately rubbed his son's red-haired head. Tom told his children to stay in the rear of the bus, where they could get warm and soon eat a warm meal! He ran to the front of the bus to talk with Thornton. Tom was worried about his wife, who remained with the monster.

*   *   *

Lukas dragged Beth into the living room, put his gun back in its holster, and then he slapped her across her face, causing her to fall down onto the old, threadbare sofa that was in the middle of the living room. "You are a poor exchange for Dagmar," said Lukas as he posed to strike her again. He stood standing over her as he contemplated his next move. "Go back upstairs," he shouted as he pulled her up off the sofa and dragged her up the stairs in a fit of rage. Once upstairs, he physically threw Beth back onto the mattress that lay in the middle of the room. "Shut up," Lukas screamed. He felt desperate to retrieve Dagmar. They were never apart, he realized.

"Beth, if Thomas hurts Dagmar, then I will kill you slowly and painfully," threatened Lukas as he nervously paced back and forth on the creaky floorboards of the second floor of the dilapidated farmhouse.

"Tom won't hurt her," declared Beth as she slowly got up off the old, dirty mattress.

"That is where we are different," said Lukas. "I will hurt you." He looked at her with his dead eyes.

He looked out the front windows and saw several vehicles parked at the end of his driveway and on the apron of his driveway. Tom's Lincoln remained parked just outside the front of the farmhouse.

He wondered if he could attempt an escape with Beth using Tom's black Lincoln Navigator. Had Tom accidentally left the keys in the ignition in his haste? wondered Lukas. But he could not leave without Dagmar. He had killed his three traitorous helpers, and he had lost Dagmar. He was desperate. He wanted to escape with Dagmar at his side with the ransom money. He had never failed, but now things looked bleak. He knew he had to calm down and sort through his options. He had Beth to bargain with, and he figured that was his point of strength.

Lukas left Beth to herself, and he walked downstairs to fix some hot coffee and to concentrate on the situation. He heated some water, then made coffee, which he hoped would settle his upset nerves. He was desperate to get Dagmar back at his side. He sat down at the kitchen table and slowly sipped his hot coffee. He could hear the upstairs floorboards creak as Mrs. Murphy paced back and forth. "She must be as stressed as I am," he thought as he continued to sip his hot coffee. "I must plan my options," he thought, "and I must turn these bad events into good ones."

*   *   *

By 3:00 PM, Tom and Checkers had moved Tom's three children from bus one to bus two, which had just arrived. Bus one was basically a command center and a communications center, while bus two was a first aid center and a mobile kitchen with warm food and drinks. The three children were moved to bus two to receive warmth, food, and first aid. Tom could not get enough hugs from his three children, who were truly glad to see their father; at the same time, he was deathly worried about their mother. Inside of bus two, Tom was helping his children get a warm mug of cocoa. Tommy looked at his dad and said, "Dad, I want to tell you something."

"Sure Tommy, what is it?"

"While all the kidnappers were downstairs, we heard three shots, and after that we only saw Lukas and Dagmar. I think they shot the other three men," explained Tommy as he sipped his warm cocoa.

"Really," replied Tom. "Checkers mentioned that on the radio just after the three shots rang out."

"Yeah, I heard the shots," said Checkers, "while I was slashing the tires."

"So maybe there aren't five kidnappers, but only Lukas and Dagmar," Tom speculated as he held Danny on his lap. "That changes things a lot."

While Checkers was helping Jenny fix a sandwich, he said, "Tom, why don't you run that idea over to Thornton and Mike?"

Tom lifted Danny off his lap, sat him on a seat, and said, "I will run this by the guys." He stood up and proceeded to leave. "Kids, stay here with Checkers while I meet with Thor and Mike in bus one to figure a safe way to get your mom," he urged his three children. He kissed Danny and Jenny on their foreheads. Then he ruffled Tommy's hair because he was too old to kiss. "I'll be back," he reassured.

Tom stepped off of bus two and immediately felt the snow in the air. He ran toward bus one and met Thornton and Mike as they reached the door to the bus. Once he stepped inside the bus, the other two men felt the warmth inside the bus. The three of them got a fresh Styrofoam cup of hot coffee, and then they found an empty table to sit at and strategize. "Listen, guys, Tommy and Checkers both heard three gunshots, and since then, no one has seen the three other kidnappers. I agree with them, Lukas may have killed them either as traitors, trying to get the ransom for themselves, or Lukas may have eliminated them to sweeten the pot in a two-way ransom split rather than a five-way split. What do you two think?" asked Tom.

"I'd like to know for sure," said Thornton.

"Can we find out for sure?" asked Mike.

"There isn't any way to know for sure," said Tom, "but maybe we'll just operate on the assumption that they are dead until we find out otherwise."

"Okay, we're going on the assumption that the three other kidnappers are dead," stated Thornton as he sipped his hot coffee and sniffed because his nose was running from the cold outside.

"Okay! Next, let's talk about trading to get Beth back," said Tom. "We gotta move fast."

"This gets tricky," said Mike as he cleared his throat and then pointed at Tom to continue.

Tom whispered, "Okay!" then he raised his hands in a gesture asking them to wait. After a moment of silence Tom said, "I want to trade Beth for Dagmar, my Lincoln, and the money. Krueger should jump at that offer." Tom waited for his two friends to respond. Tom looked at Mike, who had a frown on his face. "Mike, what do you think?" He had known Mike for years, and he could instantly tell something was bothering him.

"Tom, I think you're getting ahead of yourself. Down the road, you can give Lukas all your stuff, but for now, I see a bigger problem." Mike rubbed his hands together from being out in the cold weather, which was getting worse by the hour.

"Mike, what are you saying?"

"You exchange Dagmar for Beth, and you're left alone with two killers. Krueger could back-shoot you and Beth," explained Mike Max.

"He's right," added Thornton as he nervously rubbed his shaven head. "Even if I had my rifle, I couldn't stop them fast enough."

"What do you all suggest?"

"A substitute for Beth," said Mike.

"A substitute that could possibly take Krueger out," said Thornton as he sipped his hot coffee.

"Who do you suggest, Mike?" asked Tom, who was confused as he drank his coffee. They were all chilled from being out in the cold late-autumn snowy weather.

"I know who he's getting at," said Thornton.

"Let me explain," said Mike. "We need a capable substitute for Dagmar. Someone to keep Lukas from back-shooting the two of you."

Yeah. From a security standpoint, Mike is right on the money," said Thornton.

Tom was getting anxious for them to get to the point. He scratched his head and demanded, "Who?"

Mike leaned forward toward Tom as if he were about to let out a national security leak. "A woman named Gina Rosette."

"Gina. She works for me." Tom was suspicious and confused all at the same time. "Why Gina?" he asked.

"She is the right size, identical to Dagmar."

"Yeah, but, the hair and face are totally different."

"Tom, listen, she wants to do it," said Mike, "and right now she is at a beauty parlor having her black hair dyed blond. They are giving her a pixy cut. When she gets here, we'll just borrow Dagmar's clothes for the exchange."

Tom sat thinking. He finished his coffee and looked seriously at Mike Max for a brief moment. "Mike, what about her face?" he asked with a tone of resignation.

"Not a problem. We've already got a mask made out of thin felt, which she can partially see through, but Krueger won't be able to see her facial features," said Mike with a triumphant smile.

"Mike, isn't Gina prior military?" asked Tom with a vague recall of her background.

"Yeah. Gina has a black belt," said Mike. "She is a self-defense expert, who can possibly groin kick or sucker punch Krueger the minute they make contact. Do you see the beauty of this plan, Tom?"

"Yeah. I see," said Tom as he casually ran his hands through his coppery-red hair.

"With luck, she'll overpower him," said Thornton, "and we'll possibly capture him on the spot."

"Wouldn't that be something?" gloated Mike.

Tom started to climb out of his seat at their round table. "Wait! I gotta get a refill on my coffee," said Tom as he walked to the rear of bus one. While he was getting his coffee, he was evaluating the risk to Gina. Sure she wanted to help, he thought. But still, she would be taking a big risk. He refilled his coffee and was walking back to the table. "Guys, it's a big risk."

"Sure, but the odds are in your favor with Gina's help," said Mike. "Where's my refill?" he asked Tom, and they all laughed, letting off a little tension.

Tom agreed to the plan, which sounded safe, but not foolproof. He was concerned for Gina's safety. Mike told Tom that most likely Gina would help in capturing Lukas at the site of the exchange. Tom voiced a concern for the possible other three kidnappers, which they were not sure were not still in the farmhouse, and who could come to Lukas's aid. Thornton explained, "I could hold them off with my rifle if they were still alive and came to Lukas's aid. But I'll need to go to the facility because my rifle is in the trunk of my car."

"I'll drive you back to get your rifle," said Mike. "We have to pick up Gina at the beauty parlor anyway." Tom knew he could rely on Thornton, who was a sharpshooter with his rifle. Tom thought that Thornton should get his rifle in the event they had to hold off the remainder of Lukas's Team One. Tom and the others did not know for sure if Boris, Stephan, and Hooter had been executed by Lukas and Dagmar. Tom did not want to take any unnecessary chances.

Before Mike and Thornton left, Tom suggested they get a bullhorn from the facility in order to communicate with Krueger. Mike asked, "Did your son Tommy remember the telephone number from the farmhouse when he used it the other night to call?"

"That would be helpful," said Tom. "I'll go find out while you're gone, Mike." He doubted if his son would have had time in that dark kitchen, but he promised Mike, and so he would ask his son. "Don't forget the bullhorn, Thor. There is one in my office."

"Okay, Tom."

"So, you're going to get Gina, the rifle, and the bullhorn, but whatever you do, don't bring back any police or FBI. Try not to let them see you. Be invisible!"

"Okay, boss," giggled Thornton as he and Mike stood up from the table and shook hands with Tom.

After the two men left, Tom went back to the driveway of the farmhouse to see if there were any activities. Everything at the farmhouse appeared quiet, so he returned to bus one to talk to Leroy, who was in the rear of the bus conducting the needed communications. As Tom walked down the aisle of the bus, he saw Leroy sitting at his radio equipment. "Leroy, how is it going?" asked Tom as he reached his dispatcher.

"Boss, we're bringing all the searchers to this location," said Leroy as he pulled off his earphones. Tom wanted a show of force and his staff would provide that. He proceeded to tell Leroy where Thornton and Mike had gone and why they were there. Once Leroy was brought up to date, then Tom went to bus two to visit with his three children. When Tom entered bus two, he headed straight for his children, who were still visiting quietly with Checkers. "Hi, kids! Is Checkers keeping you company?"

Jenny stood up and shouted, "When is Mom coming out?"

"Real soon, sweetie," said her father, who stepped closer and hugged her reassuringly. After he set Jenny back down, he looked over at Tommy, and he asked, "Tommy, would you happen to remember the telephone number at the farmhouse?"

"Yes! I had a pencil, and so I wrote the number on the palm of my hand in case we might need it," said Tommy with a smile on his young, ruddy, Irish face.

"Tommy, your grandparents would be proud of you," said Tom with a proud grin on his ruddy Irish face. He turned Tommy's hand over, and there was the telephone number to Krueger's farmhouse. "Bless you, child, you probably saved your dear mother's life." Tom pulled out a pen from his shirt pocket and proceeded to copy the number on the left sleeve of his denim jacket. After he finished copying the number, he hugged Tommy and told Checkers to stay with them. He ran to bus one, hurried down the aisle to where Leroy was waiting for him, and gave him the number. Leroy tried the number by using his cell phone, and it rang. "Hang up!" shouted Tom, "I don't want to talk to him yet."

"Well, we know it works," confirmed the dispatcher.

"Leroy, can you believe my boy kept the number?"

"He takes after his father," smiled Leroy.

At 5:00 PM, Tom was sitting with his children when Thornton climbed aboard the bus and walked to the rear, where Tom and his children were visiting. Tom looked up, smiled, and said, "Hello Thor, how'd everything go?"

"Overall, pretty good. Once we switch Dagmar's clothes to Gina, I swear you won't be able to tell the difference."

"What do you mean, 'overall, pretty good'?" asked Tom suspiciously as he slid out from his seat and looked Thornton straight in the eye.

"Well, boss, we got Gina, I got my rifle and the bullhorn, but unfortunately Agent Kellogg saw us and has come along to assist us," explained Thornton as straightforward as he could be.

"I assume it couldn't be prevented."

"I was on the spot," said Thornton. "I didn't know what to do but let him come along and hope he wouldn't bring all the other agents with him."

"You did the right thing, Thor." Tom turned to his three children and said, "Tommy, keep your brother and sister here with you. Thor and I are going to get your mom." Tom looked at his oldest son, who nodded affirmatively. Then Tom turned and he and his bodyguard walked back down the aisle of bus two and exited back into the cold autumn evening weather. They made their way back onto bus one, where Mike, Gina, and Senior Special Agent Donald Kellogg were waiting. Tom stood in the front of the bus, and he first looked at the FBI agent and he said, "I'm glad you could make it, Agent Kellogg."

"Thomas, I so very much want to be involved in the capture of this supercriminal. As you know, I've chased him for many years." Tom smiled and nodded affirmatively.

Next, he saw Gina sitting near Mike in a seat near the front of the bus. "Gina! Your transformation is incredible," said Tom as he walked toward her, giving her a generous hug once he reached her. "Let me look at you," he requested as she stood up and modeled herself for him.

"Once she puts on Dagmar's clothes, she'll be identical," said Mike as he stood up next to her.

"Incredible," said Tom. "Thank you, Gina. This is very dangerous, and I truly appreciate your help in rescuing my wife." Tom told them to hurry. It was nearing sundown, and they wanted to make the exchange before dark. Mike and Thornton both took Gina to the rear of the bus, where Dagmar was being held. While they exchanged Dagmar's clothes, Tom spoke with Agent Kellogg about why he had decided to exclude the FBI and the police from the present situation.

Tom explained his troubles with Agent Barlow, then Agent Kellogg said, "I understand the problems you were having with Agent Barlow. He is very narrow-minded. In addition to that, Lukas Krueger intended to make the FBI look bad and embarrass them."

"Krueger made it almost impossible to deliver the ransom money to him," said Tom as he stood staring at Kellogg.

"That was on purpose," declared Kellogg who went on to discuss the problem. "Krueger has played a sort of cat-and-mouse game with both the FBI and Interpol for years. I've chased him for twelve years, ever since his first kidnapping," explained Senior Agent Kellogg as he fiddled with his pipe.

"Yes. I recall you telling us that at the briefing back at the FBI hotline the other night," said Tom, who did not want to revisit already covered ground.

"Yes, but what I didn't know then was that Krueger was going to explode a helicopter in the Browns' football stadium. He has gotten fanatical at embarrassing us," explained the senior agent.

"That was pretty extreme," agreed Tom.

"Let's hope Krueger doesn't get fanatical with Beth," warned the agent as he lit his pipe.

After fifteen minutes, Mike and Thornton escorted Gina to the front of the bus. Tom looked at her with amazement just as Mike tried on her blindfold. "Lukas will never know it's not Dagmar," said Tom as he had Gina turn around so he could check her from all sides. "Let's talk briefly about the exchange of Gina for Beth. I want only Thor, Mike, and Agent Kellogg on the driveway's apron. I expect the three of you to hold back the crowd of searchers, who will want to assist. Once Gina attacks Krueger, I'll help her in overpowering him. If everything goes well, we'll capture this guy at that point. You three don't join us until we have him overpowered," explained Tom sternly.

"Why should we wait?" demanded Agent Kellogg, who was obviously annoyed.

Tom was surprised by the agent's question and said, "Because the other three kidnappers may still be alive and able to shoot me, Gina, and Beth down."

"I thought they were dead," said Agent Kellogg.

"We don't know that for sure," replied Tom, who was getting annoyed with the agent's persistence. "Thor, I want to talk to you for a minute. In private," he added as he reached for his bodyguard's shoulder and gently guided him toward the rear of the bus. He led the way while Thornton followed. Once they reached the rear of the bus, Tom said, "Thor, I'm uncomfortable with Agent Kellogg and his presumptuous attitudes."

"What do you want me to do, boss?"

"Thor, stay at his side and if he tries to interfere and arrest Krueger prematurely, then stop him," requested Tom as he patted Thornton on his shoulder. Thornton agreed, and the two of them walked back to the front of the bus.

It was nearing sundown as 6:00 PM approached. Tom stood before his friends and said, "Guys, believe it or not, Tommy got Krueger's phone number. So, let's go call him." Everyone cheered and they all moved to the rear of the bus, where Leroy could call and make contact with Lukas.

* * *

At 5:00 PM, Beth was asking Lukas for a drink of water. Lukas left her by herself as he walked downstairs to retrieve a bottle of water. When he returned with the bottle of water, Beth had relocated herself from the mattress to the wooden chair by the front window. "Are you watching for your hero and waiting for him to come rescue you?"

"Tom will come for me."

"Why? Are you worth thirty million dollars?"

"It's not the money that matters."

"What is it then?"

"It's love," she said convincingly.

Lukas laughed with a hollow and hideous sound that would convince any jury or psychiatrist that he was legally insane. His laugh sounded like a bat screaming in the night.

Throughout the afternoon, Lukas had ranted and raved about Tom having taken his Dagmar, and he made all kinds of wild accusations and crazy threats. The more stressed Lukas became, the more his facial ticks occurred. It was almost sunset, and a bitter coldness was spreading from the shore of Lake Erie. Beth wrapped herself in two dirty blankets that had accompanied the dirty mattress, trying to keep warm, but it was fruitless. The night's cold was intensified by high winds. The cold winds rushed through the loosely fitted clapboards of the old, rundown farmhouse. She shivered hopelessly.

Lukas was watching Beth on the second floor when the kitchen wall telephone rang. He did not jump up in anticipation, but he did get up, walk down the stairs, and casually answer the phone. "Hello."

"Lukas? This is Tom Murphy."

"Yes. Thomas."

"I have a proposal."

"I am listening."

"I have your Dagmar, and you have my Beth."

"Is this what they call a Mexican stand-off?"

"I propose we trade women. What do you say?"

"What about my money, Thomas?"

"You can have the money. It's in two gym bags in the backseat of my Lincoln that is parked out front. Take the car. The keys are in the ignition. What do you say?" Tom asked. "What do you say, Lukas? Can we trade women?"

"What keeps me from taking the car and running?"

"My people have you trapped," said Tom. "We must first trade women!"

"Call me in ten minutes," said Lukas as he hung up the telephone on the kitchen wall. He rushed to the kitchen door, looked out the window at the car, and then he stepped out into the cold, windy night. He carefully walked to the Lincoln. Once he reached it, he opened the door, turned on his flashlight and pointed the beam of light at the ignition. He saw the keys in the ignition, then he pointed the beam of light into the backseat. He saw two gym bags, reached into one of them, and found it full of money. The second bag was also filled with money. Lukas started to pull the bags out of the backseat. A bullhorn sounded, "Leave the bags in the backseat!" Lukas dropped the bags, and he stepped away from the Lincoln. Again the bullhorn sounded, "Go back into the farmhouse." Lukas hesitated, then he heard the bullhorn sound, "Leave the bags!" Lukas closed the back door of the Lincoln, and he hurried back to the farmhouse. He figured they had not shot and killed him because they were not sure about the three other kidnappers that he and Dagmar had executed. They were dead men who still serve him, he thought. A bit of Austrian luck!

Once in the kitchen, Lukas was excited because he was closer to having the thirty million dollars, but he felt desperate to have Dagmar back at his side. He anxiously paced back and forth in the kitchen while he heated water in a stovetop teakettle. All he could think about was his companion, Dagmar, who had never been but a few moments away. After several minutes, the teakettle started to whistle. He made two mugs of tea, and walked them upstairs. The stairs creaked as he walked up them. As he reached the top step, Beth was sitting at the window but looking at the landing of the stairs. "Beth, I've brought us some hot tea," whispered Lukas, trying to be kind. He handed her a mug and smiled. "Tom called," he said casually, as if a different person had come to the surface. "He wants to trade you for Dagmar. What do you think?"

She was shivering. She heard what he had said, but she was suspicious and waited a moment before she replied. "That would be great, Lukas," she said cautiously.

Two minutes later, the wall phone in the kitchen rang again. Lukas smiled at Beth, then turned and scurried downstairs. He grabbed it on the sixth ring, shouting, "Hello!"

"Anxious, are you, Lukas?" asked Tom with a tone of confidence in his voice.

"We trade now," shouted Lukas and hung up.

* * *

It had been snowing most of the afternoon, and now it was near sunset. The snow was causing visibility problems. Tom placed another call to Lukas, who grabbed the phone on the first ring, "Hello, Thomas?"

"Yes, Lukas. This is Tom."

"Thomas, what are your final demands?"

"Lukas, I will walk Dagmar toward the farmhouse, and you have Beth walk toward me. I will be standing near my black Lincoln Navigator."

"How will Dagmar and I leave?" asked Lukas.

"Just drive away in my Lincoln. I will turn it facing the street."

"Thomas, I do not trust you."

"Krueger, I do not trust you either."

"Then it is unanimous."

"Yes."

"Good. If you trick me, I will kill your wife."

"Then I'll see you in hell."

* * *

Lukas hung up the kitchen wall phone and cursed Thomas Murphy and his wife. He walked back upstairs and checked on Beth. When he reached the second floor, he found Beth resting on the mattress. He nudged her with the toe of his boot and said, "I just talked with your husband."

"How is he?" she begged to know.

"I did not ask how he felt. Soon, he will walk Dagmar to me, and I will walk you to him. No surprises or I will kill you and Thomas." As he finished speaking, he heard the motor of the Lincoln starting. He rushed to the window and looked down at the headlights beaming as Tom turned the Lincoln so it was facing the street. "Beth, you should pray Thomas keeps to the rules of the exchange."

Lukas looked again out the front windows and screamed, "Damn, Thomas! There are people out there." He slammed his fist against the wall and then grabbed Beth and dragged her over to the window. "Look! The street is filled with people," he screamed as he showed Beth the crowds of people who were milling around the two buses and the many cars and pickup trucks. "Look, Beth," he screamed as he grabbed her by the hair. "Why has Thomas brought all these people?" he screamed as he pulled her head back and forth by her hair. "Why?"

"I don't know," she cried out in pain. "I don't know!" He watched as she cried. "The driveway is open. Tom would not lie to you. He is an honest man."

He threw Beth back toward the mattress. Lukas knew he was a man whose emotional levels swung drastically. One minute he was passive and friendly, then the next moment he would become a psychotic madman capable of just about anything. He looked closer out the window when he heard Tom with a bullhorn shouting, "Lukas. Lukas Krueger. I have Dagmar. We can trade, and you can leave in my Lincoln. Come out! Come out, now!" Lukas looked down at the Lincoln. He saw Tom standing at the front bumper holding a bullhorn, with Dagmar standing next to him. He saw she was blindfolded, and he wondered why. He checked his gun in his side holster, and then he grabbed Beth, and they slowly walked down the stairs to the main floor.

* * *

Tom and Gina stood next to the front passenger's side bumper of his Lincoln. Gina was dressed in Dagmar's clothes—a black turtleneck sweater, a red leather bolero jacket, and skintight jeans with a blindfold, so that Lukas could not see her face. Standing on the driveway apron were Mike, Checkers, Thornton, and FBI Agent Kellogg. Thornton was following Tom's advice by staying close to Agent Kellogg. Tom looked back from where he was standing, and he saw that Agent Kellogg was jogging in place nervously, which made Tom uneasy. He hoped Thornton was paying attention to the old but clever FBI agent. Tom turned back toward the farmhouse, and he saw Beth and Lukas stepping through the front door. He whispered, "Gina, they're stepping out. Now they're walking down the front porch steps." He slowly guided her forward a few feet. Then Lukas stopped, and Tom grabbed Gina and whispered, "They've stopped!" Tom looked past the Lincoln, down the gravel driveway toward the farmhouse porch steps. Both Beth and Lukas stopped at the bottom of the steps.

Tom felt scared and worried that something may go wrong. He listened as Lukas shouted, "Thomas, no more tricks, or I'll kill her." Tom wanted to hurry while the late-afternoon sunlight was still dusky and before the bright streetlights came on. Tom wanted this exchange done before Lukas could see this was Gina and not Dagmar.

"Let's do this, Krueger!" shouted Tom as he slowly started walking Gina forward. They had rehearsed what they would do. She could partially see through the thin blindfold, so when they were about six feet from Lukas, Tom tapped Gina, signaling her to pretend to trip, stumble, and fall forward toward Lukas's arms. Next, Tom rushed forward, grabbed Beth, and pulled her away from Lukas. Once Tom had Beth, he rolled her onto the snow-covered ground away from Lukas. Tom's aggressiveness surprised Lukas, who instinctively stepped back just as Gina was stumbling toward him.

The split second before Gina made contact with Lukas, he was a perfect target; while Lukas was in the open, Agent Kellogg pulled out his service revolver, swung into a shooting position, and squeezed off a shot at his longtime nemesis. At the same moment, Thornton grabbed Kellogg's hands and swung the gun up into the sky, where the shot went wild. Gina was stunned by the sound of the gunshot, and she stopped short of Lukas, who instinctively reached forward and pulled off her blindfold. Tom helplessly watched as Lukas spun Gina around, threw a deadly choke hold on her neck, and then screamed, "Thomas, this is not my Dagmar! I should break this imposter's neck!"

"No! Stop, Lukas!" shouted Tom as he lay in the snowy grass with Beth.

"You tricked me!" screamed Lukas as he immediately started dragging Gina back toward the rundown farmhouse. Tom tried to get up and rush Lukas, but he slipped and fell back onto the snowy grass near Beth.

The next thing Tom heard was Lukas screaming, "Thomas, you lied to me." He watched from the side of his Lincoln as the front door to the farmhouse closed, with Gina held captive under Lukas Krueger's control.

Once Tom realized he could not help Gina, at least for the moment, he turned to help Beth, who was lying on the snow-covered grass. As he helped her to her feet, he saw that she was chilled, wearing only a bright red T-shirt and stonewashed jeans. Tom instantly pulled off his denim jacket and wrapped it around her shoulders. "Are you okay?" inquired her concerned husband.

"I'm good, but how are the kids?" she asked as her maternal instincts went into overdrive.

"The kids are fine," Tom said as he affectionately wrapped his arms around his chilled wife, then guided her away from the dangers of the farmhouse. "The kids were afraid for you." He guided her with his arm around her waist onto the driveway and down toward the apron. As they approached the apron, Tom looked at Agent Kellogg and shouted, "What kind of stupid stunt was that, Agent Kellogg?" The agent did not reply, but Tom could see that Kellogg was embarrassed. Thornton was holding the agent's weapon and cell phone. "You could've killed someone," said Tom, who then realized he didn't need to say anything more. He walked Beth through the crowded apron, then onto the street that led to bus two, where there was a physician, a first aid station, and her three children. As they approached the bus, Tom said, "Tommy told me there wasn't much food or water given to you." Tom helped her up the steps of the bus.

"We weren't given much of anything," complained Beth.

"We'll get you fixed up. We've got first aid onboard, and the kids are anxiously waiting to see you," he bragged.

"Oh, Tom, I wanna see the kids," she burst out as she strained her neck to look toward the rear of the bus.

"Checkers is staying with the kids," explained Tom, who was more than anxious to reunite Beth with her kids.

"You mean Charles Mulroney, the field worker?"

"Yeah. Checkers," said Tom. "Lukas had two teams of kidnappers. Team One kidnapped me, then Team Two kidnapped you and the kids. After Team One worked me over, Lukas left me tied up in an abandoned old house, and the next morning, Checkers found me and saved my life."

"We owe a lot to Checkers," admitted Beth.

"Yes. We do owe Checkers," confirmed Tom.

"Tom, what happened to your face?" she asked as she noticed the entire left side, which was bruised, stitched, and swollen.

"Like I said, they worked me over while I was captive."

"Honey, they really did you damage," she said as she gently touched the stitches which held together the gash over his left cheekbone. "Your entire left side looks like it hurts so much," she observed with sympathy.

"It just looks worse than it is," said Tom stoically.

"You're so macho!" she bragged as she admired him.

After the physician examined her, he gave her a clean bill of health, then he recommended immediate fluids and a high-protein meal. She cooperated in as much as drinking a cold bottle of water. She postponed the meal and insisted she be led to her three children. Tom led her by her hand and gingerly walked her to the rear of bus two, where her children were anxiously waiting for her. The bus was crowded with Tom's employees, and so Beth could not see her children until she and Tom reached the far end of the bus. Danny was the first to see his mother, and he screamed with joy. "Mom! Mom!"

Once he shouted her name, the other two children quickly turned, and in unison they also shouted, "Mom! Mom!" Tom chuckled at their enthusiasm as he rushed their mother into their waiting arms. Beth threw herself at her children, and the entire family started to yell with joy and relief. After several minutes of hugs and kisses, Tom tried to calm his children. As he tried to leave, his wife asked him to stay, but he explained he had to go rescue Gina. He was obligated to rescue Gina. She had gone out on a limb to help him, and now he would, even if it took his life, go out on a limb to rescue her.

Tom knew he would have to call Lukas and trade Dagmar for Gina. He exited bus two, where his wife and three children were getting a warm meal and getting reacquainted. He walked up to the front door of bus one, where he met up with Checkers, Thornton, Mike, and Agent Kellogg. "Men, let's go into this bus and brainstorm our ideas," suggested Tom as the cold wind blew into his ruddy face. The five of them climbed up into the warm bus, then they all sat on a couch which surrounded a table. Tom wanted to get his ideas across to the men before they started interrupting him. "Guys, it's going on seven, and the sun has set. We have to trade Dagmar for Gina, but now it's too dark. I want to have this bus turned onto the apron of the driveway so we can light up the path from the farmhouse down to the street," explained Tom as he rubbed his hands together, warming himself.

"Tom, we can have that done," said Mike Max. "What else?" Mike took a long draw on his cigarette.

"After we move the bus, then we'll call Lukas to arrange for the trade. First I want to place a call to Agent Barlow at the kidnap hotline," said Tom. "We'll call Barlow from the rear of this bus, where Leroy can help us. Mike, go tell the bus driver to point the bus down from the driveway apron, and tell him to use his brightest lights on the path between the street and the farmhouse."

"I'll go tell the driver," said Mike as he crushed out his cigarette, climbed out of his seat, and proceeded toward the front of the bus, where the driver was sitting behind the wheel. Tom watched as Mike instructed the bus driver. The men with Tom all sat quietly while they watched the driver maneuver the bus into the requested position.

Once the bus was positioned to light the pathway between the street and the farmhouse, Tom scooted out of his seat, stood up, and grabbed Agent Kellogg's arm. "Come with me, Agent Kellogg. I want you to also talk to Agent Barlow." The two men walked to the rear of the bus, where Leroy was maintaining the communication center. As Tom and Agent Kellogg approached the dispatcher, Tom introduced the two men. He explained to Leroy that they wanted to make two calls—first to Agent Barlow at the kidnap hotline, and second to the wall phone in Krueger's kitchen.

"The kidnap hotline first?" asked Leroy.

"Yes," replied Tom. "Do you have that number?"

"Yes, Tom."

Leroy put the call through. "This is Wanda at Just Clean It Up. How may I assist you?"

"Wanda. This is Tom! Put Agent Barlow on the line."

"Tom, how is your family?"

"They're safe, Wanda. I have them back!"

"Wonderful."

"Put Barlow on."

There was a pause, then Agent Barlow shouted, "Murphy, where are you?"

"Barlow! I'm in Willoughby. How are things going?"

"We're getting nibbles."

"You are. What kind?" asked Tom.

There was a moment of silence, then Agent Barlow said, "Listen! This kind of work takes patience and persistence."

Tom laughed into the phone, loud enough for the agent to hear him, then he said, "All that is good, but I'm calling to inform you that Agent Kellogg and my searchers have Lukas Krueger trapped in a small farmhouse here in Lake County."

"How the hell did you do that?" demanded Agent Barlow.

"Patience and persistence, Agent Barlow!"

"Murphy, you're a real smartass!"

"Don't be resentful, Agent Barlow. We want you to come make the official arrest. I'm gonna put on Agent Kellogg and my communications dispatcher, who will guide you here so you can make the arrest."

"Tom!"

"Yeah?"

"Thanks," said Agent Barlow in a low and sober tone.

Tom said no more. He handed the phone over to Agent Kellogg, who brought Agent Barlow up to date on all the activities surrounding Lukas Krueger. Tom stood and listened to the conversation between the two agents, then he continued to listen as Leroy gave Agent Barlow the directions to Krueger's farmhouse. While Leroy gave the directions, Agent Kellogg looked at Tom and said, "Tom, I think we should stall Krueger until my FBI guys arrive."

Tom looked suspiciously at Agent Kellogg and said, "We can stall him, but I want to trade for Gina as soon as possible. The longer she stays with that monster the more opportunity he has to hurt her."

"I appreciate your concern," said Agent Kellogg, "but I don't want Krueger to escape because we gave him too much time." He fiddled with his pipe nervously.

"He's not going anywhere; I've got him trapped," said Tom, though he appreciated the agent's concern.

"What about your Lincoln? Didn't you offer it to him?" asked the agent as he puffed on his newly lit pipe.

"Don't believe everything you hear, Agent Kellogg. I am going to move the Lincoln after we get Gina back," explained Tom. "Did you really think I'd let him drive away after what he has done to me and my family?" he asked.

"I still think we should stall," urged Agent Kellogg, who was being pushy and controlling, which Tom noticed from the beginning was part of the agent's personality.

"Okay! I'll stall him," agreed Tom, who wanted to pacify the elder agent for the time being. He did not see any profit in arguing with Agent Kellogg, especially since Tom was in charge of the situation, and he called the shots. He heard Leroy as he finished up with Agent Barlow, and so he motioned for Agent Kellogg to wait. Then he got Leroy's attention when he said, "Leroy, lets call Krueger's kitchen phone."

"Okay, Tom," responded Leroy as he started dialing the number. It rang several times, then an anxious voice answered, "Yes. Who's there?"

"Lukas, this is Tom Murphy."

"Thomas, that was a stupid trick sending in an imposter instead of my dear Dagmar."

"Yes! That was stupid of me, and I apologize. No more tricks, Lukas. You have my word as a gentleman," said Tom as he anxiously waited to see if Krueger would accept his apology.

There was a long, silent pause. He waited until finally Krueger said, "Thomas, I accept your apology, but I do not trust you."

"Good! I do not trust you, either," replied Tom, who held his breath as he again waited for Krueger to speak.

"Good, then we trust neither. Let us trade women."

"Good, then we trade. This time, you and I stay out of it. The two women can walk alone. Gina will walk to me, and Dagmar can walk to you," explained Tom, hoping Krueger would agree.

"Good, then we trade," said Krueger. "I am ready!"

"I need time. I am not quite ready," urged Tom.

"Why?" shouted Krueger.

"Dagmar is not here," stammered Tom. "She is in a safe, dry, warm place away from here." "Now I've granted Agent Kellogg's wish to stall," thought Tom.

"How soon can you return her to me?" growled Krueger as if he had an irritable bowel.

"Soon, Lukas. Real soon," Tom stalled. "I'll call back real soon."

"I don't want to wait," said Krueger, then hung up.

Tom returned the phone to its cradle, and then he screamed, "Shit! Damn Kellogg! Krueger doesn't want to wait." He looked daggers at the old man, who nervously played with his pipe like a child caught with fingers in the cookie jar.

* * *

As Lukas walked Gina backwards up the porch steps, the wind and snow swirled around them. He had anticipated some sort of trickery by Tom. Before Tom could do anything, Lukas pulled Gina into the farmhouse and closed the porch door. He dragged her through the enclosed porch and into the living room. Once he had her in the middle of the living room, then he loosened the deadly choke hold he had on her and threw her down onto an area throw rug in front of his empty fireplace. Gina instantly jumped to her feet, prepared to attack and hopefully overpower the famous criminal. Lukas was prepared. On the coffee table in front of an old sofa, Lukas had a Taser, which he snatched, aimed, and used on Dagmar's impostor. The two electrical darts struck Gina in the chest. Instantly, she shook from the intense charge. Gina was a small woman, weighing less than one hundred and ten pounds. After seconds of shock, Lukas stopped the current, and Gina fell helplessly to the floor. She appeared catatonic as Lukas approached. He carefully pulled the two darts from her chest, and then he quickly tied her hands behind her back, then he bound her feet. He stood back from her and asked, "What is your name, you impersonator?"

"Gina …," she stuttered as an after effect of the shock she had sustained from the Taser. Lukas looked at Gina as she lay helplessly on her back on the old, dirty area rug in front of the empty fireplace in the farmhouse's cold living room.

"Gina, do you work for Murphy?" asked Lukas as he rewrapped the long cables of his Taser. "Don't fool with me."

"I'm an ex-marine," uttered Gina, "and we thought I could overpower you."

Lukas stared at her, then said, "I suspected something would be planned against me and Dagmar. Something to keep us apart." He set the Taser on the coffee table. "Do not fear me. I will keep you alive, and Thomas and I will make another exchange: you for Dagmar." He leaned down and checked Gina's bindings. "I must restrain you, or you will try to kick my ass," said Lukas with a smile.

Gina smiled back at him, a little relieved.

Lukas went onto the front enclosed porch, looked out the window, and saw that it was snowing harder. He walked back into the living room and said rhetorically, "It's now snowing!" He stood over Gina, looking down at her with a renewed, unexplained, anger. The farmhouse was silent. The silence was broken by the tinny ringing of the old kitchen wall phone. Lukas walked mechanically into the old kitchen and picked up the receiver.

After Lukas spoke with Tom, he hung up the wall phone and stomped back into the living room, leaned over Gina and grabbed her by her shoulders. As he raised her up off the floor, he shouted, "Thomas tries to trick me again,

I'll kill you." He slammed her painfully back onto the floor. "Why isn't Dagmar here?" He had became furious and out of patience.

"Tom moved her where she would be safe, warm, and dry," replied Gina as she suddenly feared for her life.

"You better be honest with me!"

"Lukas, I need water," she pleaded.

He stared at her for a long moment. He did not trust her or Thomas, but he was attracted to Dagmar's impostor, just as he was attracted to his Dagmar. "You thirst?"

"Yes, I'm dry as a bone," she replied to him.

He walked into the kitchen, opened his thermos cooler, and took out a bottle of cold water. He took the water bottle back to her, drew it to her lips, and tilted her head. He gently poured the cold water into her mouth. He tenderly asked, "Is that good?"

"Yes. Thank you, Lukas," she replied with a smile.

For the next half hour, Lukas paced throughout the first floor of the farmhouse. At 7:00 PM, the kitchen phone rang again, and this time Lukas ran impatiently into the kitchen. "Thomas?" he shouted into the receiver.

"Yes."

"Do you finally have my Dagmar?"

"Yes! We're ready to trade women," replied Tom confidently as he waited for Lukas to speak.

There was silence as Lukas thought. He finally said, "You watch Gina walk to you while Dagmar walks to me. I'll stay in the farmhouse with a rifle pointed at Gina's head. No tricks or I'll kill Gina."

"Lukas, I promise, no tricks," urged Tom, who was very anxious to get Gina safely back.

"Thomas, no tricks," Lukas reminded him sternly.

Both hung up their phones.

Lukas walked back into the living room. He looked at Gina, then he carefully checked his 9 mm, released the safety, then holstered it. Next, he turned to Gina and said, "Gina, no tricks. You walk toward Thomas, and let my Dagmar walk to me. If there are any tricks, my rifle will find you!" He knew she had not seen a rifle, but he knew she did not doubt his resolve. He intended that she would walk straight to Tom.

Lukas stood at Gina's feet, then he bent over and said, "I'm going to free your feet. Do not kick me, or I will kill you!" He pulled a knife from his boot and proceeded to cut the binding from her feet. Once her feet were free, he placed the knife back in his boot and said, "I'm going to bring you to your feet. Do not fight me!" He reached down and grabbed her by the shoulders of her red leather jacket and pulled her up off the floor. Once she was standing, Lukas jumped back away from her and drew his weapon. "No tricks, Gina!"

He looked straight at her as she steadied her footing. "I won't hurt you, Lukas. You've been good to me."

"I cannot trust you, Gina," replied Lukas as he motioned for her to walk toward the front door. He watched as she moved awkwardly out of the living room and then out onto the front porch. "I stay on the porch. I do not trust Thomas. Walk down the steps, and do not look back. When you pass Dagmar, do not speak or touch her. Good luck, Gina!"

* * *

It was time for Tom to trade Dagmar for Gina, and so Tom walked Dagmar off the bus and then onto the apron of the long gravel driveway. They stopped, faced the farmhouse, and waited until Tom could see Gina. Once Gina started walking down the steps of the porch, Tom nudged Dagmar. She started walking down the snow-covered driveway toward the farmhouse. The winds and the flurries had increased, with several inches of snow covering the gravel driveway. It was slick and icy. Gina walked facing the wind, while Dagmar had the wind to her back. Tom watched as Gina slowly walked away from the farmhouse. He sensed something was wrong because she seemed to be walking mechanically. "Something is wrong," whispered Tom.

"Her hands are tied behind her back," whispered Thornton. "She can hardly keep her balance!"

Tom stood watching from the apron next to Mike, Thornton, Checkers, Agent Kellogg, and several other of Tom's employees. He saw Gina stumble awkwardly as she tried walking faster; in order to keep her balance, she was forced to walk slower.

Tom watched as the women made their way slowly across the snow-covered driveway. He noticed that Dagmar made her way much faster than Gina. By the time they met up; Dagmar was two thirds of the way, while Gina was only one third of the way.

When they crossed each other's paths, Dagmar shouted something at Gina, but Tom could not hear because of the howling winds and because of the long distance. Tom saw Dagmar at the farmhouse steps, but Gina was only half way down the driveway. There were harsh winds, and snow was blowing in her face. The driveway was covered with slippery snow, and Tom could see that Gina was having trouble making her way to the end of the long, snow-covered, gravel driveway.

Tom watched Lukas help Dagmar up the porch steps. He wanted Gina out of Lukas's gun range, so he shouted without remembering her hands were tied. "Run, Gina. Run now!" He watched as she attempted to run faster, but instantly he regretted having shouted. As she tried to accelerate on the slushy, snow-covered driveway, she fell onto her back, hitting her head. Tom screamed, "No!" He pushed away from the crowd, and he rushed toward Gina. "Hold on, Gina! I'm coming," shouted Tom as he rushed up the driveway toward Gina. Once he reached her, he slid into her like a baseball player sliding into second base. "Gina! Are you okay?" he asked frantically as he ran his hand over the back of her head. He found no blood and was relieved.

"Get me out of here," cried Gina. "He has a rifle!"

"Okay, Gina," he said as he reached behind her back and under her legs and, lifting with his knees, he raised her up off the snow-covered gravel. "Here we go, Gina!" He started walking down the driveway and away from the dangerous farmhouse. Cautiously, he carried Gina on the slippery driveway until they reached the apron, where both Thornton and Mike and Agent Kellogg and others were anxiously waiting to help. "She is all right, guys," uttered Tom as he carried her from the apron, down the street and into the waiting, warm, first aid bus. After Tom carried Gina up and into the bus, he sat her down onto a seat. While Thornton cut the ropes that bound her wrists, Tom tensely asked, "Did Lukas hurt you, Gina?"

Once Thornton cut her hands free, she jumped up and rubbed her sore wrists and shouted, "I wanted to kick his ass!" Everyone laughed as she relieved the tension in the bus. After everyone laughed at Gina's statement, Tom took her by the arm and walked her to the rear of bus two, beyond Leroy's communication center.

Tom sat her down, then he joined her by sitting down next to her. He looked into her eyes and sincerely said, "I want to thank you both privately as well as personally. You helped save my wife's life, while risking your own life. And I thank you from the bottom of my heart." He leaned over and hugged her, showing his appreciation.

After the hug, Gina said, "Tom, after all you've done for so many folks, you at least deserve to have your wife and kids safe. I was more than glad to have helped." She smiled, then giggled a little and asked, "Who the hell fired the gun that upset our plan?"

Tom frowned as he remembered the incident, then he said, "It was the old Senior Special FBI Agent Kellogg who got carried away and tried to prematurely capture Krueger." He grimaced and waited for Gina to reply.

"Kellogg could've gotten us killed."

"If it wasn't for Thor, who grabbed Kellogg's gun hand and swiftly pointed it skyward, then the wild shot could've hit one of us," explained Tom as he anxiously rubbed his dimpled chin.

"What was his excuse?" asked Gina as she ran her hands through her new, unaccustomed, pixy haircut.

"Well, Kellogg is a legend in the FBI, and he commands a great deal of respect," said Tom, "and, so, with the approximate amount of due respect, I chewed his ass a bit." Gina laughed out loud. They both stood up, and Tom said, "We'd better get back to the group."

After Tom and Gina returned to the front of the bus, Tom went to the command center and met with Thornton and Mike. It was now dark, and the winds were blowing stronger out of the north right across Lake Erie, and the snow was accumulating on the ground as well as in the air, causing limited visibility.

Tom felt as proud as a pup. He had his family back and unharmed. He had Gina, and all his people were safe. Lukas was surrounded and about to be arrested by the FBI. In addition, Tom had not lost his thirty million American dollars, which he had been prepared to give Lukas.

Tom sat in bus one at a round couch with a table, which held a telephone. He looked at Mike and Thornton and said, "Well, guys, all that is left is for the FBI guys to come and arrest Lukas Krueger."

Thornton smiled and said, "It's been a hell of a couple of days." Again he rubbed his shiny head.

"Yes, indeed," added Mike as he lit up a victory cigar to go along with his smiling face.

"You know that Wanda is still holding down the 'now around the clock' phone branch. And keeping company with Agents Barlow and Coffee at the Kidnap Command Center," Tom said as he accepted a victory cigar from Mike.

"A-t-t-a-boy for Wanda," they all said in unison, and they gave themselves a round of high fives.

* * *

The weather was worsening. Both the winds and snow flurries had increased. Lukas looked out the kitchen windows and saw the lights of Tom's bus headlights as they lit up the pathway from the apron of the dirt and gravel driveway up to the farmhouse. The light illuminated the swirling snow as it fell to earth. "The weather is getting worse," said Lukas to Dagmar, who was waiting for the teakettle to whistle so she could make tea for the two of them. "We do not have time for tea," stressed Lukas. "As soon as Thomas moves that bus, we are going to jump in his Lincoln and drive out of here with the ransom," stressed Lukas as he looked out the kitchen window.

"I'm cold! We have time for a hot tea," she scolded.

"No, we do not!" He heard the bus's engine start, and he watched as the bus backed out of the apron of the driveway. The driveway up to the farmhouse became dark. He looked away from the window and said, "Dagmar, they are moving the bus. It is time to go!"

Dagmar walked away from the stove and over to the kitchen window next to Lukas, and she said, "Again, it is dark!"

"We must go!" said Lukas as he watched out the kitchen window. The streetlight overhead continued to spread adequate light to see the falling snow. Next, Lukas looked down where the bus had been, and he saw from the light of the streetlamp, Thornton walk up to the apron of the driveway. He was carrying a rifle, which he raised to his shoulder, aimed and shot out the streetlight. It became much darker, and Lukas could no longer see the swirling snow. Lukas anxiously shouted, "Dagmar, they've shot out the streetlight."

Dagmar, who had returned to the stove, shouted, "Why?"

"Damn Thomas!" screamed Lukas. "He is not going to keep our agreement and allow us to escape using his Lincoln." He became instantly furious as he just stood at the kitchen window staring into the darkness and wondering what was happening. After a moment, Lukas heard the Lincoln start up. He had not been able to see Tom walk up the driveway to his Lincoln, but once Tom started the Lincoln, Lukas became furious and shouted, "That damn liar! Thomas is moving the Navigator and the ransom." He slammed his fist violently on the windowsill. "Dagmar, he has lied to me once again. He cannot be trusted!"

Dagmar whispered a little laugh at Lukas's absurdity. "You certainly cannot trust Thomas Murphy!"

Lukas saw the Lincoln's headlights turn on, and he watched Tom drive away from the farmhouse, then disappear beyond the bus. Lukas became furious as he screamed, "Now we cannot drive away with the money! Thomas tricked me again!" Next, he watched as the big bus started and moved onto the dirt and gravel driveway. The bus's big, bright headlights illuminated the pathway to the farmhouse, just as it had before. The lights shone through the kitchen windows, annoying Lukas and lighting the interior of the farmhouse.

Lukas did not know that both Tom and Agent Kellogg had alerted Agent Barlow at the Kidnap Command Center. In addition, a swarm of FBI agents were headed to the farmhouse to capture and arrest him and Dagmar. Intuitively, he knew someone was coming after him.

"If Thomas and I were playing chess, then he would proudly proclaim 'checkmate,' and he would be the winner," said Lukas to Dagmar. "Thomas has removed the money and the transportation. We have lost, and he has won. We must call my brother to make our escape!"

Lukas was embarrassed; Dagmar could tell it was so very hard for him to declare defeat. He had never before been defeated. She knew he was a perfectionist who did not know how to accept defeat.

"We must call my brother!" again declared Lukas as he hung his head in shame. "I have failed!"

"Darling, we have enough to retire," said Dagmar. "Let us go home!" She draped her arms around his neck.

Lukas took his cell phone from his pants pocket, and he hit the speed dial button that was preset to Hayse Krueger, Lukas's twin brother, who was standing by with his helicopter to rescue them. The phone rang twice, then a voice answered, "Lukas?"

"Hayse, we have lost the golden goose," stated Lukas, with tears in his eyes. He realized he had never had to make this call before, even though it had been a fallback option in all six prior kidnappings. This was the first failed kidnapping and the first time he had to signal his publicly unknown twin brother, Hayse Krueger, for a rescue.

"I will be right there, Lukas," replied his brother.

Dagmar took the cell phone from Lukas, turned it off, and slipped it back into his pants pocket. "It will all be all right, my darling. You've done your best, and we are back together." She held him close and soothed him.

*   *   *

It was snowing hard, and the winds were severe. Visibility was less than a quarter of a mile, and all planes were grounded until further notice. Hayse sat in his three-seat helicopter at the Lost Nation Road Airport in northern Willoughby. Hayse was in his small, private helicopter, preparing to hop over to his brother's pickup point, in the field beside the farmhouse, where Lukas and Dagmar were waiting.

As Hayse prepared to take off, he radioed the tower, which denied him clearance. He ignored the tower and lifted off even with poor visibility, high winds, and freezing snow. He only had to fly five miles to the farmhouse, then make a return trip back north to an empty piece of property near the Mentor marsh. There, where Hayse had parked his Jeep Cherokee, they would abandon the helicopter. With the Jeep, they would travel easily across the Canadian border to their private lodge in Canada. After recuperating in Ontario, the three of them would travel to Nova Scotia, where they would take a slow, leisurely ship ride back to their base in Europe.

Hayse started the helicopter, adjusted for the wind, and then lifted up off the tarmac. The winds tossed the small, private, three-seated helicopter violently. The weather was grossly overwhelming this small helicopter. The helicopter lifted up and headed out, just clearing the treetops. Hayse pointed his helicopter in the direction of Lukas's farmhouse. Precipitation was a combination of ice pellets and slushy, freezing snow. The powerful winds from the north were blowing across Lake Erie. Within five minutes, Hayse looked down onto the open field next to his brother's farmhouse. He grabbed the onboard telephone and dialed Lukas's cell phone number; when it was answered, he shouted, "Lukas, I'm hovering above your side yard."

"Set her down," shouted Lukas. "We'll be right out."

The helicopter floodlights lit the area so Lukas and Dagmar could run to meet Hayse and his helicopter.

*   *   *

Tom and many of his men were congregating inside of bus one, facing the farmhouse. They were anxiously awaiting Agent Barlow and his group of FBI agents who were on their way to arrest Lukas Krueger. Agent Kellogg was in cell phone communication with Agent Barlow as he and his men were driving to the farmhouse. Agent Kellogg pulled his cell phone from his ear, looked at Tom and shouted, "Thomas, Barlow's men are three minutes away!"

"That sounds great," said Tom. "Krueger isn't going anywhere!" Tom motioned for Thornton to return Agent Kellogg his side weapon, and his bodyguard obediently returned the weapon to the senior agent.

"Thank you, Mr. Williams," said Agent Kellogg as he took his weapon and holstered it inside his overcoat.

"Agent Kellogg, I'm sorry we had to take that away from you," said Tom apologetically. Tom shook hands with the senior agent, then he looked at Thornton and said, "Thor, I'm going outside to watch the farmhouse."

"It's too cold out there," said Agent Kellogg.

"I'm too anxious to wait in here for Agent Barlow," Tom said as he walked to the door of the bus and pushed it open. As soon as he stepped outside, the cold, snowy wind hit his face. He walked around to the front of the bus, then he proceeded to walk past the driveway apron. He stood there thinking he had beaten Lukas Krueger, who had kidnapped him and his family. After all Lukas had put them through, Tom still overcame him and his crew of killers.

He stood alone. Everyone remained in the warm, dry bus waiting for Agent Kellogg's FBI agents. Tom heard a far-off noise and wondered what it was. Next, he saw Lukas and Dagmar come out onto the open porch. The noise got louder, then he saw a small helicopter set down in the side yard next to the farmhouse.

Tom again squinted through the downpour of sleet and snow as the helicopter landed just next to the farmhouse. He saw Lukas and Dagmar step out onto the porch. Tom was startled. He ran back to the front of the bus, and he started pounding on the front fender. He screamed, "Let's go! They're going to get away!" But no one could hear him because they were all still in the warm, dry bus. He was the first off the apron. He ran up the dirt and gravel driveway. He could see Lukas and Dagmar standing on the wraparound open porch facing the field. Tom saw Lukas staring straight at him, while Dagmar was pulling on his arm urging him to come with her to the helicopter. As Tom ran toward the farmhouse, he saw Lukas push Dagmar away; he then drew his 9 mm and quickly fired a shot at Tom. Instantly, Tom felt the bullet crease the outer edge of his left ear. He stopped dead in his tracks and grabbed his bleeding ear. Tom stood watching as Lukas dropped down to his knee, posing in a classic shooting stance. Lukas aimed ever so carefully and squeezed off a second shot, which echoed in the snowy, howling wind. Tom felt as if he had been kicked by a mule as Lukas's second shot knocked him onto his back. He felt the burn of the bullet as it penetrated deep into his upper left shoulder, snapping the bones like the splintering of a lean green stick.

With Tom flat on his back, both Thornton and Checkers ran up behind him and helped him sit up. "I'm okay!" he shouted. "Thor, go stop Lukas!"

"Go Thor! I'll care for Tom," shouted Checkers, who was helping Tom sit. Tom watched as Thornton sprinted to catch Lukas, who ran swiftly with Dagmar toward Hayse's helicopter.

Tom watched as Thornton rushed ahead of all the other men who were now chasing Lukas and Dagmar. Hayse was holding the door for them when Tom shouted, "Hurry, Thor!" Tom continued watching as Thornton sprinted toward the helicopter. But the chase suddenly looked hopeless as Lukas and Dagmar reached the small helicopter, and Hayse helped them aboard. The door closed and the helicopter proceeded to take off. Moments later, Hayse lifted the helicopter off the ground and into snowiness. At that moment, Thornton arrived under the helicopter as it slowly rose. For a brief moment, Tom saw Thornton leap up and grab the helicopter's running boards as it floated upward. The helicopter continued to rise. Thornton hung on as the flying machine rose up and away from the side yard of the farmhouse. Hayse rocked the helicopter back and forth, trying to shake Thornton off the running boards. Tom watched the helicopter sway from side to side, and, suddenly, Thornton fell to the earth. The helicopter finally ascended into the snow clouds and disappeared into the night.

* * *

Tom sat on the snow-covered driveway with a 9 mm slug in his upper left shoulder. Checkers helped support him as he sat waiting for Thornton to return. He slowly shook his head to clear the pain he was feeling. He looked down the driveway toward the farmhouse and saw Thornton and Mike running toward him. "Did they get away?" shouted Tom as his right hand held his wounded left shoulder.

"I just missed him," shouted Thornton as he reached Tom, leaned down, and checked Tom's wounded shoulder.

Mike reached Tom and said, "That was some incredible shooting to hit you from that distance and with this limited visibility."

"Mike, that was just a plum lucky shot," said Thornton as he tried to help Tom to his feet. But Tom became suddenly semiconscious and could not assist Thornton, who had to guide him back down onto the ground. "Can I have some help here," shouted Thornton as he and the others suddenly realized that Tom had gone into shock.

* * *

Half an hour later, Tom awoke. He looked around and realized he was in an ambulance. With blurry vision he tried to focus on Thornton, who was seated crouched down at the end of the ambulance. "Mr. Murphy, can you hear me?" asked the ambulance attendant, who was sitting next to Tom. "Can you hear me, Thomas?"

"Yes, I can hear you," said Tom, whose slurred speech scared him. He shouted for Thornton who reached forward and grasped Tom's right hand. "Did Lukas get away?"

"Yes, Tom, Lukas got away."

"Thor, did Barlow show up?"

"Yes, and he was pissed off!"

Tom smiled, then slipped back into unconsciousness.

* * *

As Lukas sat in the small helicopter, he looked at his twin brother and felt so grateful for his help throughout the last twelve years. Lukas reflected back at the last twelve years, when his brother stayed out of the public eye and acted as Lukas's silent partner. He used his financial genius to manage and invest and multiply Lukas's six ransoms. Because of Hayse's financial genius, the hundred million American dollars that the FBI knew about had grown substantially and was safely hidden in both Swiss and Caribbean banking institutions.

Lukas knew he was a perfectionist, and the failure of his last kidnapping would bother him forever. He knew that Hayse would console and advise him to retire with his lovely Dagmar to their dream home in the warm and sunny Caribbean.

Lukas looked out of the window, and he stared at the tumbling snow. He knew they would be all right until he could return someday to finish off Thomas Murphy and collect his thirty million American dollars.

Epilogue

When Tom awoke, he immediately felt agonizing pain throbbing from his left shoulder. Once he opened his eyes, he saw his left arm was suspended in a plaster cast over to his head. Moving his left arm hurt like hell. He looked at the cast that extended from his fingertips down his arm and engulfed his shoulder and his upper left chest. He felt groggy and assumed it was from the anesthesia.

He noticed the hospital room was dimly lit, small, and chilly, with a sliding glass door that locked him in and others out. He saw Beth dozing in a rocking chair next to his hospital bed.

All he remembered was the pain of Lukas's bullet hitting him in his left shoulder, and the force of it making him fall backwards onto the cold, hard snow. He vaguely recalled men standing over him and speaking as he lay on the snow-covered driveway.

Tom's right hand reached for and pushed the call button. Moments later, the glass door slid open and a very young nurse entered. "Mr. Murphy, you're awake!" she said as she rushed to his bedside.

The nurse's voice woke Beth, who instantly jumped to her feet and said, "Oh, Tom, you're finally back!" He could see the concern on her face as she leaned over the edge of the hospital bed and gave him a desperate hug.

"How long have I been out?"

"It's noon Monday," said Beth. "You've slept through the weekend."

As the nurse checked Tom's intravenous site, she said, "You were sensitive to the anesthesia, and it kept you asleep longer than usual."

"Did Krueger get away?"

"Yes, Tom," replied Beth sympathetically, "he got away. The good news is we have our kids and the money."

Tom thought about that for a moment, then changed the subject by asking, "Why such a large cast?" Just as he asked the question, a doctor entered the small, chilly recovery room.

"I can answer that, Thomas," said the doctor. "The bullet that struck you shattered your shoulder socket into multiple pieces, so we had to repair and re-create the socket."

"How bad?"

"It was bad, Thomas," said the doctor factually.

Tom was disgusted that Lukas had gotten away, and he was angry that he had such a complex injury. He closed his eyes and instantly drifted back to sleep.

* * *

The next morning he woke and found Beth faithfully at his side. "Good morning. How are you feeling?" she asked.

"Better, thanks. How are the kids?"

"They're anxious to see you, Tom."

"Good. I'm anxious to see them," he said with a grin.

"Senior Special Agent Kellogg is waiting outside to talk with you, Tom."

"Let me talk to him alone for a few minutes, Beth." He watched as she smiled at him, got up, and walked out of the small recovery room. He closed his eyes, still in hellish pain. Moments later, he opened his eyes and saw Senior Special Agent Kellogg standing at his bedside.

"Hello, Thomas."

"Hello, Senior Agent Kellogg."

"How do you feel, Thomas?"

"Like a bull just kicked me." Tom saw Kellogg's genuine concerned look on his face. "What can you tell me?"

"He simply disappeared. The helicopter was rented under the name of Hayse Krueger, perhaps a brother we did not know about. The three of them just flew away, leaving no trace. The good thing is you have your wife, kids, and your thirty million dollars," explained Kellogg with a sober face.

"Krueger will be back," said Tom. "He is a perfectionist, and he won't be able to leave this unresolved."

"Thomas, I believe you're right," said Kellogg as he rubbed his hands together as if he were preparing for the second round of a title bout.

Tom closed his eyes.

The End